THE SAVED

Book Four of The Taken Saga

AVERY BLAKE
NINIE HAMMON

STERLING & STONE

THE SAVED

Chapter One

GIDEON FREEMAN SLIPPED OUT of the shadows like a big cat and the fat man never seen him coming.

He come up behind the guy real quiet and slid a blade into his back slick as greased gorilla snot. Grabbed his rifle and the ammunition he was carrying and shoved him off into the river without making so much as a peep of noise. The body'd be washed downstream, would float by right below Cricket Bottom. Not that it mattered. If them Zion Village folks was right, the whole world was gonna be under water tomorrow and wouldn't be anybody interested in figuring out what happened to the man who'd had the poor judgement to step out to the edge of the dock by the elevator to relieve himself. Gideon caught him in mid-piss.

Gideon had lived inside Matheson Caverns for going on seven years. It was *his* place, he owned it way more than them Mathesons did, by virtue of squatter's rights. He *lived* here. Well, so did Taylor Matheson.

Gideon smiled.

And Gideon was glad of that, yes, he was for a fact because Kelly Jo sure knew how to grow tomatoes! Gideon had nicked some fat, juicy tomatoes off her plants a couple of days ago and they was fine indeed. He hadn't never tried none of that hydroponics stuff his own self. Didn't have to if other people near you did and then didn't keep a proper eye on the crops they raised.

Gideon had moved in the winter after Astral Day. Being a poor man of simple means, he hadn't had anything as fancy as solar panels to provide electricity for his home. When the power failed, the grids or whatever the hell they were crashed, he was outa juice. And the winters in Kentucky, as he'd learned in his previous fifty-six years, were cold enough to freeze the balls off a brass monkey. So he'd figured to stay in the cave for the winter, where the temperature, once you got far enough away from the entrance, was a uniform fifty-eight degrees year round. He had planned only to stay that first winter, until he got his feet under him and figured out how to make it outside. But he found he actually liked living in the cave. It was peaceful and quiet in there, that was for sure, and if there was one thing Gideon Freeman valued in this life it was peace and quiet. And the part he thought he'd hate, that would drive him nuts, being closed-up like that … Why shoot, he got used to that in no time, didn't mind at all. Now, he did need to get out every now and then, more in the beginning than now, but still he needed to see the sun and the sky, look at the stars, smell the flowers, hear the birds, that sort of thing. But his necessary forays out to get supplies nowadays provided all the outside time he needed.

Once he decided to stay permanent, he figured to make a nice place for himself. And he certainly had plenty of real estate to choose from! Matheson Caverns consisted of more than 250 miles of explored tunnels — probably twice that many nobody'd ever seen yet. The tunnels wasn't stretched out straight, like you could drive a train straight through or nothing like that. They was all twisted up like spaghetti, circling and looping and dead ends. The caves was on five different levels. Thinking of it like it was a big skyscraper, he had himself a penthouse apartment in the top floor.

Pretty fancy, and he'd made a nice place for himself about three miles in from the Joppa Ridge natural entrance. He'd picked a spot in the cavern where the roof was only about ten feet high, like a house sort of, and about the dimensions of the place he'd had on the ridge, built with his own two hands, with the help of his boys of, course. When they were still coming around, before Gertie died. He made a separate place for a privy, of course, even brought in a toilet seat and sat it over the space in the rock where he could do his business, then cover it up with lime, of course. He hauled in water from the river up the elevator, which was a mile farther down the cavern in the opposite direction, which meant once he got the barrels loaded, he had to put them on donkeys to haul them back to his spread as he liked to call it. He had a herd of donkeys, and some sheep, chickens and a goat — *had* a goat in the beginning but it died, like it just sort of wasted away, like it couldn't live without the sun. The other animals didn't seem to mind.

He didn't usually go out any other way than down the elevator to the river. After awhile, there was other folks moved in, too, most of them on the lower levels, and he'd seen them sometimes at the boat dock where the Three Forks River flowed through Level Five of the Caverns. But most of them had come for the same reasons he had, and they were private people, too, kept to themselves. Over time, the most people settled in by the Cricket Bottom entrance, had themselves a regular little community down there eventually.

Fact was, he didn't even know the Bickett boys had settled in the opening of the natural entrance on Joppa Ridge, drove out the folks who'd been there first, and set up their drug operation there. He stumbled upon it accidental, and backed away into the shadows so they didn't never even know he was there. He watched long enough to know they were making Methatrexidone and any fool knew how dangerous it was to make that shit outside a lab, so he got away from them quick as he could, but they blocked his natural way out, so he had to go down the tube a thousand feet to the river.

He knew when that lab blew. Even though it was three miles away, the sound of it liked to have deafened him. The concussion roaring down the cave hit him like a fist, flung him up against the wall, knocked over chairs and furniture, stuff off the shelves. He waited two days before he ventured out toward the entrance, and that musta been some blast. The cave was collapsed for half a mile. Even took out the Double Cellars Sinkhole, that had provided light and a nice breeze. All that shit was blocked up tight.

He even thought then about moving, down into Level Four, maybe, so he'd be close to the river. But wasn't no sense in that and it was a lot of trouble. He'd hauled a shit ton of stuff in here over the years before them boys blew themselves and half a mile of cavern down on top of them. Some of it was shit you couldn't even have fit in the elevator. And besides, the elevator — there was four of them — was run off them batteries connected to solar panels outside. Way up in the trees, musta been a bunch of them. It would keep running long as there was power. And if it stopped running, well, there was other ways to get down to the lower levels from his home, climbing down, through caverns maybe nobody but him knew about, maybe not even the Mathesons. Them chimney things, like hollow pillars going up through solid rock. He knew where all them was and he bet wasn't nobody else on the planet did.

Had a place where he had meat salted down, and had a VegiPac that vacuum sealed vegetables and fruit he grew in the little garden in a meadow near the cave entrance. One of the folks who lived on Level Two had a full-bore hydroponics lab, grew all kinda stuff, tomatoes, potatoes, carrots, shoot even had an apple under them lights. They were techie kinda folks, one had hooked up solar panels to batteries and used them to power the hydroponics lab. He figured it was lot easier just to keep himself a garden, if he could keep the danged deer out of it, coming in there, eating the tops off his carrots and munching on his pole beans.

Yeah, life was treating him real good, considering the rest of the world was out there dealing with them white things and the lizard-bugs with all the teeth. He'd been fine until a couple weeks ago, when all kinda hell broke loose that ruined his whole way of life.

Some little Indian girl he hadn't never met had painted a picture on the gym floor in Zion Village. He'd been there years ago when it was an academy for deaf kids, and before that as a little boy with his daddy when it wasn't nothing but Gethsemane Monastery with monks making wine and cheese and stuff.

After Astral Day, most of the folks from Jessup had moved out to the academy, turned it into Zion Village, and a little girl there had a vision. That's what he was told and he was okay with that, his granny Elberta had visions sometimes, knew when it was gonna storm or somebody was gonna die sudden. This little girl painted a huge picture on the gym floor of some big black spaceship melting the polar ice caps and flooding the earth. And they said the flood was gonna happen in six days.

And damned if all them people didn't decide to live through the flood in Matheson Caverns!

Why there musta been three, maybe four thousand people already in here and more still out there loading up stuff. Looked like every mother's child of them picked up stakes and floated on rafts here, hauling everything they owned to the caves to live on.

Gideon was by nature a scavenger. He'd amassed just about everything he owned by finding and using the cast-off belongings of others, and any other belongings they hadn't cast off yet but wasn't keeping a proper eye on. He'd not had the most highly respected job in the world before the white spots by Jupiter. He'd been the man who drove the garbage truck for TMI, the big company that provided garbage removal to small towns. Come Astral Day and wasn't nobody putting their garbage out by the curb on Wednesday nights no more.

In just a few days his whole world turned upside down. Them people from Zion Village *invaded* his home. The cave was *his* home, dammit. He'd come here when didn't nobody else want to live like a bat in the dark, made it his own special place and they didn't have no right to come trespassing in it like they done. So he figured they was fair game, he'd give as good as he got. He'd take from them whatever he could scavenge, and not just their leftovers neither. He'd take whatever they had that he wanted and if he was required to use violence to that end, he was down with that. Move into a man's house and take it over, you deserved whatever you got.

He'd hid out in the shadows out from the dock, and anytime he seen something he could use — supplies like ammunition was golden — he'd wait until nobody was looking and appropriate it for himself. He'd made a nice little stash of provisions, at the expense of three missing persons either nobody'd noticed was gone yet or nobody cared about enough to come check. He'd got it figured where he was gonna wait for the next big load of squatters. This here was Day Five and there was a whole twenty-four hours left before the Astrals did their thing. They was something like five thousand people in Zion Village so there'd be a lot more people coming. He'd just mingle in with them and go up in the elevator to Level One. And all them supplies he'd took, how would these folks know they wasn't his?

But didn't no more refugees arrive. Some kid on a jet ski showed up and talked with his hands — the deaf-person talk Gideon didn't understand — and all the people working on the dock got in the elevators and run them up to the other levels. And didn't send them back down! Dammit. He didn't know what was going on, but he didn't have no choice but to get one of them rafts, load up his stuff and float it downriver through the cave to the other end where there were stairs and an old fashioned wench-and-pulley system to use for hauling stuff up. He wouldn't get it all, but he'd get as much as he could on one load, up through Level Four to Level Three, offload it, and hide it somewhere to come back for later.

He had a raft loaded in a few minutes, pushed off, and was less than a mile from where the river exited the cave below the Cricket Bottom entrance when the impossible happened.

The water quit flowing downstream and started flowing back the other way. Squirting like from a fire hose, *flowing in*!

And the water level was going up faster than an elevator. You don't suppose … Holy shit. The flood. Water was flowing in, pushing the river back. It wasn't supposed to happen until tomorrow. But it was happening right now. He had to get off that raft, onto the river's edge and down to them stairs before the water—

But it was too late, the current upended his raft and dumped him in the water and he had to scramble to keep from drowning, barely managed to get his hands on a flashlight before all his provisions was gone. Washed him back upstream before he scrambled out ... on the wrong side of the river from where the stairs had been built up into Level Four. He knew another way, though, a chimney he could climb that would drop him out in Level Three, not Four. If the water was flowing in through the river, it was flowing in up there in Four, too, and trying to climb them stairs would be like trying to climb up a spigot with the water turned on.

He was almost to the chimney when a hand grabbed his leg and yanked him off his feet and he liked to died right on the spot from fright. Then he found himself looking at a stranger whose black eyes were as cold and as vicious as the beady eyes of a wild boar.

The man had a knife at Gideon's throat he never even saw the man draw.

"You know a way out of here, old man?"

The stranger was shouting, roaring, the sound thundering in Gideon's head so loud he thought his eardrums might explode from the pressure, though he could have sworn the man's lips never moved.

"Hell, yeah! But ain't neither one of us got time for me to draw you a map, so you best let me go."

"*Show me!*"

The words thundered in Gideon's head and he was obeying before he ever even willed his limbs to respond, hurrying irrespective of the water and the danger, rushing just to do what the man said, desperate to follow his orders, whatever they might be.

"This way," he cried, and took out running in water that was up to his knees now, had overflowed the riverbanks and was flooding the cavern.

He got to the crack in the rock and started climbing, only then glancing back. The black-eyed stranger was right behind him.

Chapter Two

PACO SCRAMBLED UP THE ROCKS, followed what looked like a crack in the rock up into the ceiling of the cave above the flooding river, much more agile and light-footed than the old man crawling upward in front of him, holding a small flashlight, the beam lighting his way.

The light from Paco's rage lit his way. He didn't need a flashlight. He glowed from the fire of fury deep inside, a fire that flamed through his whole being like that wildfire fueled by the Santa Ana wind that almost killed him.

Noah had tricked him! Had broadcast the image of the stairwell they'd passed in the shadows just to distract Paco.

Hey, motherfucker. Don't blame him. You fell for it. He's just smarter than you, that's all. Always was. Yet again, he has bested the great leader of men, Paco Salazar, who tripped over his own feet and got shoved into the pool with his clothes on.

Himself spoke with such spite and venom it was stunning. Paco reeled, as he had done when Himself finally outed himself, turned against Paco in public right there in the gym in front of all those people. Oh, Himself had become the enemy alright, no longer the voice in Paco's

11

head that warned him about the damage in his brain, that feared for his mental health, that claimed all the effort to control the minds of others, to manifest himself as an image that wasn't real had burst blood vessels in his brain, so many that the damage was now irreparable. Himself had shown him the burst vessels the night he took the ayahuasca, told him that the damage would eventually drive him totally insane. In the beginning, Himself had tried to help him. But then Himself had turned on him.

Finally figured that out, did you, asshole?

And though Himself had popped into existence as a voice in Paco's head, he had become real, a person standing beside him in the gym … how long ago? Shit, was it just a few hours ago? Had it only been that long? Himself was no longer just a voice. He'd looked so real, so lifelike Paco couldn't believe no one else could see him. He was Paco No, he was Not-Paco. He was the scrawny not-yet-sixteen-year-old kid that Spade had raped for hours and hours, laughing uproariously as he bled on the sheets on Spade's bunk.

Himself, Not-Paco had been bleeding, dripping blood on the gym floor.

Not bleeding now, numb-nuts. Got it under control by stuffing a t-shirt in my pants.

That's what Paco had done in the laundry room of that house after he'd escaped from the massacre of the prison by the Astrals.

Turn around. I'll show you. I'll prove it.

Paco didn't turn around

Himself wasn't really there. Not there. Not there!

You're going insane.

Dear God, he was!

Then Himself burst out laughing. As Paco's fingers

clutched the rocks, his feet struggling to find a foothold to climb, Himself was laughing at him.

Paco turned on him.

"Shut up, you motherfucker or I'll—"

He was shouting the words into the darkness behind him and the old man in front stopped, panting, and turned around.

"I didn't say nothing. I wouldn't, not to … you."

Ahh, the sweet sound of subjugation, of total submission, of a will bent totally to his. And he hadn't even tried, hadn't reached out to bend this man, to crush his will, blend his mind to Paco's dominion. It happened that way sometimes. When he was in the presence of those whose wills were weak, twisted in some way, they automatically fell under his power with no effort at all on his part. Good. He needed to save the reserves of his mental power. He would need it.

Taking advantage of the stop to catch his breath, the man spoke in the tone of the suck-up that he was.

"Ain't nobody else in the whole world knows about this chimney but me," he said. "Not them Mathesons, nobody. I found it my own self, but I was at the top, coming down, not here on the bottom climbing up. It's harder climbing up."

"Where does this lead?"

The old man's chest puffed out in pride.

"It bypasses Level Four altogether, goes up through the wall beside it." He waited, like a dog expecting a treat after he does a trick.

"And that is significant because …?"

"Because Level Four's flooded by now, that's why. The water flowing in the river'll be flowing in the Cricket Bottom cave entrance, too. The hole in the floor of that cavern for the stairs, water's pouring down it now. Trying to climb up out of it would be like trying to climb up through the water of a flushing toilet."

That remark struck the man as uproariously humorous and he bellowed. The laughter died in this throat when he saw that Paco was not amused.

"If this … what did you call it, a chimney?"

"Yeah, chimney. They's several of them in the caverns, holes that go through the walls from one cavern to another."

"If this chimney doesn't open in the level above it, where does it come out?"

"Comes out on Cambridge Avenue in Level Three."

"Cambridge Avenue?"

"Yeah, all these tunnels is named. How you gonna draw a map of a cave 'thout naming the passages … or numbering 'em or something. The Mathesons been exploring and mapping these caves for generations."

"Do you have a map of the caves?"

The old man tapped his dirty finger to his temple. "Right up here, know every twist and turn, been poking around in here ever day for the past five years."

The old man paused, and Paco watched him wrestle with himself, the battle of wanting to look good versus being caught in an inaccuracy warring within him. He let the fight wind down until there was a victor.

"Well, actually, not *all* the passages. These caves, there's more'n two-hundred-and-fifty miles of 'em. Don't nobody but the Mathesons know *all* the ways of them, and the younger ones might notta learnt them all. What I know is the parts of the caves that was opened to visitors, the part the Mathesons made their living showing to tourists."

"And how many miles is that?"

"It's four miles from the Cricket Bottom entrance and the stairs on the east side of the caverns to the elevators on the west, and the dock where the river flows in there — four miles 'as the crow flies.' How far it is inside the caverns is different on each of the levels, depending on how much the tunnels twist and turn and loop back around. If you's to stretch out all the twists and turns in all them tunnels and measured it on the ground, it'd be — I don't know — a fair piece."

"So there really is an elevator?"

"Oh, hell yeah. Four of them! As a matter of fact, I ... relieved a man of his belongings when he stopped to take a piss while he was loading supplies into one of them." He paused. "All that shit's gone now, washed away. Only thing left now is the supplies that's already in the cave."

"The elevator ...?" Paco prompted.

"Oh, yeah. It goes from the Styx Dock all the way up to Broadway on Level One, stops at Cambridge Avenue on Level Three and North Main on Level two on the way. That's how all them folks trucked all that shit in here for the past three days, hauled it in day and night they did, loaded it on carts and hauled it away from the elevator entrances so other folks could unload theirs."

"Carts?"

"Yeah, carts, drawn by donkeys. They's been carts in all the caves around here for hundreds of years, hauling shit. Just on Level One, though, up through Persnickety, across Smiley Face past the dome and the flow formations there, and back down Manitoba Lane to Broadway."

"And what kind of supplies do you have, Mr. ... what's your name?"

"I'm Gideon, Gideon Freeman." The man actually wiped the dirt off his hand on his pants and offered it to Paco to shake. Paco just looked at him, put him in his place with the look, and the man dropped his hand. Paco offered him no names. Names granted power. Mystery kept power private.

This was crazy. They were standing in a narrow rock passageway in a place as dark as the devil's lower asshole, and exchanging pleasantries as if they had met at a cocktail party. Though Paco had never actually been to a cocktail party, he'd seen them in old movies.

"Shouldn't we be going?"

"Ain't no hurry. Water can't come up this shaft. I heard that Noah Matheson explained it all when they had that meeting about moving in here. I wasn't there, but folks said he told them the lower two levels, Four and Five — Five being the level the river runs through — would flood. The levels above being sealed up, wouldn't."

"There are no … leaks?"

"Oh, hell no. That's the thing about the caves around here — like Mammoth Cave. You heard of Mammoth Cave, ain't you?"

Paco had, though he couldn't remember much about it, only that it was something like four hundred miles long, the longest cave in the world, and there was a national park. But he wasn't interested in Mammoth Cave now.

When Paco said nothing, the man stuttered on.

"I mean, there's been lots of geology done on it, being a national park and all, and what's true of it is true of Matheson Caverns, too. It's a dry cave. The sandstone on the surface of Joppa Ridge seals it. In a wet cave, like Carlsbad Caverns, that's how stalactites and stalagmites and flow formations and shit like that form, from water dripping down from above. There ain't but a few of them in Matheson Caverns and they's mostly in Level Four. It's under water now, or soon will be."

"Back to my original question — what do you have in the caves?" While the old man answered the question,

Paco skimmed the top of his mind. Even the effort to do that caused a dull thud behind his right eye and he didn't go deep. Got the old man's history, saw images of his homesite on Level One, and saw the latest images, of knifing the man to steal his guns and ammunition only minutes before Paco's mind had reached out in desperation, searching for any other mind ... and landed on this one. He could just as easily have come upon a priest as a thief. His luck was turning. Yes, Gideon Freeman was just the kind of man Paco was looking for. He interrupted Freeman's rambling narrative.

"You don't like that the people from Zion Village have come into the cave, do you?"

You'd have thought Paco had performed some magical feat of mind reading the way the man's face lit with astonishment. Shit.

"That's right, I don't."

"Are there other cave dwellers who are equally ... offended by the Zion invasion?"

"You bet your ass there are!"

"Good," Paco said. "Excellent."

Chapter Three

GARSON WENT LOOKING for Diana early in the morning of Day Five. He supposed it was early. And Day Five. That was going to be a problem. It was on his growing list of things to talk to Sawyer about. Circadian rhythms were strong forces in human beings. They would have to be artificially created here in the caverns. With light, somehow. He'd talk to Noah. It had to be night for everybody at the same time, then day. Establish a pattern. The everybody-working-around-the-clock thing — Garson knew both Sawyer and Nick were coming up on thirty-six hours of no sleep — would have to stop once they moved in. He didn't know the precise psychological effect it would have on thousands of people, only knew that failure to recreate the earth's rotation over a long period of time would be damaging. There had been studies. It would be fascinating to investigate, however, and maybe he could …

He rounded a corner and found Anna standing beside a curtained-off passageway. Diana was nowhere in sight. Anna would be caring for Diana now, she and Ellie had worked that out, and it was clear to see that Anna adored the child ... well, who didn't? Anna had told him that she didn't intend to tell Diana that her mother was staying behind until tonight, when everybody was sealed up tight in the ark. She and Sawyer would set the child down and deliver the news as gently as possible.

How do you say, "You're never going to see your mother again" gently? Poor little thing.

So he'd asked Anna if he could take the child on a picnic today, an adventure. The seven-year-old had never been more than fifty miles from her home in Zion Village, but Garson liked to think that becoming friends with a professor of astrophysics at Hillsdale College had granted her some insight into the wonders of the world. When Diana had heard about the petting zoo, the rock formations in Level Four, she'd talked of nothing else, how bad she wanted to see them — especially the big cricket just inside the Cricket Bottom entrance. If she didn't see them today, she'd never get another chance — they'd be under water.

This was her last shot.

He'd figured it out — they could go down Level Three — which was a superhighway compared to Level Four's twists and turns — to the Tripoli cavern and down the stairs there to Cricket Bottom, stop along the way to look at The Blarney Stone and Mount Rush-More. Garson's was not a eidetic memory but it was close and he had studied the maps of every level, knew every twist and turn. He'd asked the monks to make them sandwiches for a picnic, and the basket they gave him obviously contained other goodies, too. He thought he smelled ... could that be pumpkin bread?

He wanted to give the little girl a happy memory before ...

"Where's Diana?" he asked Anna. The little girl had

bounced up and down in place — looked like a little kangaroo — when he'd invited her. That was another thing people would need to keep in mind in the ... however-long time ahead. They had to take time to create joy wherever they could.

Anna's face was tight, her voice controlled.

"She's in with her mother now. I'll go get her."

"Her *mother*? Ellie's *here*?"

"She is. Gretchen brought her last night." Anna colored those words with layers of meaning — even Garson could see that. Before he could ask any questions, Gretchen snatched aside the curtain and almost ran into him. She ignored him and signed to Anna.

"On my way. Anything you forgot? Mother doesn't have much for me to bring. Last trip."

"Nothing," Anna signed the word. She said it out loud, too, and there were ice cubes dangling off it.

"I don't get it," Garson said to them both. "What's Ellie doing here? She didn't want to come on the ark. She—"

Gretchen turned on him, her face contorted in rage. She signed, "Sawyer Matheson told you she said that, but it's a *lie*. He was going to leave her there to die, to *drown*. He'd have *murdered* her if I hadn't—"

"Now, hold on there, young lady." Garson bristled. "Ellie *wanted*—"

"Don't tell me what my mother did or didn't want. I'll be the judge of that."

She spun on her heel and strode off down the corridor.

"How ...?" Garson began.

"Gretchen drugged her," Anna hissed, partly to speak quietly, partly because she was so angry she was leaking steam.

"With *what*?" Sawyer asked. "I didn't think there was a

good drug left anywhere on the North American continent."

"When Gretchen was packing, she knocked something into that hole behind one of the big drawers built into the walls in the girls' wing." Built in, alright, with quarter-sawn white oak trim, hand carved and stained cherry. Garson knew his wood and had noticed the first time he'd come to the academy that the rich parents of the deaf children sent here for Dr. Weiss' implant were determined that their offspring would be housed in the style to which they'd become accustomed. "She had to pull the drawer out of the wall, and she found a thirty-count bottle of Percocet stuck in the opening, a prescription for Hillary Marie Wimset, written by a dentist eight years ago. Brother Sebastian remembered the girl, said she'd had all her wisdom teeth removed."

"So Hillary lost her pain meds …"

"And eight years later, Gretchen found them."

"Are they still good? What about the expiration—"

"On a narcotic, all that means is that ten years after that date, the drug will only be ninety percent effective."

"And Gretchen gave Ellie the pills?"

"Enough to knock her out — Gretchen didn't know what she was doing. It's a miracle she didn't kill her mother, the shape that poor woman's in." Sawyer saw color darken Anna's black cheeks. "And then she brought Ellie here, *kidnapped* her out of her room."

The energy drained out of Anna and she leaned back against the wall with a sigh. "This is *not* what Ellie wanted. We talked about it for hours — how she wanted to die. Then when the ark … she didn't see any point." Surprisingly, Anna teared up. She didn't often show emotion.

"I know." Garson felt awkward, was always unnerved by the emotions of others because he didn't know what he ought to do about them, how he should respond. He settled for reaching out and touching her arm lightly. "She told me the same thing, that she planned to stay, wanted to die there in Zion Village."

"Gretchen didn't give a shit what her mother wanted, hauled her in here in the middle of the night." She stopped, banked her anger. "But I found a good bed, and we've made Ellie a room in a little cubby hole of a cavern so she can have some privacy. "

"How is she?"

"Actually sleeping right now. Those pills — what a godsend. I can make her comfortable for …"

"How long?"

"Maybe … long enough. Maybe she'll die before the pain comes back like it was before."

Chapter Four

GARSON THOUGHT of Ellie Hampton as he waited for Diana. Oh, that poor woman. Garson had met Ellie seven years ago when he moved off the campus of Hillsdale College to Zion Academy at the insistence of Sawyer Matheson, scuttling away from the facility after the Astrals had ransacked his lab there. Sawyer had pointed out that as one of the nation's preeminent Ancient Aliens expert, the Astrals might show particular interest in Garson and drawing the attention of the Astrals was not a prudent thing to do.

But privately, Garson wished again, as he had a thousand times before, that he had *not* been away from his office the day the Astrals came. That he hadn't missed probably the only chance he would ever have in his whole life to make contact with a being from another universe. In his considered opinion, one he didn't share, of course, the risk of … well, of whatever … was more than worth it for the opportunity to actually meet an Astral. Oh, he would give … well, at the time he'd likely have given his life, but it would have been well worth it. To make *contact* … sigh … that was all his life lacked for him to die a happy man.

"I'll be ready in just a minute," Diana called out to him through the curtain.

Tiny bells. Tiny bells on a cold morning, a morning in January when your breath made frost in the air. That's what Diana's voice sounded like. Just the sound alone was enough to melt the old man's heart and make him, yet again, grateful that he'd lived long enough to meet her.

"Oh, take your time, sugar plum. We're in no hurry."

Actually, there had been more hurrying around in the past four days than in all of the years Garson had been at the academy put together. What with the end of the world and all … making preparations to survive the flooding of the entire earth — well, that had caused a bit of a stir.

Because of Diana, however, Garson viewed the whole process with less detachment than he had viewed what happened to the world after they spotted the little white specks out by Jupiter. He'd been one of only a handful of scientists who hadn't been surprised, who'd been outcasts in their profession their whole careers for maintaining that there was overwhelming evidence to prove that aliens had visited the earth … more than once in the planet's history.

It was the I-told-you-so of all I-told-you-sos and he had become an instant celebrity, an astrophysicist who'd said all along it would happen. But after he had moved away from Hillsdale College and into the safety of Zion Academy, he had been removed from the academic pursuit of knowl-edge, no longer trekking all over the globe to look at cave drawings and artifacts from some new dig. There was nothing to prove anymore. Yep, the aliens had been here before, and guess what, sports fans, they've come back. Their presence established as fact everything that Garson had spent a lifetime amassing evidence to prove.

And just as he had postulated, the Astrals were, indeed, going to cleanse the planet of humanity. So there was nothing else to discover. Their little remnant might survive here, though he did have grave doubts about that. Or they might not. Time would tell. But right now, all the questions had been answered. There was nothing left to be curious about. Garson'd had to turn his scientific curiosity off like a spigot.

And, oh how he yearned for just one last ... *something* ... to investigate. He had missed all the opportunities to make the acquaintance of Astrals, and if the small community of would-be survivors were able to keep body and soul together during God only knew how much time underground, the Astrals would be gone when they poked their heads out of the hidey-hole. And Dr. Mikhail Ziegelman Garczonski, PhD, would have missed his only chance to satisfy the scientific curiosity of his lifetime.

"All done," the child burbled, reached out and took his hand in such an innocent expression of attachment and confidence, he almost teared up. "We can go now." Everyone in the village loved that little girl — she'd even captured the heart of the curmudgeon professor.

With the child holding his hand, Garson headed out into the main corridor of the cavern called Corkscrew and from it into Carnegie Hall, the largest cavern in the whole cave system that had been developed for visitors years ago. A left turn from there put them on Broadway, the main cavern that ran the length of the Level One.

As they walked along, Diana chattered like a little magpie, and he nodded yes and no in appropriate places and that's all it took to keep her going. Diana's babble was the white noise of their relationship, and Garson had to concentrate to attend to what she said when it was more than idle chatter.

27

They met people coming and going, women and children, men and families, scurrying around in an effort to get themselves ready to live here for however long it took for the flood waters the Astrals were about to unleash to go back down. Some people greeted them. Most didn't, though Diana said hello to everyone, knew every man, woman, and child in all of Zion Village, well, seemed to anyway. But the people they were greeting were not folks out for a leisurely stroll. They were people who had been convinced that the world was going to flood and their only hope of survival was to go down into a cave and live until the waters went down. Pretty preposterous, when you thought about it. But it was testimony to the people's belief in Star's prophetic ability — and the proof offered by the picture *the blind girl* had painted on the gym floor of the black death ship melting the polar ice caps.

The number of people they met grew as they turned out of the big Broadway tunnel and went into the smaller South Broadway tunnel that lead to the four elevators ending on the top floor there.

Families had been limited to what they could transport in the carts provided. Some people had simply unloaded their belongings off the elevator, loaded them into carts, hauled them a couple hundred yards down the cavern and dumped them there, prepared to camp out in what Garson considered "the middle of the street' for the duration.

There'd be more than five thousand people moving into the cave and they couldn't all unload their belongings from the elevator and set up camp right next to it! The elders had put up a large map of the caverns, next to the elevators on the three top levels, showing people the layout of the caverns. And they'd distributed brochures and "tourist guides" they'd dug out of the old Matheson Caverns Visitor's Center. Rather than having all five thousand people scrambling for the "best" sites, with the inevitable I-was-here-first disputes, the elders had *assigned* caverns based on where people had lived in Zion Village. Caverns were staked out corresponding to Zion Village neighborhoods, so people would be living in the caverns with the same people they'd lived near outside. All the large caverns had dozens of smaller, unnamed caverns branching off from them, so neighbors could set up house-keeping with total privacy from their neighbors if they so chose.

But people were frightened/angry/shocked/ whatever by the sudden turn of events, and this Level One cavern felt like the last lifeboat leaving a sinking ship — and lots of people had simply tossed their belongs aboard and jumped in, figuring they'd sort it all out later.

When Garson and Diana got to the elevators there was a crowd — some people sorting through the belongings they'd just unloaded, and others waiting to go back down in the elevator to bring up more stuff, ignoring the one-cart-load rule altogether.

Though it all around seemed chaotic right here, the whole move had been well organized, thanks to the masterful leadership of Sawyer Matheson, who, in Garson's mind at least, could have been a general or the CEO of a vast financial empire — with his intellect and people skills — rather than the sheriff of a nowhere little town in rural Kentucky. But things work out the way they were supposed to, he supposed. Without Sawyer, there might be no remnant of humanity left on the whole planet after the flood other than those humans hand-picked by the Astrals. And that seemed wrong, just plain *wrong* on a whole lot of levels.

As they stood waiting for the elevator, Garson took the opportunity to show Diana the big map and try to orient her not only to where they were going today, but where everybody was going to be living until ... well, until the water went down or they all died of starvation, whichever eventuality came first.

Noah's Ark was the portion of the caverns the Matheson family had run as a tourist business — five levels of caverns. The river flowed through Level Five, and Level Four was where visitors came in through the Cricket Bottom entrance. Both those levels would be flooded, but the remaining three levels of visitor caverns, each about four miles long, would be above the water level of the flood. Each of those four miles had dozens of other caverns snaking off them in all directions, and more caverns snaking off those ... and more ... The explored portion was a tangled labyrinth of more than 250 miles of caves.

Over the years, as the family business expanded, the Mathesons "upgraded" the tourist portion of the caves on display, though determined to keep the cave as natural as possible. The pathways on every level, stretching from the elevators on the west to the staircases on the east, were paved, wheelchair accessible, the caverns lit — in addition to the Glow Worm lights Sawyer and Taylor's father had begun putting in all the caverns as he explored them. The lighting matched the atmosphere of the cave, with lights set down behind rocks out of sight, casting shadowy illumination in every passageway. The lights operated off switches discretely set in the wall, with the cables connecting them strung out of sight. Tour guides turned on the lights in each section of cave as they got to it with a group of visitors and turned off the lights in the cavern they'd just passed through. Since the immigration of the past week, all the lights in all the caverns had been turned on and left on, no longer run off the electricity fed into the caves in cables from outside, but by solar batteries, brought in from Zion Village.

The largest cavern the Mathesons had ever discovered was on Level One and they'd called it Carnegie Hall, an open area half the size of a football field with a ceiling more than a hundred feet off the floor. A commercial kitchen was built into one side of the cavern with a dining area where foldable tables and chairs could be set up to feed a thousand people. Grandstands that would hold fifteen hundred people were built in the other side of the cavern where tourists could watch costumed re-enactments of all the cave's explorations since the dawn of history. At the height of tourist season, local vendors set up booths in the vast open area of the hall, selling everything from hand-knitted wool caps, pottery and blown-glass sculptures to antique machines like kitchen mixers and vacuum cleaners and lawn mowers. Tourists waiting in long lines in Carnegie Hall to enter Alabaster Hall gobbled up the trinkets.

Alabaster Hall.

Its splendor was so breathtaking it almost didn't seem real. It was the only cavern in the cave system that was accessed by a man-made tunnel dug out of the limestone between it and Carnegie Hall, and the "flowering gypsum" visible in Alabaster Hall was the single greatest tourist attraction. The cave limestone was composed of calcium *carbonate*, of course, whereas gypsum was calcium *sulfate*, and it was used for all manner of things — from plaster to fertilizer to wallboard.

Noah's grandfather had been out exploring when he squeezed through a crack in a cave wall, and came out on the other side in a hollow chamber lined with gypsum — floor, walls, ceiling. But gypsum in its *crystalline form* — which meant it was *made of crystals*. Prisms everywhere catching and refracting the light — crystals as big as his leg, the size of a pencil or a baseball bat, thousands of tiny ones the size of marbles and every size in between — glittering, winking, twinkling and shimmering. Besides the crystals — yellow, green, blue, turquoise, every color in the spectrum —there were naturally occurring fissures in the walls on one side of the hall. Ten sometimes twenty feet deep, the cracks were lined with multicolored crystals on both sides, above and below — each fissure's crystals uniquely shaped and colored. Since the fissures were narrow, only two or three feet wide, they were called Library Aisles because it was like walking down the aisle in an old library full of remarkable books, where you could take your time and examine every volume on every shelf.

The map showed the Level One caverns colored blue, Level Two red and Level Three green. Levels Four and Five were on the map, but not detailed, since those would be flooded when the water came and uninhabitable.

"If you can imagine picking up all the blue lines and setting them on top of the red lines and then setting both of those on top of the green lines, that's what the cave is really like. All these caverns are like the floors of a building, winding around through the rock one on top of the other."

"Uh, you wanna get out of the way, pal. We're trying to unload here," said a man trying to maneuver a cart loaded with far too many belongings out of the elevator.

Garson said nothing about the top-heavy load, which surely would come tumbling down as soon as the man tried pushing it into the cavern, just took Diana's hand and stepped back out of his way. Garson had brought almost no personal belongings into the cave. Paring them down to the bare essentials produced a pile of items that would fit into an oversized laundry basket. He had been allowed three loads of "future resources," would have brought the whole of Zion Academy's library if they'd have let him.

Question: if you know that the only information from the whole civilization of the world will be what you save from destruction today, what would you take? Shakespeare? Or the *Farmers' Almanac*? Science textbooks or carpentry guides? He had just grabbed what he could carry, trying not to linger over decisions or he'd be there still.

"See that star on the map? That's the 'YOU ARE HERE' star to show this location on Broadway on Level One. Broadway is the main tunnel that stretches from the elevators on the west side of Level One to the stairs on the east. The main tunnel in Level Two is Main Street, and on Level Three, it's Cambridge Avenue, but there are dozens of tunnels that branch off those — some of them fixed up with walkable paths, lights and railings for the visitors, and others of them in their natural states, with rocks tumbled down all around, so you have to climb and pick your way through and down them."

Once the big freight elevator was empty, Garson and Diana joined the crowd going back down for more loads, though they got off on Level Three instead of going on to the big dock on the river, which was stacked ten feet high with supplies that had to be taken up to the other levels and stored, or families' belongings for them to set up housekeeping.

Though they were headed out to see the Level Four rock formations, that cavern was narrow, and it twisted and turned and looped back on itself like tangled-up Christmas lights. Level Three was a freeway in comparison. They'd go down Cambridge to the end of Three, through the big cavern called the Halls of Montezuma — which contained the gigantic rock called the Blarney Stone — on through the smaller one beyond it called the Shores of Tripoli and down the stairs at Cricket Bottom. That's where the big cricket was!

No one got off the elevator with them because nobody'd yet moved into Level Three. Most people merely got off on the top two floors. Diana was reluctant to enter the empty chamber, where the hollow sound of their footsteps echoed in the silence.

They hadn't gone two hundred yards before she asked, "How much farther is it?" Her grip on his hand had tightened with each step and she was now walking so close to his leg he was afraid he was going to step on her.

He didn't want to drag the child along with him through the cavern. This was supposed to be a pleasant experience for her. She just needed to get used to the emptiness, that's all, so it didn't seem so foreign and frightening.

"Why, look over there at that apple tree," Garson said. Diana followed his gaze.

"Apple tree?"

He pointed to a stack of rocks near the edge of the trail that looked nothing at all like a tree of any kind.

"A pretend apple tree. That's the perfect place for a picnic, don't you think? In the shade of that tree."

Diana was instantly engaged in the fantasy. As Garson spread out the tablecloth from the monks' picnic basket, Diana prattled on. "I hope we don't get hit in the head by falling apples!"

They enjoyed a leisurely lunch, took their time, and when Garson saw Diana was still leery of the dark, empty cavern, he launched into what he did best — teaching. Time derailed, and when he glanced at his watch at the end of his description of the geologic forces that had created the caverns and the unique creatures that lived there, he was surprised to see that hours had passed. They needed to get going.

He packed up litter and leftovers in the basket, took her hand, and started back down the cavern again.

"Sugar, there is nothing to be afraid of. Like I told you before, the cavern is like an empty room. There's nothing in here except maybe a couple of blind cave crickets."

Oh, but there was. They both heard it at the same time, something scratching and scrabbling around in the rocks. Blind cave crickets didn't make noise.

Chapter Five

DIANA SUCKED IN A BREATH, undoubtedly to scream, but surprise stole the scream off her lips. A chipmunk raced across the path in front of them and hid quickly in the rocks on the other side.

"Was that a—?"

"It was a chipmunk, Dr. Garson. I didn't know there were chipmunks in the cavern."

"There aren't."

"Yes, there are, we just saw one."

"I meant there aren't supposed to be chipmunks in the cavern. They don't live there. They can't survive here. What on earth—?"

His scientific mind began to spin. Why was there a chipmunk in the cavern? Garson absolutely did *not* like where the logical sequence of that thought was taking him. The only reason for an animal from the forest to come running into the cave was …

It was running *from something*.

And Garson could think of only one thing a little beastie like that could be running from.

Maybe they ought to go back.

But now, surprisingly, Diana wanted to go ahead. The sight of the chipmunk had cheered her for some reason, and then he figured it out.

"Why don't you want to go back? Five minutes ago you were begging—"

"Five minutes ago we hadn't seen the chipmunk."

"What does that creature have to do with it?"

"The caverns aren't *empty*. They have chipmunks in them."

Then he realized that what he'd been telling her to calm her fears — that there was nothing in the caverns — had actually made her more afraid. The emptiness, the nothingness, was scary. But hey, if the caverns were for chipmunks, then she thought they might be alright too.

Diana took his hand and literally dragged him a few feet forward before the rest of him consented to go. His mind was whirring while her tiny bell voice was chirping away.

Then they both heard a whumping sound that was unmistakable. That was wings.

"Are there bats in the cave?" Diana asked. "I don't like bats."

A bat here made no more sense than a chipmunk. Oh, there were bats in Matheson Caverns, of course. Levels Four and Five were full of bat colonies because *they had outside entrances*. There were probably dozens of caves leading into Level Four, some only a few inches across, but one was so big it was called The Drain. Why would the bats have made their way up into Level Three to live?

The fluttering again. Then a sound.

Cheep, cheep!

Bats did not cheep.

Garson knew precious little about the little nocturnal

bloodsuckers but he did know they made a sound on a frequency humans couldn't hear to bounce off surfaces to operate their internal sonar.

Cheep. Cheep.

He saw something flash in front of a light, about fifty yards down the tunnel, like a bird through the headlights of a car. It wasn't a bat. Too big and not the right shape at all.

He saw another one. And another. Not mysterious creatures by any stretch.

"See," he said to the trembling Diana, "it's not a bat, just a plain old bird, that's all. A robin or a blue jay."

"I didn't know there were birds in the caverns."

Again, Garson's response: "There aren't."

A chipmunk ... a bird ...

SHIT!

"Let's go see what else is here that you didn't know about." With that, Diana let go of his hand and skipped merrily down the pathway so that he had to do his hobbling imitation of a jog to catch her.

"Wait up, little one. We're in this together, remember."

"I wanted to stay right by you because I was afraid." She looked at him with wide, compassionate eyes. "Are you afraid now?"

Hell yes, he was afraid! So terrified it was surprising he could keep the tremor from his voice and the shaking from his hands. There was no reasonable explanation for the presence of these creatures in the cavern unless ... *they were running from something.*

Had he miscalculated how long it would take for the black death ship to journey from Jupiter to Earth?

Oh, dear God, he hoped not!

They absolutely, one hundred percent, were *not* ready for it. The supplies weren't all loaded and neither were the people. He didn't know precisely what was where, but he did know Sawyer and the others thought they had all day today, planned to be moved in by midnight. So whatever they'd intended to load …

The flood.

Oh, God, the flood had come early.

When he finally let himself think the thought, the fear left him, replaced by his mind evaluating. He liked to think that his thoughts in analysis mode made a sound like a humming bird.

Not all the supplies were loaded yet.

Neither were all the people.

Sawyer!

Noah, Star, Nick, Taylor.

Eagle Feather. The lifelong friend he had met only seven years ago, but in these times that was a lifetime. The man who had chatted with him about Ancient Aliens theories and the cave drawings of the Mescalero Apache, and the legends of his family.

The detonator!

Oh, holy shit, the detonator to blow up the entrance to the mine dug by the Astrals. The last time Garson had seen it, Nick was still working on it. Had somebody — *anybody* — brought it to the caverns?

If not, they all were toast.

More scrabbling in the rocks to the right. Diana wanted to go and investigate, but Garson wouldn't let her. There was literally no telling what might have come into the caves to escape the rising water. They'd talked about that briefly in their planning sessions — not wondering what wildlife would show up unannounced and perhaps unwanted but what species they ought to strategically take with them. The only conclusion they'd reached was that the Astrals were going to destroy the earth and not for the first time. If they intended to give the human race another shot, they'd have to un-destroy the world to make it habitable for them and un-destruction would include nature, in all its particulars.

There was the sound of more scrabbling in the rocks. The farther they went, the more they heard, evidence of a growing herd of wildlife. At least halfway down the cavern by now, they watched more and more images flit in front of the lights that'd been artfully hidden behind rocks to camouflage them so the cave could look realistic to the visitors. Images of creatures larger than a chipmunk.

Off to the left, Garson spotted a large shadow. A very large shadow. It was the size of a dog or cat, but he suspected the woods around the caverns didn't boast large populations of cats or dogs. At least not ... domesticated ones.

Diana was thrilled with the new wildlife, got more excited by the minute. She peered intently expectantly around every corner, hoping to catch sight of more creatures.

Around the very next bend, they found the biggest creature so far, and not in the rocks but lying on the pathway.

It was Eagle Feather.

Chapter Six

GARSON DID RUN THEN, ignored the hitch in his gait and moved as fast as he was able to the form lying on the trail ahead.

"Mr. Eagle Feather!" Diana got there first, of course, touched his shoulder. "Mr. Eagle Feather, wake up. It's me, Diana."

Garson saw the blood before he knelt beside his friend and feared the worst. He was bleeding from a gash on his leg and another on his hand. Both had been "field bandaged" but both the bandages were soaked.

He gently turned the old Indian over onto his back.

"Eagle Feather." Garson spoke his name in a fear-hushed voice. He put his mouth down next to Eagle Feather's and grabbed his wrist, tried to find a pulse. For a horrifying few seconds there was none, then he felt it. Weak and fluttery but there.

He called again but the old man didn't respond. He was obviously suffering from blood loss and if they didn't do something to stop the bleeding, he would surely die.

Garson ripped off his long-sleeved shirt and tried to rip

the sleeve off it but couldn't, had no idea shirtsleeves were sewn on that tightly. Then he saw the knife in a scabbard at Eagle Feather's side and used it to cut the fabric. He kicked off his shoes, removed his thick white socks, and used them as pressure bandages, then he held them in place by tying the sleeves of his shirt around them, one on the old man's hand and the other on his leg.

He didn't know what else to do, only knew Eagle Feather needed much more help than the pitiful little bit of first aid he could render. He couldn't carry him, much as he would have liked to. Garson wasn't strong enough, and figured that trying to chuck the old man, who was bigger than he was, over his shoulder in a fireman's carry would be disastrous for them both, and would at the very least open up the Indian's wounds.

So what could Garson do?

Options: he could leave Eagle Feather here alone while he and Diana went for help; he'd guess it was at least a mile, maybe more, farther down the cavern to Tripoli.

He could leave Diana here with Eagle Feather and go for help.

Or he could send Diana for help and stay here with Eagle Feather himself.

"Diana, honey, you can see that Eagle Feather's hurt."

"He's bleeding. He cut himself."

"We have to get help for him. How would you feel about … being alone here — just for a short time — while I go on to Tripoli and get help?" If, indeed, there was help to be found there. When he and Diana started out on this little picnic, they planned to go down the stairs in Tripoli into the front of Level Four beside the big cricket, where there would be people. He didn't know for sure who, but thought Star was handing out maps and brochures in Bardstown and Taylor's family were finishing up dismantling their house. But now … with the *flood*. His gut clenched. Were they all out there in it — couldn't get back to the cave in time? Maybe still in Zion Village? Had they all — Sawyer, Star and Noah, Taylor and Nick and … had all of them *drowned*?

He shook off the thought.

"If we both go, we'll be leaving Eagle Feather here all alone and I don't think—"

"Somebody needs to go get Uncle Sawyer?"

"Yes."

"Then it needs to be me, not you. I can run faster than you can."

The little girl was right, of course. She could most certainly run a mile faster than he could.

"But *could* you …?"

"I don't *want* to! I want to stay with you. But I don't want to leave Mr. Eagle Feather here all by himself, bleeding."

Before he could say another word, the little girl sprang up.

"I can run fast as the wind, so fast nothing can catch me!"

She turned and bolted down the cavern toward Tripoli. She was right. She was fast.

What should he do now? Was there anything he hadn't already done?

Then he noticed the pillowcase a short distance away on the floor, looked at the wall and saw the probe stuck in the crack, saw that the lever on the toy detonator, the plunger had been depressed.

Eagle Feather had blown up the entrance to the mine!

As if he needed confirmation, that was it. He'd only have done that if, as Garson suspected, the flood had indeed come early.

As Garson remembered it, the plan had been to go up to Level One and attach the probe to a crack in the cave wall there. Garson didn't know where the Astral mine was, only that Noah had stumbled into it seven years ago when he got lost in the caverns on Astral Day. He'd blown it off for years because what he'd found that day was impossible — a chamber with smooth walls. Caves didn't have smooth walls.

Noah had found the cavern again when they were assessing the cave to serve as Noah's Ark during the Astral flood. There had been mining equipment there and Astrals. Several titans were operating robots to cut away slabs of rock to use in the telepathic lines and circles they'd created all over the globe. Garson speculated that the titans didn't do the actual mining because they couldn't be enclosed in the mine with the "telepathic" limestone all around them. If they did, their minds connecting with the hive mind on the mothership and the rocks sending those same thoughts at the same time would cause feedback, like to a microphone on a public address system.

Nick had said the signal from the detonator would travel roughly six hundred vertical feet and an unlimited distance horizontally. How far was it from here up to the top level? Garson feared it was farther than six hundred feet. Clearly Eagle Feather had put the detonator in the wall at the first available spot. He'd been bleeding, injured, had come up to Level Three on a freight elevator, that Garson noticed in a cleft in the nearby rock.

And while he was looking at it, a tarantula spider came crawling up out of it.

Garson could not have been more horrified! He was massively arachnophobic, courtesy of a truly unpleasant encounter with a tarantula when he was a little boy.

The spider had obviously been washed into the cave by

the flood — along with God only knew what other animal life and had crawled up the elevator shaft to survive.

Survive.

Yeah, that's right. That's what we need to transplant into the brave new world — populate it with hairy black spiders!

In a fit of utter loathing, which was the only thing that could have fueled such a move on his part, Garson grabbed the shoe he'd taken off, leapt up and raced across the chamber barefoot toward the spider. It saw him coming, tried to get away, but he was on it before it had a chance.

He slammed the shoe down on, hearing the unpleasant squash sound that followed. Hit it again and again and again, shuddering, until there was nothing recognizable on the cave floor except a gooey spot.

He went back to Eagle Feather's side, but kept a sharp lookout on the elevator shaft. No telling what had crawled up into the cavern through it and the other shafts like it.

Chapter Seven

Diana stopped running.

She had to. Not because she was tired but because running in the empty cavern had scared her too badly. And she had to be brave. Not get scared and go running in tears back to Dr. Garson. And besides, she had come so far now it was probably closer to the cavern called Tripoli where Uncle Sawyer was than back to Dr. Garson anyway. And Eagle Feather needed help.

She had to help Eagle Feather!

He had taken her to track rabbits one day, and another time he showed her the different kinds of butterflies there were in the meadow. He also taught her how to make a campfire without matches. He'd shown her how. She didn't ever get a fire actually started sparking those rocks together, but at least she knew how. He was a wonderful man and he needed help and she could help him.

She kept trying to think about that, fill her head with that, with helping Mr. Eagle Feather. Not let any other thoughts in her head, keep all the other thoughts in her whole brain away when she stopped running, so she couldn't think the thoughts that were scaring her. She'd had to stop running because running felt like she was running *away* from something, and she started looking over her shoulder for what was chasing her, and kept running faster and faster to get away from it. That's when she fell and skinned her knee.

She skinned it so bad it was bleeding. And it *hurt*. She wanted to cry but she didn't because Mr. Eagle Feather was bleeding, too, and he was bleeding a whole lot more blood than she was and he wasn't crying. So she wouldn't cry either.

Falling down was a good thing, though, because it proved that nothing was chasing her because if there had been it would have caught her when she fell. But if she got up and started running again, she'd feel like she was being chased again and she didn't want to fall. So she stopped running — also because running made her knee hurt where she'd skinned it.

She walked fast, though, very fast.

The caverns weren't empty, she kept telling herself. Not great big empty rooms with no furniture in them and no people. There were chipmunks and birds in the caverns. And if there were chipmunks and birds, there were other things, too. So she wasn't alone. There were—

She saw a shadow on the wall that took all the breath out of her body, that froze her to the spot like her feet had been nailed, that terrified her more than ... she almost wet herself.

Something huge had passed in front of one of those lights that were stuck back behind borders.

And then it was gone.

Had it ever been there at all, really? Had she really seen ...?

Uncle Garson had shown her how shadows were

always bigger than what they were the shadow of. So whatever she saw, it only looked big but really it was little. The shadow … it was just a cat, that's all. Or a kitten. Yes, it was just a kitten. Somehow a kitten had gotten into the cave, the same way the bird and the chipmunk had gotten in.

She kept walking fast, refusing to look to her left, where the shadow had appeared on the wall and then vanished.

It was probably just her imagination. She hadn't seen the shadow at all, not really.

It was a kitten.

Just a kitten.

She started running again, couldn't help it, just ran. And she *was* running away from something this time, the thing that made the shadow on the wall that was just a kitten. A kitten. She was crying as she ran. She thought she was because her cheeks were wet but she didn't have any air to cry.

The faster she ran the more afraid she became. Now all the shadows seemed like monsters. Like big hairy monsters with long teeth that hid under the bed in your nightmares.

She was running as fast as she could.

In her terror, in her running that didn't make her knee hurt because she didn't feel pain anymore, even … there was a part of Diana that was almost like a grownup looking at her from outside herself. That grownup whispered the truth in her ear.

There is *something here in the cavern with you!* Run!

She believed that, knew it was true in the way you sometimes know a thing is true even though you can't show how you know, you just do.

Something was in the cave with her.

Then she burst around a corner and a huge hairy animal was on the path charging right at her. Not a kitten — big, with sharp teeth. It almost knocked her down.

Pumpkin.

It was only Pumpkin!

She dropped to her knees and threw her arms around the dog and burst out sobbing so forcefully that stuff came out of her nose and ran down her upper lip. Diana was crying so loud that at first she didn't even hear it. Then she did. Pumpkin was growling. He was facing back down the cavern the way she'd come. His lips were pulled back so his teeth looked really scary, and the hair on his back was standing up and he was making a low rumble in his throat like he was really, really mad.

PUMPKIN DIDN'T DO things like that, didn't run away.

Never.

Yet, suddenly he was just *gone*, not beside Star anymore, and she saw through Noah's eyes that the dog had turned and bolted out of the Tripoli Cavern down Cambridge Avenue deeper into the cavern.

He wasn't running *away*, though. He was running *to*.

He was running to something, or someone, he knew was farther down the cavern.

Star could reach into Pumpkin's mind in much the same way she and Noah could communicate without talking. But it was an entirely different experience because Pumpkin didn't think with words. What you saw in his mind was mostly images he had gotten from something he could smell. And there were layers and layers of it. He could smell the thing that had been here yesterday and the day before that. He could smell what was going to be here in the future, if he was downwind and could smell it coming. In his mind it made perfect sense, but trying to translate that into something a human could understand was difficult, and Star did it very seldom because while it was entertaining, and sometimes necessary, it was mentally taxing to try to untangle all the images.

Here was different, though. She realized that the instant she opened his mind. There was not the plethora of smells here like there was on the outside. Outside, he could smell flowers and ants and dirt and birds and rabbits — an elk somewhere off in the woods, and … and … and …

But here, there were no growing things. No animals.

Except there *were*. She saw instantly that there were animal smells here!

Birds, squirrels, all manner of bugs and—

Something was in Pumpkin's mind that froze Star. Something large and dangerous, something that frightened Pumpkin. But Star didn't know what it could be because Pumpkin didn't know what it was either. It was something he'd never smelled before.

And then he smelled … Diana!

And Papa Eagle Feather.

She cried his name out loud.

Sawyer and the others looked around.

"What …?" Sawyer began.

"Where … is Eagle Feather—?"

"He's *here*. Pumpkin can smell him."

Noah! she cried out in his head. He understood instantly, grabbed her hand and ran off down the cavern the way Pumpkin had run.

The others followed.

In the mad scramble down the corridor, Star tried to sort out the rest of what Pumpkin could smell.

Diana!

Here?

Yes.

The boys, Sam and David, were the fastest runners, were out front. Noah and Sawyer were exhausted. Nick should have stayed behind because he was barely upright.

They came around a corner and Noah's cousins were down on their knees, comforting a frightened Diana who had a skinned knee.

Star could hear her pouring out her babbling, stream-of-consciousness monologue, only caught pieces of it.

"... Papa Eagle Feather cut himself, his hand and his leg, so Dr. Garson took his socks off and he said—"

"Slow down, honey," Sawyer said when he caught up. "Are you saying Garson and Eagle Feather are *here*, in the cave?"

"Uh huh." She pointed farther down the cavern. "He's bleeding."

Bleeding!

Star's heart froze in her chest.

The whole group went running back the way Diana indicated. Though she barely noticed it in her fear for Papa Eagle Feather, Star sensed that Pumpkin was frightened. That there was something out there — the dog didn't know what it was — that was dangerous.

Predatory.

Chapter Eight

EAGLE FEATHER OPENED HIS EYES. Saw nothing but a white
blob and closed them again.

"Eagle Feather, I saw you peeking. Open up those
pretty brown eyes again so I can get a good look at you."

He knew the voice, but it took a moment for him to
place it. Anna. Anastasia Montgomery, the nurse in the
infirmary in Zion Village.

Was he at Zion Village?

No, not there. He fumbled around in his mind, trying
of make sense of the jumble of images there. It was like a
whirlwind swirling around him. His horse threw him ... he
climbed over a fence and cut ... animals racing across the
meadow ... the detonator box ... the wolves that didn't eat
him and the old man and ...

He opened his eyes. Whatever was swirling around in
his head was making him more dizzy than looking out at
reality.

"Well, hello. Welcome back."

He glanced to his left and saw Brother Sebastian, the
abbot of the monastery lying on a bed next to his. Then he

followed the line from the needle in his own arm to some kind of machine. Brother Sebastian was connected with a line and needle to the other side of the machine. Eagle Feather thought the machine was a hematological refractor, but he wasn't sure how to pronounce it. He was sure that it performed some magic trick that made blood types irrelevant. Eagle Feather turned his eyes and saw that he had a second needle in his other arm, but it went up to a bag of clear liquid on an IV pole on his left.

"Eagle Feather, can you hear me?" Anna asked.

He almost grunted, made the Cigar Store Indian sound, but didn't. His throat felt too dry to speak but he nodded his head.

"So how many fingers am I holding up?"

"Four," he croaked. "Can I have something to drink?"

"Just what I wanted to hear." She nodded to Brother Sebastian. "He's the last in a long, long line."

Pointing to the machine, the monk said, "This thing doesn't seine out holiness — this is my one shot at converting you from your pagan ways."

Anna looked back over her shoulder and nodded and he saw that there were people gathered in the shadows beyond his bed. Star. Noah. Nick, who didn't look good himself, and Sawyer.

"You did it!" Sawyer's smile was genuine and warm, not of the drape-it-across-your-face variety.

"Stuck that detonator in the wall and *kaboom*!" Nick said.

"We're secure," Sawyer said. "The ark is sailing along under water ... and everyone on it owes their life to you."

Eagle Father brushed it off.

"Animals ... when the flood came, they all ... stampede ..." He ran out of steam.

"We saw them in the woods and parking lot," Sawyer

said. "And apparently, a few of them decided the cave was high ground because—"

"Not *a few*. Hundreds. The water herded them in — down The Drain."

Nick looked at Sawyer in alarm. After a beat of surprise, Sawyer shook his head and rolled his eyes, "Well, duh — *that* explains it. The Drain. I never thought about ... trapped at the mouth of the cave with the flood rising behind them ... nowhere else to go ... no telling *what* ..." He shook his head again. "Isn't that just *dandy*."

"The ones that didn't come in on their own steam got washed in ... unfortunately, most species of arachnids float."

The voice came from behind the others, and Eagle Feather smiled.

"Translate, that — bugs float," said Sawyer. "That part wasn't surprising. We figured we'd have some multi-legged stowaways. But ..."

"Tiny brains, engines of self-preservation. Cockroaches survived the ice age, could survive a nuclear holocaust and will most assuredly survive a flood." Garson literally shuddered. "There is one creature that survived the flood only to meet his doom at the hands of my shoe — all right, mixed metaphors. I killed a tarantula spider. I would do it again."

"How long have I—" Eagle Feather began.

"Been snoozing here like a baby while the rest of us waited on you hand and foot, provided our very lifeblood —" Garson began.

"Translate that: two days," said Sawyer. "You came around just in time for my little speech at the meeting tonight."

"I've been trying to get him to call it the State of the

Onion address — layers and layers and layers and all that," Garson said, "but he's not inclined toward levity."

"We made it this far. We're all in here together. Now the trick will be the 'all together' part — without killing each other."

"Okay," Anna announced, looking formidable with her hands on her substantial hips. "Everybody has satisfied themselves that my patient is indeed going to survive my care, now shoo out and let him get some rest."

While Anna unhooked Brother Sebastian, Star came to Eagle Feather's bedside, leaned over and kissed his cheek.

"I was so worried about you," she said softly. "And I am so proud of you. You saved us all."

The others followed Anna's directive, except for Garson.

"Oh, shoo out yourself," he told the nurse, and came to stand beside Eagle Feather's bed.

"I'll tell you what my granny always told me," she said to Eagle Feather. "If this kills you, don't you come crying to me about it."

Once she was gone, Garson got that look on his face that he got sometimes, a mixture of mischievous little boy about to chase chickens in the chicken yard and mystified scientist, intent on unraveling the mysteries of the universe.

"Wish you were up to a little trip," he said quietly. "I'm going on an adventure I think you'd enjoy."

"Every breath we take from now on will be an adventure," Eagle Feather said.

"True that. Now that you've done us all the great service of closing the entrance up tight, I plan to have myself a look at that Astral mine."

"Because …?"

"Oh, don't be obtuse, Eagle Feather. I have missed out on all the close encounters with Astrals in the past seven years, but I can at the very least explore this one last *virginal* mystery."

"Virginal?"

"Exploring the sites of previous Astral visitations is like exploring a candy store after you've loosed a whole herd of five-year-olds. Every site has been plundered by a hundred generations of humans before I got a look at it. So if the Astrals had left anything — a gum wrapper — behind to study, it was long gone."

"So you're thinking maybe the Astrals left something behind here?"

"Oh, I do so very much hope they did!" He sounded as excited as one of those five-year-olds in the candy store. "Some piece of mining equipment. If only I could study some piece of machinery ..."

The professor leaned close and Eagle Feather was aware, as he so often was, of the oddity of watching the old man's Adam's apple bobble up and down in his pencil neck like a cork on a fishing line. "You mustn't tell a soul about this."

"Why not?"

"They'd make me take somebody else along, you know they would. An amateur, polluting the study field, trampling on something of great interest. And ..."

"And...?"

"It is possible, I suppose, that there are reasons going up into that mine might not be a good idea, and you know as well as I do that if there's a reason, Sawyer Matheson will find it! He might demand to accompany me himself ... and this is *mine*! My discovery. A private quenching of one final Astral thirst. I don't want company."

"Don't get lost."

Garson gave him a fake contemptuous look and tapped

his temple with his finger. "The map's up here, every twist and turn of it."

"Be careful. Watch out for—"

"Lions and tigers and bears, oh my, somewhere out there in the dark?"

Eagle Feather thought of the vast herd of stampeding animals — every creature in the woods! Hundreds; no, thousands. He wondered which ones survived. Surely only a very few. Not the deer and the elk, certainly. But animals that could climb …

"Take a weapon with you."

Garson barked out a laugh.

"And shoot myself in the foot? I'd be safer with the lions and tigers and bears, oh my. I'll come back and report what I find."

As he lay there alone after Garson left, feeling for the first time the pain of the stitched-up hand and leg, Eagle Feather realized he should have done a better job of talking the professor out of his plan.

No telling what was out there in those once empty caverns now.

Chapter Nine

Sawyer stood tall on a makeshift stage the monks had built out of planks of wood and cheese barrels, looking out over the group of people huddled together in the stands that had been built in the cavern dubbed Carnegie Hall when he was a boy. More than a thousand visitors could sit there and watch the rangers' demonstrations and holographic illustrations of how the caverns were formed. Carnegie Hall was the largest of all the caverns, bigger than a football stadium. All the levels had a main thoroughfare and Carnegie Hall bulged out of the side of Level One's Broadway before the cavern narrowed again and led to the elevators in the western-most chimney.

People jammed the stands, and sat or stood all around in a big semi-circle facing him.

Other than the Astrals' handpicked selections from the human race, the people right here would likely be the sole survivors of the global desolation the Astrals had caused, the flood to rid the world of that pesky species Homo sapiens.

He thought he had managed years ago to squelch his

loathing for the Astrals, his rage at their un-paralleled arrogance, but sometimes, as now when he looked at the survivors of Zion Village, it washed over him in a flood and bile rose in the back of his throat.

The arrogant *bastards!*

Setting themselves up as God, deciding that they got to judge all of humanity, based whether or not they'd evolved over the years to suit their likings. And when the humans failed, the monsters punched the reset button and destroyed the world.

Then Sawyer's rage washed out as quickly as it was washed in, leaving behind something like despair. Somehow, these people had made it. But they were a straggling group of people, a random-grab from a Walmart parking lot who had managed to survive the flood, at least for now, thank you very much Eagle Feather Yellowhorse. Now they had to survive the equally precarious and in some ways more difficult challenge of living here together while they awaited the flood waters to recede.

Would they recede?

Or had the Astrals, as Garson sometimes suggested when he was being Mr. Sensitivity, picked up their special humans and zapped them into motherships, planned to keep them there in some kind of suspended animation for ten years or a hundred years or a thousand, and then plop them back down on Earth. If that was their plan, the people in this room … would be shit out of luck.

How long could these people survive? There was a way to figure that out, but it was way farther down his to-do list than getting everybody settled in here.

Right now, he didn't even have an accurate count of how many people had actually made it to the cave. He knew specifically the population of Zion Village on the day before Star sat blind in the middle of a gym and warned them of impending doom. Beth Ann Parker had had a baby, and when he'd told Lucy Pruitt about it, she'd smiled and said she'd add the baby's name to the rolls of the Village — number 5,119.

Lucy Pruitt. Paco had shot her. *Shot her!* Put a bullet in her brain for no reason whatsoever.

The rage at Paco welled up in Sawyer's throat, but he was dead and gone. Hating him was even less productive than hating the Astrals.

Of the 5,119 Zion Village residents, a surprising number had expressed their intention to stay behind. Probably three hundred people. They either didn't believe Star's prediction or, as Clarence Farmer had put it, "I just flat-out ain't hiding no more. I'm done."

Those who did want to ride out the flood on the ark had come up with a system of floating barges a mile down the Twin Forks River to the cavern, to the dock in front of the elevator, and that floating armada had moved around the clock from the moment it began until ...

The exodus was supposed to be complete by Wednesday night, Day Five, because Garson had said that the black ship Star had painted melting the polar ice caps had been parked out by Jupiter when the other ships came to Earth on Astral Day. So the reasoning, which had seemed sound at the time, was that if had taken the other ships six days to get from their holding pattern out by Jupiter, it would take the death ship the same amount of time.

Well, apparently the driver of the black monster had put the pedal to the metal, because the flood that was "scheduled" for Day Six, when everybody would be safe in their hidey-holes inside the cave — had shown up on Day Five. A few hours after Paco made his appearance.

Looking out over the crowd, Sawyer guessed there were

about 3,500 people, which meant that most of them had not gotten their whole families to safety. Almost everyone had someone back in Zion Village who had not made it, who was still there loading up the last of the supplies when Paco showed up with his army and started killing people.

He saw "vacant spots" in the crowd everywhere.

More than a dozen of the monks were missing.

One of the village elders — Erika Mason — had been left behind, though her three children had made it.

Carmen Lopez, one of the Stranded, was seated on the bottom row of the bleachers quietly sobbing. Her husband, Roberto, had been among those who didn't make it. Her twin daughters Lucy and Linda were at her side, comforting her. Sawyer had heard her tell the girls that Roberto'd stayed behind to help the Brentwoods gather up the last of their things.

The Brentwoods didn't make it either.

Dr. Paul Balforth, a dentist from Atlanta who'd been pressed into service with Bubba Blacksnake's men, had shown up at Zion Village on a chopped Harley. He'd met a woman, got married and had a five-year-old and three-year-old. He was a big, strong guy and he'd stayed behind to help load the last of the supplies. Noah said Ethan Taylor had been on the same work crew. Ethan had been shot by Paco's men.

Nick Wilson stayed "home." The bends he'd gotten from coming to the surface too fast after diving through the flood waters into the cave entrance had left him with aching joints, blurred vision and migraine headaches so severe he was unable to get out of bed. Of course, the reality of his little girl's murder was finally beginning to soak in, too, and that would knock the legs out from under any man.

Josie, precious Josie. Paco had run the child down in

the street with his monster bike as he came roaring into town.

Rage again. Useless Rage. Sawyer let it go.

People missing. Supplies missing, too.

They had made an effort to transport supplies to the cave with some level of prioritization. Food and electricity first and foremost. Water purification units and sanitary waste disposal units. Some of that had made it here, most. But not all. And food — that was all over the map. Most of the bulk items had made it, but others not. Sawyer wouldn't even let his mind slip into the same zip code as considering the scenarios of dwindling supplies and the water still out there. There was a small herd of donkeys, kept in a dead-end cavern off Broadway, but the hay to feed them hadn't made it, not all of it, anyway. Might not be long before "donkey meat" was added to the meal menu.

He dreamed about it, though, and when his mind was unoccupied, images from those dreams would flit across his mind's eye. A second here, a second there. People had brought food from their own gardens, and if it was necessary to start rationing the food supply, those people would … it would be ugly no matter how you sliced it.

Nope, couldn't think about that.

Noah threw him a nod, meaning just about everybody was here. They'd been summoned by runners hollering up and down the caverns — *the British are coming, the British are coming!* He'd also blinked the lights three times, and would tell the group today that three blinks was a signal for people to come to Carnegie Hall for a town meeting … or for some worse disaster.

He almost hung a smile across his face like a surgeon's mask, but didn't, just pulled out a whistle and blew it. The murmur of conversation stopped.

"Welcome to Noah's Ark." And suddenly his voice was thick with emotion. *"We made it."*

The tender moment was short-lived.

"I wanna know what you're gonna do about Alfred Rawlings and him moving into our cavern. You can see plain as day on the map that the folks living on Haskins Street was assigned to Chisholm Trail cavern but he just come and plopped his butt down—"

"— on Chisholm Trail *South*. You ain't the say-all and end-all authority where one starts and the other stops."

"You listen here, Rawlings, you best make fried chicken quick out of that rooster or—"

"Touch one of my birds, Carmichael, and I'll—"

"Stop!"

Sawyer roared the word so loud there was feedback and an awful squawk came out of the sound system.

But he got silence.

"I've assigned Noah, Sam and David to be the geography police. They'll be over to work it out with you as soon as they can. But right now, we need to talk about things that affect everybody."

Then he went down the list.

He talked about the disparity in the supplies, said he might have to ration some things, but none of that would be clear until the monks had made a thorough inventory of what made it and what didn't. He talked about meals in the cafeteria, how the monks were working on a color-coded schedule. As he spoke, he could tell his audience would not retain much of the information he was giving. They'd have to hear it several times for it to sink in.

Nobody could retain all this information at once. It was too much.

"I'm going to sing this song one more time. You've

heard it before, but you need to listen as carefully as if this was your first time. Your life depends on it."

He paused.

"*Don't. Go. Wandering. Off.*"

He let it sink in.

"You *will* get lost! I still get lost in here sometimes" — that was a lie — "and I've spent my life here. Stay on the *paved walkways*. Do not go down any of the side tunnels ... because they'll have other side tunnels branching off them, and those will have other ... It's a two-hundred-fifty-mile-long labyrinth. An incomprehensible maze. Even with the Glow Worm lights, one cavern looks just like another."

What he didn't say was that all the paved-walkway caverns — except for the dead-end caverns like Big Toe and Durante's Nose — were loops, started in a main cavern like Broadway and eventually returned to it in a different spot. They'd figure that out for themselves if they were here long enough. It was the unpaved caverns that were dangerous. Those could lead ... *anywhere.*

He noted as he wrapped it up that anyone still in possession of a firearm needed to turn it in.

"Tight quarters, short tempers ... no guns!"

But he was certain that some people would still refuse to relinquish them. There were always some people like that.

When Sawyer got to the end of the attention span of his listeners — the human mind can only absorb what the ass can endure — it was time to bring Garson on to do his dog-and-pony show.

"Look around you," Garson said without preamble, indeed he had started talking before he even got to the top of the little makeshift stage, made with boards stretched across four monks' cheese barrels. "You're looking at the faces of the people who will be the progenitors of humanity. The Astrals selected people *they* wanted to reseed humanity after they wiped us off the face of the planet. We're the wild card. We are what will keep the gene pool healthy through the succeeding generations because we are a random grab of humanity. In terms of dog breeds, we're mutts."

"Thanks a bunch."

"Speak for yourself."

"Woof, woof-woof."

Sawyer made a move-it-along hand motion, telling Garson to cut his rant short and get to the point.

"What I am saying is that the people sitting here in this cave will be the ancestors of humanity. Over the generations, it will be our genetics that keep the human race healthy and strong." He fumbled with some papers and Sawyer rolled his eyes. Sometimes it was a mistake to hand the platform to Garson. He hoped this wasn't going to be one of those times.

Garson gestured to a little girl with no teeth in the front in the crowd.

"These children ... what they're taught, what they know and can do, what they will pass down to their children and they to theirs is of monumental importance that transcends the concerns and hardships of the people here today."

"How about we survive first, then worry about what we're going to hand down to the rest of humanity."

Garson was undeterred.

"Matheson Caverns is the Cradle of Humanity. Think what that means. What happens here in this cave while we await the new world that's coming will become the stuff of folk tales and legends. I intend to be the new world's Josephus."

Garson was not self-aware enough to pick up on the

blank looks that appeared on the faces of at least seventy-five percent of the audience.

"Garson," Sawyer interrupted, and was rewarded with one of the looks Garson had given errant students when he was a college professor, the looks that had been known to produce internal bleeding.

Sawyer said to the crowd, "Josephus … Flavius, I think … he was a famous historian and the source of much of what we know about ancient Israel — sort of an impartial corroborator of many Biblical events."

"Oh, but he was much more than—"

Sawyer shot Garson a look and he picked up on it this time.

"My point is simply this. What happens in this cave will have import for the rest of human history and I intend to accurately document that for posterity. I hope you will not be offended if I ask to include your story in the mounting records. To that end, I shall be traveling among you as we go on this exciting journey together, a scientific nomad wandering all the caves and caverns … seeking out … truth."

Garson could have said all that in a couple of succinct paragraphs. The audience response ranged somewhere along a line from *I don't give a shit*, to *hey that's a cool idea*. If nothing else, it would keep Garson's swirling intellect occupied. That was definitely something.

"Thank you, Sawyer," Garson said and smiled, but didn't make eye contact.

That set off an alarm bell.

Something was off about that smile. Now that Sawyer thought about it, there'd been something off about the whole presentation. Sawyer couldn't put his finger on what it was. Not what Garson'd said, exactly, but maybe the fact that the whole time he'd been talking, he had never once looked Sawyer in the eye. Garson was undeniably off-the-charts brilliant. No one ever disputed that, even when his Ancient Aliens theories had made him a laughing stock in the scientific community. But there were different kinds of intelligence. Garson might be a giant in astrophysics, but he was a titmouse in interpersonal relationships. He could read astrophysics texts and star maps, but he was totally illiterate when it came to human body language. He was unutterably naive, got few jokes because he always thought whoever was talking was telling the truth.

All of the above made Garson a terrible liar. And Sawyer suddenly realized he was lying now. There was more to this than Garson was saying, more to his Josephus the Historian story than he was willing to admit.

Sawyer remembered the day more than seven years ago when he had moved the professor off the campus of Hillsdale College to the academy. He'd loaded the last of the professor's belongings into the trunk of his cruiser that day and the old man had removed his spectacles, cleaned them absentmindedly with the end of his tie, and told him the Astrals were actually mankind's ancestors.

"*IT'S REALLY VERY SIMPLE, Sawyer. This alien race seeded the planet. The evidence is everywhere if you have eyes to see it, and they have returned periodically over the millennia.*"

"*So this is just a check-in, how-ya-doing, anything-we-can-bring-you-from-home visit?*"

"*Hardly.*"

"*Then what do you think they're doing here?*"

"*They're doing what they have done every time they have returned. They are judging mankind.*"

"*On what criteria?*"

"That's … not clear. There is much speculation, but we aren't as certain of that as we are of other things."

"What other things?"

"That whatever the criteria, mankind has always failed the test."

"Failed the test?"

"My dear Sawyer, the aliens would not likely have wiped the planet clean of humanity and started over if we'd been their star pupil. We failed and they destroyed us."

"Destroyed us?"

"You have but to look at the historic and geologic record to see proof of it, that our shortcomings earned us … extinction."

"Extinction."

"Stop repeating everything I say, my boy. You sound like a parrot."

"But how …?

"Look in Genesis … the world was destroyed by a flood and only a handful of people were left to repopulate the globe."

"You think that was …?"

"I think they come, they find us wanting in some fashion I could guess at but don't quite have pinned down in my head … and so they start over."

"Start over."

"You're doing the parrot thing again." He pauses and sighs. "Look, Sawyer, don't make me draw you a picture. They started a species — us. They come back every so often so see how the species they started is faring. They don't like what they see, so they wipe out the species, leaving only a few to repopulate, and start over, hoping, I suppose, that we won't make such a mess of things next time."

A light appears in Garson's eyes then, probably best described as the glow of intellectual curiosity.

"But between now and then, oh what there is to learn from these beings! The things they know, what they have seen! Ahhh for a chance, for only an afternoon, a few hours maybe, to pick their brains. I would give my very soul for that opportunity."

. . .

THAT'S what Garson was seeing now in the professor's eyes. That light, the burning desire to *know*, just for knowing's sake. The man would do just about anything to scratch his intellectual curiosity itch. Was that all it was — he wanted to know about the people here, wanted to hand down an accurate ... no, it was more than that.

There were pioneers and there were settlers. Garson was a pioneer. It would never be enough for him to record the testimony of the settlers. There was more to Garson's proposal that he was letting on. He wanted more than just to go around asking questions. But what else could there be?

Chapter Ten

THEY HAD BEEN in the cavern for going on a week before Garson got a chance to slip away. It wasn't just the press of more than three thousand people ... actually, the exact number was 3,101 at the count. That meant that a couple thousand people in Zion Village who had planned to board the ark didn't get the chance — because the flood came early, and because Paco showed up with his army. So the ones who made it were grieving for the ones who didn't.

It could have been a morose place were it not for the tireless efforts of Star, Noah and his cousins Samuel and David. They were absolutely relentlessly positive and upbeat. They were the G.P., Geography Police — even used Fantastic Markers to write the initials on their shirts. So they spent a lot of time smoothing ruffled feathers. Noah, of course, was not by nature a gregarious young man, more introverted, but he could grind it out when he needed to. They gathered a group of their friends, and organized activities to occupy the time of the people in the cave.

For the children there was school, of course. There

were several hundred school-age children and the community of Zion Village had been providing them an education since the Astrals destroyed the winter food supplies and half the buildings in Jessup, forcing the refugees to move out to Zion Academy, turning the place into Zion Village.

Of course, several of the monks who'd been teachers in the Zion Village school were among those who didn't make it into the ark before it set sail. They had been the core of the teachers. Brother Thaddeus, who took care of the monks' herds of livestock, had made it, but there wasn't a lot of point in teaching animal husbandry anymore since all the animals on the planet had drowned. But he was a crack handyman, too, so he taught construction skills. Brother Luke, who'd been shot down by Paco, had taught history, so he was replaced by Jocelyn Conner, who'd been in charge of the surveillance room and security.

Every child had to learn American Sign Language whether they could hear or not. Many of the people in Noah's Ark were the former students at Zion Academy, a school for the deaf. But learning ASL was essential because many of them were congenitally deaf, had been born that way. Gretchen Hampton for one and there were others. Congenital deafness occurred about one in every thousand births. It was a recessive gene. But with this many deaf people … mating, becoming the parents of the next generation, the likelihood that they would pass that disability down through the next generations was high. So best they all learn how to communicate without sound.

Adults were kept busy performing necessary activities, one of those was building "houses." Gratefully, community had in storage a large number of IS packs that someone had "harvested" from the stores at Fort Campbell after the Astrals massacred all the troops. Insta-Structure packs were about the size of a laundry basket. Pull a string, and they'd inflate like a dinghy into a tent-like structure with zip windows and doors that would house a dozen people.

In addition to the IS packs, the monks had owned and used a lot of heavy farming equipment back when there'd been gasoline to run them. They discovered that stored in the barns with tractors and combines gathering dust and spiderwebs were barrels of a high creep adhesive lubricant for use on the bearings and mating surfaces. After seven years, all that was left in the barrels was a thick paste in the bottom, like sticky clay.

Somebody had discovered that if you spread that paste on fabric — any kind of fabric, sheets, table cloths, bedspreads, anything — it would harden on the surface, turning a sheet into a thin building material, a way to build walls, much like the material called washi used to build Japanese houses.

And the monks quickly recruited crews to help in the industrial kitchen where they prepared communal meals. The idle mind is the Devil's playground.

Everyone was expected to pitch in, and for the most part, everybody did.

Folks didn't think or talk much about the future, kept themselves centered on the here and now. *Here* they were safe for *now*. That was the best they could hope for and discussions of the future only lead to D and D — dissension and distress.

How long would they have to cower like rats in a hole?

Don't know.

Will we run out of … fill-in-the-blank … before the water goes down?

Don't know.

Will the world even be livable when the water goes down?

Don't know.

And there were all manner of when-the-water-goes-down D and D discussions; a herd of them went along with the original question.

When the water went down, would it simply drain away, the water running downhill? If it merely drained, then there would be ponds, lakes and oceans in every low spot on all the continents. Specific to their situation, of course, was the fact that there was only one way out of the caves — through the entrances on the lower two levels, Level Four — Cricket Bottom and various caves on Level Four— and the river entrance on Level Five. The elevation of the Cricket Bottom Entrance was only four hundred feet above sea level. Where they were standing at present, however, was about twelve hundred feet up inside Joppa Ridge. It might be years, some speculated, before all the water drained away, and by that time …

Of course, Garson was of the opinion, and had science and expertise to back up his point of view, that the Astrals had instantaneously melted the polar ice caps and they would instantaneously re-freeze them when they decided the time was right to reseed humanity. And that draining water thing — that was based on the presumption of gravity operating as it had always operated, though the Astrals had clearly shown that they could bend, stretch, and tie bows in gravity. Making water flow uphill was probably something baby titans learned to do from their cribs, assuming, of course, that there were baby titans, which begged all manner of attendant questions.

And *those* were the questions Garson wanted answered.

That was the *real* reason the old professor had sought out the role of Josephus of the Cave. He wanted to find out whatever there was to find out *about the Astrals*. He had wanted to do that since the day the white dots had appeared out by Jupiter seven years ago. But it had been his misfortune to be in the backwaters of the world, teaching at a little college in rural Kentucky. He had not been among those 20,000 incredibly fortunate people, like Star and Noah, who'd been taken up for study in one of the motherships. He would have given his right hand, *and* his left — all his appendages, leave himself a limb-less bag to use for third base — to have had that experience.

But not.

He hadn't been in one of the cities, over which the Astral motherships hung for years, had not been in one of the regional capitals they established. Of course, that was why he was still here to ask questions. All the people who had been in the cities had been destroyed on Black Monday. People in cities perished. People elsewhere did not. The tiny margin, the .000001 percent of humanity the Astrals totally ignored were the pockets of people like those at Zion Village who were out in the hinterlands, doing their own thing, not drawing attention to themselves. They were not worth the Astrals' time or attention. After all, the ragtag handful of country-mouse ragamuffins were doomed to drown in the flood anyway.

But he and this handful of Homo sapiens had at least a shot at survival. It was likely that he was now — and certainly soon would be — the only true scientist left in the whole world. The only man who might be able to transmit down to future generations not only what had happened here, but something about the Astrals themselves. Maybe Dr. Mikhail Ziegelman Garczonski, PhD, had not had the opportunity a single time in the past seven years to actually spend time with the aliens, but he had an opportunity now to at least study the works of their hands.

He would *not* pass up that opportunity!

Noah had been twelve years old on Astral day, had

been on a field trip to Matheson Caverns and gotten separated from the rest of the tour. Lost, trying to find his way out of the cave, he had stumbled into an ancient Astral mine, where they had been cutting rock during past visitations. He hadn't known it was a mine, of course, not then. All he knew was that the walls of the cave he crawled through in the darkness were perfectly, flawlessly smooth. The only explanation for that phenomena was that the stone had been cut. After Star's vision, Noah and his cousins had been canvassing the caverns to figure out how to make them a refuge for thousands of people ... and Noah found again the impossible cavern he'd stumbled upon as a child.

He had walked into a full-bore Astral mining operation, with robots cutting chunks of limestone from a mine high up on the mountainside, on the north side of the mountain. The fact that the mine was near the top of the mountain was of monumental significance because the gigantic hole the Astrals had cut into the rock there had to be plugged or everybody who was now safe in an airtight chamber with hundreds of miles of available air would have drowned when the water came pouring in that hole.

So they had sealed the entrance, Eagle Feather had come within a hair's breadth of dying to bring the detonator from Zion Village, and had pushed down the plunger after the flood had already risen above all the other entrances.

The mine had been sealed up.

The mine where there was very likely *discarded mining equipment.*

The mine where ... oh, dear God in Heaven, *please* ... there might even be the bodies of dead reptars for Garson to study, the ones who had ripped each other apart while Noah watched.

Garson had spent his life going to ancient archeological digs, where maybe, *maybe* … if you were incredibly fortunate, you stumbled upon something that indicated the presence of the Astrals thousands of years ago. Something that had been so desiccated by the years as to be almost unrecognizable. He had been thrilled beyond thought and reason to come upon such an artifact.

But now … *now*, this very moment as he breathed these very breaths, there were "remnants" of the aliens' presence on Earth in Matheson Caverns. In the Astral mine. God only knew what he might be able to find there, not withered and degraded by thousands of years of weather, but shiny new.

What if they left behind a piece of mining equipment? A robot, oh Lord what if there were an Astral mining robot in that cave? Or maybe even … a Phoebe.

In the process of fleeing the cave, Noah got tangled up in a robot … and a Phoebe showed up.

Not just one, a whole herd of them.

The first Phoebe rolled up to within a couple of feet of the still-struggling robot on top of Noah that pinned him to the floor. The little round ball was slightly bigger than a marble, and no color at all. Not clear or even translucent, though. The little balls acquired the color of whatever they were near, like a chameleon blending into different colors of leaves. But when the balls got close enough, you could see yourself in them, the image of you they were transmitting to the Astrals.

It was Star who'd named them the day the little swarm of marbles had shown up as Noah, Star and Paco sat together alone in a white room on the Astral mothership.

What if the Astrals had left behind a Phoebe? That would … Garson couldn't even describe how incredible it would be. But not, of course, as incredible as the possibility that he might actually find the body of a dead reptar. They'd gone into attack mode the day Noah'd been there, at least one and maybe more had died. What if their bodies were still there?

He didn't think that was likely, believed in all honesty that they'd removed the bodies from the mine, so he didn't let his mind consider the possibility for long because finding such a body to study would be the ultimate experience of his entire professional life.

Garson had come up with a plan. He would pretend to be studying the occupants of the cave, documenting their story. He would do that. It wasn't just a ruse. It was a legitimate scientific endeavor and he would perform that task to the very best of his ability. But while he was wandering the caverns as the Josephus of Matheson Caves, he would be looking for the Astral mine.

He knew its general location, of course, where it had to be in relation to where Noah had been on the tour that day. But its location had not been documented on any map, given that it was only rediscovered by Noah a few days before the flood. Noah was the only person who had been inside it, had gotten to the small opening in the passageway that granted entrance. But he couldn't simply ask Noah the location of the mine. Noah would ask why he wanted to know. When he told him why, the decision about whether or not Garson would be *allowed* to examine the mine would be taken out of Garson's hands. It was even possible that the powers that be, namely Sawyer, his brother, Nick and the rest of the elders, would decide it wasn't a good idea for him to go poking around in there and forbid him to go!

And what if the location of the mine became an item of idle gossip? There'd been no secrets in Zion Village even before the entire remaining population had been jammed together in a cave. Someone would overhear something. They would tell someone else. And pretty soon, the mine would become an attraction.

Hurry, hurry, hurry, step right up, see the Astral mine, the incredible equipment and the decaying corpse of a reptar.

No, this had to be Garson's information and his alone.

Chapter Eleven

DELBERT AND HERBERT.

It was a moment before Paco realized that Gideon Freeman, the moron who had saved him from drowning when the flood waters flowed into the cave, was serious.

Delbert and *Herbert*.

Holy shit.

"Del … Herb … it's me, boys," Gideon called, holding his hand out in front of Paco like a mother holding a kid against the seat when the car stops. He halted before they turned the bend into the portion of the cavern where the brothers lived, their home place kept safe from prying eyes by the deterrent of hand-lettered signs:

Keep Ot.

Who couldn't spell "out"?

That's U ASSHOLE.

I will kik your ass ot yr moth, you will have to unbuton yr shirt to shit.

Fuck me and I will fuck yr mama.

At least the morons could spell fuck. Can you say inbreeding?

"What you want, motherfucker?"

"That's Del," Gideon said quietly to Paco. "Herb's the one has a harelip."

Identical twins who looked so much alike Gideon feared Paco wouldn't be able to tell them apart except, oh by the way, *one of them has a harelip?* Shit.

Gideon must have caught the look and whispered. "It ain't like you can tell or nothin', I swear. When he was kid, they sewed it shut and you can't hardly see the scar through his mustache."

"If we'd a'wanted company, chances are we'd a'come lookin' for some. Get the fuck outta our cave."

When Paco skimmed lightly over the surface thoughts in their minds, he felt a dull ache behind his right eye. These guys' doors were open, which wasn't always the case with stupid people but generally so. Paco had learned over the years that susceptibility to his mind control was not expressly a product of lack of intelligence. It wasn't like Obi-Wan Kenobi waving his hand in front of a stupid Stormtrooper: "These aren't the droids you're looking for."

Paco had turned geniuses into virtual puppets. It was about … he thought of it as a door into the volition center of the brain. Some folks kept their will locked up tight, deadbolt and security latch. Paco could pry open doors like that, but it took considerable effort. The average person's door was slightly ajar. These assholes … their doors were hanging from broken hinges. But once inside, there wasn't much to see there, like reading a book written for a first grader. The harelip one was horny, had awakened with a hard-on, and the other one, Del, had interrupted him jacking off and he couldn't finish. He was pissed. Del was angry, too, but for no apparent reason. His mind merely boiled with rage, a primitive desire for violence — any form, just so long as it was bloody. That would be useful. Men like that were always useful.

Paco could have dived deeper, searched out their primal fears and become that in their minds, but merely nudging would be sufficient for these imbeciles.

Paco, I'd like you to meet your future as a dumbass, the new and improved mentally deficient Paco Salazar with his brain blown out his ears. All those engorged blood vessels springing leaks, spurting and spewing — that will be quite a show. Brief but colorful.

Himself had taken to badgering Paco any time Paco reached out into someone's mind, haranguing him like a fishwife.

Won't be long before you're as brain-fucked as your old buddy, Vincent, and there's no one in your life who cares enough to end your misery with a pillow over your face.

"*NOOO!*" That was a bridge too far. Nobody mentioned Vincent to Paco. Nobody! He would kill anyone who so much as thought the name. "You shut the fuck up!"

Gideon looked at Paco in alarm and he realized he'd shouted out loud.

"Who you got out there with you, Gid?" That was harelip, horny Herb, though his speech had only a slight nasal quality courtesy of his once-cleft palate. "We done told you don't bring nobody here."

"It's okay, he's good. He don't like them Zion people no more'n we do and he's planning on doing somethin about it."

"Come around the corner slow. Keep your hands where I can see them." That was probably Del.

Gideon followed the instructions, went around the bend in the cavern with his hands out to his sides, not raised exactly, but plainly visible.

Paco kept his hands in his pockets. Fuck them.

The abode of the Clarke brothers might as well have

been stuck like a stick pin to the side of some mountain in Appalachia. They'd actually gone to the trouble to haul in wood they'd likely taken off the side of somebody's chicken house, to make a house here in the cave. And if he closed his eyes, Paco could see what the front yard would look like if they had recreated it here. Junk cars. toilets. Old refrigerators and outhouses and … *that* was the stink. Outhouse. Paco didn't look around for it, but clearly it was nearby. He would have to do something about that.

According to Gideon, the Clarkes had been moonshiners long before little white spots out by Jupiter. They'd moved their still and their residence into the caverns after Astral Day and went on about business pretty much as usual. They brewed, traded liquor for anything they'd once have purchased with money and stole everything else they needed. Like most of the other permanent cave dwellers — Gideon said they numbered two, maybe three dozen people altogether — the brothers had become more and more reclusive as time went by. As the world went to shit, they dug deeper into their hidey-holes. These were Gideon's closest "neighbors," who lived in Durante's Nose, a narrow tunnel that curved off Persnickety, the cavern that opened out of Smiley Face. If you didn't know the passageway was there, you'd miss it, using only that dim string of lights overhead. They were the first Paco had met of the group of people out of whom he intended to fashion an invading army.

Gideon had warned him the twins "ain't the sharpest knives in the drawer," but with the limitations of manpower being what they were, Paco would have to use whatever he could find.

The brothers' cabin had a roof and something that was probably supposed to be a porch. Either that or they'd just put boards down on the floor of the cave there and never got around to moving them. No windows in the house/shack. To be fair: why bother? What was there to look out at? Certainly nothing like the breathtaking views from the shambling shacks he'd passed in the Kentucky mountains.

Or in West Virginia, but Paco walled that comparison off as quickly as it came into his mind. He didn't think about that time in his life, the summers he spent with his older sister in West Virginia. Those memories were kept in a special place in his mind, locked in a secure box, and he never brought them out to look at them. But he liked knowing they were there, it felt comforting to know. He absolutely, one hundred percent had *not* forgotten Vincent, would never forget him. Had, indeed, patterned his whole adult life after his friend, who planned to *go somewhere, make something of himself,* and leave his accent and his culture behind. Paco had done part of that. He had wiped his speech totally clean of the East Los Angeles Latino accent, its intonations, pronunciations, idioms and figures of speech. He had disavowed all the cultural crap that went with being Hispanic, too. Became a man of no culture, which, of course, made him a man of all cultures. He had found among the former inmates of Radcliffe Correctional Facility — surprise, surprise! — an educated man. A full-time college professor and part-time embezzler doing five to ten for cooking the books for a friend at a bank. Paco had consigned him to the role of tutor, and over the seven years since Astral Day Paco liked to think he'd earned a master's degree in subjects as far ranging as English litera-ture and quantum physics. He had honestly never realized that he was brilliant until he actually applied himself to learning — for the first time all those years ago when the only way to get to Charleston to visit Vincent was to win a school grade-point-average contest.

He hadn't "gone somewhere to make something of himself," though. Had not seen the world as Vincent had so longed to do.

"*You know the world is two-thirds water.*" Vincent spoke the words into Paco's head. "*So if you ain't in the navy, ain't no way you're ever gonna see all of it.*

That Paco had gotten caught, literally, imprisoned in Southern California on Astral Day, and any chance he had to travel had been stolen from him.

Though in life terms, he had done more traveling that just about anybody on the planet. He had, after all, been taken up into an Astral mothership, had lived there for three months, and even though there was no sense of "going anywhere," no train/car/bus sense of movement, he had gone farther than Vincent even dreamed of going.

A tiny smile chased its shadow across his lips. Vincent would have liked that. He'd have been all over going up in a spaceship.

They were talking, the three idiots he was standing in a cavern with, and Paco had been lost in his own world remembering, and missed what they had been saying.

"… don't you, Paco?" Gideon said.

"Don't I what?"

"You know, don't you hate them motherfuckers who took over our cave, just like we do?"

"I plan to take over what they have taken over," Paco said simply. "I will be in charge, everyone will answer to me. I will be the king of the mountains, so to speak, when the water goes down and there's a mountain to stand on."

"How you plannin' on pullin' *that* off?" asked Delbert. No, maybe it was Herbert. Actually, Gideon had been right, it was hard to tell them apart. They were dressed alike, not like twinsies in all-the-same-outfits, but one filthy, wife-beater tee shirt and overalls that hadn't been washed in months — years! — looked pretty much like every other one. They were both fat men, with chins marching down into their hairy chests and massive heads of hair that connected with equally massive beards so it was hard to see where one stopped and the other began. There had been a band he'd seen pictures of once in a head shop in East Lost Angeles. ZB Top or ZZ Top — something like that. These guys looked like the guys on the cover of the album. Though in truth there were no features to see except eyes, and blackened teeth when they spoke, smiled, or spit on the cave floor.

Eww. The spitting was gross. Might as well start there.

Instead of answering the man's question, Paco said, "Get rid of that snuff. Spit it out or I'll make you swallow it. Never dip snuff again. Is that clear?"

"Who the hell you think—?"

"Do it."

There was a moment of silence that was ragged on the edges, a kind of static that wasn't a noise but was. Then Delbert spit out his snuff. Herbert followed. Or maybe it was the other way around. Paco supposed he could require that they shave off their beards so he could tell them apart. Or maybe just one of them, but decided it would probably be easier on his digestion not to get a good look at their facial features.

"You ain't no Jew boy, are ya, 'cause ain't no way I'm gonna take orders from—"

"You'll take orders from me if I turn into a talking dog."

Again the static not-sound in the air. Then both men got something approaching a blank look in their eyes, well, blank-*er*, more a thousand-mile stare that wasn't exactly unfocused.

"It's Jew boys' faults," said Del.

Paco couldn't help it. He bit.

"*What* is their fault?"

"Them aliens coming. Jews was the ones flooded the earth the first time. Says so in the Bible in the book of—"

If he says Reservations, shoot him, said Himself.

"—Noah's Ark."

"'Fore the flood, we thought it was the niggers," said the horny Herb. "Killed as many as we could get our sights on, woulda got more but we finally run out of ammunition."

"Are you saying you used up all your ammunition—?"

"Shootin' niggers? Ever last shell." He looked sheepishly down at the shotgun in his hands. "It ain't loaded."

"Yeah, we shoulda slit their throats, only we didn't think 'bout that until after. You can slit a nigger's throat but you can't slit an elk's throat."

Oh. My. God.

"We ain't had no meat since we run out of ammo."

Paco turned to Gideon. "This is the best you can do? Dumb and Dumber?"

"Hey, who you callin'—?"

Paco fired a look at Herb, a reflex, the way you'd swat a mosquito — only you happened to have a sledgehammer in your hand. Herbert dropped like he'd come unhinged. Blood squirted out of his nose and he fell over on his back and lay still.

Gideon leaped back like he'd received some kind electric shock, too. Del stood gaping at his brother, then turned a murderous look on Paco.

Paco's vision pulsed with every heartbeat from the ice pick of pain that stabbed into his right eye as he pulled from his waistband the gun he'd gotten from Gideon, cocked it and aimed it at the big man's chest.

"This gun *is* loaded. I checked."

Del's gaze returned to his brother. "Dumb fuck," he said. He reached down and pulled something from the front pocket of horny Herb's overalls, a plastic bag of weed, and held it out to Paco. "It's good shit. Traded a quart of hooch for it." An expression that vaguely resembled intelligence crossed his face. "We got a couple barrels of hooch, and we growed weed but it sucked. This right here might be the last bag of good weed on the whole planet."

Paco decided he might be right.

Chapter Twelve

WHEN GARSON WENT OUT that first day actually *searching* for the Astral mine, he was so excited he might have wet himself.

The tour from which Noah had been separated as a child had come in through the Cricket Bottom Visitor's Center Entrance where it opened on Level Four, two hundred feet above the river. They had spent the morning winding their way up to Level One and when the lights had gone out in the cavern, because a terrified bus driver had crashed a tour bus into the visitor's center, Dr. Weiss had elected to take the children out the closest entrance instead of trying to find their way back down from fifteen-hundred-foot Level One to the entrance where they'd come in.

Noah had gotten separated from the group. Sawyer had told Garson the story that he'd finally wheedled out of his son, that the boy had needed to pee and had stepped out of the hand-holding line of students to relieve himself. But when he'd tried to zip his pants back up, the zipper stuck and he had stayed where he was, trying to get it free, while the tour left him behind. Because he was a Matheson, and had explored the caves his whole life with his family, the boy thought he could cut across from one cavern to another and catch up with the tour. But he had gotten confused, turned around, lost. From that point on he was wandering, climbing, ascending and descending through pitch dark caverns — the very thought of which would put Garson into cardiac arrest. And the boy was only twelve — *and deaf!* He had eventually stumbled into an "impossible cavern," a cave with smooth walls — which the surface of no cave wall could possibly be. He'd made his way through that cavern, out through an even smaller crack than where he'd entered, and found his way to a sinkhole, climbed to the surface and rejoined his tour group as they were coming out of the natural entrance.

As soon as they came up with the Noah's Ark plan to survive the Astral flood, Noah had gone with his uncle and cousins to the cavern for reconnaissance. And found himself searching for the "impossible cavern" he had found as a child. He couldn't backtrack his steps from the sinkhole he'd crawled out because it had been sealed up a few years after Astral Day. The Bickett family, who had grown dope and manufactured hard drugs for years, moved their operation into Matheson Caverns and summarily managed to blow themselves into smithereens while collapsing a substantial portion of the cave. The Natural Entrance didn't exist anymore, and neither did the Double Cellars Sinkhole where Noah had crawled out.

So Noah'd had no choice but to try to find the impossible cavern the way he'd found it the first time. He had gone to the spot where he had left the trail with the other students and gone off to do his business.

The spot where he'd left the trail … Garson smiled

when he recalled what Noah had said about finding it again.

"I thought there ought to be a bleached spot on the rock there, like a lightning strike, caused by the heat from my humiliation at getting my zipper stuck in my underwear ... and I would at that time rather have died there alone in the dark in the cave than have Astrid Kirkpatrick see me with my pants unzipped."

Noah and the class had been in Broadway cavern when he'd left the trail, so he'd returned there to retrace his steps. Noah said he had climbed "up and north," as he would have had to do, since the mine entrance was on the north side of the mountain. If Noah hadn't stumbled into the back of the mine, they'd never have known it was there. You couldn't see the opening from the ground.

Prowling his memories for every conversation he'd ever had with Noah about that mine, the cavern and the journey toward it, Garson was grateful that he didn't have to search as relentlessly as Noah'd done. Noah had left him an Easter egg. He'd said that on his return trip to the mine he'd seen what his twelve-year-old self couldn't see in the dark — the cavern that contained the mine entrance had an odd "stripe" six inches wide all the way up the wall, floor to ceiling. It was only a seam of really dark limestone but its edges were so uniform it looked like somebody'd painted it there with black paint.

So Garson was spared the task of searching through hundreds of dead-end caverns. He wouldn't accidentally pass it and continue looking ... forever. Garson would know when he found it — a cavern marked with a black stripe. Of course, then he'd have to search *that* cavern for the hole in the wall that led into the mine. Still, he was grateful for the leg up.

Starting out in the Broadway tunnel that ran the whole

length of Level One, he walked east past the first large tunnel beyond it called Pot Belly because he knew the mine wasn't that near Carnegie Hall. He passed up the second large tunnel, called Chisolm Trail, for the same reason. He went by the third tunnel, Chisholm South, because it was the other end of Chisholm Trail where it looped back and returned to Broadway. There was one small tunnel, Tigger, and two large offshoot caverns from the trail before it looped — Blind Alley, that connected it to Manitoba Lane and the tunnel called Kaboom, where an ammunition factory had once been. Along that cavern were several small-mouthed caverns that'd been fitted with doors that would lock. Those had been built decades before, would have been there when the little boy Noah was trying to find his way. If he'd come upon one of them, he'd have known instantly where he was.

Garson continued down Broadway until he reached Manitoba Lane that ran north. It connected to Blind Alley and Piglet going west and Smiley Face and Frowny Face going east. Piglet was connected to Blind Alley by way of Tigger, Pooh Bear and Eeyore. The caverns were, indeed, what Sawyer had described — a labyrinth of interconnecting tunnels in which anyone would get hopelessly lost. But Garson had come prepared.

He had made up his mind to go looking for the mine the day Noah'd told the elders about finding it, had gone digging around in the shed where the monks kept gardening supplies that very evening and found four spools of the string they weaved into garden netting, a thousand feet each. He'd stuffed all four into his backpack — would use the string to keep from getting lost.

Tying the end of the first reel of string to a rock outcrop, he stood at the tangled intersection of caverns leading away from Manitoba Lane. He let out a breath and picked randomly, the tunnel on the right — Smiley Face. He paused, reconsidered, decided on the left tunnel, Blind Alley, instead. And set out.

He looked all afternoon and had nothing to show for his efforts but a sore back.

Garson had been exhausted after just one day of searching. It was a two-mile walk out to the spot where he left Broadway. Then he searched for hours. And after that, it was a two-mile hike back.

But he refused to give up. Went out the next day. And the next. And the next. Kept track of the tunnels he'd already searched, and started his search there the next day where he'd left off.

On the day he found the black-stripe cavern, he had determined to search only ten more minutes and then call it a day. He was in a small cavern that opened off Smiley Face when he went around a bend, lifted his lantern to see how big it was and there was the black stripe on the wall. He stood looking at it for a long time, hoping his old eyes weren't playing tricks on him. It took every speck of will he possessed not to go racing off down the cavern that very day, but he made himself wait.

When he showed up bright and early the next morning, he began to systematically search the cavern for the other "landmark" that identified the Astral mine. Garson remembered specifically the description of a large, flat piece of limestone that had broken loose from the ceiling and fallen, landing so that it leaned against the cavern wall at the top of an incline. Behind the rock was the entrance to the impossible cavern.

And so he searched, investigated one after another of the rock falls looking for a specific flat rock leaned against the cave wall. He hadn't considered how many of those there might be, climbed up again and again to take a look at leaning flat rocks, but there had been nothing behind any of them.

He spotted another leaning-rock candidate up to the right. It was the biggest rock he'd found, appeared there would be plenty of space to crawl behind it. So he began climbing, slipping and sliding, telling himself that he was way too old to be doing something like this and knowing he'd still be here if he'd had to drive a motorized wheelchair up the rocky face of the wall.

He got down on his hands and knees and shined his light behind the rock.

And stopped breathing.

There was a hole in the wall of the cavern, right down on the floor. And it was clear that somebody'd been here recently. There were marks in the dirt that could possibly be scoot marks where someone had lay down on their belly and shoved through the opening.

With his heart hammering in his chest like a lunatic woodpecker, Garson edged closer. Close enough to smell it. A gagging, cloying, nauseating stink. You had to be close to the rock to smell it, but once you did, it was unmistakable.

Smelled like ... well, smelled like road kill.

Chapter Thirteen

THE GROUP of people assembled before Paco looked like the human version of the cavern's blind cave crickets, creatures that had adapted to living in a lightless environment. They were a pathetic lot, but he'd done more than he planned to do here with people equally ill-suited to the tasks. He'd taken over a prison from a monster who had raped him, paid him back by feeding him live into a wood chipper. More important than that, he had used his force of will to compel a gymnasium full of people to take his side, to cheer him on, to give up their wills and follow his.

That had taken some concentration.

Cost you a couple million brain cells, too. But what the fuck? You got brain cells to spare, don't you, Paco? So many you could donate a whole herd of them to Goodwill, for the use of people like these who were born with only a handful of them.

Paco ignored Himself. He didn't have time for the not-person right now. He had to focus and concentrate. He had to turn these people, mold them to his will and his plans and — before Himself could speak up — *using as little mind control as possible.* He was aware he needed to conserve it for later, when he might need it more.

Or conserving it for later so you'll be able to think more than a couple of four-word, drooling sentences by the time you're thirty.

Paco's right-hand man, Gideon, had assembled these good folks to audition for Paco's army.

When Noah's mind was stronger than yours, asshole, and he tricked you.

Noah would get his. Oh, my yes, he would most assuredly get his. He and the little bitch Star. He hadn't decided yet exactly how he was going to execute them when he finally laid hands on them. He wanted their deaths to be brutal, painful and bloody, sort of multitasking there, using them as an example of the tour bus destination for anybody who crossed Paco Salazar.

Clap. Clap. Clap. Himself applauded. Oh, bravo.

Paco looked out past the apparition that wasn't even there anyway, to the couple of dozen malcontents Gideon had assembled. They all had a look to them. To-the-bone stupid. And a blind-cave-fish look, the anemic skin and watery eyes of someone who didn't see a lot of sunlight and was probably in a massive Vitamin D deficit. But maybe that was just Paco's imagination, given that he knew these lowlifes had elected to live in the caves long before the cave became the salvation of a remnant of humanity. A kingdom that Paco intended to rule with an iron fist. Dear God, please let the people he hadn't seen when he went rolling into Zion Village be normal humans, someone you could relate to. Ass worth fucking. Please, universe.

But the universe had never been very responsive to Paco's pleadings and he didn't expect that to change just because the world was coming to an end.

He nudged Gideon, who was deep in discussion with a man whose high, wide forehead made his too-small eyes look like brown M&Ms and jowls so pronounced they flapped when he spoke. It was clear the man had once weighed at least a hundred pounds more than he did right now and Paco wondered if it was living in the cave that had taken off the weight or if the life that had driven him into the cave had been responsible.

He gave Gideon a nod.

"Okay, folks. This here's the guy I wanted you to meet and I ain't gonna give no I-am-so-glad-you-decided-to-join-me-here-today speech or tell you how welcome you are. You ain't welcome and you didn't come here because you wanted to. You come for the same reason I did — because we all been invaded by a bunch of motherfuckers from Zion Village and this ain't their cave. It's *ours*. We are gonna have to fight to get it back and this here man's who'll help us win that fight."

"I don't like any of you," Paco said. There was a rumble in the crowd. "Get it out there and done with it. I don't like you. You smell bad, are ugly as shit — oh, God, especially the women — and you are nobody I would choose to remain in the room with … *if* I had a choice. But I don't and neither do you. We are in this lifeboat together and we don't have to like each other to do what we have to do here — which is take over Matheson Caverns again."

"So what happens to them people from Zion village? There's a shit ton more of them than there is of us."

"And you are?"

"Gareth Johnson," said the man whose face was as sharp as a hatchet blade, punctuated by a hawk nose and lips so thin they were only visible when his mouth was open. Paco had no trouble at all imagining the man feeding on bug guts as a blind cave cricket.

"Well, Mr. Gareth Johnson … what happens to those people is whatever *I* decide happens to them. We'll kill some, of course, the meddling sheriff, the monks, the guy whose little girl …" He didn't go there. "But let me get this part straight right now. It's important, so listen up with what little brain power you possess. There is a blind girl named Star and a deaf boy named Noah. They're mine. Nobody touches them. When the shit hits the fan here, it will get bloody. They are mine. Understood?"

There was general grumbling.

Paco reached out and nudged.

"I asked you a question — understood?"

This time almost everybody answered in something like the unison of a Greek chorus. The only person who didn't was a woman with blonde hair and maybe blue eyes, hard to tell in this light. She had been pretty ten years and twenty pounds ago, but clearly she hadn't been paying attention to her mirror lately because she still gave him come-on looks like she was a prom queen. Her name was Eva Jo Proctor. He'd fuck her, maybe tonight. But right now, she needed to be put in her place. An object lesson.

He dipped only far enough into her mind to find a face, somebody she feared. Her father, likely, an old man who had … oh, *he* had fucked her, too, when she was a little girl, took her cherry and everything. Paco put on that face and watched her reaction.

Eva Jo Proctor screamed, a high, wailing cry that echoed off the cavern walls. Then she started backing away from Paco.

"No, it can't be … you're dead. I killed you, mother-fucker, stuck the butcher knife in your back."

An image of that scene filled her mind and Paco glanced at it.

"Thought you could cut my balls off and I wouldn't fuck with you anymore, didn't you," Paco said. "Well, I'm here to fuck with you all over again, and what I leave of you after I …" The image of the scene became clear. Shit, her old man had raped the kid — used a pine cone on a stick! "… give you some more pine-cone loving …"

Then Paco shoved harder, knocked her off her feet. She fell to the ground on her butt and scooted away from him, her mouth contorted in a soundless scream, shaking her head back and forth.

Then he let it go.

Eva Jo looked at him. Shook her head and looked harder. "Who are you … how?"

"I'm anybody I want to be, sweet cheeks, and I will do with you and everyone else here whatever I choose to do, up to and including fucking you with a garden claw. We clear?"

Her eyes widened, then she nodded so fast and furious she looked like a bobblehead doll on the dashboard of a car on a bumpy road.

He turned his attention back to the crowd.

"Here is all you need to know right now about what is going to happen from now on. First I am in charge. Totally in charge. You so much as shit some way I don't like and I will brain fuck you so you never do anything but drool for the rest of your miserable life. We clear?"

To a person, the crowd said some version of *yeah, we're clear*.

"Here's what I want you to do. I want you to slide into the population of Zion Village and become one of them.

He waved off the beginnings of a protest.

"You know those people. If you don't, get to know them. You are to become one of them. Are you tracking with me? I don't care what you have to do, what kind of story you have to tell, who you have to fuck or bribe or kill. But you are to become one of the fine citizens of Zion Village."

He paused. "Yes?"

This time, they all replied in unison, a little like a group of Boy Scouts responding to a take-the-grandmother-across-the-street request.

"I'm not saying you have to become anybody's new best friend. Just be a face they recognize, someone who doesn't look out of place among them. Once you have become one of them, you can start fucking with them."

He paused there, surveyed the crowd for any naysayers who were keeping their mutiny to themselves for the time being. A man named Douglas Alexander was figuring out how he was going to ditch Paco and everybody else, had in mind a cavern nobody knew about, where he planned to hole up until everybody, Paco and the crowd from Zion Village, had left. His friends called him huggable Duggable, and he'd have been handsome, but his chipmunk cheeks were too pudgy, big eyes, a large nose, lips as pouty as a woman's.

These were weird-ass people, all of them. They'd decided for various reasons, to come live in a cave for crying out loud. Yeah, there was the stability thing — always warm in winter, cool in summer, no rain/snow/weather of any kind. But that didn't seem like nearly enough motivation for such a move. Shit ... green trees, flowers, butterflies, puffy white clouds, sunshine on your skin ... It was pleasurable, normal, to want to stay in the presence of that. Not these assholes, though. They went out into the wide world only to cultivate the little gardens they survived on, trap game, trade goods with others, steal from them, whatever they had to do to survive. But then, just like a flock of cave bats, they'd come trooping back in here to the homes they'd built out of ... he'd seen some of them. Coulda just gone out and shit in the woods instead of ... how *did* they shit?

He skimmed. Toilet caverns. What must *that* smell like.

It was crazy, he could find out, dig a little deeper, had in his skimming revealed a woman named Isabel Goodridge who was running from … somebody, had taken refuge in the cave to get whoever it was off her trail. She had hooked up with Sharon Parkinson, who had the prim demeanor of an Amish school marm — when she smiled, which she did try once, she looked like she had learned how from a manual. The two of them were lovers, but also offered themselves out as whores in trade for food or provision.

He finally decided, of course, that satisfying his curiosity wasn't worth what it would cost him. They were nuts, that's all, wack-jobs. Fuck, once the water went down and they literally owned the world, he bet most of these folks would come crawling back in here just like before.

Fuck them. The people from Zion Village had at least been *forced* to come here, didn't like it here and couldn't wait to leave. That was normal. These jackoffs … they were just crazy, that's all. Chalk it up to that and move on.

"What you mean fucking with them?"

"Your job is to sow seeds of dissension." Shit, there wasn't a soul here who knew what the word meant. "Your job is to make people mad at each other. Like …" He thought of a classic old movie. These were the kinds of people who watched that shit. "The movie, *Lord of the Rings*. At the end, when Gollum was trying to turn Frodo against Sam, made it look like Sam had been stealing food."

Holy fuck, *every head nodded.* Jesus.

"Well, that's what you're going to do. You're going to steal food from their stockpile, and leave evidence of it so there's somebody to blame. Kill somebody's dog and plant the blood knife on somebody."

He caught a hint of an image and went with it.

"Rape somebody's wife so she'll blame somebody else. Or somebody's little girl."

Paco would like to think these people would be creative enough to come up with their own seeds, but he doubted it. He would have to sit down with each and give them some kind of plan.

"And I want to know about their armament ... their guns! How many do they have? Who has them? Is there a stockpile somewhere? How about ammunition? Find out everything you can about anything they have they can use to defend themselves. We're going to steal it all."

Chapter Fourteen

Dr. Mikhail Ziegelman Garczonski had been on a dig once with another archeologist, an Ancient Aliens theorist, Dr. Benjamin Bannister. The two of them were in Peru, investigating reports that caves there had drawings of large white men who local legends called the gods from the sky.

Dr. Bannister had brought his young son with him, Cameron was his name, and the boy would have accompanied them to the dig but he came down with some kind of tropical fever and Ben had to leave the boy with a local woman while the two of them trekked through the jungle to a cave probably never seen by any Caucasians. They had guides who took them through the labyrinth of caverns, a bewildering jigsaw puzzle. Garson had thought they'd get the Americans thoroughly lost and then hit them up for a higher fee on the threat of leaving them, but then he was always the suspicious one. Ben would trust a snake charmer, and managed to get through life pretty much unscathed in circumstances where Garson would have exercised far more caution.

When the two of them — sweaty, covered in bug bites

and certain to have leeches attached to their private parts — got to the cave where the natives said the drawings were located, they went alone into the chamber, with no light but the natives' torches. The top of the cavern was black from the smoke of the other torches that'd been used over the years to explore the cave, and that was an indicator of things to come, at least to Garson, though Ben would have followed a wasp into a hive in the hopes of finding something to substantiate his belief, shared with Garson and a handful of other scientists throughout the world that the earth had been visited by aliens in its past, more than once. Other scientists had found similarities among the descriptions of those beings. From Iceland to Cairo, to the mountains of eastern Kentucky to the jungles of Peru, the beings were almost always described as white giants that came from the heavens.

"There," said their guide, pointing to a wall in the shadows in front of them, using one of only a handful of words he knew in English. "Pictures."

Garson and Ben had moved slowly into the shallow recess in the cave wall and held the torches up to the drawings clearly visible on the wall. They were crude, but it was clear that the beings drawn there were white, larger than the stick figure drawings of deer nearby. Above them was a saucer-like thing that could have been described as a spaceship.

It was equally clear to see that the drawings were not ancient, were probably less than a couple hundred years old. They didn't date back into the dark recesses of human history. They were probably drawn by natives describing the Spanish Conquistadors who had had attacked their villages.

The two men said nothing to each other. There was no need. It was clear to both of them that this was another of the dozens, no, by that time hundreds, of wild goose chases they had been on separately and together that yielded them nothing but a handful of air.

Ben had sat down on a nearby rock, clearly disappointed.

"You know what I fantasize about?" he'd said. "I dream of coming upon a hermetically sealed chamber that contains the dead body of an alien. Not a drawing. A body to examine."

"Do you suppose the body would stink?" Garson had asked, and the two of them proceeded to have a heated disagreement about whether or not alien corpses stunk.

Garson was of the opinion that they did not, basing that conclusion on a comparison to the human body, whose decomposition was a consequence of what it was made of and microbial life designed to feed on it, and since alien beings clearly would not likely be similar organisms, they would not decompose in the same way.

"The levels of carbon dioxide and acidity rise in the bloodstream after death and toxic wastes build up, poisoning the cells and enzymes within the cells, and begin to eat away at them," he had pointed out. "Why would you suppose that aliens would have carbon-based anatomies?"

Ben had come back with the point that the various components might not be the same, but the process would, by its very nature, have to be. The breakdown of tissues in some form would have to occur, unless aliens had dead bodies lying everywhere, or used them for fuel, or food, or hood ornaments.

Garson had come back with the point that resident anaerobic bacteria in the intestinal tracts of humans break down after death and why would we suppose there would be bacteria of any kind in the gut of a being whose whole composition would have been different, based on the environment from which it had originated.

"Besides," he added, delivering the coup de grace, "the loss of tissue mass is chiefly the work of fly maggots, and advanced composition requires the work of dung beetles, and to suppose either of those existed in some alien world is definitely a scientific bridge too far."

"No," Garson had finished with a blast. "Alien corpses would *not* stink."

But he had been wrong. The stench that emanated from the hole in the side of the cavern was the stench of decomposition. It didn't smell precisely like a dog on the side of the road or a dead cow, not that Garson had spent a lot of time in the company of dead animals, but it was definitely something made of tissues that break down.

It was a dead reptar. Garson was sure of it. Maybe more than one, given the volume of the stench. Noah had watched the reptars attack each other, and clearly at least one of them had died from his injuries. Maybe more than one.

Garson found that his legs refused to hold him upright anymore and he dropped to his knees. Once there, the eyes that weren't what they once had been saw clearly that someone had been here recently. There were marks in the dirt. He wasn't Eagle Feather and couldn't have said if two horses or three, shod or unshod, moccasins or boots, a motorcycle or a snowmobile had passed this way ... but it seemed pretty obvious even to the unschooled eye that somebody had lain down on their stomach and shoved themselves through the small opening and into the cavern beyond.

The cavern from which now emanated a nauseating stench that smelled like roses to Garson.

"You were right, Ben!" he said aloud and was surprised

to see that his voice was so emotion-clogged it sounded like he was crying. "The corpse of an alien does stink."

Garson took a couple of cleansing breaths, tried to get his hands to stop shaking but finally gave up. He lay down on his stomach then — gratefully he was a tall man but had gotten so skinny in the past few years his belt would no longer hold up his pants and he'd had to rig makeshift suspenders to keep his pants from falling off.

He started to put his head into the opening, drew back to get a breath of fresh air — scientific wonder that it was, the stink of any dead body was still unpleasant. Then he shoved his light into the opening ahead of him and began to scoot through. Pushing with his feet and moving a bit like a worm, he made it through the opening, setting his light on the floor just inside. Then he shoved himself out, reached down and picked up the light. He literally closed his eyes, the way a little kid does to prolong the suspense and excitement of seeing a Christmas present just a little longer.

Then he opened his eyes, and couldn't see much of anything. There was nothing alien near the opening to the cavern. Darkness rushed in from all sides. He patted his pocket, oh please … yes, the second role of yarn was there. He remembered Noah saying he'd taken off his shoe to tie the string to so he could make it back to the opening, so Garson did the same. Noah had said he'd struck out right from the opening, keeping near the smooth walls of the chamber. Garson reached out, yes, it was smooth!

Moving slowly along the outside wall of the chamber, holding his lantern in front of him, he expected to see …

There was some kind of light in front of him.

No, couldn't be.

Just his old eyes playing tricks.

No way to tell except in the dark. He reached down

and turned the knob on his lantern, reducing the light it gave off little by little until he turned it completely off.

In front of him was a glow, not a light. Greenish.

His heart was doing that jackhammer thing in his chest again as he inched forward, not turning his own light back on, moving by the glow of the light ahead, going in that direction as it got brighter and brighter.

Turning off his own light had allowed his eyes to adjust to the darkness, enabling him to see what lay out there in what was not featureless darkness. There were pillars, just like Noah had described. The stones that kept the roof from collapsing while the miners removed the rock, just like in coal mines all over Kentucky.

The light grew, brighter and brighter. Definitely greenish.

Along with the light, the stench grew. It had smelled pretty rank when he first stuck his head inside the cavern, but either he'd gotten used to the stink or it had lessened because it hadn't seemed to get worse as he moved along. Now it did. Every step seemed to be leading him closer to the source of the stink, which appeared to be in the same place as the source of the light.

Might even *be* the source of the light. Finally, he took that step that put him beyond the last of the pillars blocking his view and lying on the floor of the cavern fifty feet away was a glowing mass of … something. It was the source of the green light. He stepped closer. The stink got worse, not like any smell he'd ever smelled before.

He remembered Ellie talking about her horrifying journey to Ft. Knox the day the Astrals attacked and destroyed it. A soldier had saved her life by blowing up a reptar, and splattering the beast's guts all over her and her friend. She said the stink was unspeakably bad, no way to compare it to anything in the world because it was not of this world. "Maybe rotten apples, sour milk," she'd said, then backed up. "No, not that, more like meat gone bad."

This was that, but layered over with a rotting smell that was, in his view, the stench of some form of decomposition.

The form became clearer and clearer, lit by its own internal glow. A firefly, but he was certain the glow was not a natural phenomenon associated with the creature — and it was undeniably a creature of some sort — lying on the floor of the cavern. The light was a product of the process going on, not of the creature. It was a reptar. Closer observation revealed the hoary head with the mouth full of needle teeth. Reptars glowed with blue lights, described by those who'd seen them, but this was not that. This was green light and it rose up from the fluids that Garson could now see were leaking out of the form on the floor.

Though clearly a reptar, its form was no longer that of a live creature. The scales that protected it in life now lay on top of a form like slabs of roofing tiles on a mud puddle. The scales must have been made of some substance like human bone and the skeletal form of the reptar. They were not decaying, but the body of the beast was.

Garson was now less than a dozen feet from the glowing form on the floor and the reflex to heave, to vomit up the meager breakfast of bread and monks' jam, was so great he had to hold his breath to quell it. His eyes watered. He reached up to hold his nose, then thought better of it. If he held his nose, he would have to breathe through his mouth. And somehow the thought of air clouded with that stench flowing over his tongue and into his mouth was a more disturbing and sickening thought than leaving it be, breathing normally.

He moved no closer because to do so was to invite

vomiting. He was close enough to see so much that he wanted to examine. He would have to return, of course, properly clothed with a face mask and some instruments to take tissue samples, to probe … oh my it was real.

He wished Benjamin Bannister could have been here to see it, though from what he had gleaned from news reports, Ben had come into the close proximity of far too many live reptars to be interested in the remains of a dead one.

One of the razor teeth lay only a couple of feet from his foot, perhaps knocked out in the beast's battle with the other reptar — who must have survived the encounter, or had died somewhere other than at the site of the fight because this was the only glowing green mound of goo that Garson could see.

The reptar's tooth. Right there.

He wanted it. He would take it back with him. Not that he would show it to anyone, which would beg the questions and resultant answer about how he had come to have it. But that didn't sound so bad anymore. His fears that others wouldn't allow him to come here or to study what he found here, on hindsight, were probably groundless. What possible harm was there in it?

He reached down and turned up the light on his own lantern, the glow so bright he had to squint and he lost all of his eyes' adjustment to the darkness. The corpse of the dead reptar was far more hideous-looking in the bright light than it had been in the light generated by its own demise. He saw no movement on the body, which might indicate the presence of some kind of Astral parasite that he probably didn't really want to get up close and personal with. Clearly he had been right on that point at least. Decomposition didn't seem to be aided by the presence of maggots and dung beetles.

He reached for the tooth, drew his hand back and wished he had something like a handkerchief to pick it up with. Not just for scientific purity, but the flinch factor of not wanting to touch it. He, of course, didn't have a handkerchief. But he did have a sock. He set the lantern back on the floor, took off one shoe and sock, pushed his hand down inside it, and used it as a glove to pick up the tooth off the floor. It was curved, like a scimitar, and appeared to be so sharp he was glad he had the sock on his hand or he might have been cut.

That was enough for now. He would take the tooth back and examine it, probably even show it to Eagle Feather, who might possibly have an interest in seeing it. And to Sawyer and the others, who wouldn't be interested in it. But now he thought he could convince them of the rightness of investigating the corpse, that maybe there was something to know about the creatures that might be valuable in the future.

He shoved his sockless foot into his shoe, picked up the lighted lantern in his other hand, turned to retrace his steps back to the entrance, and saw the figures that had been standing in the darkness behind the dead reptar.

Five white giants, now illuminated by his lantern, stood looking benignly at him.

Holy Jesus God. Titans.

Not dead bodies. *Live* titans.

Fuck.

Chapter Fifteen

"... so the dragon reared up on his hind legs and roared, and when he did, fire squirted out of his mouth and burned the leaves on a nearby tree ..."

The children were hanging on every word. Star had always been a good storyteller. It was a skill she'd honed when trying to translate the fortunes of people who didn't really want to hear the truth about what awaited them in the days to come. She had also entertained the other children at Uncle Claude and Aunt Mary Ellen's with stories to keep them occupied at night when Aunt Mary Ellen fixed dinner, usually some kind of Mexican food — fajitas, enchiladas — things Star hadn't eaten in years. Well, except in the mothership when the food boxes appeared bearing whatever happened to be your favorite food. It had tasted *real*. It had. She and Paco and Noah had talked about it for hours. They knew it couldn't really be human food, that it was zapped up with the Astrals' tech to look/taste/feel/smell like people food but really wasn't. They'd talked about what it was made of, with Noah pointing out that it had to be compatible with the human digestive system because they hadn't starved. Like almost everything else about the mothership, they'd never figured it out. But now, when she thought back on it, she skipped over that "facsimile" and recalled the fajitas Aunt Mary Ellen prepared, and she could almost taste them in her imagination.

Noah questioned what she should be telling the children who gathered for Stories with Star, a time for children aged four to eight or nine, like the time she'd set aside for that for years under the maple tree near the monastery in Zion Village. He pointed out that given the circumstances of the children's lives, wouldn't something kinder and gentler than tales about dragons be better fare.

He might have been right, but when she'd tried to be more sweet — fairies and bunny rabbits and butterflies — the children had complained. And she decided their world was full of monsters already, real monsters, and it might be a good idea for them, at least in fantasy, to be the slayers of monsters, to take on the dragons and beasts and trolls and best them with nothing more than a magic sword or a charmed ax.

"That's when Jason the Bold stepped out into the clearing," Star continued. "His sword was gleaming in the sunlight and—"

The image of Jason and the clearing and the dragon vanished out of Star's mind as instantly as if it had been on a juke screen and the juke was switched off. Her mind was filled then with the image of … it was *Garson*. Garson standing in the light from a lantern. All she could see of him was from the waist up, the portion of him that was lit because all around him was dark. He had a sock in his hand, wrapped around something that looked like a bone.

No, it wasn't a bone. It was the tooth of a reptar.

Then the image was gone. As instantly as it appeared, it vanished.

"... and then what happened, Aunt Star?" asked the little Rutledge girl whose name was either Claire or Clara, Star never got it right.

"Did the dragon eat Jason?" asked Sunshine Mason, who was probably destined to be either the epitome or the opposite of the name she'd been tagged with. The other kids called her Chicken Little.

Star was staggered and confused by the image that had appeared in her head and then disappeared so suddenly. She reached out to Noah, who was helping to load sacks of flour onto a dolly.

I just saw Garson, she told him with her thoughts. *His image, I mean. It was just suddenly there in my head. And I was thinking about something else entirely.*

Why would you suddenly think of Garson?

I didn't think of him. His image just appeared in my head. He was in a dark place, the only light on him the lantern he was holding. And he had something in his hand that ... it looked like a reptar's tooth.

That's bizarre.

"Aunt Star, finish the story," said Amos Kincaid, and she shushed him with her fingers to her lips.

Was it like when you touch somebody and see an image of their future, like that?

No, not really ... it was more like ... Star froze. *It was like it was when I saw the death ship. The image just formed in my mind.*

Because it was the image that was in the hive mind. They were all thinking about the death ship, all thinking the same thing.

And it spilled out of the hive mind and I saw it. Heard it, whatever.

Are you saying this felt like you could hear the hive mind? Through all the rock and the water? But it couldn't be that, because why would the hive mind have been thinking about Garson ... holding the tooth of a reptar?

I don't think so ... I don't know. It wasn't like the big, whirling, churning hive mind with gazillions of thoughts roaring through it, the one I got kicked out of on the mothership. It was smaller. I don't know how to describe it. A hive mind, but not a big hive mind.

... a hive mind ...

Like before, like something spilled out, like they all were thinking the same thing or maybe looking at the same thing and it sort of overflowed.

"I bet the dragon came down out of the sky and burned them all up," said Sunshine Mason. "Used his dragon fire and they were all fried into crispy critters."

"No!" cried Claire/Clara Rutledge. "Jason the Bold cut his head off with the sword!"

"Did not!" Sunshine said.

"Did, too!" Claire/Clara said.

I don't know what to think about it, but I can't think about it right now. The kids are about to riot. As soon as I get finished here, I'm going to talk to Garson.

Chapter Sixteen

THE ROTUND MONK struggled to get out of the chair.

He was trying hard to remain calm, positive and perpetually grateful. There was a trick to this. There had to be. There were more than 3,000 people in the cave — the census wasn't complete so it was hard to be sure — but he *was* sure nonetheless that the other 3,499 people didn't have to go through gymnasts' contortions just to get out of a damn—

He was a monk.

Brother Sebastian was the abbot of the monastery, such as it was now, the religious and spiritual leader of the community. He could not allow a stupid chair to reduce him to cursing. He should be grateful for the inflatable chair, glad he had somewhere to sit besides his mat on the floor. It was just that his considerable bulk seemed to sink down too deeply into it when he sat and his torso, which was roughly the shape of an egg with legs, combined with the floor-length brown robe somehow ...

He grunted, twisted and found himself on the floor beside the chair.

He *would* find out the trick to extricating oneself from an inflatable chair. But there were so many more important things to do and there were only twenty-one of them left. The entire Gethsemane Monastery, which in its heyday had boasted almost three hundred dedicated brothers, now numbered twenty-one. Brother Sebastian often said their names to himself, like a chant, a meditation, like he was repeating the books of the Bible, and several had taken those names. Benedict, Anthony, Thaddeus, Phillip, Mark, Ezekiel, Amos, Luke, Jonathan, Matthew, Joshua, Ezra, Jeremiah, Malachi, Zephaniah, Nehemiah, Judah, Abraham, and Joel. One hundred seventy-seven monks had risen before the sun on the day of the flood and 156 had not lived to see the sunset.

So few. So very few.

He and a handful of other monks went into the caverns with the first work teams after the Zion Village elders had made the decision to move into Noah's Ark. Sawyer had provided them their own small cavern to serve as their 'monastery.' It was one of several special dead-end caverns on Level One — he didn't know how many there were — that had been used in some way years ago when there was an ammunition factory in the caverns. The special caverns all had narrow entrances, so they had been outfitted with huge metal doors that would stop a tank — doors that could be locked! The cavern was near the commercial kitchen and Sawyer'd intended to store much of the village's food supply there behind those locked doors. But then the flood had come early and lots of things didn't go according to plan after that happened. Only a few of the monks were inside the caverns that day; most had stayed behind in Zion Village to help with the last-minute details. As he understood it, Paco had used Silas, Bartholomew, Cedric and Paul for target practice when he arrived. Shot them down for no reason, just because he *could*.

The monastery's numbers had dwindled over the years, of course, even before Astral Day. There weren't very many men who wanted to take the vows and join their order. The ones who did were older, had seen life, had — some of them — lived horrific existences, and came seeking the solitude and sanctity of the monastery as a result. But attrition had taken a toll after Astral Day, as those older monks died and there were no younger men to take their places. He'd never done the math, but he suspected the average age of the monks was probably sixty by now. And when they got out of the caverns, if they got out, their numbers would continue to dwindle until there were no monks left at all in the world. That seemed like such a terrible, terrible shame, but Brother Sebastian had tried his dead level best since he joined the order as a young man, twenty-six, to dedicate his life to unquestioning obedience. The *unquestioning* part had always been the hardest for Brother Sebastian, and it was certainly hard now not to wonder what God was doing in the grand scheme of things, allowing the desolation of humanity. And in the microcosm, the handful of cowering humanity here. Why was God leaving whatever world was left after the flood without the wisdom and guidance of the clergy?

And he was now, as he had been so many times in his life, reminded of what God had told Job when he questioned the misfortunes that had been visited upon him. "Where were you when I created the universe?"

The Astrals were *created* things, not crea*tors*. For all their incredible technology, for all their ability to cross through space, swerve in and out of wormholes, bend time to suit their needs and suspend gravity when it suited them, they remained *created* beings just as were all the humans they had massacred. Even the Astrals, sans their technology that seemed to be able to create all manner of inanimate objects, could only *copy* life, they could not *create* life. They could not create something from absolutely nothing. They could do all manner of things with what already existed — perhaps even with nothing more than a single molecule in the air — but they could not create the molecules in the air. They could not create what did not exist.

Where were *they* when God created the universe?

The twenty-one monks who were left had the huge responsibility of feeding 3,000 people three meals a day. There had been a communal dining hall at Zion Village. It had started the winter after Jessup's food supply had been destroyed and many people had nothing to eat and had just continued. Lots of people liked to plant gardens and ate their own produce, went hunting and ate the meat. But the monks provided three meals a day in the large dining hall at the monastery regardless, using the rich stores of food from the bounty of their farming operation. Steaming fresh vegetables, broiling beef, lamb, serving cheese and wine.

Now, they'd been charged with making bricks without straw.

Oh, Sebastian, how you do take on. Bricks without straw. Seriously?

Alright then, it would be more accurate to say they spent their days making bricks nobody wanted to eat. After the Astral attack on Jessup three months after Astral Day, the monastery had stored emergency food supplies in the cave. Bags of potatoes, carrots, beets, onions, turnips. They wanted to be prepared so they'd never again have to face a harsh winter.

The food was rotated out as its freshness soured, but the barrels of slurry mix had sat unused. Oil drums of it. It was basically the same recipe as what had been used in the Mobile Eats in-dash snack printer called meTouch that could produce on demand any conceivable kind of basic snack food, a menu of more than two dozen items, from a single inCarts ingredient cartridge loaded into the 3D extrusion mechanism with a multi-nozzle head to print different colors and textures at the same time. Everything from chips to chicken salad was made from a slurry of pea protein and artificial fat.

Of course, without the extrusion mechanism, and the printer head to produce colors and textures, the contents of the barrels was a soupy substance barely palatable, even with copious amounts of added salt. Brother Sebastian had lost track, but as he recalled, Garson had said there was enough of the slurry to sustain a thousand people for seven years. So they had roughly less than a two-year supply of food ... but if required to live on nothing but the slurry compound, he suspected nobody'd be interested in living that long.

They'd decided in the very beginning that *everything* in the cave would be rationed — the only possible response to having no idea how long they'd be there. The monks served three meals a day in subsistence-level portions. The menu for breakfast consisted of slurry mix and unleavened bread. They had flour enough to last about as long as the slurry mix. But the yeast to make it into bread had been in the last load of supplies that didn't make it into the cavern. Lunch was unleavened bread, cheese, smoked meat and... slurry mix. Dinner was the best meal, at least it would be while their supplies of dried vegetables held out. They made stew from carrots and radishes and onions, and had offered potatoes in the beginning — might as well eat them before they went bad.

The problem with the food distribution was the fact

that it was not equitable. Some people had gone out to their gardens and had brought into the cave with them baskets of vegetables. Until those supplies ran out, all their neighbors complained about their abundance.

Tempers were already getting short. The foul-tasting food, the inequitable distribution — some people had brought chickens and had eggs every day! — the cramped, uncomfortable housing, and the overarching, ever-present, you're-in-a-hole-in-the-ground darkness was oppressing everyone's spirits.

Brother Sebastian didn't realize that he'd remained on the floor after he fell out of the chair, lost in thought, an old man's folly. He only scrambled to his feet when he heard Brother Benedict calling for him.

"You must come," Brother Benedict gasped. The man was probably eighty years old, and had been told he had "heart issues" by Anna, the registered nurse who was the closest the community had to a doctor. He shouldn't be running. His eyes were wide and Brother Sebastian's heart leapt into his throat. Someone was hurt. Was injured seriously. Oh, please, not killed.

"What is it, man? Spit it out."

"It's Brother Ezra." The old man didn't have air enough to say more and Brother Sebastian didn't have the patience to wait until he could speak.

"Where?"

Brother Benedict pointed back across Carnegie Hall to the cavern called Corkscrew. Broadway. Brother Sebastian, who at sixty was no spring chicken himself, picked up his robes and dashed away. He hadn't gone a quarter of a mile down the cavern before it hit him.

How could it be? Here? In a *cave*?

But it was unmistakable. He rounded a corner and was almost overwhelmed. Brother Ezra stood in the center of the group of monks who had retreated as far as possible from him.

"I ... I thought it was a cat," Brother Ezra said, barely able to get a breath with the stench roiling up off his robe into his face. "How ... how did a skunk get in here?"

Chapter Seventeen

"WHERE IS IT? Did you see it?"

Sawyer peppered the people racing down the cavern in a retreating tide. He had to find the damn thing and kill it or the whole cave would smell like—

"It's in South End," said somebody.

"No, Corkscrew. Got a monk. They've got the area quarantined off until you get there."

Goody.

Sawyer ran along beside Nick, one of his newly-sworn deputies, who was fine today. Some days it was like there was nothing in the world wrong with him. Other days he was so dizzy he couldn't stand, or his joints were so stiff it was painful to move. The bubbles in his bloodstream from ascending too fast when he'd dived through the flood waters into the cave could have traveled anywhere in his body, might show up to plague him for weeks, maybe months.

Today, he was the old Nick.

No, that wasn't true. Sawyer hadn't seen "the old Nick" since the man found out Paco had run down his little girl and killed her when he came rolling into Jessup the day of the flood. There was a fire back deep in his eyes, a rage he had no way to vent. And a sorrow that Sawyer fully understood. He'd felt the same way when Rosileigh had died in the fire. There'd been plenty to do in the caverns to take Nick's mind off his sorrow. Sawyer kept him busy, had even designated him the official "Town Cryer," but without the "crying" duties. Nick had an old-fashioned watch like Sawyer's that kept track of the date as well as the time — but nothing else. Watches with other bells and whistles had all died for lack of fresh batteries years ago. Only the old wind-up variety remained. Oh, Sawyer kept track of what day it was, too, how long they'd been here, checked his watch obsessively. Nick was backup.

Brother Thaddeus came running to meet them, crying, "Stay away!"

The monk stopped, panting. "It got Brother Ezra and Brother Phillip." He grabbed a breath. "Brother Judah, Brother Abraham, and Brother Malachi are chasing it. They think they've got it cornered behind a pile of rocks."

Sawyer went to go past him and Brother Thaddeus grabbed his arm.

"You can't go down there, Sheriff Matheson," he said. "If *you* get sprayed …"

Of course, the monk was right. Sawyer certainly couldn't do his job — policing the populous and maintaining order, if he smelled like skunk stink.

"I've got this," Nick said. "I can pick it off from far enough away not to get bombed."

He held up the rifle David Matheson had used in the ambush of Paco's troops outside the Cricket Bottom cave entrance and ran off down the tunnel, leaving an agitated Brother Thaddeus with Sawyer.

"They smell so bad … dinner tonight. They can't …"

Of course, the sprayed monks couldn't go anywhere near the kitchen. Or the food stores, for that matter. Even the monks who hadn't been sprayed … those thick robes would absorb the smell. They'd all stink! Who would cook and serve meals, run the recyclable dishes through the Convo-Clean machines? Who would guard the food stores if the monks …?

A skunk. Shit! What the hell else had crawled in here besides a skunk?

~

TEN-YEAR-OLD SAMMY WITHERSPOON had not wanted to come to this stupid cavern in the first place, but he and the other kids had been run out of Broadway because they were making too much noise for the grownups. Mrs. Haversack told them to go down to Chisholm Trail — it was a loop that started and returned to the Broadway cavern, only the other entrance was called Chisholm South. Or down to Big Toe, which forked off to the right side of Broadway. But Big Toe was a dead-end cavern that only had the Glow Worm lights strung on the ceiling and not real lights so you could see to play.

Lucas Haversack had brought a ball. Sammy wished he'd thought of that, but they had had no time to prepare what they would take into the cave. His mother had grabbed her PicDisc where she stored photos, movies and stuff like that, but her father told her there wouldn't always be a juke to see them, so she'd pulled a picture of her and Daddy getting married off the wall and Sissy's baby shoes that sat in a little acrylic bubble on the table and a hair-brush, clothes and things and they went running out. He hadn't brought anything of his own to play with. His family was one of the first ones that got to the cave. And then they sat there helping other people unload stuff for four days and Daddy was mad because they'd all been told at the town meeting to go immediately to the cave and that they could only bring what would fit into one of the monks' fresh-vegetables crates. That's what they used to haul stuff down the river and load those crates on rafts. But other people didn't come to the cave right away like they'd been told, and they brought way more than one crate full.

Daddy said it wasn't fair that they had played by the rules and the Brunswicks, whose igloo was two down from theirs, had brought all kinda books and games and toys for their kids. He and Mr. Brunswick had a big fight about it and almost started hitting each other.

Sammy wished he'd thought to grab a ball when he went running out of his room. It was right there, but he hadn't. Which meant, of course, that as far as he knew, Lucas had the *only* ball in the whole cavern. And that meant he was in charge. He got to pick what games they played, he got to choose sides first, he could get all pouty, the way he always did, and take his ball and go home.

"You missed it, Sammy," Haley Abernathy called, pointing to a stack of rocks and dirt behind him. "It bounced into the rocks."

Sammy sighed. It was hard enough to catch a ball outside in the bright sunlight. But the light here in the cave was shadowy and it was hard to see. It wasn't his fault he missed it.

His eyesight wasn't as good as other kids'. He could see the ball, but couldn't seem to judge where it was going to land. His mother said that in Before, there had been doctors who'd give you thin plastic things to put in your eyes to make you see better, and then when you were thirteen and your eyes stopped growing, they would cut into your eye with a laser — which sounded totally horrifying — and fix it so you could see as well as everybody else. Now, he just had to live with the world being kind of blurry, and it seemed to him like it was getting worse all the time.

Sammy turned, feeling a kind of sadness he didn't understand, but believed if he could just go out in the sun, he'd feel fine again. He went to the rocks Haley'd pointed to. He heard a sound then, a strange sound, like maybe something he was supposed to recognize.

It sounded like a baby rattle.

He reached down to pick up the ball which had lodged in a crevice between two rocks. He saw a flash of something and felt a tingling or burning sensation on his wrist. Then he saw it in the rocks only a few inches from the ball. A snake! He flailed out at it instinctively to knock it away and felt the pain again, higher up his arm. He understood then that the snake had bitten him. Twice.

Chapter Eighteen

ALFRED RAWLINGS LET FLY a string of obscenities that would have seared the ears off a sailor. He wasn't a man prone to swearing, but he wasn't mistaken about what had happened here. He'd come in this cavern with four chickens — three hens and a rooster — had bullied the guy operating the raft floating supplies into the caverns to get him to allow the extra cage and had listened for days to his neighbors complaining 'bout the crowding and whining that *they* didn't have fresh eggs every morning for breakfast like *he* did.

Fuck them. They wanted fresh eggs for breakfast, they shoulda had the presence of mind to bring some chickens along to lay the eggs. Their lack of foresight wasn't his fault, and be damned if he'd be shamed into sharing what was his. Calvin Masterson down in Butler Bulge Cavern had brought a goat and every morning he was milking that goat, drinking the milk. If Calvin could have a goat, Al could by God have chickens.

Al lived at the end of the row of "houses" in Chisholm Trail *South* cavern that branched off Chisholm Trail

135

cavern, had to fight all the folks who'd lived on Haskins Street in Zion Village to stay where he was but he'd stuck. He kept his chickens cooped up in a pretty good-sized area in a cleft in the rock out behind his igloo. Area was way bigger than a chicken yard and he'd used broke-up pieces of crates to pen them up. Wasn't no way for them to get out by themselves and just wander off. Yesterday, when he'd tossed out the last feed for the night, they'd all been there.

Now wasn't but one left! *One damn chicken.* Somebody'd took the three others and wasn't no mystery who that had been! Al had listened to Seth Carmichael mouth off about the chickens since that first day in the meeting in Carnegie Hall. Complaining about the rooster crowing, saying the only good bird was one frying in a pan. Wasn't no doubt who'd done the stealing. The bastard had better not have killed them chickens yet, or he would strangle the son of a bitch.

Alfred marched down the corridor to where Seth Carmichael and his family had set up their igloo.

"Get your ass out here, Seth," he called. "And bring my chickens with you."

The flap on Seth's igloo swung out and Seth appeared. Clear as day he was stoned off his butt, on something.

"I ain't got your damned chickens," he said. "You can't keep up with your chickens, ain't my fault."

"I am warning you, Seth. I will come in there and tear your whole house apart if you don't bring my chickens back out here right this minute."

"You and whose army?"

Alfred threw the first punch, caught Seth square in the mouth and knocked him backward where he fell into the wall of the igloo and moved the whole structure. Seth's wife, Daisy, stuck her head out the flap and cried at Al, "What are you—?"

Seth's teenage son shoved her aside and leapt outside.

"You hit my dad," the boy said. "Whaddaya think you're doing hitting my dad?"

"Stay out of it, boy. All I want is my chickens back—"

"I ain't got your damned chickens," Seth said.

"The hell you don't and you better—"

"You go near my husband again and I'll blow your guts all over the cave wall."

Daisy Carmichael stood in the doorway of the igloo about fifteen feet away, leveling a shotgun at Alfred. Everybody was supposed to surrender their firearms to the sheriff, but didn't hardly anybody follow the rules. Lots of people had guns, but weren't many people still had any ammunition for them. Trouble was, you didn't know who did and who didn't.

Daisy pulled back the hammers on both barrels. The woman was batshit crazy and everybody knew it. She used to show up at dinner about twice a week back in Zion Village, with her hair all wild and wearing them Spanish dresses with the bangles and jangles, acting like she was some kind of flamenco dancer or something. It was her baby brother Arliss Jenkins who had seen the shuttle crash outside Jessup. Him and Big-un Blocker and some other boys went barreling to the site in a pickup truck, ready to bag themselves an alien. They'd been torn to shreds by reptars, and Daisy lost it after that. Never was the same. Sometimes she'd rant on about how it was the sheriff who'd killed her brother and other times she'd claim that Thelma Whittle down the street had called the Astrals to town as revenge when her boy Silas got locked up for being drunk and other times …

You couldn't trust Daisy. Wasn't no telling what she'd do.

"Put that gun down, Daisy," Alfred said, and took a step toward her. "You ain't gonna shoot me or anybody else with it." He held out his hand. "What you're gonna do is give me—"

The blast from both barrels of the shotgun literally cut Alfred Rawlings in half. He flew backward from the impact, landed on his back and slid another couple of feet, leaving behind a blood snail trail.

Some of the witnesses said Daisy hadn't really meant to pull the trigger, that she was just bluffing like she always did and accidentally … Others said Alfred lunged at her, tried to take the gun away and she fired to protect herself. Well, one witness said that, Sherrye Lumpkin, and she was the closest thing to a friend Daisy Carmichael had.

The only thing not in dispute was what happened to Alfred Rawlings when she pulled the trigger. Daisy's husband, Seth, got to his feet, his eyes the size of saucers. Daisy just lowered the gun, turned and went back into the tent.

Chapter Nineteen

SAWYER COULD HEAR THE SCREAMING, the echo of it, bouncing off the walls of the cavern. It was a wailing, the mournful cry that had stopped every man, woman and child in their tracks, listening. Sawyer had started running as soon as he heard it, but even so there was already a crowd gathered around before he got there, standing in an ever-broadening semi-circle, scooting out so the others behind could see. He shoved his way through to the front to the tableau in the center of the almost empty cavern.

Sawyer rushed instantly to the people kneeling beside the edge of the trail.

Anna was there. Someone had called Nick and he'd made it before Sawyer. The woman who was screaming was kneeling beside the body of a little boy. The woman was just screaming, while a man kneeling beside her tried to calm her.

When he got closer he recognized Norma and Edgar Witherspoon. The boy must be Sammy.

"Snake bite," Nick said.

"Snake ... how ...?"

He knew how.

Anna was working furiously on the boy. His mother was cradling him, apparently at Anna's directive, and his left arm was hanging down on the ground. It was ugly and swelling — Sawyer could actually see it getting bigger.

"Twice, two bites," Nick said.

Sawyer swore without even realizing he was speaking.

"No, let it bleed," Anna told Norma, when she tried to blot the blood seeping, not gushing from puncture marks on his wrist and upper arm. Not good locations for snakebites. "He's going into shock. Let him lie back, but keep his head lower than the rest of his body. Elevate his feet. Somebody, get me a blanket."

"But shouldn't we cut the wound, suck the—" somebody offered.

"Wive's tale," Anna snapped, as she unbuttoned the boy's shirt, unbuckled his belt and unfastened his jeans.

"A tourniquet, then? I can make one." Edgar was frantic to do something. Norma just continued to scream. The boy in her arms was unconscious.

"Neither," Anna said. "Where's that …?"

Then two monks emerged from the crowd with the stretcher from the infirmary, put it down, but Norma wouldn't let the boy go.

"Norma, we need to get him to the infirmary," Anna told her.

Norma just kept screaming, her head thrown back, her eyes shut, making a wild, keening sound.

"Norma!" Edgar cried. Then he slapped her. Not gentle either, so hard the crowd gasped. Blood flew out of her nose as her head snapped to the side and she was suddenly silent. And in the moment of shock that produced, Edgar took the boy out of her arms and placed him on the stretcher.

Norma looked at her husband uncomprehendingly, then at the boy being lifted off the ground on the stretcher.

"It wasn't poisonous," she said, to everybody and nobody. "Just a garter snake. I saw it in the rocks over there. Just a hog snake, that's all."

Edgar helped her to her feet so she could scurry along behind the people bearing her son on a stretcher to the infirmary.

"Anybody *really* see the—?" Sawyer began.

"Barring a massive allergic reaction, you don't go into shock from a non-poisonous snake bite," Nick said. "I'm betting rattlesnake. We got to keep the kids from playing in these rocks."

He and Nick stood as the procession with the stretcher hurried down the corridor. Keep the kids from playing in the rocks. Where else were they supposed to play?

"Sawyer! Sawyer, you gotta come quick," a man was yelling as he ran toward Nick and Sawyer from the other end of the cavern. "Daisy Carmichael's gone and done it now!"

By the time they got to the grisly scene in the Grisholm Trail South cavern, Eagle Feather was there. The wounds the old Indian had suffered escaping from Zion Village had not been serious. It was the blood loss that had put his life at risk. Once the blood had been replaced, he'd recovered remarkably fast.

He was on one knee outside Al Rawlings's chicken coop, holding a lone chicken feather. He touched something dark in the dirt, a spot that could have been blood, then stood.

"They leave no evidence, maybe a stray feather." He held it up in his hand. "Like they were cleaning up after themselves."

"They who?" Sawyer asked.

"Foxes. They carry off their kill, sometimes bury part of it to come back to later." He pointed to Rawlings's makeshift pen. "A fox can jump more than five feet — they're more like a cat than a dog."

"You're saying Seth didn't take Al's chicken, a fox did," Nick said. It wasn't a question.

"Couldn't have been a raccoon. They make a mess, kill multiple birds if they can get to them and leave the bodies where they're killed. Usually just eat the contents of the birds' crops and some of the chest, almost never the whole bird."

Less than half an hour later, the chicken thief was spotted, skittering across the rocks and back into the darkness at the end of the cavern. Several people tried to catch it, but the fox seemed to vanish.

~

SAMMY WITHERSPOON only lived a few hours after he was bitten. A small boy. A big snake. Multiple bites. The outcome was never in doubt.

Sawyer felt so bad for the grieving parents but he had to shake off the pall of empathetic sorrow because the nitty-gritty details fell to him. *He* had to figure out where/how to bury the body of Sammy Witherspoon. And Al Rawlings, too! He also had to come up with some way to confine, contain … *jail* Daisy Carmichael. And Sawyer suspected she would be only the first of a growing number of people who would need restraining or incarceration. Probably sooner rather than later.

Then what? A trial? Execution?

It was coming apart. It had held together for longer than could reasonably be expected, he supposed. The blessing of geography and isolation had made it possible for the community of Jessup, Kentucky — that became Zion Village — to continue to function as a respectable society, a place where the rule of law held *even without* the whole infrastructure of jurisprudence to back it up, without courts and juries and jails. The norms of right and wrong still applied there and people abided by them, kind of an honor system. Oh, they weren't perfect, but there were few surprises. Even with silver marbles in the sky and saber-toothed monsters prowling the earth, there was right and there was wrong and for the most part people in Zion Village kept each other inside the fences.

It had been getting harder, though. Every year. More contentious. Rowdier. Sawyer kept the lid on the pot, but the contents had been gradually heating up and the lid was jiggling, bouncing in his hands. Zion Village had *grown*, more than double the number of refugees who'd straggled out to Zion Academy after the Astral shuttle destroyed Jessup. People kept coming and they were always welcomed. Some wonderful people came, drawn by the strange pull of Noah and Star. But even those were strangers … *survivors*. And the trouble was, survival of the fittest often … *usually* … meant survival of the meanest or the most ruthless or the craziest.

This final challenge, clawing at the last possible hope of survival *in a cave* — that was a bridge too far. The fabric of society was coming apart. Sawyer could almost hear the awful sound of it ripping.

He felt something like a shudder go through his whole body, held his hands out in front of him. They were not shaking. He remembered Astral Day when he'd sat in his office and tried to figure out who the sheriff of McClintock County, Kentucky could reasonably be expected to save. He'd acknowledged he couldn't save the world, that loading all the passengers and crew of the Titanic on his little lifeboat would sink it and everybody would drown. He'd selected his little corner, his town, people he knew and understood, and he'd pledged himself — not in so many words but that's what he'd done — to saving *those people.*

But the *number* of those people and the *character* of those people had morphed over time. His father's sage advice — you can't save every puppy in the pound — came back to him. Sawyer Matheson had had no alternative but to *try* to jam every puppy in Zion Village into Noah's Ark. And some of those puppies ... weren't house broken.

He looked at his steady hands, felt his quavering insides, and forced all those thoughts out of his mind. What was the next right thing to do? He had to concentrate on the next right thing now and forget everything else.

Bury the dead.

He'd talked to Garson about it and his clinical mind, devoid of emotional complications, had come up with a solution that would work. The barrels that had contained Blue Goo. Use them as sealed caskets. The "caskets" could then be placed in a remote, dead-end cavern that'd be re-named The Cemetery. They couldn't dig graves in the solid rock, of course, but they could make cairns of piled stones. They'd even put up crosses. The families would need somewhere to go to. That would have to do.

The next right thing?

Create a jail.

Actually, the jail was the simplest of his problems to solve because he didn't have to do much of anything. There were seven dead-end caverns, scattered along the miles of twists and turns in Level One, that had small entrances with doors that had finger-print-opening locks. They'd been built years ago when Matheson Caverns had its own ammunition factory — mined the saltpeter and the gypsum on site, stirred in some charcoal and "boom," gunpowder. The production of gunpowder and ammunition necessitated building heavy metal doors with sturdy locks.

One of those caverns opened off the east side of Carnegie Hall and that's where the monks had located their "monastery" — so they'd be close to the commercial kitchen where they'd be working. Another of those caverns could easily be converted into a jail.

The largest, most secure of those caverns had been built in the tunnel called Kaboom, a couple of miles from Carnegie Hall, depending on which connecting caverns you took to get there. The cavern lay behind what Sawyer called the Drawbridge doors — huge, metal behemoths that had been transported into the caverns in sections and assembled there. The lock on those doors required the fingerprints of two elders to open. Behind them were three caverns that also had doors and locks. One was the armory, for the guns they had brought with them from the academy plus the ones they had confiscated from the people coming into the ark. The second was loaded floor to ceiling with kegs of gunpowder.

The third was what Sawyer'd designated Home Base. It was a small room behind an enormous door ... inside the Drawbridge doors — the safest place in the caverns. It *might* even be water tight if you closed the air vents, though if the caverns flooded, who'd want to be stuck in there to die? More than just an empty cavern, it had battery-powered electric lights, a couple of tables, a dozen empty powder kegs to sit on, two sets of bunk beds, blankets, pillows and cots. At one time, it'd also been outfitted with enough freeze-dried food and water to last a dozen people a month. Now, most of the furniture had been commandeered for Ark residents' housing and all that remained of the supplies was the water and a couple of tins of freeze-dried "beef stew." Sawyer'd made the existence of Home Base known to a handful of key people, told them it was where they should go if the shit totally hit the fan. Garson had insisted on calling it the Doomsday Room.

Right now, Daisy Carmichael was in handcuffs, guarded by two deputies. Her presence was yet another bone of contention in the grumpy, irritable, growing-more-disgruntled-and-contentious-every-day residents of Noah's Ark. Getting her out of sight and out of mind would at least put on the back burner the legitimate questions about what came next. A trial? When she'd shot Al Rawlings in cold blood in front of thirty-five eyewitnesses — and didn't deny it — what was the point of a trial? Why stage some kind of performance with the outcome known before the start?

But wasn't that her *right* under the law? Should they still abide by those rights now? Back in the day, she'd have gotten off with an insanity plea. Since her only possible defense wasn't an option, why play all the other reindeer games?

Fine then, say she was guilty of the crime of first-degree murder.

Then what … execute her?

Seriously.

He swallowed. This was Kentucky and Kentucky was a death penalty state, had been, at least, when any of that kind of shit mattered.

Okay, forget the execution part, just keep her locked up … for how long? Forever? The logistics of that — the manpower — were staggering.

So Sawyer stopped thinking about it. One issue at a time.

Chapter Twenty

GARSON MADE HIMSELF BREATHE. Forced himself to release the gasp he had sucked in at the sight of the beings in the cavern with him. If he didn't let it out and breathe, he would pass out.

He knew he was gawking, staring, being rude, but — was there any such thing as being rude to a titan? Clearly, the Astrals didn't have the same rules about behavior that humans did.

Focus.

Everything you have ever wanted in your whole scientific life is standing right there in front of you. For the love of God, man, do something.

"Hello, I'm Garson. What's your na—? Who are—?"

Focus!

"What are you doing here?"

It was at least a rational question, though certainly not the kind of probing inquiry he had always envisioned his conversations with beings from another world would be.

None of them spoke. But words formed slowly in Garson's mind.

Gathering our equipment and the remains of … the one that does not function. An explosion sealed the exit.

The Astrals had returned to retrieve the mining equipment from the cave. Duh. Of course they had. In all the visitations Astrals had made to Earth in the past, they had never left anything definitive behind. Not some gadget the Aztecs couldn't operate, or some substance an ancient race couldn't have produced. They'd cleaned up after themselves nicely before they left Earth, erasing their presence from all but the most prying minds.

The Astrals had come to this mountain to mine the limestone rock here during the previous visitation because Noah had found the impossible cavern with the smooth sides on Astral Day, six days *before* the ships arrived.

They had returned on *this* visitation to continue the mining operation.

Garson's best guess was that they'd used the rock for the seeing stones they'd laid down in lines and circles all over the earth as their first act when they arrived seven years ago — the stones that enabled them to gather the mass thoughts of a group of humans. Apparently, they needed new rock for every visitation or they wouldn't have come here to cut it out of the mountain this time — they'd have used the rocks they left behind the last time they were here.

All that was merely sequential reasoning, of course, without any empirical data or confirmation. It just *made sense* … until it didn't.

Why were they here *now*? Why had they been cutting limestone *this week*? They'd laid down stones seven years ago, used them to examine mankind. Mankind flunked, they passed judgement and were preparing to annihilate humanity.

What'd they need new rock for now?

Necessary component for—

The words appeared in Garson's mind even though he had not asked the question aloud. But the word beyond "component" was no word in the English language, or in any one of the seven other languages Garson spoke. It didn't even sound/feel like a human word at all.

The titans made no effort to define it, merely stood, looking at him.

What difference did it make— that was a rabbit trail. Clearly they used the rock for *something* or they wouldn't have come here … and gotten trapped here by the explosion.

The silence lengthened.

Garson stood in the dark cavern with five live titans and one dead reptar. But he knew the silence was only on his end. The titans could, if they chose, go through the thoughts in his mind like fingering through the shirts on a rack in the final clearance aisle.

But they didn't put any more words into his mind and so he stood.

And they stood.

Enough shock had worn off that he was able to be more observant. Three of the titans appeared male, the other two female. They wore robes not totally unlike the monks and equally unadorned. They all had pleasant, if blank, looks on their faces. None of them smiled, but Garson remembered Noah's description of his interaction with titans on the mothership when he was kidnapped. He said when they smiled it looked like they'd learned how from a manual — probably had — and it wasn't a pleasant sight.

Okay, sports fans, now what?

He now had before him the single most important scientific find of his entire life, the doorway to knowledge beyond his imaginings. He also had before him, oh by the way, creatures that at any moment could morph into the murderous reptars like the dead one stinking behind him, whose tooth, he just realized, he was clutching like a light saber in front of him.

No. We cannot change.

There was no further explanation. They were saying they couldn't become reptars. Why the hell not?

Images formed instantly in his mind, horrifying images of reptars *killing each other*. The most efficient killing machines imaginable intent on destroying their own kind. Ripping off scales with their slicing teeth. There was utter silence, though. The expected accompanying sounds — screaming, sucking, purring sounds — were absent as blue and red blood squirted everywhere and—

The images vanished. There. Then gone.

We cannot change.

There was no emphasis of any kind on the words, but they hadn't said "will" not, as if it were some kind of promise or pledge. They'd said *cannot*.

The images instantly returned, reptars attacking each other just like Noah had seen when he came to the cavern. But this time, the scenes were accompanied by a horrifying sound — a high-pitched shriek Garson could feel in his teeth, a sound so painful he dropped to his knees, put his hands over his ears. But the sound wasn't coming from outside, it was inside, a static, buzzing squeal. He shook his head, couldn't *stand*—

The images and the sound stopped. There. Then gone.

Garson got slowly to his feet, swiped at his upper lip because it felt like his nose had been bleeding but his hand was dry.

The sound. The attack.

The sound had *caused* the attack.

Garson's off-the-top-of-his-head explanation of the phenomenon to Noah had been correct! The limestone they'd cut from the cave had some component that transported human thoughts to the hive mind. That's what the Astrals used it for, they laid out lines and circles of stones all over the earth, carrying the thoughts of humanity to the hive mind of the Astrals.

But apparently the limestone didn't just transport *human* thoughts. It transported *Astrals'* thoughts, too — at least reptars'.

So you're a reptar, whose thoughts are always connected to the hive mind ... and you're surrounded by limestone, which *also* transmits your thoughts to the hive mind. Both at the same time: *feedback!* The reptars' thoughts *already* in the hive mind, transmitted to the hive mind a *second* time would create a continuous loop. Like the high school auditorium sound system squawking because the microphone is transmitting sound to the speaker ... and the microphone picks up that sound and transmits it *back* through the speaker ... which the microphone picks up again and transmits back ... a continuous loop.

The limestone caused feedback in their minds, an awful screeching, squawking sound that drove them bonkers, made them so crazy they attacked each other.

We cannot change, they'd said.

The titans were standing here calm as newborn lambs with limestone all around them. The effect limestone had on reptars was to transmit their thoughts in a continuous loop that created feedback. Clearly, it didn't do that same thing to titans. Apparently, the effect it had on titans was to prevent the transmission of thought altogether. In titans, the limestone *blocked* their connection to the hive mind. Period.

The titans were telling him that they couldn't become reptars or they would go nuts. And they couldn't communicate at all with the hive mind on the Astral mothership.

These guys couldn't turn into Astral killing machines. They were stuck as harmless white giants that weren't at all dangerous, at least not that Garson had ever heard, and they couldn't rat the humans out to the other Astrals in the mothership, at least not now, not surrounded by limestone that blocked their connection.

He made a decision then. Or maybe he only recognized that he had already reached a decision in his mind. He would not tell the others about the presence of the titans in the mine. The titans were defenseless surrounded by limestone, and the others would cheerfully massacre them. And it certainly wasn't that the creatures didn't deserve death, a death as horrible as it was possible to administer, repeated a hundred times over, a million times over ... seven BILLION times over.

But Garson could see no moral point to be made by holding these particular five titans accountable for the sins of their whole species. In their hive mind form, every one of them — acting as a single being — was responsible for the deaths of billions of humans. They were *all* responsible ... but none of them was individually responsible.

He wouldn't let the others kill these beings. There was no reason to do so. And alive, he could ...

Oh, come on, Garson, who do you think you're kidding? You want to keep these creatures alive because you want to study them.

And he *did* want to study them. If they would allow it. But that was a matter for another time. Right now, the practical matter at hand was that he had a job to do. He would return to the others and *not* tell them that he had searched for the impossible cavern … and *not* tell them he had found it … and *not* tell them what he'd discovered there.

He was simply carrying out his original mission, what he'd planned to do when he got out of bed this morning. Only, instead of hiding the existence of one dead reptar, he would be hiding the existence of five live titans.

Chapter Twenty-One

Jackie Carlisle would soon be eight years old and not once, not ever in her whole life had she ever won when she and the other kids played hide-and-seek. And that made her mad! They always found her. No matter where she picked to hide. In the village, they'd played outside on the grounds or in designated areas of the academy — empty classrooms, or the administration wing on weekends when nobody was there, and sometimes in the monastery. The monks would let them play there, but the rooms were so bare there was nowhere to hide.

And ever since that little boy got bit by a snake, the grownups had said the children couldn't play in the rocks, that they had to stay on the trail.

Where could you *hide* on the trail?

Oh sure, there were houses beside it. People had made houses out of all kinds of things, inflatable tent-things and real tents and poles with sheets and those kinda-paper walls where you smeared that stuff on fabric and the fabric got stiff and would stand up so you could make a wall out of it. Houses were everywhere, up and down the caverns around that big one called Carnegie Hall. And she'd heard the grownups talk about the houses down in the level below and the one below that but there weren't as many there and her mother said that was because those people were Aunt Social — even though Jackie didn't have any aunts and uncles at all.

Some people would let you hide in their houses, but most people wouldn't and it was no fun anyway because the grownups always gave your hiding place away.

But this time, it was going to be different.

Jackie's mother sometimes said she was headstrong, and she didn't know what that meant except maybe that her head wouldn't break if she bumped it. Her older brothers, Gus and Arlo, complained that their mother let Jackie get away with stuff, didn't make her obey, and Jackie knew that was partly true. She could usually wiggle out of punishment. That's why she wasn't worried about getting in trouble now. Her mother wouldn't really spank her. She might say she would but she wouldn't do it, not with so many people so close to hear Jackie cry. And Jackie was really good at crying so it sounded like she was about to die.

Jackie had made up her mind that this time, *this one time,* she was going to win at hide-and-seek!

How could she not? The others would be stuck behind somebody's clothes pile while she would be off by herself, hiding where nobody'd think to look.

She saw the entrances to lots of caverns off the main trail called Broadway. Those trails weren't paved and didn't have lights or anything because they hadn't been on the tour where people paid money to look at the cave. There were the Glow Worms on the ceilings there, of course. The Glow Worms were everywhere. They didn't give much light, but when your eyes were adjusted to the darkness, you could see as well as you could playing outside on a summer night, the backyard lit by a full moon.

Nobody was allowed to go into the caverns without lights. Not even the grownups! That was a big important rule. You could fall into a crack in the cave floor — there weren't cracks in the paved cave floors. Mostly, it was because there was the possibility of getting lost, no trail to follow in those caverns, just the natural cave bottom and you had to pick your way through, around rocks, over hills and stuff ... at least that's what Bobby Hardesty said. His father was one of the deputies that helped the sheriff and he'd been in some of those caverns so he should know.

She would be breaking all the rules if she went down one of those caverns to hide, but Jackie didn't care. Her brothers teased her about being so easy to find. Arlo was always the one who did and he laughed at her when he'd see her under the bed or behind the shoes in a closet when they lived in the village. Well, Arlo wouldn't find her where she was going to hide today!

As soon as Melissa Jamison put her hands over her eyes and started counting — One. Two. Three. Four. — all the children ran off to find places to hide. Holly Bradshaw squatted down behind a pile of solar batteries next to the Crenshaws' tent, which was the tent next to the one on the end. Melissa would find her quick. Jackie made it look like she was hiding in the shadows behind the last house that had walls made out of flowered sheets with that stiff stuff on them. But when Holly wasn't looking, Jackie jumped up and ran off down Broadway as fast as she could because it was a long way to the entrance to the unlighted cavern she'd picked and she had to get there without any of the other kids seeing her leave the trail. She'd get in big trouble if somebody tattled and somebody was always a tattle-tale. If she was going to win the game, Jackie would have to make it to that cavern without *anybody* seeing her. Then when she heard the "All Free." which meant the person who was it had given up trying to find her, she'd dart back out onto Broadway and go running down it and nobody would ever know where she'd hidden.

When she got to the forbidden cavern, she was panting and her side hurt, but she had made it without being noticed.

Now, she crept back into the cavern, climbing over rocks and piles of dirt and places where pieces of the ceiling had fallen down. She was very careful, looked really hard before she took a step to be sure there wasn't a snake anywhere near. She wouldn't have to go far back into the cavern. Nobody would be looking for her there. In fact, she'd have to listen real hard to hear them call "All Free," when they had looked everywhere and couldn't find her.

As her eyes adjusted to the dark, she saw the perfect place. There was a big rock, like a rock as big as a car. If she squatted down behind it in the shadow, nobody'd ever see her.

She climbed behind the rock and got on her knees so she could peek around it to the lighted corridor beyond. It was farther away than she thought. She hadn't realized that she had come such a long way into the cavern.

Her breathing slowed. Everything was quiet and still. The IT person had ten minutes to find everybody before they called out All Free.

Jackie decided she needed to know how long she had been here so if she didn't hear the All Free, she would know when it was safe to go back. Jackie could count to a hundred. She could do that a couple of times. That'd take ten minutes.

One. Two. Three. Four.

She thought she heard a sound behind her, turned to

look but no one was there. How could anybody be behind her, unless …

Billy Joe Bennett.

He always won, like almost every time, because he was small and could run fast, so he got away quick and fit into little places nobody thought to look.

He had figured out this was a good place to hide just like she had!

Jackie was so angry she wanted to cry.

"Billy Joe," she whispered, but she whispered loud. "I know you're there. How did you get here before me?"

Billy Joe didn't answer.

Well, she'd show him! She'd climb up higher in the rocks, higher than he was, find a place so small even little B.J. couldn't fit into it. She turned and scrambled up the loose rock piled up behind her, got to the top of the pile and looked up at the tumble of boulders behind it. There was a big rock there that jutted out from the others.

She froze. Didn't move. Couldn't. Just stood there. She wanted to scream but she could only whisper. "*Mommy!*"

Jackie Carlisle won the game. Nobody ever found her.

Chapter Twenty-Two

GIDEON HAD BROUGHT it to Paco last night. Or yesterday, what the fuck — in here a day was whatever you wanted it to be. That was a problem for Paco because he had always suffered from insomnia. And n*ow* — too many things in his head boiling and bubbling, to let them all rush in into his higher consciousness when he was not vigilant, too vulnerable in sleep. So he hadn't slept in … how the fuck did he know?

He shivered when he held the small bottle in his hand, and not because it was just what he'd wanted, was such a classic *fuck you* to the universe, either. He shivered because he was cold. Fifty-eight degrees was *cold*.

But the smile on his face was in appreciation of the cosmic irony.

"This work?" Gideon had asked as he set it down in front of Paco, proud as a kid with a report card with nothing but A's.

Paco had sent Gideon out to find poison, some kind of poison, either among the belongings of his small-but-loyal band of followers or among the conglomeration of pathetic belongings Gideon'd brought into the cave with him in the past seven years. Gideon was a hoarder, and Paco doubted he would be able to find any poison if he had any. Paco knew from his study of the subject — years ago, that poison was all about dosage, that any number of common chemicals or plants could be lethal in the right amount. He didn't really care about lethal, just very sick would do.

And then Gideon had handed him the bottle of rat poison. And Paco had thrown his head back and laughed. That was what Spade had used on the prisoners in Radcliffe Correctional Facility to instigate his insurrection and it was certainly fitting and right that it should be the method by which Paco overthrew the ruling regime in the *last bus-full of humanity on the planet* and set himself up as king of the mountain. Just as Spade had done.

Rat poison.

Paco held it up and continued to laugh, didn't even bother to ask Gideon why the fuck he had a bottle of rat poison. Fate. Karma. Random. It didn't matter. It was here and Paco intended to put it to good use.

The next day — was it fucking day? — when Gideon lifted up the blanket door and allowed the young woman to enter the room, he knew it had been one of the best decisions he'd ever made, as strategic as any decision he'd ever made to send Gideon out looking for her.

When she saw him, she gasped, took a step backward.

"You're dead," she said, her voice flat, with that nasal quality of deaf people. "You ... Noah said you drowned."

"And so I would have if he'd been in charge of the universe. But he wasn't."

She was a beautiful young woman, but the expression on her face ruined the whole look. Thick chestnut hair that hung down to the middle of her back, pulled back in a ponytail. Dark blue eyes and a pouty chin. He'd thought she was pretty when she'd tipped him off that Sawyer and company were sneaking up on him, in front of the whole gym full of people. But she'd been kind of out-of-sight-out-of-mind in his memory since then. Actually, it had been Himself who'd mentioned her.

You know, someone who has an IQ that's bigger than a two-digit number might be better qualified to do what you want them to do.

And he'd thought of the young woman.

"You're Gretchen Hampton," he said, and nudged his way into her mind. It took some nudging. Hers was not like the average person, the door propped open to let the fresh air blow through. She was closed up, locked up tight, everything about her. That's what spoiled her beauty, her demeanor. One look from those blue eyes could cause internal bleeding. He held out his hand to her. "I'm Paco Salazar."

"I know who you are." She turned on Gideon. "This is who you meant, somebody who could do something about the balance of power in Noah's Ark?" She turned back to Paco. "You'd be shot on sight."

"Which is why I'm staying out of everybody's sights."

He edged his way farther into her mind, didn't feel the familiar pain behind his right eye, and pushed more boldly ahead. The darkness he saw there both chilled and excited him.

"I think we might have some common goals and objectives."

"For instance?

Now, he began to push hard. Getting someone to do what you wanted them to do was certainly an art, not a science, even if you were able to dick around with their minds to make it happen. It was a difficult thing, indeed, to make it happen with a group, took a lot of energy.

His right eye socket began to throb.

But with this young woman, he was only nudging her toward where she already wanted to go. The boulder at the top of the hill. Didn't take much more than a gentle shove to get it rolling. It would gain speed on its own, fueled by its own prerogatives. He just needed to give her the little shove.

Changing the power structure. Getting rid of those in authority. Making our own decisions.

He shoved those thoughts into her mind.

And suddenly, he went blind in his right eye.

He'd been standing beside the table where Gideon had paltry supplies he'd been sent for, things that might be useful in the insurrection. Paco put out his hand now, grabbed the table for stability.

I'm sorry, sir, you'll have to pull over to the curb. It's illegal to drive with only one headlight.

Then Himself burst into maniacal laughter.

Paco blinked, dug his knuckle into his eye, squeezed it shut tight.

"Is something wrong—" Gretchen began.

"Shut the fuck up!"

Paco realized he was trembling, and a wave of nausea swept over him when he opened his eye again. Still nothing. He reached a trembling hand up to his left eye and covered it.

He was totally blind.

There was nothing but darkness where there should have been input from the right eye.

The optic nerve is a curious little doodad. You've been putting pressure on the blood vessels that feed it for way too long. You haven't totally blown out the blood vessel, though. You just ... how can I describe it? You put a crimp in the hose.

Paco wanted Himself's voice out of his head, out of it. He put his hands uselessly over his ears.

What, you going to shut me up by plugging up your ears? Stupid fuck. I'm in here with you. Knock knock. I don't shut up until you shut up, which will be — I'm calculating just on conjecture here, of course — but I'm thinking a matter of days.

"No."

Himself's face appeared on Gideon's head. Paco's face, *Not*-Paco's face, a mocking smile on his lips. Paco punched the smile off his face, landed a blow that broke his nose!

Broke Himself's nose.

No, Gideon's nose. The man went down like you'd pulled tight the noose round his neck and let the body fall through the trap door at the bottom.

Over here now!

Himself was giggling like a child playing a game.

You can't catch me. You can't catch me.

Gideon lay sprawled in the dirt. Gretchen stood staring at him, looking from the bloodied man at her feet to Paco and back again. Gideon groaned, rolled over and rose up on his elbow.

"What the fuck …?" The man's words were garbled and he spit something out his bloodied mouth. A tooth.

"Just a practice shot," Paco told Gretchen. "That's what I'm going to do to Noah when I catch up with him — smash his perfect nose all over his perfect face. I'm going to … I have plans, big plans."

He turned the full force of his one-eyed gaze on her.

Can she tell I can't see with my right eye? Is it … does it look funny, from the outside?

"And you're going to help me do it, all of it. Aren't you, Gretchen?"

He didn't dare push any harder. A crimped hose … that

wasn't the same thing as a busted hose, not the same thing at all. You could straighten out a crimped hose, let the water flow back through it. He'd see again. Of course he would. Himself was a stupid fuck and didn't know what he was talking about.

He pushed just a bit harder, felt an ache behind the eye he could no longer see out of, then he felt the boulder begin to move, roll a few inches. A little more. A foot.

Whoosh! It was gone, rolling down the mountainside.

Then she threw back her head and laughed. She laughed and laughed and laughed.

Chapter Twenty-Three

"WHY DO you want a bucket of the slurry soup, Uncle Garson?"

Diana had caught him draining out the dregs of the soybean slurry from the barrel. He'd volunteered to help in the kitchen after the Monk/Skunk Stink Catastrophe had rendered one whole section of tunnels unfit for human habitation and half the workforce of monks unable to do their jobs. It was the perfect cover for Garson to steal food for the Astrals he was hiding in the mine. He had put together a concoction using mostly the ingredients of gun powder — charcoal, saltpeter and gypsum — along with vinegar and detergent to soak the monks' robes. Garson had told them the robes needed to soak for two days when in reality they'd be fine in a couple of hours. After the mixture proved successful, they'd use it to scrub down the monks and Garson would lose his access to the human food supply.

He was already part of the rotating detail of people assigned to feed and water the small herd of donkeys, and that had made it easy to steal both food and water without raising suspicions. Unfortunately, Diana had fallen in love with one of the baby donkeys, named it Donkey Ho-tee, and spent every available minute with it. So Garson had be careful that she didn't see him stealing there. But he hadn't expected to trip over Diana here.

Eventually, when the rationing system fell apart, which of course it would eventually, stealing even a small portion of food would be a challenge. But he'd worry about that when the time came.

"You promise you won't tell?"

The little girl put on a solemn face and crossed her fingers across her heart. Then she did the most adorable lip-zipping gesture that made him burst out laughing.

"I'm testing it."

"Testing it for what?"

"I'm trying to figure out a way to make it taste better."

"It's gross. Everybody says it tastes as bad as Applebee's. What's Applebee's?"

"That's just a word that means foul-tasting. It came from a restaurant chain that was around a long time ago." He couldn't help pontificating. "The food in the restaurants was good, nothing unconventional, I don't think. But it was 'plain' so the young people — they called themselves 'foodies' — made fun of it." At the time, Garson had wanted to ask the students in his classes, 'Have you *ever* actually eaten there?' To Diana, he continued, "They eventually put the restaurant out of business and almost a hundred thousand people lost their jobs."

"Why did the foodies do that?"

He wanted to tell her the truth: "Because they were totally self-absorbed assholes." Snobbery in any form, particularly the kind that involved people flicking their intellectual ashes on whatever dared to commit the most egregious of all sins — "ordinary" — was a pet peeve of Garson's. But he softened it, instead quoted *Forrest Gump*, Diana's favorite vintage movie.

"Stupid is as stupid does."

She caught the reference and grinned.

"Why is what you're doing a secret?"

"I don't want to get everybody's hopes up because I really don't think my experiments are going to succeed."

"You think maybe the Astrals would think it tastes good? Or do they even eat the same foods humans do? And do they poop like humans poop?"

His head snapped up at the question, but it was innocent.

"I really don't know what they eat."

And that was the truth. Hiding the Astrals was like buying a pet gerbil without knowing what to feed it. Or how much.

He had provided human food because he didn't have anything else to provide, but they had never reacted to anything he brought with any emotion whatsoever. Certainly didn't act like they were hungry the first time he hauled a container of slurry mix in to them and one of water. They should have been starving, close to dying from thirst. Clearly, their metabolism was not similar to the metabolisms of humans.

Apparently, they didn't get "hungry" or "thirsty" as an indication that they should take nourishment. Maybe there was some other indicator. They were, after all, only components of a central, all-encompassing intelligence, not individuals, and the hive mind would certainly take care of its own.

Garson had given names to the five titans because he'd

wanted to keep them separate in his mind, even if they had no desire to be separate on their own.

Of course, they looked so similar it was difficult, particularly in the dim lantern light, to tell them apart. But one of the males was considerably larger than the other two. And of the other two males, one's eyes were lower on his forehead than the other's, accentuating the lack of hair on his head. It was a slight difference, but discernible. He had always been a fan of *The Three Stooges* slapstick humor. So he'd called the males Big Moe, Curly (the bald one) and Larry. He and some of his students would often get together on weekends and make pizza with the inCarts machine in his house. Though now that he had eaten the components of the food dispensed by the machine — soy-like organic substances and artificial fat — sans all the artificial color, texture and flavoring, it made him slightly nauseous to consider how much of it he had eaten voluntarily in his life. He and the students would binge-watch the classics, the real oldies from waaaaay back when the juke was called television and its content was cut up into pieces you could only see one time a week. He didn't remember why that was.

They watched a space program called *Star Trek* and had rolled on the floor laughing at the ridiculousness of the science it was based on. Of course, laughing uproariously and binging on the food in the inCarts was probably more a product of the weed the students were smoking than the excellence of the entertainment they were watching, but Garson hadn't been high and he'd loved *The Three Stooges*.

The two females were harder. They were so similar he suspected he wouldn't be able to tell them apart even if he'd had sufficient light. There were no discernible differences — size, height, facial features, stature. So he had dubbed the two of them Laverne and Shirley, from another tv program, and reconciled himself to not knowing which of them he was talking to at any given time.

Not that that mattered either. Talking to one of them was talking to them all and he could not discern a speck of difference in the replies that formed in his head, no matter who he was talking to.

When he had taken the food to them the first time, he'd been scared to death somebody would catch him with it and wonder why he needed a bucket of slurry and two gallons of water. But nobody cared. The longer they stayed in the cavern, the more chaotic the situation became. People were too concerned about their own circumstances to worry about what the old "mad scientist" — he knew that's what they called him when he wasn't around — was doing.

Of course, that was the reaction of the general public. If he had encountered anyone he knew well — Star/Noah, Nick, Sawyer, Eagle Feather — the guano would most certainly have connected with the air conditioning.

He gave the food and water to the titans and the words *thank you* appeared in his mind. It was not a sign of grati- tude on their parts, of course, just that they had learned from their study of human interaction that you said that when someone did something for you.

They had eaten the food and drunk the water, parceling it out among themselves to grant equal portions, but didn't seem glad to be eating, or thirsty.

He asked how much food he should bring them and the reply was *whatever amount you choose to bring.*

So he stopped worrying the creatures were going to starve if he didn't bring them enough food and contented himself with sneaking out only half his own rations.

He spent as much time as he dared with the titans,

tried to get some time every day. But the mine was a *hike* from the living spaces in the cavern. At least two and a half miles — five miles round trip — and the climb up to the opening was … daunting. The exercise was good for him, though. He felt better than he had in a long time, courtesy of the exercise and the totally balanced, if disgusting, diet. But he'd lost weight. No one would notice, because everybody was losing weight.

Whenever he could create the time — using his survey of humanity as a ruse — he would sneak off to pepper the Astrals with scientific questions and almost always come away more confused than he'd been in the beginning. Quantum physics was way less complicated than first grade math to them. Often they'd answer a question with symbols instead of words, and he decided the symbols were an iteration of numbers. Not the next iteration, the 100th iteration.

He framed a list of questions every night as he lay on his bunk, even though the list he'd asked about the day before had provided him with little understandable information. His mind was spinning so fast all the time trying to assimilate what they were telling him, that he was not "present' in any real sense to humans most of the time, and was for the first time grateful for his reputation for strange behavior. It served him well now. He wanted so badly to understand how they had come to Earth, how they had propelled the crafts through space and time, how they defied gravity, how they … how they *everything.* They never refused to answer his questions, but neither did they try to explain when he didn't understand the answers they gave him.

Sometimes he thought of himself talking to Diana, how he tried to simplify things, get them down to her level so she could understand. The Astrals didn't grant him the same courtesy.

After a while, he thought he saw a very subtle change in them. He could see tiny sparks of individuality in them, which either hadn't been there in the beginning, or were only just now manifesting themselves. He suspected the phenomenon was a product of being cut off from the hive mind for such an extended length of time. These beings had never thought without their every thought flowing into the massive stream of consciousness that was the hive mind. Now, the hive mind had been shrunk to the five Astrals themselves. It might be subtly changing them, that and their forced proximity to a human as their only interaction.

Moe smiled the most of all of them. It was a learned behavior for Astrals and looked learned, like they'd had to practice which muscles on their faces to employ to get the corners of their mouths to turn upward properly. But it seemed to Garson, *seemed*, that Moe might have been at least mildly glad to see him when he arrived. He also liked to think, though he had no basis for the assumption in reality, that the words which appeared in his head in response to his questions usually came from Moe.

Laverne and Shirley, Tweedledum and Tweedledee, Pete and Repeat, my brother Darrell and my other brother Darrell, were sock puppets, the kind of totally interchangeable beings it was not hard at all to picture being the totally lacking-in-individuality cogs in the hive mine wheel.

Curly sometimes did not come to "greet" Garson when he arrived with food and water. Sometimes, he merely stood off by himself doing ... nothing. Which, of course, begged the question, what *did* they do when he was not here? Locked up in the mine in absolute darkness, unless they produced some kind of light when he was not around. Apparently, the stench of the reptar's decomposition did not bother them. It certainly did Garson. And on his third visit, the body was gone. When he asked where, a purposeful "blankness" appeared in his mind, which he took to mean it no longer existed.

What did they do with their time? When he asked that, he got images that he finally interpreted to mean their consciousness existed inside all their heads, and stimulus or lack of it from their environment was inconsequential.

Big Moe was the largest titan and he sometimes, not often and maybe it was wishful thinking on Garson's part and not reality, but sometimes Garson was certain that Big Moe had made actual eye contact with him. Briefly, fleeting, less even than the kind of connection humans made to the woman who'd got caught in a long elevator ride.

Of course, the titans never engaged in anything even remotely resembling a "conversation" with Garson. They contributed nothing, answered questions if asked — though sometimes they "said" nothing at all in response. All questions about the flood, how long it would be before the water receded, what the world would be like when it did, how long the Astrals would remain on Earth afterward, were greeted with a mind full of nothing.

Other times, he was sure their silence was because the answer to the question he'd asked was so complex it would have been useless to try to dumb it down so Garson could understand it.

They never asked him questions because — duh — they could read his mind to find out anything they wanted to know. But he wasn't sure they were doing that. There was no way for him to know, but he suspected the reason they had not gone prying around in his mind had nothing to do with any sense of respect for him, or kindness on their part. His conclusion was far less flattering than that. Garson believed they didn't read his mind because they didn't choose to. Apparently, he just flat out didn't interest them enough for them to go to the trouble.

Eventually, he'd have to fess up about the titans' existence, or somebody would catch him feeding them. One way or the other, he couldn't keep their existence a secret forever.

And once the others found out about them, the humans would kill them. Just because they were Astrals, had massacred *billions* of people, was certainly reason enough to execute them, but in far more practical terms, the humans could not allow the Astrals to leave the cave when the water went down. As soon as they stepped away from the blocking force of the limestone, they would instantly connect with the hive mind in the mothership. The Astrals there would learn that a group of pesky humans had refused to go gently into that good night, and they'd never allow the pollution of the gene pool of humans they'd hand-selected to repopulate the planet. They'd wipe out the Matheson Cave survivors as casually as stomping a bug.

Actually, the titans wouldn't need the mothership to wipe them out. When they were no longer surrounded by limestone, the titans could shape-shift into reptars without the maddening feedback that drove reptars insane. Five reptars would make short work of almost totally defenseless humans. Ellie's description of the massacre at Ft. Knox made it clear that even trained, equipped soldiers were no match for them.

Clearly, it was better to fess up to Sawyer privately — "They followed me home, Mom, can I keep them?" — than to wait until he was found out. Better to discuss the issue with a few trusted people than to allow the whole cave full of humans to discover that, oh by the way, there were five titans living in the same space with them. Human-to-human relationships were getting more and more unstable and finding out about the Astrals could very well be the bomb that set everybody off.

Chapter Twenty-Four

THE WOMAN WAS HYSTERICAL, or close to it, and she'd brought with her a group of equally hysterical friends and neighbors. Sawyer went out to meet them, hoping he'd be able to separate those who really had valuable information from the yeah-what-she-saids, but the dwellings in the cave only offered visual privacy, not auditory. There wasn't anywhere he could take them to talk where the others standing nearby couldn't hear. The only silencer was distance, that's why he'd put the prisoner Daisy in the most isolated metal-doored room. She hollered incessantly and she'd have driven anybody within earshot bug-shit crazy.

"... find her anywhere ..." Mrs. Carlisle was crying so hard as she spoke it was hard to get much more than garbled half sentences. "... looked and looked ... other children said she was with them ... got the neighbors to look ... been gone for hours."

Mary Carlisle was a woman in her late thirties who looked older. On Astral Day, she hadn't even known she was pregnant with the little girl now missing. Her husband had been deep sea fishing off the coast of Bermuda with some friends from college. Cell service was spotty there even when aliens weren't attacking. She was never able to contact him and had no idea what happened to him. Unfortunately, just about everybody had a similar story.

News of the worldwide flood hammered Mary, like it did everyone else in Zion Village who still had loved ones out there in the world — maybe more than most, since she'd never given up hope on Jackson. Even after seven years she still believed she'd look up one day and there he'd be, told her children and anyone else who'd listen to fanciful conjectures about the adventures he was having in his journey home to his family, laughed about how surprised he'd be to discover he had a little girl named after him.

If Jack had still been out there somewhere, he was dead now, though, had drowned when the whole world flooded. Now, her dead husband's namesake was missing.

Sawyer took her gently by the shoulders.

"Mary, I know this is hard, but you have to concentrate, focus and tell me what happened."

She hugged herself, digging her fingers into her arms, and gritted her teeth to get control and described how the group of about ten children had been playing hide-and-seek and when all the other children had been found, they'd called out to tell Jackie she'd won. But she never answered.

The children had looked, then Billy Joe Bennet had come running to Mary saying they couldn't find Jackie, that Holly Bradshaw saw her running down Broadway away from the houses. Mary'd looked, so had all the neighbors. They'd looked everywhere!

And had trampled underfoot any evidence there might have been to find.

Several other adults and children offered other versions

of the same story. By the time he'd heard them all, Noah, Star and Pumpkin, Taylor, Samuel, Nick and Eagle Feather had arrived.

"Stay here, everybody—"

"I'm coming with you," Mary cried. "That's *my little girl.*"

"And she needs her mother's help right now. The best way you can help is to stay out of the way. All of you. Let me do my job."

Nobody liked it, but they did what they were told.

As soon as they were out of earshot of the crowd, Nick asked Sawyer what he was thought might have happened to the child.

"I think she's lost," he said. "That's the only explanation that makes sense. She went down one of the side tunnels to hide and then couldn't find her way back." He sighed. "And after everybody has scuffed up the ground all around in the main cavern, I'll never be able to figure out which way she might have gone. We'll have to split up."

He assigned Taylor, Samuel, David and Eagle Feather to go east on Broadway. Nick, Noah, and Star went with him west. He had brought a blind girl along on a search because of Pumpkin. The dog wasn't trained at tracking, but because Star could somehow get into the dog's mind and see what he was smelling she might be able to sift out something valuable.

"Don't go farther than half a mile or so down any of the tunnels. No little girl's going to go down a dark cave farther than that by herself."

"I'm surprised she was willing to go far enough to get lost," Nick said.

Sawyer exchanged a look with Nick. Neither of them said anything, but they were both thinking the same thing. That little girl hadn't run off down some dark cave all by herself, so far she couldn't even see the lights of the big cavern behind her. If she went down one of the non-commercial caverns, she hadn't been by herself.

It was more than an hour later when Samuel came to get him, said that Eagle Feather had found something. The other searchers were already there when he arrived. Pumpkin sat on the ground next to Star, whining.

"What is it?" Eagle Feather asked her. "What does he smell?"

"That's just it. He doesn't know what it is. There's no image in his mind, so it's something he's never smelled before. But he doesn't like it, whatever it is."

"There," Eagle Feather pointed to a spot on the ground behind a large rock. All Sawyer saw was scuffed dirt.

"She was hiding here, behind this rock."

"Okay," he said, taking the old man's word for it.

"Then she went this way." Eagle Feather began to climb up the pile of loose rocks behind the hiding place. He was an amazing old man, seventy-eight years old and he hopped from rock to rock with the balance and agility of a teenager.

He didn't go all the way to the top of the pile, stopped short and pointed to the rocks. They were scattered around, the dirt disturbed. And there were spots where something had dripped in the dirt.

The spots lay in the beams of several flashlights. Clearly, they were drops of blood.

Star didn't ask what the others could see that she couldn't. With Noah around, she could almost forget she was blind. When she was inside his head, she could see whatever Noah saw.

"A struggle," Sawyer said. "Someone—"

"There could be more," Eagle Feather said, and started

up over the pile of boulders behind the smaller rocks. He stopped before he ascended to the largest rock and pointed the beam of his flashlight at the dirt at the base of it.

Sawyer's heart leapt into his throat.

His head shot up and Eagle Feather's eyes met his. The old man shook his head slowly and said a word that froze all their hearts.

"Cougar."

Chapter Twenty-Five

ELLIE HAMPTON never dreamed because dreaming was a product of sleeping and she'd been in such excruciating pain for so long she couldn't remember the last time she'd actually slept, closed her eyes and opened them and it was morning.

Not real sleep. There had been that nightmare barely conscious time when nothing was real — Gretchen had drugged her and brought her to the cave. And when Ellie woke up, she was not in pain.

She remembered it the way you remember all the things that aren't real anymore. For a hazy time after, Anna had given her pills and her pain was gone.

It had returned, of course. Anna tried to make the pills last as long as possible, but …

They were gone now. Ellie knew she ought to feel gratitude to Gretchen for finding the pills and giving them to her for her pain. She didn't. She understood Gretchen's real motivation, knew exactly why she did what she did. Gretchen was ever only about Gretchen. Gretchen didn't want her mother to die and she had her reasons. It was that simple.

She supposed it might be morning, but the only way to tell was the changing of the big sign dangling from the ceiling in Carnegie Hall, the one Diana'd described to her, said it had a smiley face sun on one side and a smiley face moon on the other. Somebody — she thought maybe it was Garson, but her memories were too foggy to be sure — had said it was not psychologically healthy to live in perpetual darkness, that awareness of night and day, even if it was artificial, would help regulate the cave population's circadian rhythms. So the powers that be, whoever they were right now, had designated that certain times were "night" and the "street lights" (cavern lights) were dimmed in an effort to get the populace to go along with the ruse and sleep during those times and stay awake during the times designated as day.

That was one of a dozen attempts to make the world inside the cave conform to the world they'd left behind, exercises in futility that included assigning home plots in the caverns based on the old neighborhoods in Zion Village, the thought being that seeing the same next door neighbor every morning in the cavern that you'd seen for the past seven years in the village would be less jarring than taking the whole population of the community and shaking the people up in a Mason jar and dumping them out willy nilly all over the cave.

The efforts also involved holding regular school hours with required attendance, organized sports for young and old alike at "ballfields" set up in caverns with high ceilings, broadcasting a ridiculous, fingernails-on-a-blackboard grating "dinner bell" to announce mealtimes, and appointing "neighborhood watch" captains to report to Sawyer the "state of the union" in the neighborhood a couple of times a day. An effort to head off conflict that had completely bombed given that Sawyer had stepped in it from the beginning by having the audacity to select the captains, infuriating his constituency who were angry at not being allowed to "elect their representatives."

Now, several weeks in — Ellie didn't know exactly how long — the Matheson Cave Experiment in Human Survival was pretty much going to hell in a handbasket. Who knew if any of the people in this hole in the ground would ever again see the light of day. Only one person was absolutely certain of her fate. Ellie Hampton knew she would die here. And as soon as possible.

Ellie often thought of Dr. Henderson. Though she had spent not even five minutes in his presence, and that had been seven years ago, his face and words came to her mind often. She'd had to kill three men to get to him and she'd done it without blinking. Fighting her way to Ft. Knox after she discovered there was a functioning hospital there had not been nearly as harrowing an experience as living through the massacre of twenty-one thousand people, as Astral shuttles destroyed the military base, unleashing legions of reptars and firing death destruction rays to turn people, buildings, tanks, whatever into piles of black dust.

As far as she knew, she and Diana were the only survivors — Diana still in her mother's womb. The only building left standing had been a Burger Kastle.

Dr. Henderson had examined her — well, took a look at the lump, the first one in her right breast, the one she found standing in the shower on Astral Day. She still believed, chose to believe, that if she'd been able to find treatment for that one soon enough ... but who knew. In Before, she would most definitely have survived. She'd have been given the latest chemotherapy. The death rate for breast cancer had been hacked down to less than one percent. But in After, with no medical treatment, the cancer had *spread* ...

She drew her thoughts back to Dr. Henderson again. The cancer was in her brain now, she was sure. Her thought processes were becoming more and more unreliable and erratic. Given the level of pain she endured every second, her mind had begun deteriorating rapidly, starting about six months ago. Maybe if she waited long enough, the cancer would eat out her brain and she wouldn't even know she was in agony.

Dr. Henderson! She yanked her wandering thoughts back. Yes, he had been about to remove the lump that day at Ft. Knox, literally had the scalpel in his hand about to make the incision, when the shuttles showed up and wiped the fort off the map. He'd explained to her that what he was about to do, without benefit of putting her to sleep, would merely numb her breast and when the numbness wore off, he had no drugs to give her.

Then he had asked the question, the question that clanged in her mind the day she heard it and had in recent years taken up residence in her frontal lobe, and built a fortress ... now, after seven years, she heard the question clanging like a gong struck into the frigid clear air of a Tibetan mountainside.

Do you have a high tolerance for pain?

And at the time, the question had totally flummoxed her because she didn't have an answer. How the hell did she know what her pain tolerance was since she'd never in her privileged life — with the exception of a finger slammed once in a car door — experienced pain?

It was prophetic, that question. It haunted her, even in the early days when the only pain she felt was from the infected incision the abortionist Dr. Hank had performed to take out the breast lump. She thought about that pain, how it had immobilized her and demoralized her. It hurt and she was ashamed of her "low tolerance" for pain because it had HURT.

She would laugh at that level of pain now, if she could laugh at all. It was so inconsequential, so infinitesimal, so … now, compared to the agony of cancer in just about every organ in her body. How she longed for that time, the joy of feeling that pain again … and *only* that pain.

Did she have a high tolerance for pain? Hell no! But in the past seven years, she had developed one. Only that calibration was sliding sideways in her mind. All her tolerance defenses were crumbling around her, and she could not hold onto sanity for very much longer.

All she wanted in life was to stop hurting. She wanted to die. Had tried to die. Wanted to drown with the rest of humanity when the flood came. But Gretchen had snatched death away, and when Ellie thought about that time now she understood with an emotional pain equal to the pain in her body that the girl had *not* done it out of love.

It had taken a long time for Ellie to figure it out. Years. It wasn't even something she "figured out." The understanding just settled around her, inexorably. Like sitting in a cold bath and turning on the hot water … feeling the temperature change all around you.

No, Gretchen had not been saving her mother's life. She didn't want to *save* it. She had been intentionally *prolonging the agony*. Gretchen wanted her mother to suffer for committing the unpardonable sin of loving another child, of not making her the total center of her universe. Maybe Gretchen was unaware of her true motivation. Ellie didn't think so. She knew exactly what she was doing and why.

Consequently, she had become a helicopter daughter,

hovering over her mother's every move, determined not to allow her any possible chance that might present itself to die.

So Ellie would have to do this the hard way.

When Anna brought in the foul-tasting gruel — not hospital food, but what the whole population of the cave was choking down every meal, she had turned her head and refused to take a bite.

"Now come on, Miss Ellie," she said in her lovely Georgia drawl that sounded like honey pouring out of her mouth. "I know it tastes like shit, but you got to eat same as the rest of us."

"Take it away. I won't eat it."

"Now, come on—"

"Enough with the cajoling. I'm not going to eat. Or drink. Or allow any more transfusions."

"You know you have to take the transfusions."

Absent drugs to kill the cancer cells, Anna had come up with the only treatment option. Ellie's blood was drained away and completely replaced every other day, by the blood from donors, using hematological refraction, a technique that made it possible to transfuse blood for one person directly into another even if their blood was not the same type.

There was a rotation of blood donors. Just about everybody in Zion Village had signed up. Those transfusions had kept her alive, not killing the cancer cells, but providing healthy cells with healthy hemoglobin oxygen content and new white blood cells to fight the battle ... for a couple of days at a time. Anna had begun the transfusions about eighteen months ago and Ellie should have refused then, but there'd been that tiny ghost of hope.

"I'm done, Anna. This one thing I can do to end my own suffering. I will stop eating. I will stop drinking. I will not take another transfusion. I am a rational adult, over the age of twenty-one last time I looked and legally I have the right to decide. I want it written up so I can sign it, so we're all clear. No heroic measures. No IV fluids. No feeding tube. No forced transfusions. You do not need the advice or consent of a next of kin if the patient is capable of making the decisions. I am and I do."

Her throat felt like it was on fire and waves of agony flowed over her like surf at the exertion. She'd have to stop now, save some strength.

"Would you please … Sawyer. Get Sawyer for me."

Chapter Twenty-Six

EVERYTHING INSIDE SAWYER rebelled at the idea that there was a dangerous animal, a predatory animal, here in the cave with them. He stared at Eagle Feather, willing the old man to come up with some other explanation for the track there in the dirt.

Eagle Feather spoke softly, not in the way of someone who doesn't want to be overheard but like a person who doesn't like what he's saying, doesn't want to say it, but has to.

"The print of a wolf or dog, the pad here" — he pointed to a large indention below four smaller ones — "would be solid. This is not. See the three lobes?" Sawyer couldn't see what he meant, but it didn't matter. "A wolf or a dog, you'd see the marks for the claws in front of the toes. Cats retract their claws. From the size of this track, I'd say it's an adult male, ninety to a hundred ten pounds."

"Jesus," Nick gasped.

"How did it …?" That was Star, but it was a denial statement, not a real question. Sawyer knew that Star had seen — through Noah's eyes and Pumpkin's sense of smell — what he had seen the day of the flood, the number and kinds of terrified animals racing in blind panic away from the rising water across the parking lot in front of the Cricket Bottom cave entrance. Eagle Feather had told them all about the sight of hundreds of forest animals being herded by rising water into the hole in the mountain called — appropriately — The Drain.

The snake. The skunk and the fox. Two hundred fifty miles of explored caverns, all of them with Glow Worm lights. And no telling how many miles of unexplored caverns. But a mountain lion! Sawyer's mind rebelled at every image those words conjured in his mind.

He finally found his voice. Even to his own ears it sounded airless and whispery.

"What are, could she have survived …?"

Eagle Feather shook his head.

"A cougar attacks from the back. Often jumps off a high place." He indicated the rock that hung over the spot where they'd found the scuffed ground and the blood drops. "It can leap as far as fifty feet without injury. It crushes its prey's head or bites through the back of the neck, instantly severing the spinal column. Then it carries the body off to …"

Sawyer shuddered, couldn't help it.

"How has it … what has it been living on all this time?" Taylor asked.

"Its natural prey," Eagle Feather said. "The wild animals in here have — for the most part — been living off each other. But I imagine game is getting scarce by now."

"We haven't kept good track of the livestock," Sawyer said. "That was Brother Luke's job and he …" He shook his head. "There are all kinds of domesticated animals here. Calvin Masterson in Butler Bulge Cavern has goats. Alfred Rawlings *had* chickens. The monks brought sheep and lambs, I think, plus the donkeys. I don't know how many donkeys there were in the beginning, so I don't know if any are missing."

Sawyer thought about Diana's pet, the baby donkey Donkey Ho-tee. He couldn't allow her to visit him anymore.

"Small animals, too. Susan Collins brought in two cats and she can't find—"

"You mean this thing has been prowling around *where we live*?" David was horrified.

"The cougar came in on Level Four and made it up through Three to Two and to One because this is where the *food* is," Nick said. "The livestock—"

"And us," Eagle Feather said.

Though Sawyer had plotted out "neighborhoods" in all three caverns where people could settle, spaced them out evenly, people had huddled together instead. The intimidating darkness all around — couldn't blame them. Everybody refused to build in Level Three. It seemed too remote. Levels One and Two were more full than they had to be — there were *miles* of caverns, and there was no need for crowding. But the population of Noah's Ark all congregated at the west end of the top two levels near the elevator. They'd rather bitch all the time about neighbors too close than pick up and move farther out into the cavern where there was plenty of space … and plenty of darkness.

Star began to cry quietly and Noah put his arm around her. Taylor looked like he wanted to be sick. Nick kept his face emotionless. Sawyer hoped he was doing the same.

"How long?" Nick asked and for a moment Sawyer didn't get the intent of the question.

"A mountain lion this large would normally eat eight,

maybe ten pounds of meat a day, so it usually kills prey the size of a deer once a week."

"So we've got a week." Sawyer paused. *The size of a deer.* "Okay, less than a week to find its den and kill it?"

"Cougars don't live in dens."

"But I thought…"

"Wolves," Eagle Feather said. "They're a pack. They mate for life, they make a den to birth and raise young. Cougars are solitary hunters. They stay on the move, shelter in crevices, behind rocks during the day, seldom in the same place two days in a row. They hunt at night."

"In here, it's always night," Taylor said.

"So what's our next move?" That was Nick. The buck stopped with Sawyer. Taylor was so rattled he was doing well to hold it together. As was Noah, though he was being strong for Star. Star had gone from crying softly to sobbing.

"I have to tell Mary Carlisle that her daughter … is dead," Sawyer said. "We have to come up with defensive measures for everybody, while Eagle Feather and I hunt this motherfucker down and kill it."

EAGLE FEATHER'S voice was soft, but the room was so utterly silent nobody had trouble hearing him.

"Travel in groups," he said. "Don't go anywhere alone. Make a lot of noise, sing or talk loud, but not in a high-pitched voice."

Three thousand or so people sat in the stands, on the floor or stood in small groups in the vastness of Carnegie Hall, trying to come to grips with what had happened. The sound of Mary Carlisle's screams when he'd told her about her daughter … Sawyer would go to his grave with that sound echoing in his ears. So would the others who heard it, and *a lot* of others heard it.

"And what if we see it, the … *mountain lion?*" The voice from the crowd seemed to be saying the word out loud to somehow make it real. "What do we do?"

"Don't turn and run," Eagle Feather said. "Cougars attack from the back, go for the back of the neck or the head. And don't play dead. Make eye contact and maintain it. Throw rocks at it, hold out your coat or shawl to make yourself look bigger than you are. Use anything you have on you as a weapon. If it decides other prey would be easier than you, it'll back down."

"Other prey? What *other prey?*"

"You need to understand that the cat will become more and more bold. It's been in here as long as we have, with not much to eat except small animals — squirrels, foxes, moles, rabbits. It's a predator. The only food that exists in this cave is what we brought into it. And us."

Eagle Feather talked about keeping the few pets that had made it into the cavern tied up.

"That's easy for you to say," called a woman's voice. "You can put a leash on a dog, but I can't tie up my cats!"

"Either tie them up or just send them out into the tunnels … bite-sized snacks."

The woman gasped.

"I meant to shock you," Eagle Feather said, his voice cold. "You have to take this seriously. I don't want to sound harsh, but the presence of food — *prey,* is why it's here. Trash … food left out, your cats or dogs, anything edible will attract it."

"It can have my share of the Applebee's," someone said. That was the name they had given to the slurry mix that, though a totally balanced diet, did … taste like Applebee's.

"We have moved the donkeys to the cavern behind the chapel, so we can keep a better watch on them."

Not all the donkeys, but the whole crowd didn't need to know that one of the donkeys had been selected to use as bait. Eagle Feather said trying to track the cat would be useless. Miles of tunnels, with the big cat crouching behind rocks near the ceiling, moving like a shadow from boulder to boulder. Its eyesight was such that even with nothing but the Glow Worm lights on the ceilings it could see like broad daylight. You track it, you could end up becoming prey instead of predator.

Eagle Feather had told Sawyer his plan right before Sawyer blinked all the lights twice to indicate that everyone should go to Carnegie Hall immediately. The Indian intended to stake out the donkey, and then station sharp-shooters as far away as possible, but with sight-lines. Given the sophisticated scopes on most deer rifles, even a non-hunter could sight in on a buck at a hundred yards. But hunting was about more than what you could see through the telescopic sight on your rifle. Timing, steady hands, understanding your prey. And for very long-distance shots, knowing how to work the rise on the shot because the bullet would drop lower and lower the farther it traveled.

Unfortunately, there were no tunnels that ran straight far enough to offer the kind of distance sharp shooters had mastered — and all the Mathesons, fathers and sons, were sharp shooters. In fact, Taylor's wife Kelly Jo was the best shot of the lot. Broadway ran the whole width of the cavern from west to east — and on beyond the section of paved tourist caverns on both ends for who knew how far. The elevators opened into the west end of Broadway with the stairs on the east. The villagers who'd moved into the caverns had hovered together near the elevators — leaving miles of Broadway uninhabited. Eagle Feather selected a section of the big cavern about two miles from Carnegie Hall to bait his trap.

Chapter Twenty-Seven

HENRY LEWIS LOST IT. Something just came undone inside and he went for it.

He had eaten that slurry shit, that *Applebee's* for as long as he could stand it. He was fifty-four years old, had owned a dress store in Jessup, and his wife and kids were ... he didn't think about that. They'd been among those who were scheduled to board the ark on the last day. Henry had gone ahead to get everything in order, to build the walls made out of sheets and some blankets smeared with that Blue Goo stuff so they'd have somewhere to live. Janice was staying with the boys and Henry was glad to go. *Glad* to go. He was glad to get out of the house where Janice did nothing but complain, morning, noon and night. She didn't have the sense to be grateful they'd had a warning, that, unlike everybody else in the whole world, *they* had somewhere to go to hide from the flood. Hell, no, it was just bitch, bitch, bitch and finally he'd left her home with Andrew, who was sixteen and wanted nothing more out of life than to get laid, and Stanley, fourteen, who was as dumb as a box of rocks though Janice defended every stupid thing he did.

He'd liked the cave the first time he came in, which was when he off-loaded his family's things and was shown where he was supposed to put up their dwelling. It was quiet here. Even with the voices of all the people, the space, it was so big and open it ate up sound. He'd liked being here, liked the peace and quiet, was dreading—

But that didn't mean he was *glad* his wife and sons hadn't made it!

It didn't mean that at all! Didn't. He made a point of telling everybody how he was grief-stricken that he'd made it onto the ark and they hadn't. And he *was*! He was grieving, he was.

He couldn't sleep, couldn't make himself finish building the house, just left it. Couldn't think of nothing else but how ... much he liked being alone. Oh, dear God, he *was* glad they hadn't made it, which was the same thing as *killing* them. Same thing. And he was going to burn in hell for them drowning just like he'd held them underwater in the bathtub.

The food was the thing, though. He wanted the peace and the quiet, yeah, but if there was one thing you could say about Janice, it was that she was a good cook. A fabulous cook. Why, that woman could whip out the best fried chicken you ever put in your mouth ... with gravy and mashed potatoes that hadn't been quite as good as they used to be because the secret ingredient was mayonnaise and they'd run out of that five years ago.

No fried chicken here. No gravy. No mashed potatoes, even without the mayonnaise. Nope, not here. Here it was gruel in the morning. Gruel at noon. Gruel at night. At first with a handful of vegetables, raw, to go along with it. And beef jerky. Oh, and there was lots of butter and cheese and milk but he was lactose intolerant and hadn't gotten the annual shot that fixed it in years.

Gruel.

Then a fella told him what Timothy Willingham had hid away.

He couldn't place who the fella was, thought it was that Gideon Freeman but wasn't sure. What he was sure of was that soon's Freeman told him about Timothy's stash, Henry couldn't think of nothing else.

Finally, he had to go see, passed by and the tent flap was up and you could look inside and *there it was*. Neighbors musta thought it was a beach ball, but Henry knew better, remembered when Tim used to pile them up in his front yard and sell them out of a stand on the street.

Watermelons.

It was a *watermelon*.

And he broke. Just lost it. He didn't even wait until nobody was around, just run into the house and grabbed it. Neighbors saw. Eric Jones had just sat there, but Cynthia Rosenberg called out, "Is that a watermelon? Where'd you get a watermelon?"

And then the Hendersons heard her, of course. She had a voice like the foghorn on a tugboat. He turned and ran then, just ran. And when people seen what he had, they followed him … no, *chased him*.

It became a mob, him dodging around people, tripping and almost falling, seeing the faces of people he passed, watched their looks change soon's they seen what he was carrying. Seen the longing in their eyes.

Arnold Patel was who brought him down, jumped on him from behind like a tackle in a football game, and he fell forward on the watermelon. It busted, went splattering everywhere. He started grabbing pieces of it, shoving them in his mouth.

"It's *mine!*" he cried, though it wasn't, of course.

Then Charlie Weatherford yanked a big piece of it right out of Henry's hand and when he tried to grab it back, Charlie hit him. *Hit* him. Somebody screamed. Where did the blood come from? Then he saw he had a gash on his shoulder, looked up to find Timothy Willingham, screaming obscenities about *his* watermelon, that it was his, dammit, *his* — holding a bloody knife, slashing at everybody within reach, trying to grab the pieces for himself.

Then everybody was fighting everybody. Henry grabbed the biggest piece of the watermelon off the ground, and got one bite of it before Tim stabbed him in the neck.

~

MAXINE MILLFORD just leapt at her. Charlene Pendleton was walking down the tunnel and suddenly Maxine was up in her face, screaming.

"Where is he? What'd you do with him? His barking didn't hurt nobody!"

Charlene shook her off. Maxine was a skinny little thing and Charlene didn't even take shit off people her own size.

"Barking didn't *hurt* nobody? Keeping people awake night after night with that yap, yap, yapping."

"What'd you do with him?" Maxine came at her again, her fingernails like claws, scratching down Charlene's arm. Charlene screamed, grabbed Maxine by the hair and threw her to the ground.

"He didn't hurt nobody!" Maxine was snarling.

People were trying to pull them apart, Maxine

screaming about her stupid dog, Charlene trying to hit Maxine.

Benton Saunders grabbed her arms, pinned them behind her back, and Maxine's husband Belmont had his wife, trying to hold onto her, but she was a madwoman.

"She killed Bitsy," Maxine shrieked. "She killed him. She didn't like him barking so—"

"I didn't never do no such thing! I didn't like him barking, up in the middle of the night yap, yap, yapping. Yappy little bastard, somebody'd ought to have killed him, *but it wasn't me.*"

"Yes, you did!"

"You ain't listening — I didn't kill your—"

"Then explain *this.*" Maxine shook one arm free of her husband and held out a little dog collar, black with rhinestones on it.

"What about it?"

"I found it right *there,* that's what about it." Maxine pointed to the end of the pole that held up Charlene's roof. "It was hanging there in plain sight, like you was *proud* of what you done. Where is he?"

"I never saw that damn collar in my life. I didn't hang it there and I didn't do nothing with your dog, neither."

"Liar!"

Maxine lunged at her again and her husband kept her from swinging. But Charlene wrenched free from Benton Saunders's grip and landed a fist right smack in Maxine's face. Blood went everywhere, and then Maxine's husband came at her.

"What do you think you're—"

Then Charlene's brother, who was nearby, weighed in, shoving Maxine's husband out of the way.

Then everybody within earshot started screaming, yelling and hitting.

~

DOROTHY PARKER DOUBLED over and began to scream, holding her belly, screeching. She fell to the ground and her husband Robert dropped at her side.

"Dotty, what in the world …?"

Then Dorothy spewed out vomit everywhere, only it wasn't just vomit. It was blood.

"Help me," Robert cried, kneeling beside her. "Somebody go get Anna."

Dotty rolled over onto her side, heaving out gigantic mouthfuls of blood, gurgling and coughing.

The people around had jumped back away from the vomit, didn't leap to help. Just stood back away, gawking.

"She sick or something?"

"Oh shit, if what she's got's contagious, she got puke on my shoe."

"We're all gonna get it!"

"It's the plague. I read in history it was like that. People puked blood."

Then the others were running away instead of helping. Leaving Robert kneeling by his wife's side, pleading for somebody to—

A pain like nothing he'd ever experienced stabbed into Robert's gut and he fell forward, literally right on top of his wife. The agony was more than he could stand and he began to scream, his eyes blurry. It happened so fast.

The crowd running away included Isabel Montgomery and Hazel Wilkerson. The most distinguishing thing about the two women was that there was nothing distinguishing at all. They were totally unremarkable, from their not-memorable faces, to their ordinary ever-expanding waistlines, to their Kentucky accents that pronounced "can't" "cain't" and "Pentecostal" "penny costal." They were infinitely forgettable.

The two of them had grown up together in Jessup, played together in elementary school, giggled together in high school and worried over new babies and diaper rash as they raised their kids. Once the kids were in school, they both got jobs at the company called Kwan Glass in Louisville that made car windshields and windows, glass tabletops and the screens for tablets and jukes. Got up at four o'clock in the morning every day for thirty years.

On the hour-and-a-half commute, Isabel used autodrive, and spent the time hand sewing. She made quilts, clothing, wall hangings, drapes, curtains, table cloths — wasn't a person in Jessup, well, in Zion Village, who didn't own something Isabel had made.

Hazel used her commute time to write novels, trashy novels — they had sex in them and not the normal private kind, neither! She never let nobody but Isabel read them and Isabel confided that her husband, Winthrop, had a better sex life than any man in town because of what she read.

The two of them moved in together — just as roommates, they wasn't queer or nothing like that! — after Winthrop failed to come home from Louisville when he went up there two days after Astral Day. Isabel didn't know what happed to him. And Hazel's husband, Morris, died of a heart attack before the Astrals had been on Earth a month. They were closer than sisters.

Isabel fell first, just dropped to her knees and began to cry out in agony. She was bleeding, you could see the blood running down her legs and not just from there. Her nose and oh, glory be, she was bleeding from her eyes, too. Hazel took one step back toward where Isabel lay wringing in agony on the trail, then turned and kept on running.

The blood running out of Isabel's eyes had done it. *Bleeding out her eyes.* Hazel made it probably fifty yards down the tunnel, where people were in hysterics as one person after another was falling to their knees in sudden agony. When Hazel fell — she only tripped, didn't fall because of pain in her gut — people were running so fast, they just run right over her.

One of them was George Albertson. He had been one of the original grocers whose stores Sawyer had closed on Astral Day and he'd raised all kinda holy hell about it, but Sawyer'd had his way, as Sawyer always done. He kept people from looting, and they woulda. But within a few days, it didn't matter. People came in to buy groceries but their credit cards didn't clear, and those who had money, pretty soon he couldn't make change anymore because the registers were out. So what difference did it make? People looting his store was the same thing as people buying what they came for with money that was worthless.

But Sawyer's lockdown had given George a jump on things. He had managed to stash away in the basement boiler room a supply of non-perishables, cans of vegetables, fruit, cans of anything he could haul down there, literally filled the room so full it was a good thing the door opened *out.* He and his wife June and their kids actually managed to keep their larder a secret, lived off it for the first winter, when they chose to stay in Jessup instead of moving with everybody else out to the academy after the Astrals destroyed the town's food supplies. Not a single neighbor ever suspected they were able to stay because they had enough to eat from what was in their basement.

They had lived two doors down from Hazel and Morris Wilkerson, and when George saw Hazel lying there in the floor of the tunnel where she'd got knocked down, he wanted to stop and help her. The two of them had had a thing, back in the day; she'd sneak away from Morris by saying she was going to bunco and he'd say he was going bowling with some boys in Bardstown, then they'd shack up in that motel on the Bluegrass Parkway. The affair lasted almost a year and a half and then June began to think something might be up, started accusing George so he broke it off. The sex wasn't that good anymore anyway. When George saw Hazel lying there, he remembered they'd had good times together and he wanted to stop and help her, but he couldn't, had to *get away*. There was some awful disease and he'd probably already been exposed. But he got too close, tripped and fell on Hazel. His knee caught her in the neck and smashed her throat. He didn't mean to, but she couldn't breathe anymore and … oh, dear holy God, did he kill her? Did he *kill* Hazel? He just rolled off her and tried to keep going but somebody fell on him, on his knee and bent it backwards and he started screaming.

SAWYER FELT like he was trying to fight a malicious ghost, a poltergeist, an evil that had come out of nowhere and popped up everywhere at the same time. But it wasn't out of nowhere, not really. The pot had been simmering, the lid jiggling, threatening any minute to boil over. It finally had. Spontaneous conflict, like spontaneous combustion, was going on everywhere in the cave, a fire breaking out in one spot and before Sawyer could put it out, another one broke out somewhere else. Several of his deputies got to the first riot before he did, trying to quell the chaos that somebody said had started over watermelon. But what it had started over didn't matter. The wood was dry and all it'd needed was a spark.

They'd dragged out Arnold Patel and Charlie Weatherford, who appeared to be hurt badly, stab wounds. Henry Lewis was dead, his carotid artery slashed, and people were saying it was Timothy Willingham who had done it. He was the man who'd owned the watermelon.

And then some kind of fight broke out about a dog. Sawyer didn't even make it to the scene of that one because people came streaming down the cavern at him screaming, literally like they were running from a fire. He tried to stop someone to ask what was going on, but nobody'd stop. They all were panicked, screaming, "Plague! Bubonic plague. It's spreading everywhere."

It was hours before a tentative peace was restored, which only meant that the active fires were at least dampened.

The population of Sawyer's jail was growing fast. He'd locked up several of the loudest rioters, just to give them time to cool off. Maxine Milford, Charlene Pendleton, her husband and brother, Charlie Weatherford and several others. Sawyer fully intended to let them go after he'd had a chance to talk some sense into them. And realistically, he had no choice but to let them go because soon enough they'd figure out he couldn't keep them there. The age-old mommy threat — "I'm bigger than you are and it's my house" — only went so far. The prisoners outnumbered him now, and it wouldn't take them long to figure out that he might *threaten* to shoot them ... but other than protecting life, Sawyer Matheson wouldn't shoot anybody.

But he wouldn't let Timothy Willingham go. Like Daisy, he'd killed somebody — Henry Lewis.

"I'd do it again, a thousand times over," Timothy was screaming as Sawyer led him away. "He stole my watermelon."

It hadn't been bubonic plague, of course. It had been, at least the best Anna could tell, poison. Strychnine or arsenic, one of the kinds that in the right dosages caused symptoms like hemorrhagic fever, or maybe the plague, he didn't know the symptoms of plague. He counted an even dozen people dead — eight had been poisoned and four others had been trampled in the resultant panic or had been killed in riots and fights. Five other poison victims were sick and Anna gave them zero chance of survival. Nineteen people were in the overflowing infirmary, suffering from non-life-threatening injuries, which included six broken noses, half a dozen broken limbs, one dislocated shoulder, four with missing teeth and two who clearly had internal injuries but Anna could not tell what the injuries were and couldn't have done anything to help them if she could.

Though everybody on Noah's Ark ate exactly the same thing, it turned out that everyone who'd gotten sick had been sitting at the same table for lunch today. That's *where* it had happened, which begged two more pressing questions:

What possible reason could there be to poison people?

And why was Gretchen Hampton the only person seated at that table who didn't get sick?

Chapter Twenty-Eight

EAGLE FEATHER LET the others wrestle the stubborn donkey to the spot far down Broadway they'd selected as the best place to set their trap. He had scouted out locations and this one offered a clear line of sight from rocks on the north end, where Taylor would be stationed to the sacrificial donkey. More than a dozen other, smaller tunnels fed into it where the cat could possibly be hiding. Eagle Feather didn't think the trap had much chance of success, at least not on the first day. Horrifying as it was to think about it, the cat had recently made a kill and might not yet be hungry. Star's face, when she was seven years old, flashed into his mind. No teeth in front, and talking with that special toothless sound kids had at that age. To think of the little Carlisle girl as "meat" … it made him sick.

But this was a big male, from the size of the tracks, and even the average male cougar typically consumed ten pounds of meat a day. Cougars dragged their kill to a place where it was safe to consume it, and would return day after day until there is nothing left to feed on.

Eagle Feather had tracked a cougar only once in his

life. Hadn't set out meat to lure it, just went hunting for it. The cat had been feeding on Jim Sleeping Bear's cattle, had taken out three already and he couldn't afford to lose anymore. It did no good to go to the Reservation Council, ask for their help. In fact, they might have discovered, if they'd asked — which they didn't — that some government agency was "re-seeding" the big cats into the New Mexico mountains and killing one would be against the law.

Eagle Feather had not brought the cougar down. Jimmy had, shot it as it stood on a rock two hundred feet away — with no laser sight.

What Eagle Feather remembered most about the kill was approaching the cat where it lay in a crevice in the rocks where it had fallen. It was not dead, but near. It had looked at him with eyes he remembered to this day. And he'd felt the kind of empathy that could only be understood by somebody who himself lived off the land. Predators killed to eat. The cat had only been doing what millions of years of instinct had programed it to do. Only man killed for sport.

"Here will do," Eagle Feather said and Taylor, Sam and Kelly Jo pulled the protesting donkey into position. Eagle Feather could tell from the animal's eyes that it could smell the presence of the cougar and that was why it hadn't wanted to come.

Taylor, his wife and his sons were the best shots in Zion Village. They'd demonstrated their skill when they'd ambushed Paco and his troops the day of the flood. But long before that they had sat in many a deer blind over the years, bagging meat to grace the tables of the village. Game, of course, had grown more and more plentiful every year after Astral Day, as one species after another had moved back into the hills and mountains around the academy as soon as the biggest and worst predator of all — man — was no longer polluting their environment.

And with the game — elk, mule deer, antelope — came the predators who fed on them, the coyotes, mountain lions ... and the wolves.

Eagle Feather tried not to think about his hallucination, borne of exhaustion and blood loss. The wolf pack, their eyes on him, ears laid back, growling. It had been as horrifying an experience as he'd ever known. Even during the days when he regularly smoked peyote, he'd never had any vision as vivid as that one. And the old man. Eagle Feather wished that part of the vision had been real. He would have liked to have talked to all his ancestors.

"Hold his head," Eagle Feather said, and once they had grabbed both sides, Eagle Feather made a quick slash across the animal's throat and it folded up on the ground.

"Just the throat?" Taylor asked.

Eagle Feather had considered cutting into the animal's guts to expose them and provide more allure, but cougars weren't scavengers by nature, though hunger had clearly driven this cat to do a lot of things that weren't in its nature, getting that close to the man smell to poach the dogs and stray kittens ... and grab the little girl. The way it had been living were the acts of a desperate animal.

"I think that puts too fine a point on it," he said. "Let's go."

The cougar would know the hunters were in the cavern. Had Eagle Feather done this in the wild, he would have stayed downwind of the bait. Here, there was no wind. He knew the cat would be able to smell their presence, and with its extraordinary eyesight, pick out where they were. Under normal circumstances, that would be more than enough to spook the cat. What would swing the balance was the big cat's hunger. Hunger had made it desperate enough to get close to the village, with the overwhelming human smell.

Would it be willing to chance taking this bait, even knowing there were men around? That's what they were here to find out.

"Let's do this."

He and Taylor had arranged a place for the trap that provided all three of them a good sightline to the cat when it took the bait. None of them had a perfect shot for a certain-kill shot, but they were close enough. One of the three of them would take the animal down.

That is, if the cougar accepted their invitation to dinner.

Chapter Twenty-Nine

STAR ASKED Noah to go with her. She had told him about the vision she'd had, what felt like a spillover from the hive mind, the vision of Garson, standing in a dark room, and the two of them could come up with no possible explanation for it. Maybe Garson could shed some light on it.

She took Noah's arm to guide her so she didn't need Pumpkin. Turning back to the dog, she said, "Stay" and the dog dropped back to the ground where he had been lying with a sigh.

He was a "senior dog" now. Twelve. In dog years that was, she didn't know how old — just old. She could see his aging in how his movements had slowed, how he'd no longer jumped up into the bed beside her in Zion Village, likely because it pained his joints to jump now. He had lost some teeth. She had felt inside his mouth and found them missing. And his appetite was not what it had been. Mostly, she noticed that his whole muzzle had turned pure white.

But he was still Pumpkin and she adored him beyond all reason, and in the same breath knew that she wouldn't likely have the wonder of his presence in her life for many more years … that's how she thought of it, how she *had* to think of it. She was going to live for years and years to come and so was Pumpkin, at her side, allowing her to fumble around in his mind trying to make sense of the things he could smell that were mere images in his mind.

They found Garson in his "office" tent. If he'd had to decide between packing a bed and packing books, he'd have selected books and would have slept on the floor. So they granted him extra space.

"Well, hello you two. Haven't seen you since …"

His voice trailed off, probably because he had no idea when last he'd seen them, or maybe just felt socially awkward with such a shallow greeting. Shallow had gone the way of the buggy whip in the years since Astral Day, and had died altogether after the village moved into Noah's Ark. It was real here, twenty-four/seven, gritty. Nobody wasted time making nice.

"What can I do for you?"

"We need your help to figure something out," Noah said.

"Glad to be of service, but I can't imagine what I could contribute to any problem your mind has not yet solved."

"It happened during Stories with Star with the little ones. I was describing a scene … how Jason the Bold stepped up with a gleaming sword when … something … *came into my mind*," Star told him. "That's the only way I have to put it — almost like the vision of the death ship melting the polar ice cap but not that strong."

She couldn't see his face, but Noah could, and she saw through him Garson had frozen like a statue.

"It was like the vision of the black ship because it felt like … spillover from the hive mind. It was like I told you before — all the Astrals in the motherships were thinking about that one thing when they decided to annihilate the whole human race, and the force of all those thousands of minds thinking the same thought … slammed the vision into *my* mind and knocked me out."

"What was the vision?" Garson's voice sounded airless.

"*You!* It was you, with darkness all around you."

"Just … *me*?"

"Why would you be a vision in the hive mind? And why/how could I see it here, under all the rock and water?"

What Noah saw, and Star through him, was Garson's ashen face. He looked like he had swallowed a live goldfish.

THOUGH NOAH HAD NOT BEEN LOOKING at Star to read her lips, he knew what she'd said from her mind. What had so upset Garson about seeing the image of a hive mind?

The professor sat very still, saying nothing. At that moment, he looked very old.

"I want to show the two of you something." He sat his cup down and it rattled in the saucer. "But you have to promise you won't ask questions until you've seen *everything* I have to show you — and that you'll *listen* when I explain it to you. Agreed?"

They both nodded.

What in the world was wrong?

Garson led them out of the tent, across the width of Carnegie Hall and off down the Broadway passage. They walked in silence. No one said anything, at least not out loud. But Noah and Star were engaged in endless speculation about what Garson …

Then Noah began to get an inkling where they were

going. As it became more and more familiar, he asked. "Why are you taking us—?"

Garson snapped at him: "You agreed not to ask questions!"

Noah nodded. Then Garson just started rambling, speaking to them, but somehow to himself, too.

"I spent an entire lifetime expostulating about the aliens that'd visited Earth thousands of years ago and being laughed out of every lecture hall across America. White spots by Jupiter, presto chango, I'm a hero. But whether outcast or savior, all I have *ever* been is a scientist. I study. I learn. I figure out. And once the Astrals arrived, *there* was the answer to every question I'd ever asked. Everything I ever wanted to know, they knew. For example …"

He began spouting what Noah called astrophysics-ese — big words, even bigger concepts, and nobody but another astrophysicist would have understood any of it. They kept walking. Garson kept talking. Every now and then a word surfaced that Noah understood, but not very often. But by this time, a terrible sense of foreboding came over Noah and he didn't know why. Then he realized the feeling was pulsing off Star.

He tuned back in to Garson's monologue when he started making sense again.

"But I never got a chance to ask any of those questions. And I wanted to know so desperately. I may be the only human on the planet who was disappointed the earth was going to flood because I was going to die before I got my questions answered."

By this time they had gotten to a cavern with the odd stripe of dark limestone that looked like it'd been painted on the wall. Noah recognized the slope he had climbed in the dark as a small boy, alone and terrified. Then Noah got it.

Garson could see Noah knew where they were.

"Why did I come here — because I hoped beyond reason that they had left *something behind.* It was possible. Maybe a piece of mining equipment. A robot. Shoot, even a screw or bolt … anything."

Garson went before them. They got to the top of the slope and Noah helped Star up the last part of the incline.

"I even dared to hope that maybe … you had said the reptars were fighting, that's how you got away. So I wondered, hoped maybe … what if they left a body of a reptar behind? Do you know what I'd have given when I started just to be able to study the body of a dead reptar?"

That was an odd way to put it, but Noah let it go.

Clearly, someone had been here since he left — in a mad flight of terror from the Astral mine and the reptars there. Someone had been here more than once, he thought, wallowing out the ground in front of the opening, even widening the opening that led into the plugged-up mine. Garson had found something in there and he'd been coming back here to study it, probably because he couldn't get some big machine out through the little hole in the stone.

"I'll go first," Garson said, and before Noah and Star could say a word, he plopped down on his belly and began to scoot into the opening. Obviously, this wasn't his first rodeo.

Once he was inside, he called out, "Star next."

Star got down on her hands and knees, then on her belly. "This is a small opening. How did you ever get out through it?"

"Desperation is a great lubricant."

Once she was inside, Noah lay down on his belly and

began to scoot through. There was no light ahead. Garson had been holding a lantern, but had turned it off. What for?

Noah got to the end of the tunnel and stood up in the darkness of the vast mine beyond it.

"If your lantern's not working, we've come a long way for nothing," Noah said. "You should have let me bring a backup. Let me see if I can fix—"

The light burst from the lantern, turned up full power.

Noah gaped. Lost his breath. Star beside him suddenly gasped, seeing what he was seeing.

"It can't be …"

Standing before the three of them were five titans.

Chapter Thirty

IN THE BRIGHT glow of the lantern, their white skin almost iridescent in the gloom, were three male titans and two females. One of the males was very large. Just standing there with the idiotic smiles that were always on their faces. Noah felt a mix of fears that churned around in his belly so fast and furiously all they did was make him nauseous, but he couldn't hold onto any one of them long enough to really feel it. He was scared of—

Garson touched his arm and Noah turned to him. He held the lantern up so Noah could read his lips.

"They're harmless," Garson said. "Just titans."

Yeah, right, titans that could at any second transform into reptars.

Noah turned to Star and cried, "Run."

He shoved her toward the hole before Garson grabbed his arm, and mouthed, "They *can't* change into reptars. They're trapped — as titans, just like they're trapped in this mine."

Noah had never been angry with the professor, but

right now he would cheerfully have punched him in the mouth.

"Trust me!" Garson said, got in his face and mouthed it again, slowly. "We're safe. *Trust. Me.*"

Noah froze — there was such pleading in Garson's face and eyes. When Noah hesitated, didn't bolt instantly out of the mine, Garson rushed ahead.

"You promised you would listen to my explanation." He nodded toward Star, too, knowing she'd see it through Noah's eyes. "You both *promised.*"

"Okay." Though Noah could not hear his own voice, he didn't need to hear it to know it sounded angry, cold and scared. He was definitely all three.

Garson began babbling. "When we blew up the entrance to the mine, these five were inside. Trapped."

"What were they doing here? They knew the flood was happening. Why didn't they leave?"

"They came in to remove the last of the equipment and they sensed … what they thought was another hive mind. It was you and Star, I suppose. When they went deeper into the mine to investigate, to get closer — we blew up the entrance and they couldn't get out before the flood."

"So they were stuck here," Star said, but it wasn't a question. He could feel her hand shaking in his.

Garson looked uncomfortable.

"In a manner of speaking."

"What does that mean?"

"Obviously, they couldn't have fit through the opening in the bottom of the rock where we came in. But this is a mine and the equipment was sealed in here with them."

"So you're saying they could have used it to dig through the wall into the caverns?" Noah was again horrified and terrified.

"They could have, but why would they? They knew we were on the other side of that wall, and they're defenseless."

"You keep saying that — defenseless. A being who can change into a killing machine in under a minute is not defenseless."

"They *can't* change into reptars. If they did, they'd tear each other apart, just like the ones you saw trying to kill each other when you were here before." Garson gestured all around. "Limestone. Remember, I explained it to you, why the reptars went nuts. It causes feedback in their heads, that horrible buzzing sound, makes them crazy."

Noah was trying hard to process all that he was hearing. He couldn't dispute what Garson was saying — he'd seen it for himself. The reptars had been trying to butcher each other the last time he'd been in this mine.

"So they can't transform," Star said. "They have to remain titans — is that what you're saying?"

"It is. And as titans … they're harmless."

Noah relaxed a little, no longer hypervigilant. And once he did, his thoughts were easier to order.

"How have they—?"

"I have been bringing them food and water. They don't seem to think the gruel tastes like Applebee's at all." That was Garson, totally inappropriate. The remark wouldn't even have been funny under other circumstances.

"You've been hiding them, feeding them — why?"

"Well, why do you think? So I could study them."

Finally, the professor had gotten what he'd wanted all his life. He wasn't just left with the crumbs, the picked-over leftovers of what ancient alien civilizations left behind when they booked. He had actual aliens to study. Noah could almost understand. Almost.

"What were you planning to do, Garson?" Garson was

a smart man — what had he been thinking? "Were you planning on keeping them hidden until—?"

"Oh, heavens no. I never planned to keep the secret forever. Just long enough so I could ... you know ... talk to them."

You were on the mothership.

The words just appeared in his mind, and in Star's too. Noah was suddenly furious.

"Yeah, I was in the mothership. You sent down one of your zapping beams and yanked me up out of my life and stuck me on a pin like a bug to study. Surprised you didn't bisect us like frogs."

Why do you keep us out?

He didn't know at first what the Astral was talking about and then he knew. Star wasn't letting them into her mind. She was blocking them. Way to go! Of course it was a futile effort on her part and they all knew it. Unfortunately, Noah wasn't as psychically strong as Star. He couldn't stand up to their probing fingers in his mind. They just walked right in, and made themselves at home. And since Noah knew what Star was thinking ...

This isn't a group mind. It belongs to me. It's mine and you're not welcome in it. Get out!

Star was as pissed as Noah was.

Noah turned his attention back to Garson, who babbled out answers to questions he hadn't asked yet.

"I was going to show them to you and to the others — and after that I didn't have a plan because I knew that as soon as your father found out there were Astrals in the cavern with us, he'd come in with guns blazing, massacre them — not that they don't deserve massacre, you understand — but they'd all be dead before I had a chance to demonstrate that they're really quite harmless."

Noah couldn't argue with that.

"Noah." Garson was speaking softly. "I didn't 'rat them out' because I knew that would get them killed. They can't hurt anybody. Do *I* ...?" He paused, made a gesture that included him and Star. "Do *we*, the three of us, have a right to decide whether they live or die? I don't know about you, but I don't want that responsibility."

Noah discovered that he didn't want the responsibility either.

Chapter Thirty-One

THEY STOOD TOGETHER IN SILENCE, the three of them, in the glow of Garson's lantern — in an Astral mine with five titans.

The titans were as expressionless and emotionless as all the other titans Noah had come across over the years. They weren't afraid. Likely didn't understand human fear at all — maybe *that's* what they'd been studying in him, Star and Paco. If they had been, the three of them had provided terror on display, in all its various forms. They were just kids and they'd been scared spitless.

A wave of rage passed over Noah, then receded as inexorably as a wave sliding off the shore and back into the depths of the sea. These beings were waves in the sea. They weren't individuals. They were an indistinguishable part of a whole. Whether or not these five titans ceased to exist didn't seem to make any difference at all to them.

But it did to Noah. Garson and Star, too. That's how humans differed from the Astral hive mine. Individuals mattered. Every one of them. Ending a life — a *harmless* life, even one of the Astrals' — wasn't a decision to take lightly.

"The elders should decide," Star said, her voice soft.

She was right, of course. Star always was about such things, about matters of right and wrong.

"So we go tell them about the titans and then … somebody comes here and carries out—?" It was clear Garson thought he knew what the elders would decide.

"No!" Star said.

Noah heard her in his head, of course, but he could tell she had shouted the word. She looked from him to Garson, and spoke again. "No. This is the only chance humanity will ever have to hold Astrals accountable for what they've done. But *we* don't kill indiscriminately. We're better than that."

She turned to Noah when she continued, seemed to need to look into his eyes. He could see the turmoil in her mind, the warring emotions. She was having trouble tacking words onto her thoughts. He understood without words, but she needed to say it, articulate it.

"The new world … it starts here, now, in this cave. We need to establish from the very beginning that *this* is who we are, this is what humanity is about — justice."

"That's quite a lofty goal, but how do you plan to pull it off?" Garson said. "Take them out of here" — he lifted an eyebrow and gestured to the hole the three of them had barely been able to squeeze through — "and march them off to the elders?"

Noah almost felt the idea pop into Star's mind.

"Wait a minute. This is a *mine*. They were in here cutting slabs of rock out of the walls. They came back for the equipment, so it's still here. Why couldn't they just … I don't know, cut a hole—?"

Showing ourselves would not be prudent.

228

The words formed in all their minds.

"You got that right, pal!" Noah was surprised at how hard it was for him to hold onto his temper. He had every right to be furious, but if he went there, even stuck his big toe into those waters, he'd be swept away. Now wasn't the time for emotion.

"Even if you could get them out, do you reeeeeally want to drag these guys through the cavern to stand trial?" Garson asked.

"Oh God, no!" Noah said. Given the tenuous state of the population's mental health right now — finding out there were five live titans in here with them — it would be a nitrogen bomb.

An image streaked like a comet through his mind — Medieval villagers brandishing torches. "Grab your clubs and pitchforks, boys!" He shook it off.

"Maybe there's somewhere they could cut a hole into where nobody'd see ..." Garson began. "How big is this mine?"

The Astrals said nothing and no words formed in their minds.

This wasn't at all like talking to Star telepathically. They had conversations, didn't just move into each other's minds and put their feet up on the coffee table and light a cigar. But they had developed that mind control over years of practice. Respect for the other. There was a room in each other's heads where they communicated — at least that's the way he thought of it — and the rest of the building was off limits. He supposed either one of them could have gone wandering around. But they never did.

The Astrals, on the other hand, were blunt and intrusive — and it didn't feel like they were ignoring the question.

"They can't answer," Garson said. "I've ... experienced this. There's no way to respond that we could understand."

"Aw, come on," Noah barked. "Is it bigger than a bread box?"

Suddenly, an image formed in the darkness between them and the titans, a holographic image. It was a view from high in the air, looking down on Joppa Ridge. Then the top portion of the mountain vanished and they could see down into what lay below — Level One of the caverns.

And the mine.

Noah couldn't breathe. He shot a glance at Garson, whose mouth literally was hanging open.

The mine was as big as the cavern!

For a few moments, Noah's mind flatly refused to accept the reality.

The Astral mine lay next to the whole length of Level One — a hole cut out of solid rock winding along beside miles and miles of caverns!

A response formed in Noah's mind to the question he had not yet formulated.

We mine stone. The caverns are holes *in the stone.*

The Astrals had never broken through into the space of the cavern because they were mining rock — the caverns were *holes* in the rock, empty air.

Noah's hole was in the eastern wall of the Astral mine that stretched beneath the sandstone cap of the mountain all the way across the mountain to the gypsum deposits on the west side and stopped there. That rock was useless to them.

What had formed over millennia in the gypsum deposit on the cavern side, however, was Alabaster Hall — the staggeringly beautiful display of flowering gypsum crystals. Noah could see it sparkling next to the western wall of the mine even in the hologram. His great grandfather had discovered it, crawled through a small opening into it when he was exploring, much as Noah had crawled into the Astral mine. His grandfather had excavated a narrow tunnel to the hall from the north side of Broadway near Carnegie Hall.

That winding, narrow tunnel was the *only way in or out.* If it were blocked off — say, with deputies stationed there — the residents of Noah's Ark would have no idea what was going on inside it.

No idea that five Astrals had been called before the elders, whose members would determine their fate.

Yes, we can cut into that cavern from the mine.

The Astrals had seen his plan and understood that it would work.

"We won't bring the elders here; we'll bring these guys to the elders," Noah told Garson — Star already knew what he was planning. Then he explained what he had in mind.

For the first time since the three of them had entered the mine, Garson spoke directly to the Astrals, to the big one.

"And you agree to all this?"

Yes.

"Why?"

It occurred to Noah then — duh! — that there was no reason for the Astrals to go along with the plan. Why not just remain here in the mine until they died, or wait here to be killed, maybe hide from—?

Why not?

He got it then. The Astrals flat out didn't care. The fear of death was not a concept that translated from Astral to human and back. Oh, there must have been some kind of primal survival instinct that prompted titans to transform into reptars, but he didn't think it could be triggered by anything less than the clear and present danger of imminent death. And even then, he didn't think they were afraid to die.

Humans could not countenance the Astrals' staggering disregard for life — massacring a whole planet of people, and the Astrals could not countenance why it mattered. There was no possible bridge of understanding. The species were too fundamentally different. The Astrals were a hive. One mind more or less … what did it matter?

Chapter Thirty-Two

"I HEARD THAT," Ellie gasped.

Sawyer had just stepped into her private cavern from the curtained-off area outside and he wasn't completely certain ...

"The gasp."

"Gasp?"

"Everybody does it." She paused to get another breath to continue. "Everybody ... stops outside ... to steel themselves for having to see me."

"Ellie, nobody—"

"Shut up. No bullshit. I don't have time or energy for bullshit. I know I am ... a pathetic husk of a human being. Be real."

He said nothing. What was there to say?

She smiled at him then, or he thought she did.

"Just for the record, fifty-eight degrees is fucking freezing!"

Ellie was covered up with a mountain of blankets; she wasn't the only one who'd complained about the cold. You'd see people everywhere with blankets and shawls and coats. Seriously. Some people actually thought the constant cave temperature was cold. But Ellie got a pass on that. Ellie got a pass on everything.

"Did Anna tell you?"

"That you told her you wouldn't eat or drink or take transfusions … yes, she told me."

"Please tell me you're not going to try to—"

"Talk you out of it? No. Gretchen's not going to like—"

"I don't give a fuck what Gretchen likes. It's not her decision to make. It's mine and she's already stolen it from me once."

She took another breath.

"She could do … something again, maybe. You won't let her …?"

"I won't."

"Promise. Pinky swear?"

"Pinky swear."

"You know you'll have a fight on your hands."

"I know. I'll just have to put on my big boy pants and stand my ground."

"About Diana …" Sawyer knew Ellie and Anna had worked all that out.

"She knows you're dying."

Ellie said nothing. Her expression was so frozen, the way your face freezes when you've just hit your thumb with a hammer and you're trying not to scream. Ellie's face looked like that all the time. So it was hard to tell, but he though she looked surprised.

"She and Garson have talked about it."

"Garson."

There was a ghost of a smile then.

"He adores her. He'll slide right into grandfather role."

"Yes, that's how it … what did she say?"

"She told Garson that Aunt Ellie was going to go away soon." Sawyer felt his voice catch in his throat and he had to grab hold of it to keep the emotion out of it. "She told him not to be sad when it happened, that Aunt Ellie was going somewhere that she wouldn't hurt anymore. I think she's been talking to Brother Sebastian and the other monks about it."

Ellie nodded, a slight movement, and then gathered up strength.

"Prisoners on death row get a last meal, right. Do I?"

He struggled to keep his voice level.

"What would you like?"

"I want … a glass of wine. With you, please. Some kind of fresh vegetable … I know those are in short supply."

"Actually, they are literally under lock and key, but I have connections."

"Carrot, bean … shit, not a radish but a tomato would be nice. Something."

"I can arrange it."

"And then I want you to squeeze my hand, get up, walk out of here and promise me you won't come back until I'm dead and you have to remove the body."

"Ellie …"

"I'm the one dying. I get to make the rules."

"Okay."

When Sawyer brought Ellie's tray to her room, he had a candle set in the middle of it. That had been a special touch added by the monks. He'd wanted to bring her a flower, but that had been a bridge too far. The monks had produced at his request a tomato — a real, red tomato, and both carrots and beans. They'd cooked the carrots and beans so they would be soft enough for her to chew, added lots of butter.

"Knock, knock," he called out softly. "Room service."

There was a sound from within that he took to be assent, and he brought the tray in and set it on the table by her bed.

Ellie was dressed for the occasion. She wore a yellow-flowered dress, the last one Sawyer had seen her wear before she gave up trying to get out of bed. After that, only nightgowns. She must have gotten Anna to slip it over her head. Sawyer couldn't imagine how painful that must have been. It fit like a grocery sack.

"How …?"

"I hope you like red wine." He had a towel over his arm as if he were a waiter and he poured from the bottle into the two crystal wineglasses on the tray. "I'm just a country boy, don't know which goes with what — white with fish, red with meat? — but it doesn't matter because we're not having either."

With a flourish, he lifted the cover off the plate where a freshly sliced tomato lay on a saucer and a small bowl of carrots and beans floated in butter.

She looked from the tray to his face and back to the tray. Tears began to slide down her face, but she couldn't cry.

He leaned over and held the wineglass to her lips and she took a little sip.

"Ahhhh. I'd … forgotten …"

Her voice sounded like wind through dry wheat. He took a sip from his own glass of wine, but if it had any flavor at all, he couldn't detect it.

Then he cut off a small piece of the tomato and offered it. She took it off the fork and swallowed, but he could see what the effort cost her. Then a spoonful of carrots and beans. He got the spoon to her mouth, she opened her lips to the edge of the spoon, maybe got a few drops of the liquid. Then she closed her mouth and her eyes and he knew she'd reached the end of her strength and endurance.

He set the spoon back down in the bowl.

"I love you, Sawyer Matheson." Every word was an effort, and she even tried to sound normal. "I fell for you that day you grounded my helicopter."

He remembered how she'd looked that day in the tight designer jeans and the clingy blue blouse.

"I love you, too, Ellie." He was aware that tears were streaming down his cheeks but he didn't reach up to wipe them away. "I fell for you the day I squirted you off with a hose at the car wash. In case you didn't know it, with your clothes soaked you could have won a wet t-shirt contest, you might as well have been naked."

"I wish..." But she didn't finish. He reached out, took her hand and squeezed it.

"Thank you." She was whispering again and he could tell she was crying, too, but just didn't have any tears to shed. "Now ... kiss me goodbye."

He leaned over and lifted her chin, and placed his lips gently on her parched, cracked ones. He closed his eyes and imagined.

Then he stood up, squeezed her hand, turned and walked out of the room.

Chapter Thirty-Three

TIME GOES by slowly when you remain absolutely still, and learning how to be that still took a lifetime to learn. His grandfather had taught Eagle Feather. From talking to Nick, he learned that the Navy used some of the same techniques to teach the same skill to SEALs, and to snipers.

The secret of concealment was remaining still. Absolutely still, so still you almost went into some kind of yoga state where your heart rate and breathing and blood slow and your blood pressure lowers. The eye is drawn to movement, even the slightest. He had demonstrated that skill when he had escaped from Paco and his men ... right before their eyes, and he practiced that stillness now.

Lying half prone with only his arms holding the rifle and his head visible above the rock, he got comfortable. Which was no easy task for someone who had the aches, pains and joint-crying-outs of a seventy-eight-year-old man. And there were the wounds he'd gotten on the shards of glass in the top of the fence the day he'd eluded Paco, one on his forearm, the other on his leg. They had been sealed up by Anna with the help of some tissue glue and were healing nicely. But just because only a red mark remained on the outside didn't prevent the ache and throb they made to make Eagle Feather aware of their presence on the inside.

He relaxed and stilled his every movement, starting with his legs and moving up his body, he relaxed each muscle group and concentrated on not moving anything. His breathing slowed. His heart rate along with it.

Then he concentrated on the scope of the rifle he held in his hands and the small circle of magnified world it displayed. He didn't normally use a sight when he hunted, but he hunted in the daytime, not at night, and in this portion of the cave the only light came from the Glow Worm lights strung on the top of the cavern above. That light was something like the light in the desert on a clear, starry night under a full moon. It was perfect light for the cougar to hunt. With its acute eyesight, it could count the grains of sand on the top of a rock, if cougars counted, that is.

He was using a sight now because he had to get so far from his target, had to get that far away to lure the big cat. He wasn't accurate at that range without a sight, and wasn't nearly the shot with a sight Kelly Jo and Taylor were. The safe money was on Kelly Jo.

One hour.

Two.

Three.

The hunters didn't move, and Eagle Feather was profoundly grateful that he hadn't had coffee to drink this morning or he could add a full bladder to the other aches and pains that had cropped up as the seconds ticked away.

He had arthritis in—

Movement.

Just a flicker. He would have frozen from the surprise

of it if he hadn't already been as still as a statue. He didn't move his head away from the sight on the rifle, but looked out both eyes and blurred what was in front of him and he could see the big cat approaching, on the rocks, just sizing up the bait and the situation. Waiting. Cats were very patient animals. Eagle Feather returned the focus of his eyes to the sight on the rifle. Then he waited. He was a patient man, too.

Four hours.

In the hour the cat had been visible, Eagle Feather hadn't seen it so much as twitch. He wasn't even sure if it was visible to the other two hunters. Their sight-lines were likely blocked by the big rock it knelt beside.

It finally began to move toward the bait.

Eagle Feather didn't have a shot at it where it was crouched, could only see the back flanks and tail, the tip of an ear and part of a shoulder. He couldn't chance a bad shot — the cat would be gone in an eye blink.

The cat didn't approach the kill down the slope of rocks the three hunters had hoped it would. It came down a different a slope, from a different direction. It had apparently kept out of sight behind the rocks at the top of the cavern near the ceiling and somehow went undetected. If Eagle Feather had known that, he — he shoved the thought away. There was nothing left of the little girl to find. What? A *piece* of her? Her mother was better off without that horror.

Slowly, the big cat moved down the rocks, beginning now to come into the sight-lines of Kelly Jo's rifle, but not yet into Taylor's.

He was inching along, but was not in pounce mode, didn't have its ears back, claws extended. He knew he didn't have to bring the donkey down, knew it was dead. He could carry the animal's carcass … who knew how far.

Eagle Feather had heard stories of a cougar that dragged the carcass of an elk more than a thousand feet and then up into a tree.

The cat was now about three feet from the donkey, coming at it from the side. It might pause to rip out its guts and feed before it dragged the donkey away. It might simply clamp its massive jaws on the animal on the back of its neck and drag it away. This cat was even bigger than Eagle Feather thought it would be. He had a shot now, of course, but didn't take it. Kelly Jo had a broadside shot, a bigger target.

Bam!

The sound of the rifle echoed like there'd been a gunfight going on in the chamber. The cat fell backward from the impact, but it didn't lie still. It made for the rocks again. Now, Eagle Feather had a shot and watched the bullet ping off a rock the animal's body had just passed behind.

As the closest, Eagle Feather jumped to his feet and moved across the tops of the rocks on the side of the cavern. He knew the other hunters were closing in, too, and was conscious of not moving into their lines of fire.

"He's wounded," Eagle Feather called out. Didn't warn them to be careful because he didn't need to. The only thing more dangerous than a cougar was a wounded cougar. Eagle Feather reached the point where the animal could be tracked by the blood on the rocks. It was bleeding badly, wouldn't make it far. Taylor was running along the trail. Kelly Jo was climbing down off the rocks to run on the trail as well when Eagle Feather sensed it.

Not sensed, *knew*. It had nothing to do with the five senses available to him. He didn't hear a thing, see a thing, feel any change in the air, but he knew the big cat had circled around and was making for the rocks above him, might be there already.

He whirled to the right and leapt under a rock over-hang, his eyes scanning the nearby rocks for drops of blood. There, just ahead, where the cat had started up the incline. Eagle Feather inched in that direction, slowly peeked around the corner of the rock and the big cat was lying there panting, blood gushing out of its side.

Even so, the cat got to its feet when it saw him and faced him, and let out the cry that was among the most horrifying sounds in nature. The cougar couldn't roar because of the way its larynx was built, so it cried out in a sound more scream than growl, a cry that seared the soul.

Its ears were laid back as it backed away. It would protect its own vital organs, would reach out with massive paws and swat at whatever came near. Eagle Feather wasn't even aware of raising his rifle, of sighting without the stupid scope, of squeezing the trigger. The cat was knocked backward by the force of the shot that had caught it in the middle of the chest. It lay still. Dead.

Kelly Jo got there with Taylor a step behind. Eagle Feather nodded at her, acknowledged her kill. Now, they'd have to drag the carcass of the dead cougar to a low spot and pile rocks on top of the body.

Chapter Thirty-Four

"HE'S GONE!" Diana cried, anguish in her voice. "He was in that pen Uncle Noah made for him. I know he was. I put him there, but he's gone now. Oh Uncle Sawyer, find him, please, find him."

The little girl had come running at him, crying out her story before she even got to him. He got down on one knee in front of her and tried to calm her enough to get the story out of her.

"He's gone. Donkey Ho-tee. He's *gone*."

"Did you leave the gate open?"

She stopped at that question, and then said confused, "The gate isn't open. How did he get out without somehow opening the gate? But it's closed."

"I tell you what," Sawyer said. "You go find Garson, tell him about the donkey. He's the smartest man in the cave. Maybe he can figure out how he got out of the pen and where he might be."

It was just a ruse, of course, to get rid of her for the moment.

After everybody'd been warned to keep their animals

close, that the tunnels were *dangerous* ... yeah, Sawyer thought he might have a pretty good idea how the donkey had gotten out of the pen without opening the gate, or how it had left and then closed and latched the gate behind it.

Sawyer found her in the kitchen washing dishes. He didn't have the kitchen rotation sheet and didn't know who was scheduled to work, but he did know that Gretchen hadn't been on the detail in the beginning. If she was there now, it was because she'd asked to be. She'd *volunteered*. Gretchen had never done work like that in the kitchen — it was beneath her.

He touched her shoulder and when she turned, he signed, "Gretchen I need to talk to you for a minute."

She looked up at him and the anger in her eyes was so strong he almost took a step back.

"I don't have anything to say to you," she spoke aloud, in a nasal toneless voice.

"What did you do with Donkey Ho-tee?"

The question put like that, so blunt, staggered her mentally for a moment. He saw the response and she saw that he had seen.

She held her arms out to him.

"Okay, fine. Here. Put the cuffs on me and haul my ass to jail. I have committed the heinous crime of latch-breaking. I'm sure the death penalty is involved."

Her rage was somehow pathetic. It had always been sad.

"Why?" Though he knew why. The real why.

"Because I was sick and tired of Mother's room smelling like a donkey pen, that's why. She'd come in there after playing with that ... that thing, smelling like a goat."

Donkeys smelled nothing like goats and he suspected Gretchen had never smelled a live goat.

"The final straw ... she climbed up on the side of Mother's bed and she had donkey shit on her shoe. Got it everywhere. I am *not* going to allow that child to ruin the final few days my mother has to live, thanks to you."

It was all so distorted; she had twisted reality around to match what she wanted to believe. It wasn't Sawyer's fault Ellie would die soon. Gretchen had come to him — as he knew she would, and demanded that he somehow force her mother to take liquids and nutrition and blood transfusions and whatever else Anna had been giving her to keep her alive. He had refused. Gretchen had exploded. Now, in her mind, he would be responsible for her mother's death.

"Diana's not the one ruining the final few days your mother has to live. *You are.* Diana brings light and life and love into her world for Ellie to enjoy in the time she has left. You bring jealousy, anger, retribution, and spite, spoil every moment with your self-centeredness. *You* are the one ruining your mother's life."

There, he'd said it. He'd held onto it for so long, but it had finally exploded out. He wasn't sorry.

"You're just like everybody else, charmed by that little witch so you can't see what a monster she really is."

He swallowed his rage.

"What did you do with the donkey?"

She said nothing.

He ground out the new next few words in his most professional, *you-in-a-heap-of-trouble-boy* sheriff's tone.

"I will ask you only one more time. What did you do with Donkey Ho-tee.

She wouldn't meet his eyes.

"I took him down Broadway and let him go where that little girl disappeared. It's too late now, the stupid little fucker didn't even have enough sense to follow me back. He's dead, is now battling the gastric juices of a cougar."

He had to stifle an almost overwhelming desire to slap her. Instead, he turned and headed toward Broadway. He feared she might be right.

He searched for the animal for more than an hour, knowing it wouldn't have ventured far on its own, hoping against hope that it hadn't fallen victim to the teeth of the big cat his brother, Eagle Feather, Kelly Jo and Sam had gone out hunting.

Then he spotted a place where the trail was scuffed. There was solid rock beneath his feet with a layer of dirt on it. He knelt on one knee and shined his flashlight down at the dirt. It was disturbed. That was all he could tell. Eagle Feather could have read those scuff marks and told you the life histories of every being who had ever passed this way, including the prehistoric Indians that had drawn the pictures on the cave walls thousands of years ago.

Even Taylor would have been better at this than Sawyer. He was the hunter in the family. Sawyer was into fishing, or had been until his son was abducted from the side of their pond. Even though he was returned three months later, Sawyer never saw a pond that he didn't think of diving into the white light to save his son and grabbing nothing but air.

He backed up to get a better, wider view and it was clear something had happened here recently to disturb the dirt. He had no idea what—

Wait. What was that?

He'd seen … something. Making a wide circle around the suspect piece of ground, he came at it from the other direction. He knelt down and focused the flashlight beam on the ground. A drip. He put out his finger and touched it, brought his finger to his nose. Blood … maybe. He moved back farther, shined the light round and could see a dark spot beside a rock he had thought at first was a shadow. On closer inspection, it was a large spot of ... *blood*.

Donkey Ho-tee was gone.

A wave of anger flashed over him at the spiteful cruelty of taking a little girl's pet. He noticed something at the edge of the beam of his flashlight. It was a track. In all the scuff marks, this was the only visible track.

He wasn't an old Indian who could have told you what the animal had to eat three days ago. The track was shallow, not as deep as the one Eagle Feather had pointed out when they found where the little girl had been taken. He leaned closer. It was an animal track, alright. Clearly visible was the pad. He looked for the three lobes Eagle Feather had pointed out and couldn't see them. It appeared to be a single, straight lobe. But then, he hadn't been able to see the lobes with Eagle Feather right there beside him pointing them out, either. There were the six circles in front of the larger one, and the marks where the claws had indented the dirt.

He looked for a moment longer, something niggling in his brain, but it was a moth around a flame, fluttering and then gone.

Squaring his shoulders, he started the long walk back to find Diana and tell her that her pet wouldn't be coming back.

He was all the way to the edge of the village before the moth finally lit and was still.

There hadn't been any marks in front of the toes of the track he had looked at with Eagle Feather. Eagle Feather had said it was because cats retracted their claws. So why hadn't the cougar done that this time?

Chapter Thirty-Five

SAWYER SAID the words out loud for the same reason he had said the words "alien invasion" aloud in his office on Astral day. To make them real.

"There are five Astrals, titans *here*, in the cavern with us."

Noah nodded.

He spoke and Sawyer couldn't help marveling at how almost normal he sounded, because he had the one thing the other deaf people trying to speak didn't have. He could hear how he sounded, through Star. That feedback over the years had made it possible for him to sound like he could hear.

And he sounded perfectly normal now, as he explained about the trapped Astrals, Garson, and the stolen food. Sawyer felt lightheaded. How could there possibly be so much going on that he didn't know about while what was going on that he *did* know about was falling totally apart?

He was listening to Noah, but not. Heard him, but through that cotton of shock/disbelief that makes words kind of foggy.

"… have to seal off the cavern with deputies so nobody can see what's going on in there. Once the place is secured, the Astrals will dig through the wall from the mine into Alabaster Hall."

Noah might as well have said the Astrals would make cream cheese out of the moon.

"Drill through the wall?" Noah had explained about the geography of the mine and the caverns, but still … "You don't think anybody's going to hear that drill and think, 'Oh, gee whiz, wonder what's going on in there?'"

"There won't be any noise. Our mining equipment roars and rumbles and sputters. Theirs … melts."

Okay, that made sense. Melting wasn't a particularly noisy process after all. Sawyer felt giddy.

"And I'm to have the elders in Alabaster Hall and the Astrals will dig a hole in the wall, waltz in and we're supposed to … what?"

"Decide what to do with them. Somebody's got to decide. Who if not the elders?"

Everything Noah said was accurate and true. But … *damn!* Five live Astrals in the caverns. As if he didn't have enough …

He let it go.

"So later this evening, then — seven. Everybody will gather out of the way in Carnegie Hall, eating or waiting in line." He looked at his watch — the one Erika Mason had given him, the elder who wouldn't be here tonight because she hadn't made it into the ark before the flood. He thought of it as the countdown watch. It was tracking how many days they'd been underground.

"Eagle Feather and Taylor aren't back yet from hunting. Nick and Fred …"

"I'll find them."

Nick hadn't been feeling very well the last couple of

days, the nitrogen narcosis thing. It popped up unexpect-edly — sometimes annoyed, and sometimes debilitated Nick, then vanished just like it'd come.

Sawyer's head was still reeling when he passed the deputy-enforced "limits" of human habitation on Level One. It wasn't like he needed deputies to enforce it. Not a person in the caverns could be dragged away ... into the darkness.

He met the hunters and Taylor held out a thumbs-up. And Sawyer wanted to cheer. It was wonderful news. There had been a killer out there and now there was no more danger. No more hold-onto-your-kids and don't-let-the-pets-out.

No more patrolling deputies to enforce a perimeter.

But the feeling of celebration died in his throat. That cat had killed and ... *eaten* ... seven-year-old Jackie Carlisle.

"What did you do with—?"

"Buried it," Taylor said. "Made a hole the best we could, put the cat in and piled on rocks on top."

That was the only thing they could have done, of course. They couldn't very well have brought the body back here ...

"It got Donkey Ho-tee, too," Sawyer told Eagle Feather. "Diana will be devastated when I tell her, which I've been putting off. At least I can tell her now that the monster that killed her pet isn't going to threaten anybody anymore."

"Killed Donkey Ho-tee?" Eagle Feather looked confused. "When?"

"Don't know exactly when. Hours ago." There was no reason to tell him that Gretchen had been the real killer, that she'd put the baby donkey out all alone because she wanted it dead. "Down on the other end of Broadway."

Eagle Feather shook his head.

"Couldn't be. If the cougar had just made a kill, it would have hauled Donkey Ho-tee's body off somewhere and lived on it for a few days before it went hunting again. It would never have taken our bait. The cougar we killed today didn't kill Diana's pet."

"You saying there are *two* of the bastards?"

Kelly Jo had gone on but Taylor hung back and must have caught the end of the conversation.

"Two? Are you telling me we have another one—?"

"No," Sawyer said. "That's not what I said. I don't know … I need to do some more digging around and right now I have bigger fish to fry."

Taylor gawked at him, incredulous.

"There's a bigger fish to fry than a killer mountain lion on the loose in a cave with three thousand people? Then it must be Moby Dick."

Sawyer almost smiled. "Well, it is big and white, so yeah, Moby Dick."

He took a deep breath, didn't even bother to try to prepare them with a "You're not going to believe this, but …" He just laid the whole thing out for them, as Noah had told it to him, didn't omit anything.

When Sawyer was finished with his story, the looks on Taylor's and Eagle Feather's faces must have mirrored how he had looked when Noah had told him.

"Are you sure this is real," Taylor said, but it was denial, not a question.

"Hell, no, I'm not sure of anything anymore. But we're talking Noah and Star here. And Garson. Of course it's the truth."

"Well, son of a bitch." Taylor let fly a few more colorful expletives. "And what are we supposed to do with five Moby Dicks … the key word in that sentence being dicks?"

It was almost humorous, if there was anything about any of this that anybody could find amusing. Still, telling the other elders Noah and Star's story and watching the looks on their faces, their reactions ... it was at least mildly entertaining.

When he told Nick, he looked worse than he had after he came up out of the water suffering from nitrogen narcosis.

And Fred Schwartz. He'd debated leaving Fred out of the mix. The man was in his late eighties and moving to the ark, life here — it had aged him fast. He was feisty but fragile. If telling him there were five titans here might ... no, Fred was an elder same as Sawyer was, had the same never-spelled-out rights and all-inclusive obligations he did. And often it was Fred whose wisdom prevailed.

When he finished his spiel, Fred looked heavenward. "What, we don't have enough troubles?" he said. "You give us *this*? Seriously?"

Sawyer stopped by to check on Ellie, but her eyes were closed and he didn't want to disturb her. Her breath was so shallow. It barely moved the sheet. The look Anna gave him said that the vigil was almost over. Not days, hours now.

When he got to Alabaster Hall, everyone was assembled except Nick.

"Last I saw him, he'd just left the jail, releasing the troublemakers, I think," Taylor said.

"Was he sick?"

The effects of the bends were sometimes bad, but this must have been spectacularly awful. Nick would have crawled over three miles of broken glass to get to Alabaster Hall to help the elders deal with the Astrals.

"No ... not *sick*. He said to tell you he had bigger fish to fry."

Taylor held up his hand before Sawyer could ask. "I don't know. He wouldn't say. But the look on his face ... *I* wouldn't have crossed him."

What could *possibly* be a bigger fish to fry than five aliens in the cavern?

Chapter Thirty-Six

NICK'S MIND WAS SPINNING — five Astrals *here* in the caverns! — whirling around so fast he almost missed it.

After he had finally managed to wrench the jail supervision responsibility out of Sawyer's hands — he couldn't do *everything* — and Sawyer'd given him the keys so he could oversee the release of the last of the troublemakers from the riot. He'd do it on his way to Alabaster Hall.

Most of the people who'd been locked up were malcontents Nick didn't even know. He could only place a few of them as people he'd ever seen in Zion Village. So where had the rest of them come from?

Some of them had friends and family members milling around, waiting for them to be set free — a disgruntled lot, but then most of the people in the caverns these days were discontented, pissed off about something.

As he was working with the big padlock on one of the cell doors, he tuned out the grumbling and belly-aching. But a single word floated up out of the torrent of speech around him, hung suspended there, didn't wash out with the others.

Phoebe.

"… hadn't ought to a'locked us in the first place …"

"… didn't break no law …"

"… probably got a bunch of Phoebes watching everybody …"

Nick and the other deputy unlocked the cell doors one at a time and dragged the inmates out into the corridor.

"… who's gonna replace them tent posts they busted …"

"… shoulda kicked his ass into the middle of next week …"

But the word, the single word … still floated free in Nick's head. Then it landed gentle as a single moth on a dry limb. A little moth on a branch. And hung there.

Phoebe.

"… got the same rights as everybody else …"

Where had Nick heard—?

Then he *knew*. When Noah had been telling the elders about his harrowing experience in the mine, he'd described the Phoebes that had kept him under surveillance as he lay trapped beneath the malfunctioning robot.

That's where Nick'd heard about Phoebes — from Noah. Noah had said he, Star and Paco had often encountered the little marbles when they were on the Astral mothership.

So how did the jackass he'd just let out of a cell hear about them? More important, how did he know Star had named them Phoebes? Had he been there when she did it — overheard? Nick looked the guy up and down. Naaaaa. If this man had been one of the people the Astrals took to the mothership to study they'd have decided on the spot the human race wasn't worth saving.

"Hey, you," he said to the smarmy, fat man shuffling

away down the corridor. The man ignored him so he took two huge steps and grabbed him by the collar.

"I'm talking to you."

"What?" he whined, wiggling pathetically to get free. "What do you want from me? I ain't done nothing."

This was one of the people Nick couldn't place, didn't think he'd ever seen him before, looked like he had crawled out from under a rock. He was filthy, stank worse than all the donkeys in the pen put together, had a mop of dirty black hair and a beard. Beneath the hair, the guy was as pale as a blind cave fish. Looked like he hadn't seen the light of day in years.

"What's your name?"

"Who wants to know?"

"Deputy Sheriff Nick Wilson. Now answer my question."

"You ain't no lawman. Ain't no sheriffs in here. Ain't nobody can tell us—"

"What's. Your. Name?" Nick slathered the words in menace.

"Delbert Clarke, okay? Now, let me go."

"Where in Zion Village did you live exactly, Mr. Clarke?"

The man wouldn't meet his eyes, and there was nobody around who'd come to welcome him out of his cell.

"Here and there. I moved a lot. Ain't none of your—"

"Where'd you hear about Phoebes?"

"Huh?"

"Phoebes. You said there might be Phoebes watching. What do you know about Phoebes?"

"Ain't none of this any of your business. You ain't got no right—"

In a motion almost too fast to follow, Nick let go of the

man's bunched up collar, grabbed his wrist and twisted his arm up behind his back.

The man cried out and dropped to his knees. All Nick had to do was exert the slightest pressure on the man's arm, and he was in agony.

"I'll ask again. Where did you hear about Phoebes?"

The man screamed. "I don't know. Somebody was talking about 'em, that's all."

"Who?"

"I don't know!"

He was either lying or too stupid to remember. Nick wouldn't let it go, though. Couldn't. The word had raised the hairs on the back of his neck, had set off some primitive alarm he had learned from bitter experience not to ignore.

But couldn't find out what he wanted to know here with the other deputy and all the released and soon-to-be-released prisoners and their friends and family milling around. He was starting to attract a crowd.

Turning to the deputy who'd accompanied him, he told the man to let the other detainees go, then he hauled the fat man down the passageway and around a corner, using his pressure on the guy's arm to keep him going. Nick found an empty tunnel leading off into darkness and he dragged the man into it and dumped him on his belly in the dirt.

Before the man could get to his feet, Nick put his foot on the back of the man's neck.

"Here's how this is going down," Nick said. "I'm going to ask questions and you're going to answer them. If you don't answer my questions or you lie to me, I will break one of your fingers. Lie again, a second finger. A man would have a lot of trouble doing up his fly with all his fingers broken."

Nick picked up the guy's hand, twisted it backward, lifted the pinky finger and said, "Where did you hear about Phoebes?"

"I done told you I don't know where I heard it."

Nick snapped the finger at the middle joint like a brittle twig and the man howled in pain, blew so much snot out his nose it made a puddle of mud in the dirt in front of him.

"Shut up, stop your caterwauling."

Nick emphasized his words by wiggling the guy's broken finger and he squeaked out a muffled moan and was silent.

"Phoebes, remember? Where did you hear about them?"

"Please mister, I don't know you, I ain't hurt you. What you doing this to pour old Delbert for? I don't know nothing. I swear to Jesus, Mary and Joseph, I don't. They was just talking about … I don't even 'member what … and then this dude said they was things the size of marbles called Phoebes that could watch what you was doin'."

"What dude, what was his name?"

"He didn't never give his name."

Nick wiggled his finger. The man strangled a cry and spoke fast.

"Just a guy, you know … a dude, didn't nobody know him … he was who sent Gideon Freeman to find us, to ask me and Herbert did we want to help him."

"Herbert?"

"My brother."

"Is he around here?"

"Naw. The dude … zapped him."

"*Zapped* him?"

"Kilt him. Looked at him mean and kilt him."

Nick let that go.

"What'd he want you to help him do?"

Nick let off the pressure on the finger and the man took heart and babbled on.

"Start some trouble, that's all. Just start a little trouble."

"Trouble?"

"Nothing bad, just little stuff. Get people mad at each other, like that."

"And what did *you* do ... and don't say 'nothing' or ..." He wiggled Mr. Clarke's broken finger and he whimpered.

"Please mister ... I didn't do nothing bad, just kilt a little yappy dog is all. Hung his collar out where his owner'd find it and get all upset about it. Didn't hurt nobody."

"The guy who wanted you to start the trouble, tell me about him."

"Ain't nothing to tell, he was just weird."

"Weird how?" Nick wiggled the finger next to the broken one.

"You know, strange, had funny eyes you couldn't look at and he ... did weird shit."

"Don't make me drag this out of you."

"No, *please*. I ... he just said crazy shit, that's all. He talked to himself all the time, and I don't mean like to himself, but like Himself was a person standin' there, called him by name."

It felt like Nick's blood froze, but not into a solid stream. As individual drops, cold little stones in his bloodstream. Lying, oh so still in his veins.

STANDING *in the gymnasium with Sawyer and Noah and the monster who'd murdered Josie — so close his fingers ache to throttle him. The monster speaks to somebody, to nobody, to empty air.*

"You turned on me, Himself. You're ... the enemy, now."

Then he giggles, replies to what he'd just said, in a different voice entirely, "Finally figured that out, did you, asshole?"

PACO.

Had to be.

Paco was alive.

He'd somehow escaped drowning and he was here in the cave.

Which meant Nick would have the opportunity to choke the life out of him and watch him die.

Chapter Thirty-Seven

THE ELDERS WERE ASSEMBLED in Alabaster Hall, all of them quiet. Waiting. Waiting for … no, this time Sawyer didn't say it out loud to make it real because he flat out didn't want to make it real. They were waiting for the Astrals to drill a hole through the wall. The opening would be on the western side of the room, the only side where there weren't any of the naturally occurring fissures the Mathesons had dubbed Library Aisles.

Because they were narrow and deep and lined with beauty worth spending time to examine.

Garson had gone back around and into the mine through the "Noah entrance" and was apparently somewhere on the other side of the wall — in the mine the Astrals had dug *the last time* they came to Earth and wiped out humanity.

There was no sound at all. There was not even a sizzling like you'd expect to hear when something melted.

The wall they were standing in front of just became "not solid," not a substance that was stiff, not a rock. It became something like liquid, hung there, and then the edges of it ran to the sides, like beads of water on the surface of something lifted out.

Now there was a hole in the wall of Alabaster Hall and in the hole, the doorway, stood Garson and five gigantic white beings.

Mother fuck the queen, it was all true, every word of it.

Five titans.

He heard a gasp from the side and turned to see that Fred had taken a step backward and was trembling all over. Sawyer shouldn't have told him, shouldn't have brought him. But when he put his hand on the old man's shoulder to steady him, that's all it took. He firmed up and shook off Sawyer's support.

Garson lead the five Astrals into the room through the opening and Sawyer couldn't help the association. Garson looked like a ringmaster leading the elephants into the center — to do amazing tricks to dazzle and amuse, come one, come all, see the behemoths balance on a ball, stand on their hind legs.

"I am the one got us into this," Garson began without preamble. "But in my own defense, I should point out that *I* am not the reason these beings are here. Those of you who blew up the mine entrance and trapped them get to take that rooster home to your own chicken houses to roost … however, I did conceal their presence, and for that I owe you all an apology."

"Why didn't you tell anybody?" Taylor asked.

"Because I am a self-absorbed old fool, a forever-scientist, and the opportunity to talk to beings who had bent time and gravity — I'm sorry. I took it. I have no other defense."

Words formed in Sawyer's head and he could tell from

the looks on the faces of the others that the same was happening to them.

Have to meet us eventually.

Have to cut our way out, or die of thirst.

It was like it was the same voice but different and Sawyer looked from one of them to the other, trying to figure out which one had spoken. Okay, not *spoken* but …

"Moe talks more than Curly," Garson said, "but none of them have ever spoken anything out loud."

"Moe? Curly?"

"Don't be obtuse, Sawyer, I had to call them *something*."

"And the …"

"Laverne and Shirley." Garson paused for a beat for Sawyer to get it and when he didn't, went on. "We didn't force them to come here. They agreed."

"How very gracious of them," said Jessica Maddocks, her words slathered with sarcasm.

Sawyer took over then.

"Now that we know about them, we have to decide what to do with them."

"What's to decide?" Taylor turned to Garson. "You're saying these dudes can't become reptars, right? Something about feedback."

"Yes, I did, just so," Garson said. "Their thoughts transmit to the hive mind at the same time limestone transmits them, causes feedback, maddening, deafening. Noah watched two of them rip each other apart because of it, remember."

A fleeting thought beat its wings in Sawyer's mind like the moths around the light on the back porch when he was a kid. Just fluttering there, waiting to die.

Like the thought he'd had about the cougar's tracks where Donkey Ho-tee disappeared.

Fleeting, fluttering thoughts — a sense of urgency to them, but then they were gone.

"Original question — what's to decide?" Taylor looked from one to the other of the people in the room. "We have to kill them. Am I missing something here? I don't see that there's any controversy, is there?"

"They're harmless beings." Garson was pleading a hopeless case but that didn't stop him from trying. "They can do nothing to harm us."

"Not now, they can't," Noah pointed out. "But if they ever step foot outside this cave after the flood, they will immediately hook up to the hive mind in the mothership. And milliseconds later we will have shuttles hovering over us, waiting to take their buddies back home and kill us for the unpardonable sin of not being their hand-picked survivors."

"I'm not so sure that's accurate anymore, Noah," Garson said. He paused, and without turning he spoke a word. "Moe."

The titan turned to him.

"Did you see that?"

"And it means …?" Jessica Maddocks was getting frustrated.

What does that possibly mean?

"It means these five titans aren't little cells in the blood-stream of the collective consciousness anymore. They have been cut off here with nobody but me for a companion, picking their brains, and allowing them to rummage through mine to their heart's content."

"And …?" Taylor, prodded, but Sawyer saw where he was going.

"And they're *individuals* now! One cell out of a billion doesn't respond to a name. They've changed. I don't think they'd be able to hook back up to the hive mind even without the limestone blocking transmissions." He looked from one to the other. "They can't hurt us, not now, not later. They're harmless."

Garson had pleaded his case, arguing eloquently for the lives of Moe, Curly, Larry, Laverne and Shirley — the five Astrals that had been trapped in the cavern by the explosion.

When he was done, no one else spoke. The silence that followed was so profound Sawyer fancied he could hear the ticking of his watch, though it didn't tick and he wasn't wearing it.

"We can babble about this until the flood water goes down." Disgust turned Taylor's voice hard and cold. "What do we do with them? My vote is *kill* them."

Comets streaked across Sawyer's mind. Noah in the beam of light. His deputies—

"Mine, too." He heard his voice before he even thought the words.

Star said nothing, then lifted her chin and fixed the white giants with sightless eyes.

"They should die."

Noah nodded agreement, but said nothing. The expression on Eagle Feather's face never changed.

"Death."

Jessica Maddocks sounded like an echo. "Death."

Brother Sebastian shook his head sadly and said only one word. "Mercy."

That left Fred. The group turned to the old man, who had been watching the debate but had not once entered in. Now, he stepped forward — literally. He crossed the few feet separating the elders from the titans. So small and bent, he looked unutterably frail standing before the white giants.

"I am a man of God, a believer in the Torah. You don't even know what that means."

Words appeared in Sawyer's mind.

An ancient book.

Fred's head snapped up. "You got something to say to me, schmuck, *talk.*"

The smaller male titan, the one Garson called Larry, spoke, sounding like an automated attendant.

"It is an old book."

Fred shook his head and wagged his boney finger.

"Oh, no, not just old, *holy.* That word, you don't know. It is from the hands of God himself."

Maybe it was Sawyer's imagination, surely it was. Still, it seemed to him that the old man's tinny voice deepened, rumbled.

"In Exodus 21, Jehovah commanded, 'If there is harm, then you shall pay an eye for an eye.'"

Alabaster Hall was a chamber too small to form an echo. But there was one. Fred's words repeated. Then again, quieter. Then silence.

"So that totals what — *fourteen billion eyes* you owe mankind?"

He cast a glance at Brother Sebastian. They were dear friends. Their eyes met and locked.

"If my great grandparents had been allowed to vote on whether or not to execute the Nazi murderers of six million of our people, *nobody* would have cried mercy."

He straightened, defying the arthritis that bent his back.

"Leviticus 24 … 'The one who has inflicted the injury must suffer the same injury.'"

He lifted his cane and poked it into the belly of the titan called Moe.

"If I had the power, I would *burn* you, all five of you,

until there was nothing left but little whirlwinds of black dust. And I would do it" — with all his strength, he jabbed the Astral on every word — "Seven. Billion. Times."

Lowering his cane, he turned his back on the giants, a gesture meant to be as dismissive as it appeared.

"Kill the motherfuckers," he said.

Chapter Thirty-Eight

IT HADN'T TAKEN a whole lot of persuasion for Nick to get the man named Delbert Clarke to roll over on Paco and give his location. When he was done questioning him, Nick hauled him back to jail and told the deputy in charge to hold him. Sawyer'd want to have a go at him later, once he learned the riots hadn't been spontaneous combustion but fires intentionally set.

He saw Taylor in the corridor and gave him a message for Sawyer, that Nick would be missing the elders meeting, had bigger fish to fry — that's all. And he was sure Sawyer would wonder what fish could possibly be bigger than deciding what to do with the five Astrals they had inadvertently trapped in the cave with them.

Nothing else in all his life would have kept Nick from going to that meeting. This and only this. Finding the motherfucker who had killed Josie and choking the life out of him.

He didn't let himself think about Josie. Couldn't or he would have gone mad. The end of the world, as a matter of fact, was the only thing powerful enough to force him to put what had happened to her in the background of his mind. He'd learned how to do that, take what had happened and put it on a back burner in your mind, as a soldier. When the three villagers were killed, or the day the IED blew Richardson's legs off and he kept asking if he'd ever be able to kick a football again. Nick didn't think about those things when they happened, he couldn't have or he would have been as dead as his buddies. The tyranny of the urgent was also the deliverance of the urgent, because it rescued you from reality that would shred your soul to ribbons without the distraction.

In the little pieces of downtime since they'd gotten into the ark, he had managed to occupy his attention and thoughts with pressing, life-and-death matters. But now, as he headed down Broadway to Manitoba Lane, and down it to Smiley Face, he allowed himself the luxury/agony of remembering, of attending to a random-grab of any one of the thousand little memories that added up to the sum total of the person, what they had left with you when they moved on. A total that was never enough, never captured the essence, always left you wanting more.

He and Michelle had made a conscious decision to have Josie knowing from the amniocentesis test that she would be born with Down syndrome. They had talked about it, prayed about it, and in the end it really didn't seem like a decision at all. It was a mere acceptance of the reality that their little girl would be born special and different. Neither of them had ever considered the option of abortion. She was their little girl. She'd have issues. Next.

Michelle had given her life to bring Josie into the world.

And when he held her for the first time, the image of Down syndrome stamped on her face even as a newborn, he tried to imagine having made any other decision than to be her father and raise her with all the love that'd welled up in his heart for her.

Oh, he knew every father probably thought his little girl was unique, was in some way the single most incredible human being to ever grace the planet. He knew that. But his little girl really was. She was. Seriously.

There was no other child whose eyes were more blue, a blue you could fall into, into the depths of them, that single clear blue of the ice in a frozen pond reflecting a cloudless winter sky.

She probably wasn't the most beautiful child in the world. Nick didn't know. He honestly could not look at her through the filter of oh-she's-handicapped that other people did.

Josie woke up with a smile on her face every morning of her life. She would reach over and grab her glasses off the night table. He had looted an optometry store in Lexington a couple of weeks after Astral Day to get glasses for his very pregnant wife. Michelle had never gotten around to having the surgery to correct her farsightedness. In the past seven years, he'd found glasses from among his haul that made little Josie see better. Then she'd snuggle them on her face, throw her arms around Nick's neck and hug him with a strength that couldn't possibly be in the arms of a tiny little girl. And she'd tell him, "It's gonna be a good day, Daddy. You'll see. Special good."

Oh, he might be editing history, rearranging what had happened, wallpapering over … but he wasn't. He really could not remember a single day in the child's life that had not been good, had not been special, a glow-around-the-edges kind of special just because she was in it.

And this monster … he couldn't even make himself say the man's name out loud for fear the filth of it would stick in his mouth and he'd be able to taste it for the rest of his life. This monster had run her down in the road. Nobody told him that part, but he overheard it afterward from the people who'd been there, who'd seen. The monster didn't accidentally hit a child who popped out into the road in front of him and he didn't have time to stop.

No. He had *aimed* at her. He had *intended* to hit her. He *planned* to kill her and when his monster machine had mangled her poor little body and threw it out behind him, he had turned back forward with a look of delight on his face.

The moment Nick's eyes first fell on the man in the gym, he memorized his every feature, every detail of his face and body, imprinting the image on his soul. He had known then, with the kind of gut-level certainty reserved for the inevitability of sunrise, that he would kill this man. Even when Nick was hauled here to be executed, it hadn't mattered. He had known, *known* that that man would not continue to draw breath in the same world with Nick.

Of course, he'd been glad to learn the man was dead, that he'd drowned. But he'd been disappointed that the task of ridding the world of such filth had been taken from him.

Except the monster wasn't dead. He was here. He had somehow escaped the flood waters Noah was certain had drowned him. Had somehow managed to get into the cave, and to amass a group of followers, with the intent of "taking over the place," as the Neanderthal Delbert had put it.

Nick was under no illusions about the cleverness and danger that was inherent in the whole being of Paco Salazar. Nick and Star had told him story after story about their triad — NoahStarPaco — that the Astrals had kidnapped to study. He had genuine power. He could control minds, had done it successfully with the idiot

Delbert, though there was little there to control. Still, Nick had no idea what he might be facing when he finally confronted the murderer. And he didn't give a flying fuck what it was.

The motherfucker was *going down*.

Nick was going to wrap his fingers around his neck, and look into his face as he squeezed the life out of him. He would watch the eyes go dim, slide sideways into the death stare.

No, it wouldn't bring Josie back. But this wasn't really about Josie and Nick knew it. It was about Nick. If he could only find the monster who'd killed her and make him pay, he would spend his rage. Then he could treasure the memories of his precious child, could look at them and grieve.

Chapter Thirty-Nine

ALL THE ELDERS heard the words at the same time, though they were not spoken aloud.

There is one broken among you.

And then, in all their minds bloomed a face. *Ellie.*

Sawyer drew in a breath to speak but his throat locked up.

Taylor spoke the words his brother couldn't. "What's Ellie got to do with any of this?"

She is broken. We can … repair.

"Repair? Fix?" A breath. "Do you mean *heal?*"

The word became a bowling ball in Sawyer's head, banging onto the hardwood, rumbling down the lane, crashing into the pins with an explosive clatter.

Heal.

"What are you saying?" he demanded. He could speak now.

The hive mind can—

Garson's head snapped up and he leapt at the one called Curly, shouting at him. Sawyer had never seen him angry.

"*Hive mind?* Are you telling me that you have been

tapped into the hive mind of the mothership *all along*? It's all been a lie, a ruse—?"

The horror of that reality crashed into the room, this time a wrecking ball.

All they had done, all their effort. Their fear. Their *hope*. Gone. The moment they stepped out into the fresh air of a new world, assuming any of them survived long enough to do that, the Astrals would be dangling up there in little silver balls waiting for them.

Fear of just that had been growing in Sawyer's mind as the days ticked down to Ground Zero. The image formed out of the fear. Looking into the clear Kentucky sky. Breathing pure, fresh air. The sun shining down.

Not there. There. Shuttles blink into existence, shiny silver balls hanging over the trees. There were always three shuttles.

Always three.

There's one heartbeat, maybe two. Time to take no more than one breath of the sun-warmed air and then the bottoms of the shuttles begin to glow red. The pathetic tatters of humanity come scrambling up out of their hidey-hole after the end of the world, and Astral shuttles make black dust of them all.

No, we are unable to join unity in the mothership.

It looked like Garson and Curly were having an argument, except only one of them's lips were moving.

"Then what the fuck are you talking about?" It was the first time Sawyer had ever heard Garson curse, too.

"He's telling the truth," Star said. "They aren't tapped into the mothership. I'd hear the hive mind if they were."

Garson dialed it back. "If you're not connected, how can the hive mind heal Ellie?"

We *are a hive mind.*

Five titans. A hive mind.

The import of that was more than Sawyer could fit into his head without pieces of it dangling out his ears.

"Are you saying that *you*, the five of you, can …?" The words were there, but suddenly the strength to propel them into the room was not.

We will actualize a new idiomatic reality.

Garson looked at the one called Moe, as if asking for more explanation.

Change brain structure on a molecular level.

In some way Sawyer could understand but could never have explained, the voice in his head remained there, just didn't say anything.

Garson turned to the elders.

"I know that sound. That *not-sound*. That's what you hear when the answer to your question is too complex for you to understand." The professor actually smiled a little. "Some concepts can't be dumbed down enough to communicate to humans." Then Garson started down one of his rabbit trails. "The space-time continuum, for example. Scientists on earth think it—"

"I don't give a fuck about the space-time continuum." Sawyer was shouting now, couldn't control his voice. He stepped to the nearest titan, the big one called Moe and grabbed him by the shoulders. Somewhere Sawyer's mind filed away the random factoid that the Astral's skin was not warm. "What about Ellie?"

We can make her well.

Shocked silence.

"*Well?*" His voice broke and he was crying. "How?"

Astral silence.

Then simply: *Hive mind.*

Sawyer was so stunned, he thought he might need somebody to direct his steps to a chair so he could sit down. Then the overwhelm washed away and the world returned crisp and bright, and with it the realization. His eyes met Taylor's and hooked there. Clearly the brothers were thinking the same thought.

The hive mind might be able to heal Ellie ... oh, dear holy God, Jesus, Joseph and Mary! But they wouldn't be able to *resurrect* her. What if ... what if Ellie were already dead?

Chapter Forty

PACO'S HEAD SNAPPED UP. He'd been pacing the cavern, figuring out which of his pathetic goons he would send to break into the armory. He didn't want their guns, didn't need their weapons. The trick was ammunition. Gideon had explained to him about the ammunition factory that had operated in the caverns — barrels of gunpowder and—

HHMM.

A sound spoke in his head and he dropped the mug of awful-tasting coffee and it clinked on the stone floor.

HHHHMMMM.

Just a hum, that's all, the sound of an old refrigerator in his aunt's trailer on that West Virginia mountainside kicking on. A hmmmmm.

But it wasn't a refrigerator.

It was a hive mind.

An active hive mind.

He stayed down below its consciousness, could picture in his head being outside a house looking in the window, bending down below the window frame and slowly lifting his head up just enough to see inside. He couldn't be seen. He had been doing something similar with Noah and Star ever since he'd flopped up on shore after the Astral flood, after he didn't conveniently drown as Noah had intended when he tricked him. He could sense them like they were music playing loud in the next room. But he didn't go into the room, and he sure as fuck didn't sing along with the tune. He just "knew they were there."

The trick, of course, was they *didn't know* he was there. He had been pondering how he would come at them. Physically first, not in their heads. But he'd make it somehow … he'd work it out so he could see their faces. Then he'd jump up in their heads, like people hiding behind the furniture at a surprise party, and yell *Boo*.

And watch the color drain out of their faces, which, of course, would make Noah the color of a titan.

HHHHMMMM.

Paco hid down below it. Peeked up over the window sill just a little. Just enough.

Titans. There were titans here.

There was absolutely no fucking way in the universe that it could be so, but he knew that it was. He could *hear* them, *sense* them. They were all concentrating on something together — that's what had produced the hum.

How had titans gotten in here?

Clearly, they didn't just arrive. They had to have been here since before the water rose, but he hadn't been aware of them until now because they hadn't exerted the force of their hive mind until now.

If he put his head up just a little further, he could see what it was they were concentrating on, the same way he had seen the image of the annihilation.

But he didn't dare. They could catch him. Star and Noah were in each other's heads all the fucking time and they thought he was dead. They would never think to feel him. He had been very, very careful indeed not to come up into the level of their consciousness. But this hive mind. Astrals. More than one. It wouldn't take but a little slip for them to recognize there was somebody in their hive mind with them.

So he didn't look, didn't try to see what it was they were concentrating on, just stood there with spilled coffee soaking into his sock wondering ... how could there possibly be Astrals in the cave?

Terror gripped Paco's belly, the kind he hadn't felt since his time in the yard of the prison, when the reptars had stepped out of the shuttle and eaten half the prisoners. The scene came into his mind in full technicolor. Why was it that memories like that were always so vivid?

I'm turning up the volume, asshole.

Himself. Paco ignored him, but couldn't ignore the memory.

He was that kid again, the scared kid, running for the door with Tiburon behind him. Only a step or two ahead of the reptar. He remembered falling through the doorway, sliding on his back across the floor, the whole thing playing out in hideous slow motion. The decision. Right there in front of him.

Did he ensure his own survival?

Or put his life in danger to save his best friend?

He'd picked Option Number One. And he'd made it. He'd kicked the door shut in Tiburon's face. Had saved himself by sacrificing his friend.

Self-serving motherfucker. You been betraying friends your whole life. Tiburón sure as fuck wasn't the first.

No. Not Vincent. Paco wouldn't allow those thoughts into his brain and if Himself tried to make him think them, he would put up a fight, even if it would do all the shit Himself had been warning him it would — blow all the circuits.

Two can play at this game. You *dare* ... and I'll kill us both.

Himself just leaned against a door frame that wasn't there and said nothing.

And his mind snapped back like a fully extended rubber band. Astrals here. Then how was anybody here still alive?

Somehow, they had gotten in before the flood, unless they'd dug a hole in Noah's Ark, in which case all the humans would be dead, too. So they had been here all this time and they hadn't kicked ass, hadn't ripped the population apart.

Why not?

The only possible explanation was that the Astrals whose hive mind he could hear humming along out there, were titans.

So why hadn't they *become* reptars? It wasn't like they were stuck in their white marshmallow suits. They could become killers in a heartbeat. Why hadn't they? Why hadn't they become reptars and killed everybody?

No answer came to mind. Himself was blessedly silent.

Then an answer began to bubble up out of the mud in the bottom of his consciousness, like a single bubble easing up the side of an aquarium. The only possible explanation for why the titans had not turned into reptars was that they couldn't. For some reason — Paco couldn't begin to guess what it was — the titans were stuck as titans. They couldn't change or they would have. The other way around — they would have changed if they could have. As Astrals, it'd be their job to get rid of this little pimple of humanity. Quickly and efficiently. Reptars would have killed everybody by now.

There were titans in the cave and as God made little green apples, the "powers that be knew about it."

Of course they did. Sawyer and that Nick — the image of the little girl turning to look at him — flashed in his mind and for a heartbeat or two he could see nothing else. Then it was gone.

Himself was standing beside the pathetic tent Gideon Freeman had erected for Paco. It was such an unutterably odd sensation to look at the fellow standing across from you and see yourself looking back, only it wasn't a mirror. But, of course, Himself wasn't really there at all.

If I'm not here, how can I do this? Himself picked up a stone off the cave floor and threw it at him.

Paco reached up to catch it before it smacked him in the face.

And it wasn't there, of course.

Himself doubled over with laughter.

Concentrate. Focus.

There were titans here in the cave and the folks in charge knew they were here. How did that benefit Paco?

Well, if he were a citizen of the fine little town of Zion Village — Noah's Ark — it would sorely piss him off to learn that the powers-that-be were keeping secrets. His "elected" officials — Paco didn't know how they'd gotten to be in charge, elected or power grab — were hiding something. If he were one of the plebes, he would be madder than dammit to discover that the leaders had Astrals in the place and hadn't bothered to tell him.

Yes sir, that'd make him mad.

Paco needed to act fast. If he was to make hay of this, he had to deliver the bad news about the titans in the worst way possible, before those in charge had a chance to fess up. He had to send his little bugs out into the villagers to plant the information, let the cat out of the bag.

This was the opening he'd been looking for, a way to divide and conquer, separate the leadership from the folks they were leading. Paco couldn't fight three thousand people, but he could take his pathetic little band of soldiers and beat the shit out of half a dozen leaders.

He quieted his thoughts. Eyed Himself standing on the other side of the cavern and ignored him. Himself said nothing. Did nothing. Just watched.

Then Paco began to glide into the minds of his insurrection army.

In the cool and dark of their minds, he came. One at a time. He slipped into their consciousness and once he was in, he began to take over.

And an amazing thing happened. Nothing. No pain. No pressure. Oh, he still couldn't see out of his right eye, but he would. The vision would return. It would. But right now he was enjoying the pleasure ... *pleasure* like it used to be years ago. When he was young. Before Himself. Before the ayahuasca drug. The simple pleasure of gliding into the mind of another human being, getting them to scoot over in the front seat — because *you* were driving.

One after another, Paco took control.

And then he reached Gretchen. He slid into control of her last. She was stiff, unyielding, not compliant as she had been before. But he bowled over her and then he had them all. *All!*

He had watched a magician years ago perform an amazing trick. He balanced plates on sticks. Started out with one. Balanced the stick in the center of his right palm, balanced a plate on the other end and spun it. He did the same with the left hand. Then added more sticks and more plates.

That's what Paco was doing, spinning plates. Like that magician, he had to constantly reach out and re-start the spinning plates that were faltering, hopping from one mind to another. And as soon as he got one going good, another would begin to wobble, someone would try to exert control over their own mind and Paco'd be there, nudging. If nudging didn't work, pushing. Shoving.

Spinning the plate.

He was having a wonderful time. A *glorious* time. Taking the lives of these people and owning them. His mind was dominating the minds of forty-seven people at once — gliding from one mind to the next — overruling their wills.

He was in charge — roaring down the street on his black motorcycle with the shark face, his hair slicked back. He was the Man.

Himself sat impossibly behind him on the bike, but Paco refused to acknowledge his presence, refused to hear the words when Himself shook his head slowly and spoke.

Any time now … any time.

Chapter Forty-One

ELLIE FELT ALMOST DETACHED, watching herself from somewhere in the upper right corner of the cavern, floating there maybe, looking down on the pathetically ravished body of Elliot Thurgood Hampton.

She was glad now she'd gotten Anna to help her into the yellow-flowered dress. She didn't want to die looking like a sick person.

Die.

This is what it feels like to die.

So far, it was not nearly as bad as she'd feared. So far. Of course, it could all go to shit in a heartbeat.

Speaking of heartbeats, she wasn't sure she could hear hers anymore. Or feel it. She had been losing the sensations in her outer extremities for the past couple of days, so she wasn't surprised. The plumbing all had to shut down, didn't it, for the dying thing to happen. Maybe that part was starting now.

She had intended to talk to Diana about it, the whole dying thing, comfort the little girl. She needed to understand that Anna and Sawyer, Eagle Feather, Star, Noah and Garson … would be there for her in the way that Ellie had been for the past seven years.

That had been the plan.

Then … it all went to shit.

Something happened to Diana's pet, a baby donkey named Donkey Ho-tee. It had been tucked safely away in its pen and then it had suddenly disappeared, at least that's what Ellie could glean from the conversations outside the flap door of her room. Did the people who talked there honestly believe she couldn't hear what they were saying? Actually, maybe they did. Maybe that was the point. It was a way to say hard things without really acknowledging you were saying hard things.

Diana had been too upset by the loss of the donkey, so none of it had gone down as Ellie had planned. And maybe that was for the best. Maybe making a big production out of it … some kind of pass-the-baton ceremony … would make it harder, not easier on the little girl.

Because Ellie was shutting down, so were the nerves, the monsters who had been screaming in agonizing protest at the cancer's assault on them for months. Years. That was a good thing … well, relatively speaking.

Ellie had asked Anna, straight up, "So what happens when you die?"

Anna had answered just as straight up — used a medical phrase Ellie liked. What are the symptoms of "active dying"?

"When your organs start to shut down, you will begin to lose the feeling in your extremities."

"My extremities being all the places that hurt? Hallelujah chorus, I won't be able to feel it anymore, you don't think. I will have some time, if only a little while, before I die when I don't hurt. Not anywhere?"

Anna had, of course, pointed out that every death was

individual. Exactly what Ellie would and wouldn't feel was an unknown, but so far it was feeling better all the time.

Do you have a high tolerance for pain?

That doctor at Ft. Knox told her as he was set to make the incision in her breast to take out the lump that he couldn't put her under and didn't have any good meds for pain anymore. Said it was going to hurt.

Hurt. Shit. A stubbed toe hurts worse than what she had felt when the monster abortionist finally did remove the lump.

Oh, at the time, she hadn't thought that. At the time, she had thought it hurt like hell. That kind of thing was a matter of perspective. From here, looking back, the original lumpectomy was so painless she could have fallen asleep right in the middle of it.

It was good to be alone here now. Anna wouldn't be gone long, had just stepped out for a minute to go to Alabaster Hall because Sawyer'd said he might need her there for something. In a way, Ellie hoped she'd die before Anna got back. She felt like she had been giving a series of farewell performances since she stopped eating and drinking. They were wearing her out.

Alone. Quiet now. Yeah, that was as good a way to go as any.

And the pain. The pain was easing off for the first time in … ever. Gradually going away.

With the release from pain, she could feel her body settling, relaxing back into the sheets, as the muscles held rigid to contain the agony began to unwind. It was a little like floating must feel. Weightless above the sheets, slowly settling back, her head making a dent in the pillow, her body was so desiccated, it barely did the same on the mattress.

With the release from pain, she could think. A clarity

of mind came to her she hadn't experienced since, shit, she didn't know how long. She could think. Thoughts, clear thoughts. Her mind felt sharp, bright.

Then the brightness began to pale, a light on a dimmer switch, shadows moving out longer from the walls, pooling and puddling in the middle of the room. She had felt blessedly, gloriously alive for those few vivid moments. That was her gift, that bright sparkle of life, that's what she would carry with her …

Yeah, with her *where*?

She had no idea what she believed about such things, refusing with a great act of will not to submit to foxhole mentality … there are no atheists in foxholes … as she approached the end. But she was ever so curious, and maybe she would have been afraid, maybe she would have been utterly terrified if death were not such a release.

Yeah, it sucked to be dying. It sucked more to stay alive in agony.

It had been awful over the past months to watch her own body deteriorate right in front of her eyes. Anybody who got old, lived past the age of fifty, had experienced it. But over time. Gradually. Brown spots, white hairs — her mother had complained far more about white eyebrows — gnarled hands. The body going to shit. Every day, Ellie would look down and see more deterioration.

She was getting …

Say the word.

No!

Okay.

"Ugly."

Ellie Hampton had been a beautiful woman and liked to think she would gradually have surrendered that beauty to the ravages of time with grace. Now, she was no longer what all those nannies years ago had told her she was. No longer beautiful.

She hated to die like that. Ugly. What was it her grandmother always said: a closed casket hides a multitude of sins.

And Woody Allen. He had said he wasn't afraid of dying, he just didn't want to be there when it happened.

Her mind was jumping around, hovering over thoughts but somehow not thinking them either, not deeply.

Symptoms of active dying:

Hallucinations, delirium, agitation.

Shit, all she got was foggy.

Not fair. She didn't get the full technicolor show and she'd always wanted to have a hallucination, just one. She should demand her money back. And now, when she was actually entitled to one, had earned one, she couldn't conjure so much as a single image.

Then she brightened. It was a game. A contest. No, more like an Easter egg hunt. You looked around for the Easter eggs that'd been deposited in your body and that were the symptoms of active dying.

And she'd found another one!

Long pauses in breathing.

Why, she almost had to think to breathe, to make it happen, air in and out.

She held up her arm to look at it ... she was so weak.

That was one, wasn't it? Weakness. No. But it didn't hurt to lift it. She didn't know if that was one, but even if it wasn't, she was profoundly grateful to have this time, this time of "active dying" when she didn't hurt anywhere.

She looked at the arm she held in front of her. She'd been looking for something. What was ...?

Skin changes color.

No spots yet, but Anna said everybody's death was

individual, their own. She might not get them all, but in the end, she'd still win the contest.

Ten things I would do if I weren't dying:

Okay, five.

But she could only think of one: she'd make love with Sawyer Matheson.

Chapter Forty-Two

SAWYER RACED out of the Alabaster Hall, around the bend in the corridor and found a crowd in the passageway, held in place at the police line by the deputies. Sawyer barreled through the piece of black and yellow plastic — a sprinter crossing the finish line — and kept going through the cavern, knocking people aside, shoving them out of his way.

What were all these people doing here? Some of them shouted at him as he shoved his way through them, not friendly shouts.

He didn't care. He would have mown down Mother Teresa if she'd been standing there. He'd have mown down anybody who got in his way.

He had to get to Ellie before it was too late.

He rounded the corner and raced down the corridor to the special place they'd made for Ellie right outside Carnegie Hall, so she could feel a part of what was going on. Thank God they hadn't given her a room where she would have solitary and quiet.

"Sawyer, what—?" Anna began.

"Is she …?"

And suddenly he didn't want to know. If she was dead, if here at the end of all things he had been moments too late. He wasn't at all sure he could live with that.

"She was fine a few minutes ago. She seemed to want to be alone." Anna smiled a little. "Said she was 'damned tired of the series of farewell performances she'd been giving.'"

"But she's all right?"

Anna looked at him quizzically. "No, she's not alright. She'd dying, very close."

"But she's still alive — right now, she's alive?"

He realized he was yelling at Anna, that she didn't understand his intensity.

When Anna nodded, Sawyer passed her, literally knocked her out of the way and yanked back the curtain that separated Ellie's room from the little anteroom, the small portion of the cave where Anna kept her supplies, where people gathered themselves, steeled themselves to go in.

"Ellie!" he cried.

Her eyes opened.

Oh, thank God.

"Go … away, Sawyer." Her voice was a whisper on a breath. "I want to do this by myself."

She looked past him and he realized Anna had followed him into her room.

"This is one, isn't it, Anna?"

"One what?"

"Hallucinations. One of the symptoms of active dying—"

He didn't let her finish, just stepped to the bed and started to pick her up.

"What the fuck do you think you're doing!" Anna

grabbed his arm. "For God's sake, Sawyer, leave her alone. Let her die in peace."

"She's not going to die."

"Please … don't touch … You might make it hurt again."

She was fighting back weakly, protesting, trying to push him away with no strength at all in her arms. She stopped pushing and got a funny look on her face.

"I have to breathe," she said. "To think about it."

"What do you mean she's not going to die?" Anna demanded.

"Not if I can get her there in time."

Sawyer reached down and began to lift her up off the bed, ignoring the smell of … he didn't know what all. The smell of impending death. And she cried out when he did, with no air to cry out.

"No, it hurts."

Anna literally attacked him then. Grabbed his arm and yanked him aside with her considerable strength.

"Leave her alone! Can't you see she doesn't hurt anymore? Lots of people hurt right up to their last breath, but she's free. Stop it!"

Sawyer literally shoved Anna into the wall with a shoulder block, where she hit something on the table, knocked it off and grunted from the force.

In one movement, he scooped Ellie up off the bed, turned and started running with her. With her body, that's all it was, a shell. She had so little hair it didn't cover her scalp, which was a sickly white color and peeling. Her eyes were sunken holes in her face, looked like cigarette burns in a table cloth, and she weighted almost nothing, like a child.

She was crying. with gasping breaths.

"Please, no… it *hurts*!"

It didn't hit him until that moment and it could have stopped him dead in his tracks.

What if the titans were wrong? What if they couldn't do it, couldn't heal her?

No …what if they were *lying*?

Buying time once they knew they were about to be killed.

What if they were doing it for spite? Just one final Fuck You before he and the others offed the motherfuckers. It wasn't like that wasn't something they would do, that such cruelty was beneath them. These were beings who had wiped out the entire population of a planet. It's not likely they'd balk at sticking it to the humans one more time before they died.

He had bought it.

He was running, knocking people out of his way, but then he slowed. Ellie was making strange sounds in her throat, her breathing was ragged.

That's what it was, a final fuck you. A final in-your-face, we're-smarter-than-you-are. A final jab of pain before they felt pain of their own, if Astrals even felt pain, which he didn't know.

And he had punished Ellie for his gullibility. She was dying, had been dying *pain free*. But he had picked her up, had hurt her, had reawakened the dying nerves.

She was in agony again and it was his fault!

He staggered past the broken police tape a few more steps and then he was crying as he stood cradling her, trying to be tender. Not to hurt her. Would it be more painful to carry her back—?

And he was babbling through his tears, begging her forgiveness, telling her how horribly sorry he was for this final indignity. Garson rushed out of Alabaster Hall when he saw him approach and then stop.

"Sawyer," he said. "Come on!"

No need for haste.

Of course there wasn't. As soon as they all found out it had been a lie, these five Astrals would die ... or whatever happened to them when their bodies were destroyed.

"No hurry now," he said. The cold steel in his voice even frightened him. "*We* aren't going to kill these bastards. *I* will do it. All by myself. The five of them, and they won't die easy. I'll make them pay!"

"Is she ...?" Garson asked.

Sawyer looked down at her. Her eyes were closed and she wasn't breathing.

She was gone.

Sawyer had been crying, openly nakedly crying, but now the tears stopped as if he'd turned off a spigot.

He bent to lay her gently on the floor.

"Stay with her," he told Garson, his voice tender and quiet. Then he ground out the next words, "I have things to do!"

He kissed her softly on the forehead.

And she took a breath.

Then another.

Chapter Forty-Three

NICK HAD COME prepared to fight his way to Paco. He had unlocked the armory near the jail on his way and armed himself with a pistol, a rifle— and a bayonet. The bayonet must have been part of the original Zion Academy armory because it didn't fit on the end of any of the rifles they currently had. That didn't matter, though. Nick intended to use it as a knife.

He'd assumed he'd need all the weapons he'd taken to kill or disarm the "soldiers" who were protecting Paco. But he'd have gone in after Paco armed only with his bare hands if he'd had to — there was nothing and nobody who could have kept him away. No living soul could have protected Paco from the engine of death that was Nick Wilson.

But when he found Paco, the man was alone. Nick didn't have to fight his way through an armed cadre of body guards. Didn't have to take needless lives to make his way to his prey. He leaned out around the edge of the final corner of rock, peering into the cavern where the man named Gideon Freeman had built his home, and found Paco alone.

He was standing with his arms slack at his sides, a really strange look on his face and a thousand-yard stare in his eyes. Nick realized he was doing something with his mind, using his psychic powers to make something happen out there in the world.

Golly, gee … Nick hated to interrupt.

"Hey motherfucker," he called out and then advanced boldly into the cavern. "That little girl you ran down, the child you butchered when you came roaring into town like the conquering horde? That was *my* little girl. Her name was Josie and she was just seven years old."

Rage stole his voice for a moment. When he continued, he growled out the words.

"Starting right now, you have fewer than a dozen breaths to breathe before I kill you."

Nick started toward Paco.

The world went wonky.

It was a little like in the Middle Eastern desert when the heat distorted the horizon, split it up into layers of blurry misshapen images. That's what happened to the air in the cavern. It got that distorted, broken-into-layers, this-is-not-reality look.

Bright light speared into his eyes, blinding him. Squinting into the brightness, he could make out *something* coming. Like watching a convoy come toward you out of the desert, watching reality take shape out of the formless morass of mirage lines, Nick watched a form emerge from the distortion of light.

It was at least twenty feet tall and so wide its scales scraped against the cavern walls.

Nick felt the scream form in his throat, but couldn't tell if he actually gave it voice.

Huge and black and hairy, it scuttled at him in a spurt of speed the way they always did, its pincher six feet across and snapping — he could hear the clacking sound. Its bifurcated tail reared up and bent over its back five, six, seven sections, each three or four feet across. The two eyes on the top of it fixed him with a malevolent hatred that stopped his heart, the curved stinger dangling a single drop of venom that could kill a grown man in a few hours. A few hours of agony.

Unlike other scorpions, this one was angry and aggressive, attacking instead of scampering away, using its strong pincers to capture what it was hunting, or just tear it apart with the claws.

The thing had been under Kincaid's pack, so black you couldn't see it in the dark, but it could see you just from the light of the stars.

Hendrik had caught movement and fixed his flashlight beam on it. Four inches long, running in fury at Beetle's boot, attacking, ready to kill anything it could get its stinger into.

Hendrik and Beetle had scuffed at it, doing a dance with it in the sand. That's when it happened, though later the captain said it couldn't have been that way, that Arabian fat-tailed scorpions didn't jump. But this one did. It crawled up on the toe of Beetle's boot and launched itself at Hendrik's bare leg. Nick watched it fly through the air, clacking its lone pincher — apparently the stomping had broken one off. But it didn't need both to grip the instant it came to rest and it buried the stinger up to the hilt in Hendricks's calf.

They knocked it off him, trying to kill it, stomping it into the sand but the motherfucker was hard as hell to kill, kept sinking down into the sand and coming back at them, again and again.

They killed it, though, finally. But it took half a dozen men stomping it with their boots before they dragged its mangled corpse out of the sand.

Nick had heard the screams of dying men before. He was a soldier. But he had never heard the kind of cry that came from Hendrik as the poison of the monster spread out through his leg into his blood.

He screamed until his voice was completely gone, maybe ripped out his vocal cords, and he kept screaming in silence after that. They said he died in the chopper before they could get him to the aid station.

And the snapshot image — the monster grasping with one pincher, the other missing, superimposed on the image of Hendrik's face contorted in agony …

Nick couldn't move. Couldn't breathe. Couldn't run. The terror so real it tasted like vomit in his throat, slathered him with fear sweat, turned his knees to bags of water.

The giant scorpion stopped short in its rush at him. Stood twenty feet away, wagging that tail back and forth. Snapping the one whole pincer.

The other pincer was broken.

The other pincer was broken.

This wasn't *a* fat-tailed scorpion. It was *the* fat-tailed scorpion. The one that had leaped off Beetle's boot and sunk its stinger into Hendrik's leg.

The fat-tailed scorpion in Nick's mind.

It wasn't real. It was one of Paco's illusions.

It looked real, though. How do you fight a monster that isn't there?

The same way you'd fight it if it were there. No sense in sending bullets pinging off the body armor. He dropped the pistol and rifle and drew the bayonet. He'd kill it with his bare hands.

Nick took two steps toward it.

And it was gone. Poof. No afterimage, sparkle, no trace. Gone. And Paco was standing where he had been when Nick came in. Only he had dropped to his knees.

And he was the one screaming now.

His head was thrown back. He had grabbed handfuls of his own hair and seemed to be trying to rip it out of his scalp. He was shrieking — a sound like Hendrik had made. Wailing.

Blood welled up in his eyes and flowed down his face like tears.

Chapter Forty-Four

ELLIE'S BREATHING was not labored as before. It was stronger.

Sawyer stopped babbling his apologies for hurting her needlessly, begging Ellie's forgiveness. Was he imagining it? No, there was some pink coming back into her skin.

She moaned. Her voice wasn't cracked and rough.

He started running again into Alabaster Hall where the titans stood, not doing anything.

Not sitting in the lotus position, focused looks on their faces, their eyes in a thousand-yard stare, not holding hands and singing Kumbaya. As far as he could tell they hadn't moved at all, were standing where they'd been when he had left the room.

"Here," he said, not knowing what else to do, and he put her down on the floor in front of them.

Not necessary to bring her. The words appeared in his mind. *It is done.*

Done?

Sawyer sat back on his heels, gaping, at Ellie. His heart

was pounding so hard each explosive beat seemed to throb somewhere behind his eyes.

Her breathing was gurgley at first, then a bit of a wheeze. Then normal. He felt the presence of the others gathered around him, but he paid them no mind. He saw Ellie, only Ellie.

It happened so fast.

No, it took hours.

Days.

It took forever.

Time wasn't hooked up to Sawyer's train of reality and it ceased to have form or meaning.

Ellie's lips had been parched and cracked, so dry they were flaking. The scaly skin dropped off, the cracks healed, just closed and were gone and the tissue beneath her lips, the lips began to puff out into what they had once been.

He couldn't take in every change anymore because they were everywhere and when he looked at any one of them, other changes happened that he didn't see.

Her breathing was not just normal, but deep and refreshing, each breath like she'd just come up out of the water and was gasping in the first breath. It slowed then. Became … normal.

Her hands. They'd been like bony claws, fingernails broken and yellowed. The fingernails changed, and bright, sparkling fingernail polish formed on them.

It was like she was a deflated balloon and somebody was slowly, gently blowing air back into it. Her face began to fill out, the tissue under it … growing? Healing? Swelling? The hollows in her cheeks vanished. The hollows under her eyes vanished, too, the dark circles pinked up.

He looked down at her legs and feet and the skin was becoming pink instead of gray.

When his eyes returned to her face, she had eyebrows

now. They had become so thin you couldn't see them. It wasn't even like they'd grown out — like a fast-forward video of planting a grass seed and watching the blades burst up out of the soil. It was faster than that. One second there were no eyebrows, the next they were dark feathers above her eyes, with long lashes. When had that happened?

And her hair.

It was coming back in. He caught sight of her scalp and saw that the scalp was pink, not pasty white, and then he couldn't see the scalp anymore because her hair covered it. It grew and grew, he couldn't take his eyes off it. There were other changes happening he should take note of, wanted to take note of, wanted to capture as snapshot memories he would carry with him to his deathbed.

But he couldn't take his eyes off her hair. He couldn't remember it when it had looked normal. One of the first of the ravaging effects of the cancer was most of her hair fell out in great handfuls and what was left was limp and ... not colorless, but the brown of dirt. It had been like that for ... years.

The hair now was full and lustrous, looked like it did when she stepped off the helicopter that day in front of the administration building at Zion Academy. She had come running across the grass toward him ... he'd replayed that memory over and over and over in his mind in the years since. Until about a year ago. He stopped, refused to think of it again. It didn't seem right to harbor some fantasy of her and cling to it, when the real Ellie was still here and needed all the care and attention he could give her.

He thought it now, though. Her hair was totally ruffled by the downdraft of the helicopter blade, in total disarray, but when she got to him, she stopped, a little winded, and shook her head. That's all it took. Just shaking her head and her hair fell naturally back into place, a cap of chestnut brown that flowed with the breeze. She'd told him once that she had paid three hundred dollars for a haircut the day before Astral Day.

Her hair now was as it had been on that day.

What was it the titan had said?

Change brain structure on a molecular level. Change every molecule … to what? Back to what it had been — what it was supposed to be before every cell had been invaded by cancer and her immune system had been overwhelmed by it.

Molecules, cells in the human body changed constantly, millions of them died and were replaced. Someone had told Sawyer once that it was a seven-year cycle. That it took that long for every cell in the body to be replaced by a new one just like it, so the person you were seven years ago, you literally were not that person anymore, had none of the cells in your body that you'd had.

The titans were altering the molecules that formed Ellie's cells, transforming Ellie back to a previous form, at a specific moment in time, the particular structure and nature of the molecules in her body as they had been *on that day*. And when the transformation was complete, Ellie Hampton would be the Ellie Hampton who had stepped off the helicopter seven years ago. Exactly, down to the last cell.

Chapter Forty-Five

PACO WAS ZONING, cruising, skirting through the minds of one person after another the way he hadn't done in years. He didn't know why, didn't question it, just put the pedal to the metal and roared on.

He now resided in the heads of dozens of people, just had to keep spinning those plates to stay there. Nudging them all into starting a riot. Speaking into all the minds at once:

THERE ARE *titans in the cave with us.*

THEN HE WATCHED THEIR REACTIONS. One man turned to another. "Did you know there are titans in the cave with us!"

The second man didn't believe. "Naaaa, that's crazy ... not in here—"

"Hell yeah, I *know*!" said a third man. "My brother seen 'em."

"How'd they get in here?" cried the second, the one who hadn't believed.

SAWYER, *Noah, Star, Eagle Feather … they hid the titans.*

"THE SHERIFF AND HIS BROTHER, the Indian — they're all in it together, hiding 'em from us!"

"Why would they do a thing like—?"

"They been running things like they own all of us, like we ain't got no say in what happens—"

A woman overhears and squeals, "Did you say titans — in *here?*"

"They're liars and sneaks," said the man who'd started it all, "smuggled titans in when we wasn't looking—"

"Titans — *titans!*" the woman wails.

FIND THEM. Stop them. *Kill them!*

"WE GOTTA FIND those motherfuckers and kill them."

"Where could they be?"

"Split up — look!"

"Tiiiiitans," the wailing woman never let up, and she wasn't even one of Paco's troops. "They're gonna butcher us all!"

Oh, this was so much fun! Paco didn't feel any pressure in his brain at all, just gliding through, like he was on ice. Himself spoke in his head, but Paco ignored him.

Well, you got part of that right, motherfucker. It is slick, but it's not ice. It's blood, you've sprung leaks everywhere.

While Paco had been spinning plates, Himself had

vanished, probably went back to wherever things that don't exist go. He had vanished because Paco's brain was functioning well now. It was working just fine! Himself wasn't a consequence of the damage to it anymore.

Wrong again, asshole. That's two for two. I am standing here in your brain right where I've always been. But funniest thing ... I'm ankle deep in blood. You better figure out a way to stick a finger in this dike, metaphorically speaking, or this shit's gonna get deep.

It was easier to ignore Himself when Paco could see him, could look at him, see that he was just an image of himself, like in a mirror, not real. But when he just popped up in Paco's head, it was harder—

Paco thought he heard a movement behind him. Ah, Himself had returned.

Paco turned toward the movement but it wasn't Himself standing in the entrance to the cavern. It was that man, Nick Wilson.

"Hey motherfucker," the man called out and then advanced boldly into the cavern. "That little girl you ran down, the child you butchered when you came roaring into town like the conquering horde, that was *my* little girl. Her name was Josie and she was just seven years old."

And for an instant, for a tiny split second, Paco wanted to apologize, to tell the man it'd all been a mistake, that he didn't know she was special, that if he'd known he wouldn't have touched a hair on her head, that he would have done anything to protect her, in fact, would have killed anyone who got near enough to harm her.

Only for a split second, though. Then it was gone. Replaced by self-preservation. Paco took the blame for this one without any prodding from Himself. This was what you got when you gave *anybody* a pass.

Paco had three, maybe four seconds to come up with a way to fight this man or he would be as dead as the little girl whose body had wrapped around the front tire of his motorcycle.

He leapt forward psychically, like one of those cliff divers from high off the rocks in Acapulco, plunged into Nick Wilson's mind.

And when he did, he felt an odd tearing sensation, like something inside him was ripping.

The images in the man's mind were raw and brutal. He had been a soldier, one of those special ops guys who didn't officially exist and did shit nobody was supposed to know about. And he had done some bad shit!

The images of dead bodies. Mangled men. Tortured …

A scorpion. It bloomed big and black and ugly *and beautiful* and Paco stepped into the image like sliding into the seat of a sports car. He revved the engine, so to speak, and then went after Wilson. He'd have this Nick fellow screaming in no time.

But he had to keep the plates spinning. Keep them spinning.

Nick had gone as white as a gym sock. He *believed* it was real. Hell yeah he believed, Paco's scorpion was huge and realistic and terrifying.

NOT JUST TERRIFYING BUT EXPENSIVE, *too. You have no idea how much that image is costing you, Paco, but any second now, you're going to find out.*

SPINNING. Spinning. There were other plates besides the scorpion, more going on than that one thing. The other minds, forty-seven of them, had to keep them spinning. Each one. Every one. Spiiiiiiin.

. . .

"YOU'RE TALKING NONSENSE, Sawyer wouldn't never—"

Paco nudged and his puppet turned and smashed a fist the size of a canned ham into the non-believer's face.

"Out of our way!"

"They're in Alabaster Hall!"

"They got a hundred titans in there — selling us out to the Astrals."

THE SCORPION WAS big and detailed, not just a flat image, and Paco had to move it, had to scare Nick with it ... but it was a little like one of those gigantic, dancing blow-up figures with a hole in the top. The only way it would keep its size and shape was for you to keep blowing air into it from the bottom.

And so Paco blew, pumped the image up, kept it there in the air in front of Nick.

And he kept the people whose minds he occupied angry, too.

The scorpion.

The people.

The scorpion.

The—

Then the imaginary mirror image of Paco let fly a peal of maniacal laughter so shrill it shredded Paco's eardrums. Paco grabbed hunks of his own hair to rip his head open so he could reach in and silence Himself.

Chapter Forty-Six

ELLIE WAS DEAD.

So how could she think she was dead if she was dead?

That wasn't circular logic, she didn't think. It made sense — what in her brain was left to know she was dead if she was dead?

What difference did it make?

Ellie had been having trouble remembering to breathe, and then she tried to look at her arm to see if it was spotting. Anna said that was part of active dying, the skin turning a mottled color.

But she hadn't seen any spots on her arm, not yet. She'd just as soon pass that one up anyway. Who wants to die spotted?

Then ...

Then she had the most amazing dream.

She dreamed Sawyer came to her, picked her up and carried her somewhere. And she'd felt light as a feather when he lifted her. But the pain came back, not all of it, but some, and she cried out. It had been so good not to feel

... though the feeling of pain this time was distant, like she didn't feel it all the way down.

That was an odd way to put it, but the pain was happening, and her body was responding, flinching away, and it hurt ... but there was a sense that only a small part of her was feeling the pain, was participating in the agony. She wasn't. The essential Ellie was just aware that she hurt, but it wasn't important. Nothing seemed important now because she was so sleepy.

Was that it? You just fell asleep? She wanted to fall asleep. She wanted ...

She forgot to breathe. And decided not to bother. It was a lot of trouble, breathing. In and out all the time. She let that part go, she let it all go and embraced the death she had looked forward to for so long.

She was dead.

Ellie was dead.

And it was true.

All the things people said about how your body was restored after death, how you became the person you once were, that you were ... what was it the Christians called it, living in a glorified body?

Brother Sebastian had talked to her about that when she had finally gotten around to talking to him about what was about to happen to her. Purportedly, anyway, he was the one person who could give her good insight, because he purported to know what happened after.

What happened *After.* The big question. The only important question, really. What happened to you after you died?

Well, Ellie was in After now. And she was aware only of good feelings, of returning strength.

She took a deep long breath and it didn't hurt taking it in and she didn't cough letting it out. It felt so good to breathe. And the tiredness, the overwhelming fatigue that made her limbs feel like they were made of anvils. It was gone.

Ellie was in After. And she *liked* After.

Shit, if she had known how good she would feel after she died, she'd have done it a long time ago.

That struck her as humorous, but not funny enough to laugh about.

She could hear sounds, conversation that she took to be people talking in her room after she died. She didn't listen to any of it. She was too busy enjoying how wonderful she felt.

A glorified body, that's what Brother Sebastian said would be given when she crossed over, when she went to heaven. She would be Ellie, but all Ellie was ever meant to be, no flaws or limitations.

Glorified.

She didn't want to open her eyes, though. That was the thing. She was afraid of what she might see if she did. What if she was in some terrible place, some horror, some hell? What if she really wasn't as she felt, that her body was rotted and decayed and her mind was just refusing to accept it?

She didn't open her eyes, but she did steal a peek out through a forest of lashes.

She was lying on the floor of the cavern. Why was she on the floor? She couldn't see much, but could hear the voices. The volume gradually turned up in her ears and—

"Ellie."

Her name. Someone had called her name. Not someone. Sawyer.

Was he here, too? How the fuck could Sawyer be here with her in After?

"Ellie, open your eyes. Look at me."

321

No.

Okay, yes.

Ellie opened her eyes, blinked and closed them again. Obviously, she was finally getting what she had wanted, the only thing she had wanted from the menu of active dying symptoms. A hallucination. She was hallucinating that she was lying on the floor with Sawyer bent over her in a room with … titans. Astrals.

No. Goddammit no.

There couldn't be Astrals in After. No!

After was for *people*, for humans, and those monsters had exterminated humans. How could they be here in After?

She opened her eyes and looked, actually looked into Sawyer's face.

"You look like shit on a cracker," she told him. Her mouth worked, voice was normal, it felt absolutely natural to speak. There was … nothing wrong with her. Not here in After.

There was an explosion of laughter behind Sawyer, and she looked to see …

Where the fuck was she? This couldn't be After. She was still in the damned cave.

"What am I doing in … no, what are *you* doing here? How can you be in After with me and why is After still in a cave?"

As she spoke, she rose to a sitting position, looked down and she was wearing the yellow dress Anna had put on her. But it didn't hang on her like a garbage bag. It fit! It fit in all the right places.

"You're alive."

That's all Sawyer said. There were others here. Star and Noah, Taylor, Eagle Feather, Fred, Jessica Maddocks and Garson. Why were they all dead?

"What do you mean I'm alive? I'm dead."

Sawyer laughed, tilted his head back and bellowed out a laugh so full of happiness and pure joy it warmed her all over.

"No, you're alive. And you got granted a do-over. Oh, how I wish I was the man I was seven years ago, but you *are* the woman."

Then they told her the tale. She sat up and listened, then realized it was stupid to sit on the floor and started to rise and Sawyer started to help her but she didn't need any help.

As they spoke, she held her arms out in front of her. No, not the mottled flesh of the dying. She … shit, she had a real tan, though, from being outside. Not a perfect tanning-machine tan. Still.

Her fingernails were polished, manicured.

She reached up then, and felt her face. Felt the softness of the skin. The smoothness of it. The firmness of it.

Dear holy God, it was true.

She turned then toward the titans. Five of them standing in the middle of the room.

She waited a moment for her emotions to resolve themselves. But there were no emotions to resolve. She hated them, loathed them, knew she should be profoundly grateful to them for giving her back her life, not just her life, but her *life*.

She didn't, though. She hated them on behalf of a soldier with beautiful blue eyes who had died so she could survive in a dumpster. Who had died with 21,000 other people.

"Fuck you," she snarled.

Then louder, "I don't care if you did heal me, fuck you!"

Sawyer took her into his arms and held her, hugged her

so tight she couldn't get her breath, but it wasn't the same kind of can't-get-your-breath as when your lungs are poisoned.

She was alive.

Holy shit she was *alive*.

And she was well.

She froze then, pulled back out of Sawyer's arms, and without embarrassment, unbuttoned the top buttons of the dress and reached through the opening, ran her hand over her skin and slowly lifted her fingers up to her breast. She hesitated, then resolutely felt the bottom portion of her breast, felt for the scar where the lump had been removed.

There was no scar. She felt around frantically on her other breast. No lump.

Oh, Jesus. There was no lump, no scar. She was well. She was healed.

She turned back to the titans ... tried to summon some shred of gratitude ...

No, it was useless. She didn't say it out loud this time, but she thought it. Fuck you!

And someone else was saying those words, or words to that effect. Someone was shouting them. A whole bunch of someones. As Ellie attended to her surroundings, she heard what'd been there in the background all along.

Out in the hallway leading into Alabaster Hall, a crowd had formed. A mob. A pissed-off mob, but maybe there wasn't any other kind.

Chapter Forty-Seven

HANK AUSTIN CAME RUNNING down the hallway to Sawyer, cast a glance at Ellie standing there beside him but clearly had no idea who she was.

"You gotta come, sheriff." Anytime one of the residents of Noah's Ark called him "sheriff," it was something bad. Oh, he'd heard the building rumble of angry talk out in the passageway, but he was choosing to ignore it for now. He didn't want to go anywhere. When Ellie had pulled out of his arms to feel if the lump was still there he had let her go, but only reluctantly. Now, he found that his arms ached to hold her. To touch her. He never wanted to let her go.

"They found out about the titans."

"Who found out?"

"*Everybody*. At least now it's everybody. It started out just a few knew but word spread."

Sawyer looked at Taylor, the question hanging between them.

How could anybody have found out about the titans? Nobody knew except the elders.

He looked around for Nick but he had not shown up

yet. Best not to take Garson out into this kind of fray. God only knew what he might say to set everybody off.

Sawyer and Taylor ran down the hallway with Hank to where Taylor's sons Sam and David stood with two other guards back from a "police line" tape they'd stretched between two empty flour barrels the monks had rolled into the passageway to get them out of the way. Sawyer had broken through the tape, but somebody had tied the broken pieces back together. An angry mob was on the other side of the tape, barely kept at bay by the threat of the deputies' rifles.

"Keep them out of Alabaster Hall," Sawyer told the deputies.

"How?" David asked. "If they're determined to go see, are we supposed to shoot them?"

"If you have to, yes, shoot them." But he knew as he said the words David wouldn't do it. He'd been willing to ambush Paco's men from the trees the day of the flood, but this was a bridge too far.

Then he turned and strode ahead with his brother at his side.

"What are you going to say to them?"

"Shit if I know."

But he did know. He was going to tell them the truth. All of it.

The narrow passageway was jammed! Hundreds of people, jockeying for position in front for the best view, angry and frightened. The low grumble turned ugly as soon as Sawyer came in sight.

Angry shouts came from all over the crowd.

"… all gonna die!"

"You got titans in there, doncha!"

"What's wrong with you? Why …?"

"They said they was more'n one of 'em."

"… gonna turn into reptars and kill us all …"

"My wife and kids is in there eating and you brought a—"

"Them titans is just waiting 'til you give them the signal and then they're gonna start ripping—"

"Shut up, Sid," Sawyer said, with sufficient menace to silence the man. In the breath of silence that followed, he called out.

"I need volunteers to be reasonable. Anybody here willing to volunteer to calm down for five minutes and listen to reason, to give me a chance to explain? I only need a few volunteers, come on … *somebody*."

The belligerence level of the crowd dialed down.

"You got titans in there, yes or no? That's all we wanna know."

Sawyer did not recognize the man who was speaking. How was it he didn't know the guy?

"And who are you?" Sawyer shot back at him.

Arnold Fletcher, a carpenter who'd helped construct the rafts to float supplies downriver, was standing next to the guy. Fletch backed up and took a better look. "Yeah, who the hell are you?"

The man got flustered, but had enough bluster to save the day.

"What difference does it make who I am? You need to be asking him" — he pointed to Sawyer — "who he is, or who he *thinks* he is bringing titans in here to kill us all."

"Obviously, you're not a volunteer," Sawyer said. "But the rest of you are, so let's be reasonable together. I want to tell you what we've discovered." He climbed up onto the top of one of the barrels and yelled out into the crowd. "Titans can't transform into reptars when they're surrounded by limestone. It's impossible."

That set off a bomb of grumbling and rumbling, fear

and confusion, a bubbling pot that any second would boil over.

"Listen! This is what we know and how we know it." As he began to explain, folks quieted to hear what he had to say. He told them about Noah, Astral Day, the impossible cavern, the mine and Noah's encounter with the reptars.

He was cashing in all his chips, here. Betting them all on one throw of the dice. Every bit of good will, gratitude, believability and understanding he'd accrued in almost twenty years of helping these people — he used it all.

"You sayin' them reptars attacked each other?"

"That's exactly what I'm saying — ripped each other apart. And we know why." He gestured all around him. "Limestone. Limestone causes feedback in their heads like the squawk of the amplifier used to do in the gym in Zion. Drives reptars crazy and blocks the titans' connection to the mothership."

Sawyer spotted Taylor's wife Kelly Jo in the crowd, motioned her forward and whispered something into her ear and Kelly Jo took out running back toward Alabaster Hall.

Sawyer continued the story, about planting charges to blow up the entrance to the mine, Eagle Feather, and about Garson finding the trapped titans when he went looking for a piece of mining machinery to study. He didn't mention the fact that Garson had hidden them and fed them — this crowd would never understand — just elaborated on Garson's explanation of "closed loops' and "feedback," drew it out slightly, gave more detail than he really needed to, so Taylor would have time to do what he instructed him to do.

"So limestone's kryptonite?" somebody asked.

Before he had a chance to answer, another question

came from a man in the back, who years ago had been one of the guides in Matheson Caverns.

"And so's gypsum — that's what you're saying, right?"

That's when the moth that had been flitting around in Sawyer's brain settled on the bulb. Gypsum. There was *no limestone* in Alabaster Hall. The crystalline palace was formed of flowering gypsum.

Sawyer couldn't get his breath for a moment, his mind stumbled and he grappled to find anything — *Garson knew that*, and if *he* wasn't worried about it … after all, the two were essentially the same rock. It was just that limestone was ugly and crystalline gypsum was beautiful, but the composition of the two was almost identical. Both were minerals that formed from calcium salts. Limestone was calcium carbonate rock and gypsum was calcium sulfate.

It was the *same thing*! It *was* … wasn't it?

He had no time to puzzle over it now. He had to finish the story, about how Noah and Star and Garson decided to bring the five titans before the elders … and about the elders voting to execute them.

"If you voted to kill them, why are they still in there?"

"Why haven't you shot the motherfuckers?"

"What were you waiting for?"

Taylor showed up right on cue. Ellie was beside him.

The gasps were slow in coming because for those who knew her well, had visited her as she declined, the transformation was so incredible they literally didn't recognize her. For those who didn't know her well, she was a face they'd seen around, and then she left.

"*Ellie?*" someone said.

"You can't be … are you Ellie Hampton?"

Then the wonder and joy and surprise and shock and all the other glorious emotions erupted from the crowd and the women who'd been her friends swarmed over her, touching her, running their hands through her hair, hugging her and crying. There were at least half a dozen women and every last one of them was bawling.

Before attention could return to what the riot had started over, Ellie asked Taylor to lift her up onto the other empty flour barrel beside Sawyer's.

"Can you hear me, back in the back?"

Now she could be seen by the whole crowd. In the form-fitting yellow flowered dress, she was so beautiful she took Sawyer's breath away.

"For those of you who don't know me, or don't remember me, I am Ellie Hampton. I have been sick ever since I got to Zion Academy, flew in on a helicopter on Astral Day. Breast cancer, and I've been fighting it for years. It was winning, though. I was dying. In fact, I thought I *had* died when I opened my eyes and saw ... this."

She held out both arms, then gestured down at her own body.

"Aw, come on, admit it. I am *smokin' hot*."

There was a stunned moment before the crowd roared with laughter.

She was a natural in front of a crowd. Who knew?

"So what happened to transform the dying shell of a woman, with no hair — and no hope — into this one, healed and healthy? The five titans in Alabaster Hall did."

You could have heard a mouse tiptoeing across a cotton ball in the shocked silence that followed.

"I was *dying*. Literally end-stage dying, vital organs shutting down and all that. And I was *glad*. I had been in such agony for years. But they made me ... *new*."

Sawyer didn't think anybody had breathed out the communal gasp they'd all sucked in when she said "five titans."

Ellie's gaze shifted to the left. He followed her look. Gretchen was there in the crowd alongside all the troublemakers.

He flashed on the poor donkey, but let it go.

Ellie suddenly jumped down off the barrel and pushed her way through the crowd toward Gretchen.

As soon as she no longer had their attention, the crowd began to heat up again. Sawyer didn't understand it. Every time he thought he had things calmed down, somebody would shout something incendiary and it was off to the races.

He fielded questions, one after another, fired by people who genuinely didn't understand but were trying to — but mostly by people who sounded like they were just trying to start a fight. His eye was ever on Ellie, though — yanked back like a fully extended rubber band. Ellie smiling, Ellie laughing, Ellie hugging Gretchen, Ellie *alive*.

With a great force of will, Sawyer remained calm and reassuring, trying to keep the crowd he'd talked off the ledge from leaping up and threatening to jump again.

"So you're saying we'd ought to give them their lives because they gave that woman back hers?" called out one of the men in the crowd who was unfamiliar to Sawyer. There seemed to be a disproportionate number of people out there in front of him who had been cave dwellers before Noah's Ark. "Well, sorry about your luck, lady, but they didn't give life to all the people out there they turned to black dust or drowned and I, for one, don't think one life for billions is an even trade."

"Nobody said anything about giving them their lives back," Sawyer said, taking control of the crowd once again. "I said I'd tell you everything that happened and I did. You asked why we hadn't killed them yet." He pointed to Ellie standing with Gretchen. "She's why. We gave them time to heal her."

Before anyone had time to mount a protest, he contained.

"Now, the decision of the elders *will be carried out!*"

That silenced the crowd.

"But we're not going to hand them over to a mob to tear them apart! They judged us inferior and we're about to demonstrate that we're lightyears ahead of them in what really matters. We'll give them the justice they wouldn't give us."

It appeared the fire was finally out, that Sawyer had extinguished the spark of "grab yer pitchforks, boys" before it could spread again, and he decided to quit while he was ahead.

"Go home," he said. Some people were already turning to leave, people with families.

"Let us—" His eye fell on a woman he knew to be a cave dweller, a tall, ugly woman with a voice like a crow, who was holding a baby — not newborn, but only a couple of months old. He intended to shut her up quick if she started instigating again, but she didn't. Instead, she dropped ... literally *dropped* her baby on the cave floor. Just dumped it out of her arms. Grabbing handfuls of hair on both sides of her head, she began yanking furiously, trying to pull it out as she shrieked maniacally. Then she launched herself at the woman beside her and started biting her face.

Between one heartbeat and the next, the woman had gone completely insane.

Chapter Forty-Eight

"*THAR SHE BLOWS!*" Himself cried in triumph, not just in Paco's head. He took control of Paco's voice and cried out loud, though the voice was clotted, like it came from somewhere underwater.

Say goodbye to Paco Salazar as you have always known him.

It felt like a pressure valve somewhere let go.

And I have brought a guest, flown here in secret from Hell itself, to give you a very special sendoff.

Suddenly, someone else was standing where Himself had been standing in Paco's mind. He had his back to Paco and there was something familiar about him but Paco couldn't quite track where …

He turned around. Vincent. Dead Vincent. Been-dead-for-years-and-years Vincent. The mouldering corpse that stood in front of Paco bore only enough resemblance to his friend for Paco to know who he was.

Rotted flesh hung in hunks from the bones of the arm of the figure standing in front of Paco.

Vincent.

His feet scraped along the rock, the bones digging small trenches in the rock face.

His face. Vincent's face. There were no eyes in the sockets of the white skull that rested on the spindle pedestal of bone that was his neck. The mouth still had teeth and lips and a tongue, however ... rotting. So falling apart that when he did speak, pieces of his tongue fell off and plopped on the floor and fat green worms crawled out of them.

"You *killed* me."

The words were the sound of rusty chains dragged over a metal floor. A horror of sound that tore at Paco's ears.

"Vincent ... they were going to take you to that place where your grandmother was ... remember, she showed you, human bite marks on her arm. You told me you'd rather die than be in a place like that — don't you remember? You have to remember."

"So you put a pillow over my face and I struggled and fought. Didn't that tell you something, asshole?"

He had struggled, had fought with incredible strength. Paco never thought to wonder why that was, why he would have fought if he was brain dead. But Paco thought about it now and the horror of the possibility ... the horror was more than Paco could stand. He put his knuckles in his mouth to silence the scream but it ripped out of his throat anyway.

"I wasn't brain dead. I knew everything that was happening, heard every sound and every word. Every day, I struggled, fought to come back, to climb back into control, to move a finger or something to signal that I was in there. I was in there *alive*. On Halloween, I moved a toe! Nobody saw, but somebody woulda noticed. A toe, then the leg, then … I would have fought my way back. I would have been fine."

Horror washed over Paco in waves.

"But you murdered me."

Then the spider appeared in the right eye socket of the skull, it crawled out, one black hairy leg at a time, and then crawled up to sit on top of the skull. The snake that slithered out of the left eye socket was a coral snake, alternating bands of red and yellow scales, just like he'd told the tattoo artist to make it.

Paco tried to make his legs stay upright, but his body didn't give a shit what he said anymore, and he sank to his knees.

"You stole my life, my future." Worms and bugs dribbled off Vincent's rotting tongue as he spoke. "I was going to join the Navy, see the world. You were my *friend*!"

On his knees, Paco was able to command his hands to reach down and lift his shirt, to show Vincent the tattoo of the spider and the snake, to prove to him that he loved him and had meant only to save him from a fate worse than death.

But when he looked down, the tattoo on his chest had come to life. Under his skin were spiders, dozens of spiders, hundreds, all of them trying to get out the hole in the skull on his chest, fighting to crawl out, biting him and each other, as the snakes were doing on the other side. Paco was screaming when Vincent got to him, when he lifted his hands and showed Paco the pillow he was carrying.

Paco felt himself shoved off his knees onto his back, felt a form hover over him.

Vincent lowered the pillow. And since he was above Paco, the hunks of rotted flesh, green worms and black bugs fell off and landed in Paco's open mouth as he screamed. The white came closer and closer to his face.

Something was grasping his neck, squeezing.

The pillow — he couldn't breathe.

His neck — he couldn't breathe.

And he felt a *pop*.

Not really much of a sound at all. Not an explosion. More the sound of a balloon. A small balloon from a child's birthday party.

The pop was Paco's brain exploding. The world turned red as his own blood drowned him

… as Vincent smothered him.

… as Nick strangled him.

Blood squirted out of his mouth, his eyes, his nose. The world was red as his brain was drowned in a tsunami that blew out all his higher-order thinking in an instant, blew apart everything about Paco that was Paco. Exploded the mind that could think and reason and left nothing behind except instinct.

Not just Paco's mind, though.

He had been connected psychically to forty-seven people. He had totally subjugated their wills to his. His mind was in control.

When Paco's mind exploded, that connection broke. But not before the minds of those forty-seven people exploded, too.

Chapter Forty-Nine

GRETCHEN STOOD FROZEN, watching Ellie's progress through the crowd. Then a little hole opened up among the people with Ellie on one side and Gretchen on the other, only a few feet apart. It felt like a thousand miles.

"Mother."

Just the one word. But she'd spoken it aloud, didn't sign it.

"Gretchen, I ..." Ellie spoke and signed at the same time, couldn't get out the rest of it. She was still getting used to ... no she would never get used to the new body she'd been deposited in. Never get used to or take for granted that she felt young and alive, alive, *alive*! She could laugh now, and nothing hurt. Nothing. *Nothing hurt*.

There was nothing to say or sign that mattered and Ellie merely flung herself at her daughter.

Gretchen stood stock still for a moment before returning her mother's hug and even then it was a moment before she matched Ellie's strength and intensity. But then she did hug. The young woman squeezed Ellie so hard Ellie thought her ribs would break.

"Mother," she kept crooning aloud, though she couldn't hear the word herself.

"Mother … Mother …"

Gretchen pulled back out of the hug, and began to sign. She didn't like speaking for the same reason most deaf people didn't. Of course, for her there had always been the added wrinkle that signing with Ellie was a bond to her mother that Diana didn't have. But now she was just signing furiously, faster than Ellie could keep up.

"Gone … you were gone … needed you but you were sick. Wanted you to sign me a story … you felt bad."

Then she stopped signing, put her head in her hands and sobbed.

Ellie wrapped her arms around her daughter and let her cry, realizing anew how profound an effect her illness had had on her little girl. She'd understood it at the time, of course, but couldn't do anything about it. It was what it was. Gretchen had been frightened by her mother's condition, afraid she would go away and never come back. And finding her mother expending precious energy on Diana when she had so little to give. It had at first made Gretchen angry. Then it had made her sad. Then it had sunk deep into her and poisoned the well there, changing the tenor of every thought and action, made her—

Gretchen suddenly got a funny look on her face, backed up and called out in her flat, nasal voice, "They've been hiding the titans from us and we had a right to know."

Where did *that* come from?

Actually, Gretchen seemed to feel a bit the same way because as soon as the words left her mouth, she shook her head, stared for a moment, then seemed to come back to herself.

"What happened to you, Mother?" She signed and spoke. "How—"

"The titans."

"Titans?"

"Did you hear Sawyer's story about the mine and Eagle Feather and Garson? It was all going on the past week when I was …"

Say it out loud to make it real. Then let it go.

"… *when I was dying.* I didn't attend to everything around me, caught pieces of it. The Astrals were mining limestone on the other side of the mountain and Garson said we had to seal the hole—"

Gretchen got an odd expression on her face and shouted, "Find them! Find the titans and kill them!"

Ellie was startled into silence. Then she said/signed tentatively, "What are you saying, Gretchen? Why are you …?"

Then the girl's expression shifted again, and she was just Gretchen — so thrilled to see her mother she couldn't quit touching her. "You're … you're … *you* again, Mother."

Ellie reached out and pulled Gretchen back into her arms and hugged her tight, tears running down her face.

"I'll be the mother of the bride on your wedding day. I'll hold my first grandchild. All the things I'd given up, knew I would not live to see, I'll—"

And then Gretchen did it again. Pulling away, her face changed and she took two steps and said to the women standing there, "They kept the titans a secret to use against us. What other explanation is there? We can't trust them. Can't trust any of them."

Ellie put her hand on Gretchen's shoulder and turned her around.

"What did you say? You can't trust Sawyer, Noah, Star … what are you talking about?"

Gretchen looked surprised, a little embarrassed.

"There was this … man. He looked Hispanic, good-looking, but … scary. He … talked to us."

"Us? Us who?"

"I'm not sure." Then Gretchen was all the way back, looked deep into her mother's eyes, connected with her, teared up again.

"I can't believe you're … you were so sick and now you're … well."

Ellie was seriously freaked out by Gretchen's behavior. Why was she … it was just the shock of seeing Ellie well — that's all. Your dying mother shows up breathing and smiling and healthy. That'd mess with your mind!

"Oh, Gretch, think about it. I get to watch you grow up. I get to see you and Diana become young women, beautiful—"

"Diana." Gretchen said that one word aloud, didn't sign it.

And at that moment the little girl appeared as if she'd been summoned. She burst through the crowd, looking for someone, glanced up at Ellie, looked at Gretchen — then her eyes snapped back to Ellie and grew wide with astonishment. Her mouth formed something like a little O, but she didn't make a sound.

"Mommy!" she squealed and she threw herself at Ellie, grabbed her in a hug so tight Ellie couldn't breathe.

"Haven't we already settled the Mommy thing?" Gretchen signed and the look, the awful, downward, dark visage began to eat up her face. Ellie could see her actually fighting against it, though, struggling. She kept looking at Ellie, gobbling her up with her eyes, like that was the salve that would heal all the wounds — Mother was going to live after all.

"Maybe we did." Ellie smiled as warmly as she could at

Gretchen, reached out and took her hand. "But now we're *un*-settling it. I'm your mother, Gretchen." Then she looked at Diana, "And I'm *your* mother, too."

Diana was dancing around on the spot with glee, heedless of Gretchen and her coldness, squealing, "Mommy, Mommy."

"That's me." Ellie tried to sound matter-of-fact, but so much was riding on Gretchen's response. So much. "That's the new normal. You both have a mother who loves you more than you can imagine."

She opened up her arms, and Diana cried, "Group hug!" The little girl leaned into it. After a second's hesitation, so did Gretchen. Maybe now they could start over. Now, they could—

Gretchen suddenly pulled out of the hug, and like some kind of sock puppet, called out, "If we don't kill the titans, they'll kill us."

It was like she was reading a script. And she was shouting. Out loud. Gretchen never spoke aloud if she could help it. Why now? Why this?

And she seemed to realize how odd it was, too, at least to some extent. She looked back at her mother, confused.

"I didn't say that," she said.

"Oh, yes you did!"

Ellie's confirmation frightened her. "No, I didn't. I wouldn't. I ..." Her eyes clouded and she spoke aloud, as if to herself — and Gretchen never *talked* to herself ... she was *deaf*. "He wants bad things to happen."

"Who does, sweetheart? What bad things? What are you talking about?"

"The dark-haired man, he wants—"

And then Gretchen ... left the building. Her face went slack, expressionless, her arms went limp and hung at her sides. It was like she'd been put into a sudden trance waiting for a magician to tell her to bark like a dog.

Her face was emotionless, totally without personality. Soulless. A mannequin. Her chin dropped down on her chest and Ellie reached out, cupped her chin and turned the girl's face up to hers.

"Gretchen, honey—"

Gretchen's face twisted into a mask of animal hatred and rage so deformed by lunacy that it wasn't even her face anymore. Ellie let go of her chin and actually took a step back.

Then Gretchen … *growled.* An ugly sound came from deep in her throat, no deeper, from somewhere in the depths of her chest, her heart, her soul.

She looked from Ellie to Diana. And she bared her teeth like a dog.

Ellie knew what she was about to do and before she had a chance to leap, Ellie shoved Diana violently away from her and cried, "Run."

Then she turned back to face a raging thing that happened to be residing in the body of her daughter.

Gretchen was not there anymore.

Chapter Fifty

SAWYER SUSPECTED that one day he would look back on the events of this day as the most amazing he had ever lived through, far eclipsing Astral Day, the day Noah was taken and the day he was returned. Not that he had great hopes to live long enough to look back on any of these days in the cave. Two astonishing, unexpected, without precedent in his or anybody else's lives events had occurred back to back in less than half an hour.

Ellie was healed. He hadn't wanted to let go of her hand when she spotted Gretchen in the crowd and rushed to her. He'd wanted to hold it, feel the plump, normal softness in a hand that only minutes before had been dry, bony and cold. Cold because she was dying.

Now she was Ellie. *Ellie!*

That was the good astonishing thing.

The bad astonishing thing was what happened to dozens of people — forty, maybe fifty of them. Random people. They were the people who'd been the most irate, the most belligerent when the near-riot broke out. Unreasonable, infecting others with their anger. But for all that, they were normal, ordinary men and women. He knew some of them as the cave dwellers who'd been here when Zion Village had come storming into the cave. Most hadn't been happy about it, but they'd settled into reality with mumbling and grumbling.

Those people had tried to get the others to stay and keep escalating their protest. Troublemakers.

Then his eye had caught the big, ugly woman holding the tiny baby. She'd been one of the troublemakers, kept trying to stir anger back into the crowd. He'd stared slack-jawed as the woman dropped her baby on the floor! Dropped it like was a grocery sack and began trying to pull her own hair out … right before she attacked the woman next to her — no weapon, just her own teeth.

Before he could react to that, he made eye contact with a woman named Norma Blackaby. She was built like a mailbox, but with an annoyingly high, squeaky voice. As he looked at her … something happened. All the expression drained off her face, her arms fell slack to her sides. He could see the same thing happening to others in the crowd, but his attention stayed focused on Norma's face. And it was clear from the look that came over it that Norma Blackaby had left the building.

There was nothing behind her eyes but blankness, and though whatever was wrong was clearly mental, her whole body responded to it, sort of collapsed on itself, a loss of muscle tone, though she remained standing. He wondered if she'd had a stroke.

Then something happened in her eyes, and what he saw there was primal, primitive, mindless fury. She tilted her head back and let out a scream, wild, Jurassic, more animal than human. So was her attack on the man standing next to her, who was in a grumbling conversation with two other men. She leapt on him in a wild animal rage that knocked him to the floor and then she tried to … rip him apart with her bare hands. She clawed at him, at his face and arms and hands with her fingernails, poked at his eyes, bit him. Tore a hunk of flesh out of his defending arms with her teeth, and all the while making a grunting, growling sound of some wild beast.

Between one heartbeat and the next, the crowd literally exploded into violent, bloody chaos. Everywhere you looked, the same scene was playing out. Men and women became … *animals*.

A man grabbed a young woman next to him and started ripping her clothes off, clearly intent on raping her right then and there. When her husband tried to drag him off her, the wild man leapt at him and tried to rip out his throat with his teeth.

All this happened in seconds.

Sawyer was rooted to the spot in horror, mindless horrible violence everywhere he looked.

Ellie!

Oh, dear holy God what had happened to Ellie?

In that moment, Sawyer Matheson finally let the mantel of "sheriff of McClintock County, Kentucky" fall off his shoulders and he never put it back on again.

Who could he reasonably be expected to save? He had wondered that on Astral Day a lifetime ago. Why, this one little community, he'd thought, and he had spent the past seven years doing just that, providing protection, order and the rule of law — even in the face of the end of the world.

Now, he leapt down off the empty flour barrel, a man intent on finding the woman he loved and protecting her, protecting all the people he loved. Everybody else in Noah's Ark, well, they were on their own.

That's when somebody noticed the pile of tobacco sticks.

They'd been lying in the corner gathering dust since Astral Day, awaiting a work crew to use them to construct a wooden tabletop on the long registration counter. Most were about five feet long, cut thin enough to fit comfortably into a man's hand. *Sharp on one end.*

As Sawyer bullied his way through the hysterical people, he watched Basil Stonewall die just four feet away. Freddie Pence had picked up a tobacco stick and plunged the pointed end into his chest like a spear. Sawyer became aware that his gun was in his hand, though he had no memory of pulling it from its holster, and when Freddie yanked the bloody stick out of Basil's chest, his eyes like a crazed animal, and turned to use the weapon on Basil's wife, Sawyer shot him in the back, point blank, from a range of ten feet. He dropped like a stone.

The gunshot caused a heartbeat pause. The sound — the understanding that somebody had a gun in here and was using it! — caused a frozen tableau that didn't last more than two seconds, then the riot took up where it had left off and Sawyer clawed his way to the back of the crowd to where he'd last seen Ellie.

Chapter Fifty-One

EAGLE FEATHER and the others could hear the growl of an angry crowd outside in the hallway, down the cavern at the entrance of the branch that lead to Alabaster Hall. The louder shouts were audible, too.

"They're pissed because we didn't tell them about the titans," Taylor said. "Shit, we just found out ourselves."

"They're pissed at the titans," said Fred. "As well they should be. We should feed them to that cougar out prowling around looking for food. Hope it likes white meat."

"The cougar is dead," Taylor and Eagle Feather said at the same time.

Eagle Feather was uneasy. "It sounds ugly out there."

The five titans were standing on the western side of the room close to the hole in the wall they had dug/melted to get into Alabaster Hall from their mine. Shirley and Curly — had Garson thought those names through before he adopted them? — were standing together closer to the hallway that led into the rest of the caverns. Just standing, their arms at their sides, identical blank looks on their faces. No, they weren't exactly blank. In fact, if Eagle Feather'd had to guess, he'd say there was more individuality to their blank looks than to any of the hive mind's other cookie-cutter participants. They'd gotten infected with human individualism.

Eagle Feather and Taylor made their way to the back of the room on the side opposite from the hole into the mine, where they could get a better angle to see out into the winding hallway. Star, Noah and Garson followed.

Brother Sebastian was near the entrance to the cavern, talking to Kelly Jo and Anna, who had been slapped down so profoundly by the healing of Ellie Hampton she couldn't seem to draw in a whole breath. Fred looked like all he asked of life at that moment was a place to sit down.

When the human explosion happened, geography in Alabaster Hall mattered, because those out front got mowed down.

Suddenly, a man covered in gore came barreling down the hallway toward the chamber and without even breaking stride launched himself at Samuel Matheson, stationed as a guard just outside. Even though Sam had a rifle, the man had taken him so totally by surprise, Sam fell backward with the man on top of him. Out of nowhere the man produced a stick, pointed, a tobacco stick. The pointed end was bloody and he lifted it high into the air and without the slightest hesitation plunged it down into Sam's chest.

Kelly Jo saw it all, screamed, shrieked. David launched himself at the man and knocked him off Sam's body and the two of them grappled for the stick. In seconds, the riot out in the hallway mowed down the deputies and bubbled over into Alabaster Hall and the room began to fill with people, an outlandish mismatch of predators and prey. People were running in terror from other wild-eyed people who seemed bent on killing everybody in sight. It was utter pandemonium.

Noah had heard Kelly Jo's scream through Star, was looking around, trying to locate where — but Eagle Feather grabbed him by the upper arm and shoved him toward the back wall. He staggered, didn't understand.

"The Library Aisles!" Eagle Feather cried. "Get Star into a narrow one and go back as far as you can."

He shoved Noah toward the wall opposite the opening into the Astral mine, kept his eyes shifting from one part of the deadly brawl to another, his knife drawn as their only defense, as he backed up after the others.

The carnage all around was swift, brutal. They hadn't even made it to the Library Aisles when a woman with a bloody stake in her hand rushed at the titan nearest the hallway entrance. Curly, the smaller male, was standing passively with Shirley when the woman ran up to him and stabbed him in the chest, lodging the spear deep into his body, laughing in animal-like hysteria.

The titan collapsed dead on the floor.

Anna began to scream when a man leapt on her and started tearing at her clothes. He was literally foaming at the mouth.

Bam! A gunshot sounded, but it was out in the hallway. Nobody in Alabaster Hall was armed now except David Matheson. He hadn't fired, though. Eagle Feather last saw him in the hallway entrance fighting the man who had killed his brother, with Kelly Jo trying to help.

Taylor had been at the back of Alabaster Hall when the world exploded, but Eagle Feather couldn't see him at all now.

Star and Pumpkin got to the Library Aisles first and she turned sideways to squeeze between the shiny crystal walls and wedge herself into the back. There was not even enough room to turn around. Noah shoved Garson in behind her. Eagle Feather intended to position himself in front of the fissure with a knife to defend those hiding inside, but before he could push Noah through the opening, Noah turned away and raced into the fray.

Two crazed people leapt on Shirley, brought the female titan down like wolves bringing down a deer, and began to tear at her with their bare hands. Biting, going for her throat.

What the fuck was going on here?

Garson was in analytical mode, engrossed in observations and evaluations — with no apparent fear that Eagle Feather could see. Either he was braver than Eagle Feather would have suspected or dumber.

Dumber.

No, he just didn't attend to the situation as "danger" because he was too busy examining and analyzing it.

"The id — they're operating on primal urges," he said, as if that made any sense at all to Eagle Feather. "Animals, don't you see. Something destroyed their superegos and they have nothing regulating their primitive blood lust."

Star cried out, "Noah, come back!" and Eagle Feather knew the out-loud words were instinctive shouting, that she was yelling for Noah much louder *inside* her head.

Fred went to Anna's aid, uselessly pounding his fists on the back of the man who was now on top of her, struggling with her clothes while she writhed and screamed. Some unknown man in the crowd kicked the would-be rapist hard in the side of the head and he dropped, unconscious on top of her. Anna shoved the body of the rapist off hers and with Brother Sebastian's help staggered to her feet.

The struggling female titan was no match for the ferocity of her attackers, crazed maniacs. She tried to fight them off but the man who had jumped on her, bit through her neck with his teeth!

She made choking, gurgling sounds as blood gushed out the gory wound. The remaining three — Moe, the largest male, Larry and Laverne were near the mine entrance and something was happening to—

Jesus, they were turning into reptars.

The white-skinned titans were bending at the waist, touching their hands to the ground, beginning to change. Eagle Feather watched their limbs elongate. Their movements become more like an insect. They grew the long torsos of animals, their skin now black scales laced with a haunting blue glow. All three titans in the hall turned into reptars in seconds, beasts with mouths with rows upon rows of needle-tipped teeth, arranged in concentric rings.

"Papa Eagle Feather, help Noah!" Star cried. "It's Taylor!"

Eagle Feather looked around, frantically searching for — and saw Noah dragging the body of his uncle across the floor toward the crevice. Eagle Feather took a single step in that direction and a man appeared between him and Noah, swinging his bloody tobacco stick back and forth, maniacal glee on his blood-covered face. He lunged with the stick like a sword, Eagle Feather sidestepped and buried his knife in the man's belly, ripped the knife sideways and let the man fall. Reaching down, he grabbed the man's stick, turned, stepped backward three or four steps and shoved it toward Garson, who took it like Eagle Feather was handing him a dead mouse by the tail.

The Indian sheathed his knife and ran to Noah. Blood was streaming down Taylor's face from a nasty scalp wound, and he was only semi-conscious. Eagle Feather grabbed Taylor's other arm and dragged him to the crack. They'd have to get him on his feet ... Noah grabbed his uncle under the arms, hauled him upright in a single motion and stepped into the fissure, dragging Taylor, staggering along with him. It was too narrow inside the crack for Taylor's body to collapse. Garson dropped the stick and pushed Taylor farther, Noah pulled from the other side and they got him inside. Garson turned sideways to slide in behind him.

Now, there was no room for Eagle Feather.

Turning his back toward the crevice, he pulled his knife and swung it back and forth in front of him.

"Scoot back," Garson grunted at the others, shoving Taylor farther into the crack. "*Back!*"

"It gets bigger at the end," Star cried.

Garson reached out and grabbed Eagle Feather's arm.

"Come on, there's room!" he said.

Eagle Feather turned sideways and wedged himself into the narrow opening between the crystalline walls until he was deep enough that it would be hard to get to him — then Garson pulled again, he stepped sideways another couple of feet and now he was back so far that anyone who had in mind to attack him, and those behind him, would have to face his knife in a close fight.

The opening was too narrow for a reptar to fit. He hoped.

And from the tenor of the screaming in Alabaster Hall, the titans' transformations were complete. He heard a rough, purring sound, but could see only the slice of the world visible between the two walls of the crevice ... and he was not inclined to move forward for a better view. He knew the sound, though. And when a headless body dressed in a brown monk's robe flew across the room and landed with a sick thud against the far wall, he knew the reptars had set about conducting business.

He heard a woman shrieking and the voice of the old

man, Fred Schwartz, screaming obscenities before his cries were suddenly cut off.

"My fault," Garson said. Eagle Feather didn't turn his head to face him, but his voice sounded utterly devastated, cast against a backdrop of dying screams. "Alabaster Hall is lined with gypsum, not limestone. Calcium sulfate and calcium carbonate have almost the same configuration of atoms and I never dreamed they wouldn't have the same effect ... the feedback in the Astrals' hive mind ... I should never have brought them—"

"They'd have cut their way out of that mine eventually." Eagle Feather said. The old Indian gestured out into Alabaster Hall, where they could hear the carnage. "None of this is your fault. Everything bad that has happened on this planet for seven years, *they* did it. We're just doing the best we can to survive!"

The mindless wack-jobs were now meeting their fate in the meat grinder that was the knife-lined mouth of the Astral killing machines. The nutcases went after the reptars as recklessly as they had the titans. No fear. No acknowledgement of any kind of higher-order thinking. And the reptars returned in kind and slashed them into bloody hunks of unrecognizable flesh.

It began to dawn on Eagle Feather the position he'd gotten them into. They were safe from the reptars stuck here in Alabaster Hall that couldn't leave. If the beasts stepped out into the limestone mine or the limestone passageway, they'd have that feedback thing going and they'd go crazy.

The reptars couldn't leave this room. And as long as the reptars were there, Eagle Feather, Garson, Taylor, Noah, and Star couldn't leave the room, either.

Chapter Fifty-Two

SAWYER COULD NO LONGER SEE Ellie and her daughter in the crowd, a crowd gone wild crazy where people were literally ripping others apart with their bare hands. He pushed a fat man violently out of the way and without even breaking stride, slammed his pistol into the side of the face of a man who had something ... he had bitten a piece of somebody ...

And there they were. It took a full second for the magnitude of it to sink in. Ellie backing away. Gretchen in front of her, ready to pounce like a lion. He knew he wouldn't get there in time, but he cried out.

"Gretchen, no. Stop!"

Even though he knew the girl was deaf and wouldn't hear the cry, Ellie would and did. She'd know he was coming. Shoving people out of the way, scrambling, clawing, he pushed his way through a glut of three terrified people literally holding onto each other and screaming.

Then Gretchen leaped. She was as graceful as a cat, and Sawyer thought of the big predator mountain lion Eagle Feather had tracked down and killed, the one

Gretchen had sacrificed Diana's pet donkey to. He was sure the lioness had looked no more feline, graceful or deadly than Gretchen when she leapt across the space between them, shoved her mother aside with a backhand that caught Ellie in the face and sent blood squirting from her nose.

Ellie wasn't Gretchen's prey. Diana was.

And Sawyer felt like he had the day the Astrals took Noah. He'd dived for Noah then, too, and his hands had come up empty. He didn't make it this time either, but he got closer, close enough to get a hank of Gretchen's hair and yank her head backwards seconds before she would have seized Diana's throat. Not to strangle her. To break her neck.

Gretchen was crazed, had the strength of some monstrous super-being. Sawyer didn't let go of her hair, but she yanked her head sideways and ripped the hair and a piece of her scalp off with it as she flung him aside, murderous intent in every syllable of her body language. The glancing blow sent Sawyer sprawling on the floor, sliding. He was turning as he slid, grabbed for his pistol.

It wasn't there.

He had hit the man with the pistol and then returned the gun to its holster, but it was gone now. He scrambled to get up, knowing without looking that Gretchen had reached Diana, had grabbed her by the throat and would snap her—

There was a gunshot, the report so close to his head …

He watched Gretchen pause.

It seemed she hung there in space for a long time, suspended between one reality and another. Then she crumpled to the cavern floor.

Who? What the—?

Ellie stood with the pistol in her hand that had slipped

out of Sawyer's holster. She had picked it up, turned it on her own daughter, and blew most of the back of her head off. She was rooted to the spot, and Sawyer knew her mind had gone into an adrenaline loop, that she wasn't able to think for herself right now.

Diana had been knocked off her feet and he pulled her up. The child was crying, horrified and apparently right now couldn't talk. So she signed.

Why did she do that? Why did she want to hurt me?

And Sawyer realized the child could sign, had always been able to sign, but had let that be a special thing between Gretchen and her mother.

"She was crazy, sweetheart. She couldn't think."

He reached out and gently pried the pistol out of Ellie's hands and returned it to his holster. Chaos reigned around them still, screaming, blood, horror and insanity.

Something else, too. Ellie heard it first, her head snapped that way and her eyes grew huge. There was a rattling sound, then a purr. Something sucking, and the clack of claws on rock.

The titans were now reptars.

Sawyer grabbed Ellie's hand and wrapped it around Diana's and shifted into combat mode. Any soldier knows what the shift feels like and no matter how long ago you served, the way of thinking returns in a heartbeat.

There are only two kinds of soldiers here, private — the quick and the dead. Which are you?

The quick, sir!

That was combat mode. The narrowing of vision, the survival instinct turned up to maximum power, your head on a swivel, your danger antenna working like an ant's. The adrenaline dump into your brain as pure instinct — fight or flight — took over. And compartmentalizing. The bad that happened, the horror of it, all the emotional wires disconnected. You stuffed that away for later. Somebody got killed — into a compartment. You killed somebody — into a compartment. You'd think about it sometime, maybe remember every detail and maybe nothing but the essential truth of it, but you did not engage with sorrow at the time.

The quick and the dead. Which are you, private?

The quick, sir!

In combat mode, you made decisions in a nanosecond, based on whatever information you had. If you were right, you survived. If you were wrong, you might make it, but not likely. And two bad decisions in a row — toast.

They had to move now. Ellie and Diana were totally at the mercy of the mindless murdering maniacs and he had to get them out of the crowd and to safety. But to do that, he had to run *toward* a reptar. Correction: three reptars in Alabaster Hall.

Where his brother, his son … where all the other people in the world he cared about were—

Let it go.

Reptars, not titans, which meant they'd shifted. Then the tiny niggling itch of what's wrong with this picture finally got scratched. *Gypsum.* Not limestone. The titans wouldn't have transformed into reptars knowing they'd just tear each other apart. But they also knew they were in Alabaster Hall, shielded by the alabaster from the insanity-inducing limestone.

"Stay with me, understand?"

Ellie just looked at him, blood dribbling down her upper lip where Gretchen had hit her.

"Ellie!"

When her eyes met his again, she was *there.*

"No matter what happens, stay with me."

He saw something change in Ellie's eyes, too, or thought he did. A hardness came into them, and he remembered that she and Diana's mother had been the only two survivors when the Astrals massacred twenty-one thousand soldiers at Ft. Knox seven years ago.

"Go!" she said, and he turned and started battling his way through the crowd of insanity, back toward the Alabaster Hall tunnel — and beyond it. The only safe place in all of Matheson Caverns right now was on the other side of the Drawbridge door.

The others would go there to Home Base, too, when they could. They would. *They would!*

Chapter Fifty-Three

EAGLE FEATHER and the others were wedged so back far in the Library Aisles he could see only a thin slice of Alabaster Hall. That was enough. Like everyone else on the planet, Eagle Feather had seen news footage of the creatures, the monster death machines called reptars, had watched a live real-time report where there were closeups of the creatures ripping people apart ... until they ripped the cameraman apart. But even with a mind image of them, nothing could prepare a human being for anything so totally foreign. It wasn't some movie animation. He watched one flash across his field of vision. Huge, the size of a moose. If the proportions remained the same after the shapeshift, the big one was the titan Moe as a reptar. Did the reptar have the titan's memories? Did he recall at all that Garson had fed them and brought them water? Maybe.

But if they did, they also remembered that the elders had voted to kill them and the outbreak of — whatever it was — was the only thing that'd saved them.

The claws of the reptar tapped like women in high

heeled shoes on the polished floor of Alabaster Hall, the bodies of beasts, with movements like an insect. The smaller one — either Larry or the female, Laverne — came into almost full view, far enough away from the crack to see all of her. She held a screaming, kicking woman in her claws and she opened her mouth to reveal row upon row of needle-tipped teeth, arranged in concentric circles. Her jaw unhinged and then flattened out and she shoved the woman's whole upper body into it, and then bit down. Eagle Feather would have turned his face away if he could have moved his head that far. He settled for closing his eyes, but listening to the sounds was its own horror. They moved like insects, on too many legs — how many? He didn't know. But they didn't race forward like a cockroach caught in the glow of the kitchen light. They scuttled forward and then stopped, then made another movement. Like a spider, defending itself from attack.

Eagle Feather had heard of the armor plating that covered their bodies, but up close it didn't look as fearsome as it had seemed. Just ebony scales configured like a suit of armor on the beast. The carapace might not have looked substantial, but he recalled Ellie's nightmare description of the massacre at Ft. Knox. How soldiers fired everything they had at the beasts and the bullets bounced off the armor with little sparkling lights. The skin beneath the armor plating gave off a blue glow.

Suddenly, a claw on an insectile arm shot through the opening in front of Eagle Feather and he cried out in fear and surprise. The claw was razor sharp and attached to legs that looked like swords. He heard the sucking sound and a gurgle as the talon on the end stretched out toward him.

"Back up," he cried.

But Star was at the end of the crack, up against the

wall and the others were scrunched up against her as tight as they could.

The claw reached out and fell short by maybe twelve inches. The creature clawed out again, and came a little closer, but only marginally. The base of the appendage was too large to fit between the rock sides of the crevice.

The claw disappeared and was replaced by a face, horror too awful to consider, too monstrous to behold. Dual sets of eyelids over eyes with irises that changed colors, shifted from yellow to green to blue and then to brilliant red, perhaps as an indication of the attack status of the creature.

Maybe you could tell by the colors if the thing was pissed. He heard an inhaling, grating rattle, something wet and slurpy turning into a gurgle. Something about the beast was sucking, you could hear the awful slurpy sound, some internal organ, sucking in the remains of humans the beast ate.

The face jammed into the crack roared, its breath the smell of blood and some other odor unidentifiable that Eagle Feather suspected did not come from this world at all. It roared, pieces of tissue and bone shards flying out of its mouth like somebody spitting when they talk. In its eye was rage. The creature knew he could not get to the humans. It wouldn't fit into the crack and couldn't reach far enough into it to snag one.

It roared again, then stepped back and the face vanished. That's when Eagle Feather knew it was the female, Laverne, because the other two reptars he could see mowing down the humanity at the opening of the hall were larger. Which meant they were safe here. Laverne had the smallest body. If she couldn't jam her — what was the name of where the appendage joined her body under the armor — shoulder? If she couldn't fit hers far enough into the crack to reach them with her talon, the other two bigger creatures couldn't reach them either.

"What's happening?" Star cried. Only Garson, who was directly behind Eagle Feather could see anything at all and it was precious little. Eagle Feather was a big man, jammed tight, leaving little space to look past him. Star and Noah could see nothing at all.

"The reptars are … killing the people in the room. But there are crazy people, the ones who attacked them — they're not running away, they're running toward the reptars, trying to attack them, rip at them with bare hands and the reptars are … tearing them apart."

"*Everybody* in the room?"

It was Taylor's voice. He'd come around, had reached up and was trying to swab the blood off his face.

Eagle Feather paused.

"Sam and David and Kelly Jo are out there!" He would have shoved his way out into the open to help them if he hadn't been jammed so tight in the crevice.

The volume of screaming in the room reduced drastically, then stopped altogether. Either the reptars had killed all the nearby humans or the people had managed to make it out into the hallway and escape. There was no sound but the growling, gurgling and sucking sounds the beasts made, and the purr. A giant cat.

"Why is it quiet?" Garson asked.

"They're all dead, everybody they can get to." He heard Taylor gasp. "Some people ran out into the hallway and got away. The reptars are just standing there in the hallway entrance."

The beasts paced back and forth, almost like lions in a cage at the zoo. And Eagle Feather suddenly had a horrible thought.

"Limestone … their kryptonite blocks titans' communication with the mothership and makes reptars crazy, but here in Alabaster Hall—" Star figured out where he was going and answered the question before he had a chance to answer it.

"No. If they had hooked up to the hive mind in the mothership when they got to Alabaster hall, I'd know."

"So there must be limestone above the gypsum in the roof of Alabaster Hall, beneath the sandstone cap on the top of the ridge," Garson said. "Apparently the limestone has to be exposed to do its job."

Suddenly the three reptars stopped pacing.

Laverne, the smallest, took a tentative step out into the hallway.

Eagle Feather couldn't help a gasp.

Then another step. She moved slower than he'd ever seen a reptar move, almost carefully, the way you'd walk across a frozen pond you weren't certain could bear your weight.

"She's … *going out into the hall.*"

"She who?" Garson asked.

"The smallest, the one you called Laverne. She's sort of inching her way out into the hallway."

"But she can't. As soon as she's surrounded by the limestone, the feedback will start squawking in her head."

Like she'd heard his words — and shit, maybe she had — she began to shake her head back and forth. Wag it like there was something going on in there that was … at the very least distracting and unpleasant. She took another step, though. Then another. Not moving fast and sure and like a scuttling spider, but moving, walking on all those legs.

"*Grumphdh,*" Laverne *said.* The sound came out her mouth — so that was speaking, a word, wasn't it?

"I didn't think they could talk," Eagle Feather sputtered.

"Why talk when your thoughts are in each other's heads?" Garson said. "But clearly they *can* speak."

"That's it, then," Noah said. He used his own voice so seldom it was possible to forget he could talk, too. "They are talking out loud — some kind of *language* — because they've unhooked from each other's minds to prevent the feedback."

The reptar moved on down the hallway. Slowly, not quite staggering, but close. And resolute.

"And from the look of her, unhooking is hard to do," Eagle Feather said.

Laverne turned her head back toward the other two reptars standing in the entrance to Alabaster Hall.

"*Druundletes.*" It must have been a word, though it was one no human mouth and throat could have produced. The voice was deep, rumbling, like the purring sound the reptars made when they killed. It was just a sound, though, as devoid of tone and expression as an automated attendant.

The big reptar, the one called Moe, began to move slowly out into the cavern behind Laverne. He stepped back momentarily, like he'd put his toe into cold water and was reluctant to dive in. Then he plunged ahead, wagging his head from side to side as if there were bees inside his skull.

"What's happening?" Garson cried, like a little kid. "Can you see what they're doing?"

"They're leaving," Eagle Feather said.

Chapter Fifty-Four

SAWYER HEARD a gunshot echoing in the cave. Clearly, not everyone had obeyed his directive to surrender their firearms before they came inside. Good. The crazy people weren't using weapons, just knives or clubs or their bare hands. If someone was firing a gun, it was somebody defending themselves against the people monsters.

He had made it through the thickest part of the crowd, dragging Ellie and Diana behind him, when a smallish woman came out of nowhere, just came running through the dispersing crowd, going against the flow of people away from Alabaster Hall.

She was waving a pipe and ran at the first person she saw — Jocelyn Conner. Jocelyn had worked in the surveillance room in Zion Academy and later in Zion Village. She was helping an older man with a limp flee down the corridor, but he wasn't getting along very fast. The woman with the pipe was making for them, howling a sound that was like a wolf's growl, only more squeaky.

Sawyer would have sworn he had never seen the woman before in his life. She lifted the pipe to bury it in

Jocelyn's head and Sawyer fired, dropped her to her knees, then she fell over and was still.

"Why?" cried the old man, probably Jocelyn's father. "What's happening? Why are they—?"

"I don't know," Sawyer said. "Figuring out why is for later." He spoke to Jocelyn, "Hide! Find somewhere, anywhere and stay hidden until I flash the lights. Don't come out until then."

"What are *you* going to do?"

He didn't know until he heard the answer come out of his mouth.

"I'm going to hunt down every crazy person in these caverns and kill them," he said. "Now go."

And that was the plan that was forming in the back of his mind that he was ignoring — except not. He had guns and ammunition. Even if they were completely nuts, the crazy people didn't seem to be armed, or if they were, only with primitive weapons. It actually appeared that they had … regressed to the point they couldn't even operate a gun. Hand them a rifle and they'd use it as a club.

Sawyer needed to find Nick, hoped he'd be at Home Base when he got there. Then Sawyer had to find the others, who might still be in Alabaster Hall. Or not.

They'd been there when the shit hit the fan. Now, they were either already dead or they had gotten away. Maybe they'd leapt through the hole the Astral mining equipment had dug in the wall. Once in the mine, there'd be limestone to protect them — from the reptars, anyway. Or maybe they'd made it out into the hallway, or hidden … shit, they could have hidden in the Library Aisles. But wherever they were, they were beyond his help now. Their fate had already been decided.

He had to go after the maniacs, find them, kill them, and then figure out what the fuck to do with the three reptars trapped in Alabaster Hall. The titans were easy. They would simply have executed them. He hadn't figured it out completely in his head how it ought to be done, but it would have been possible to do any number of ways. Probably a bullet to the brain, but he hadn't gotten that far.

But what about *reptars*? The monsters were trapped, so he could sit in the hallway outside Alabaster Hall with a rifle and a box full of ammunition. Shooting ducks in a washtub. Eventually, he supposed, if he fired enough shots, he'd eventually hit an eye, or a place between where the plates fit together. But the thought was utterly horrifying. Everything was horrifying since he discovered they were sharing Noah's Ark with the enemy who was trying to eradicate all humanity.

Noah's Ark.

Noah.

He was fine. Not now. *Noah. Was. Fine!*

The three of them ran past the nearest opening, the cavern called Pot Belly that angled north, and continued down Broadway. They turned into Chisholm Trail, and ran down it past the spot where it intersected Blind Alley and Chisolm South to the cavern where the Drawbridge doors were located — appropriately named Kaboom. They passed fewer and fewer people as they ran. They could hear distant screaming. Even gunfire.

They arrived, panting and sweating, in front of the Drawbridge Door that opened into the cavern where the ammunition factory had been. It required the fingerprints of *two* elders to open the lock — which had sounded like a good idea at the time. But now … There was a workaround that involved touching different parts of the door in a particular sequence, but he'd have to get his breath and calm down to remember it.

Sawyer turned to Ellie, standing beside him catching

her breath, and the shock of seeing her took his breath away. She was here, she was alive and well and … he had not had nearly enough time to engage with that reality, too much had happened since then.

Still, he just stared at her, said nothing, just stared.

She was scanning the corridors looking for lunatics and her eyes came to rest on his face. She froze there, too.

"Me neither," she said, still getting her breath. "And maybe none of this is real, maybe you can stop rushing around trying to save everybody because this is just the final hallucination of a dying woman. Anna told me that one of the stages of *active dying* …" — she paused, seemed to savor the words — "was hallucinations. Maybe that's all this is. If it is, I hope I die all the way before I wake up."

"It's real," he said. And he took her into his arms and kissed her. He didn't intend to, had no mind to do a thing like that here and now. It had just happened, kissing her had become as essential to his survival as taking the next breath. Without it, he would die.

She melted into his kiss—

"Anybody want to tell me what the fuck's going on?"

Nick's voice boomed out behind them. Sawyer and Ellie reluctantly pulled apart. When they did, Nick leapt back, his face suddenly white and for a moment Sawyer and Ellie didn't know what was wrong.

"What the … how did …?"

"Oh, this," Ellie said, still breathless, from running or from the kiss. Sawyer couldn't tell. She gestured down at herself. "It's just an old rag I picked up at Walmart. You like it?"

He stumbled another step backward. His eyes were huge.

"The titans did it," Diana told him, startling Sawyer. In his moment of passion Sawyer had all but forgotten the little girl was there, that they had been dragging her along with them at a dead run. "They were a hive mind and they did something with moles and cubes."

"Molecules. They did something to my brain on a molecular level."

"How did—?"

"Explanations later. We have to get them safe in Home Base. Now that you're here, I can open the door." He pressed his thumb to the fingerprint reader, Nick did the same, and something inside the door clunked as the lock disengaged.

"Where have you been?" Sawyer demanded.

"Killing Paco."

Chapter Fifty-Five

EAGLE FEATHER COULD HEAR the sounds moving away from Alabaster Hall, the horrified screaming and the massacre that was sweeping through the cavern as the reptars proceeded. They couldn't stay hidden in here forever. They needed to get to Home Base. The others would be there if they ... the others *would* be there.

"We aren't planning on staying here all day, are we?" Garson offered. "I am an old man with a weak bladder."

Noah heard the remark through Star's brain.

"Needing to pee got me into shitload of trouble in this cave once."

Eagle Feather marveled at the resilience of the human spirit. The few remaining people on planet Earth were tough. Their relentless fight for survival had built into them a strength none of them even realized they had.

Inching slowly out of the crack, he told the others, "Stay here. Far back. Leave me room to dive back in."

They all remained in place as Eagle Feather ventured out into the battlefield carnage that now littered Alabaster

Hall. There were … he looked around, didn't count, at least twenty people lying dead or dismembered.

Taylor's sons and wife lay among the fallen. So was Fred. But he didn't see Anna. Perhaps she made it.

And two titans sprawled in their own blood, which was an odd shade of dark purple.

There was nobody to save here. Nobody to rescue. Everybody was dead.

He edged along the rounded walls of the Hall, ready at any moment to make a dash for one of the cracks. It might not be impossible now to outrun a reptar. Hard, but maybe not impossible. Unless Garson was wrong in his interpretation of why the reptars had been able to leave the haven of gypsum out into the limestone without going nuts.

"They've consciously turned off their hive minds," he said, when Eagle Feather relayed to him what he was seeing.

"Yes," Star had cried. "They aren't … together anymore."

"But apparently it's a feat of some difficulty," Garson said, "judging from what you're seeing. Clearly the effort to disengage from it, and to remain disengaged, is substantial."

What Eagle Feather was seeing were reptars carefully venturing down the cavern the hallway, Shaking their heads from side to side instead of zipping around like water spiders.

From what Eagle Feather could see before the three reptars disappeared around the bend in the now empty caverns were three deadly beasts moving slowly. Not creeping or tottering, but not bounding, either, not so quick the movement was almost blurred. And carefully. Maybe so much of their mental activity was tied up in remaining cut off from the others of their kind that there wasn't enough

left over to move fast. Maybe they felt the human equiva-
lent of dizzy. Maybe their other senses were off. He didn't
know what would happen when one of them was engaged
in … what would happen when one of them became the
killing machine it was designed to be. Maybe it would
move and behave just as they'd always seen reptars fight.
But maybe not. He was sure they could eventually run you
down, if not as fast as before, the result was likely to be the
same. Reptars would win the race, humans would lose.
And their ability to fight with their slashing saber legs, their
pointed talons, was impaired … but then they were
fighting against beings that didn't have the armament
they did.

As if Garson were thinking the same thought, he said,
"I suspect those beasts could kill humans with one eye tied
behind their backs."

And even if they were slow, they were still unstoppable
and it was still impossible to kill one of them. Sooner or
later, they would win the war.

Eagle Feather could neither see nor hear any movement in the tunnel outside the opening into Alabaster Hall,
that was littered with more bodies than there were inside.
He made a hand motion, and Garson stepped out. He'd
been the cork, holding the others in, and Taylor almost
knocked him down when he lurched out and … stood
gawking at the carnage. The others inched their way out
of the crack.

He spotted his oldest son's body first.

"*Sam!*"

Taylor rushed to his boy and dropped on his knees
beside his lifeless form. Noah knelt beside him. Then he
saw David and Kelly Jo, both lying dead nearby. He
gasped, maybe stifled a cry, then dropped his chin on his
chest and collapsed back on his heels.

"Kelly Jo? Davie?" Taylor whispered the names. "No." He shook his head in denial, flinging blood from his head wound like a dog shaking off water, splattering it on Noah's face.

Eagle Feather went to him and put his hand on his shoulder, but he didn't look up.

"We have to ... *go*. Now." Taylor didn't move. "We have to get Noah and Star somewhere safe." Eagle Feather gestured with his chin toward Star, who stood sightless amid a mindless horror it was a blessing her eyes couldn't see.

Still Taylor didn't move and Noah stayed with him.

Eagle Feather played the only card he had left. "I need your help!"

Taylor made some kind of sound deep in his throat — a strangled sob, then held his hand up for Eagle Feather to help him to his feet. In that gesture, Eagle Feather glimpsed his older brother in him, the strength that Sawyer always displayed to *do the thing*, the whatever-needed-to-be-done, no matter what. Noah rose beside him.

Chapter Fifty-Six

SAWYER HUNG on every word Nick told him, as he related the bizarre discovery that Paco was indeed alive, and that he had been in the caverns with them all along.

"I don't know how to describe it, but he wasn't really *there* when I showed up," Nick said, shaking his head. "It was a little like watching Star and Noah."

Sawyer and Nick were going through the weapons they'd gotten from the armory as they spoke, strapping on ammunition vests, preparing to "hunt down every crazy person in this cave and kill them," as Sawyer had promised Jocelyn Conner.

Ellie and Diana sat nearby on empty kegs, watching.

Sawyer couldn't keep his eyes from straying to Ellie, again and again. How could it be? How could he be so damned happy when the whole world was flooded, there were crazy people loose everywhere killing indiscriminately and he wasn't sure of the fates of his brother, nephews, son and dearest friends.

And it wasn't that he didn't care about those things. He absolutely did, but he was in some kind of offshoot of the combat mode thing, the compartmentalizing thing. Only now he found himself able to compartmentalize not only the bad, but the good, too, wall it off so at least briefly he could enjoy it even with all the bad in nearby compartments screaming to get out.

"Paco was doing something with his mind," Sawyer said. "Noah talked about it sometimes." Noah and Star were usually closed-mouthed about the things the three of them could do in each other's heads when they were on the mothership.

Nick described how Paco had died, that he didn't even realize Nick was strangling him to death. "He was *gone*."

"Just like the crazies walking around out there are 'gone.'"

"Could there be a connection, you think?"

"Maybe we'll find out."

"And maybe not."

The two of them were armed and ready to go. Nick stepped out of the Home Base door into the cavern first, and Sawyer knew it was to give him and Ellie a moment alone.

"You'll come back, right?"

"I won't be long."

"Don't you dare let anything happen to you, do you hear me?" There was real anger in her voice and terror in her eyes. "I was supposed to die today and I didn't. Don't you dare die today. You hear me? Don't you *dare*."

He didn't kiss her goodbye, was afraid if he touched her he wouldn't be able to leave her.

The former soldiers fell back into the routine faster than Sawyer would have believed, though he often felt like Nick had never left the SEALs.

"We'll make a sweep back down Kaboom to Chisholm Trail, take Blind Alley to Tigger and then to Manitoba

Lane," Sawyer said. "I say we make for Broadway then. I don't imagine anybody ran as far as Smiley Face or Frowny Face. So we head west on Broadway back toward Carnegie Hall. I know there are several families in Big Toe. We check it and the side caverns and see if anybody's seen the crazies. If we can find anyone. People went running wild everywhere."

They didn't even know how many nutcases there were. Carnegie Hall had been full of people eating or getting ready to, when the trouble started, and only a small percentage of the population of the cave had shown up in front of Alabaster Hall engaged in what felt like a planned, forced riot. But other people all over the caverns could have caught the craziness. They could be anywhere.

Nick touched Sawyer's arm. "Deadly force. Nothing less."

Sawyer looked him in the eye and nodded.

Translate that: shoot 'em on sight.

Chapter Fifty-Seven

EVERY SHADOW WAS a crazy person in hiding, waiting to jump out on him, though he didn't really think they were into stealth. They had been more like rabid dogs, biting and snapping at anything that came near them, not planning out an attack for even a few seconds ahead. Primal violence, untamed by so much as an animal's instinct for survival.

No, the crazies wouldn't be hiding, waiting for him. But the reptars.

Avoiding the Chisolm Trail cavern because he wanted to get farther from Carnegie Hall, Eagle Feather led them toward where the cavern completed its loop back to Broadway down the Chisolm South cavern. They went from empty dwelling to empty dwelling, making their way as fast as they could to Home Base, running low, hiding behind the walls that wouldn't even stop a whisper, let alone a pointed tobacco stick, a dagger or a reptar's talons. But it was something to hide behind. And if hiding were possible, it was a much preferable alternative to fighting.

They stepped up into an open area and a woman's

stifled sob came from a few feet away. Noah stepped over to her dwelling and moved the curtain aside. Inside was a woman and three small children. She had blood splatters all over her. She had been in close proximity to violence, was near somebody a crazy person attacked, or near a reptar. The blood was shiny, still wet.

She gasped in a breath to scream but Noah put his fingers to his lips and some part of her recognized the non-threatening body language and she strangled it back.

"Where are they?" Eagle Feather asked.

"He just clubbed Michael. Just hit him over the head with a pot. No reason, just …"

"Ma'am, have you seen any of those people, the crazy ones?"

"… had to get back here to the kids. Left Becky" — she nodded to the oldest, who couldn't have been more than twelve — "just so I could go find Michael. He went to see what was going on in Alabaster Hall, and he didn't come back. And then …"

Noah patted her on the shoulder and said aloud, in his just-a-little-toneless deaf speech.

"You stay right here. Don't make any noise."

And he let the curtain drop back in place.

He looked at Eagle Feather, nodded and they moved on. Noah was holding it together pretty well, but Taylor was staggering along with them like a blind man. Eagle Feather knew he was reeling from emotional wounds, not the cut on his head.

Running from one hiding place to another, they could hear the echoes of screams, maybe in the next cavern over, maybe half a mile away. The way the caverns distorted sound, it was hard to tell. They came around one bend and a group of people leapt to their feet and raced away in fright, assuming they were as nutty as the other people who had killed indiscriminately."

They came up Chisolm South to Chisholm Trail and the large open space where it joined Blind Alley. Chisholm South was behind them, Kaboom farther down, beyond the little cavern called Piglet ... that led off into a maze. They'd have to cross the open space to get to Home Base, and when they did, they'd be visible from the two large caverns and several other small ones — any one of which could hold an enemy.

"I will go first," Eagle Feather said. He turned to Garson. "How fast can you move, old man?"

"Depends on what's chasing me."

Eagle Feather felt a ghost of a smile whispering on his lips.

"Noah and Star will come after me, then you. Taylor will be last. When I motion for you to come, haul ass. Do you understand?"

"My goodness, dear friend — do I understand? It was a simple declarative sentence. What was there not to understand?"

Eagle Feather shook his head, peered out to get the best view he could get, and raced across the open area and into the shadows on the other side. Nothing stirred. Maybe there was some movement down Blind Alley, but it could have been a shadow, a play of light in the darkened interior of the cavern.

He made a hand motion and Noah guided Star across the open space. They both looked both ways and when Noah got to him, Star said, "There's something or somebody in Blind Alley. Noah saw movement."

That's where Eagle Feather thought he had seen movement, too.

Something was definitely there, down that passageway.

But it could be people as scared as they were, not a crazed maniac or a monster. Eagle Feather made a come-here motion and Garson took out at what was for him a run across the open area toward them, got to them gasping.

"There's something … moving … down there," he panted, pointing to Blind Alley.

Eagle Feather gave Taylor the nod and he came running across the open area toward them.

Then he stopped.

Stopped!

"Uh oh," he said, and looked out across the distance separating him from the other four. "We've got company." Then they heard the clattering sound of claws on stone and the purr.

Eagle Feather's stomach turned to a stone. He could hear it approaching down Blind Alley toward Taylor, but it wasn't the skittering, scuttling too-many-feet movement of a reptar. At least not a normal reptar.

Eagle Feather opened his mouth to scream, "Come on!" but before he had a chance, Taylor turned and looked down the cavern leading back to the empty Chisholm Trail South. Then he called out — to nobody in that cavern, "Wait. Don't leave me. I'm coming."

Taylor looked back over his shoulder at what was relentlessly approaching down Blind Alley and when he did, his gaze raked over the others huddled in the shadows. He let out something that sounded like a faked scream. Then pointedly called out, "Go on, save yourselves."

He turned then and took off running toward Chisolm South where nobody was waiting for him. Noah took two steps and started to cry out, but Eagle Feather grabbed his shoulder and dragged him back into the shadows.

The reptar appeared then, wagging its head from side to side. Shaking it now and then, like a dog trying to shake something out of its ear. It was moving slowly, for a reptar, scuttling along without the quick, jerky motions that made its attack so spider-like. But it was moving fast just the same. It was moving faster than Taylor.

It passed by them, headed down Chisolm Trail after Taylor. Eagle Feather and Star had to drag Noah away in the other direction toward Kaboom and Home Base.

Chapter Fifty-Eight

NICK HAD ALWAYS SAID Sawyer Matheson was the guy you wanted with you in a foxhole. As they moved stealthily down the shadowy caverns he discovered quickly how true that statement had been.

Sawyer's descriptions of the nut-case people had sounded so bizarre to Nick he could barely countenance it. Just went crazy, nuts, for no reason. Violent, ultra-violent. Why? His quest to find Paco had taken him to Persnickety, a cavern almost all the way to the stairs that led down the east side of the caverns to Cricket Bottom. A lot had happened in the rest of the cave while he was gone. Including the crazies.

The two men alternated movements forward — Sawyer on one side of Broadway, Nick on the other, going from cover to cover, staying low. According to the descriptions the others had given, the nut-cases weren't likely to be stealthy, lie in wait for a victim. They appeared to be unable to control their impulses enough to hide out, or, if Sawyer was right, even use a weapon.

Both of those things were good.

Still, they stayed low.

Nick had had trouble with his hearing ever since he'd surfaced in the cave, but it appeared to be working fine now. But not up to the acuity of Sawyer's, because the man on the other side of the cavern held out his hand in a stop gesture. He had heard something. Then he made the hand signal for proceed slowly. They did. Then Nick heard it too. It was sobbing, a woman crying.

They came upon the ruins of dwellings everywhere, destroyed by the mad flight of people from the crazies who were chasing them, or in terror from reptars they'd heard were in the caverns, didn't know those monsters were stuck in Alabaster Hall.

That was another thing they would have to attend to, but one crisis at a time. The sobbing was coming from a partially destroyed dwelling halfway down a short side tunnel. It had two remaining walls, but the third had been knocked inward and the crying was coming from under that. Sawyer held up his hand for them to stop. Then Nick took up a position with his rifle aimed at the pile of shattered walls, ready to shoot dead whatever might come out of it that looked dangerous.

Sawyer called out softly. "Hello in there. It's me, Sawyer Matheson."

The crying instantly stopped. A tear-clotted voice asked, "Sawyer?"

Sawyer still approached the downed wall carefully.

"Are you alright?"

Then a woman stuck her head out from under the debris and looked pleadingly at Sawyer.

"Are they gone now? Did you kill them all?"

Sawyer lowered his weapon and so did Nick.

"We're looking for them now, Betty Jo. Have you seen—?"

"Shirley Thompson — do you know her, because I sure don't. Never met her until she showed up in the cafeteria line serving with me."

Her eyes filled with tears.

"She went crazy, chased me here. I didn't know what to else to do. I'm sorry. I'm so sorry."

The woman had gestured to a pile debris about fifteen feet away. Nick approached it cautiously, used his foot to shove aside the fallen wall. Lying beneath it was a woman with a butcher knife sticking out of her chest.

"She's dead, isn't she? Dead."

She couldn't see what Nick saw, so he nodded to Sawyer, who told her, "Yes, she's dead."

"I'm sorry, I'm so sorry." The woman put her head in her hands and began to cry again.

"Where are Sidney and the boys?"

"I don't know. We got separated and I didn't know how else to find them but to come home and wait for them." She looked around at the abandoned dwellings. "Most people didn't come back home. I don't know where they went — just running away down the caverns. I got here and I was looking for some kind of weapon. I'd just picked up the knife when ... she came at me and her eyes were ... and she had blood on her face, in her mouth ..." The woman began to cry again. "Where should I go to be safe?"

There was no safe place until he and Sawyer eliminated the threat.

Sawyer got down on one knee in front of her and patted her on the shoulder.

"I don't know anywhere that's safer to go than right

here. You're right — eventually your husband and the boys will come back here. If you go looking for them …"

"I'll stay here, then." She looked around fearfully. "Hidden."

The woman burrowed back down among the fallen ruin of her dwelling.

Sawyer looked at Nick, and the two of them started back down Broadway when a whispered voice said, "Sawyer, is that really you?"

A man of about fifty-five straightened up and came out from behind where he had been crouching.

"Where is everybody?" Sawyer asked him.

"Scattered! Running away, scared. I seen people getting in the elevator to go down to the lower levels, thinking maybe it was safer down there. I figured just to stay here. Kinda hard for me to get around."

Nick knew the man — Parker Holt. He had lost a leg in a freak industrial accident a decade ago and had a prosthetic limb. It had been computerized and worked so well he didn't even limp. But in recent years, it began to fail. Maybe it needed some kind of adjustment to the computer mechanism or a new battery. Whatever it needed, there was nobody around to provide it and eventually Parker was stuck with a stiff leg, which was only slightly better than no leg at all.

"I just told Betty Jo to lay low. I'd advise you to do the same thing. Nick and I are hunting down the—"

"What happened? Why did those people—?"

"I don't know. Now's not the time to be asking why. We'll figure out all that later. Right now you need to concentrate on staying safe." Sawyer gestured to the man's hiding place behind the collapsed tents of his neighbors. "That looks like as good a place as any."

"How will we know when—?"

"I am building this airplane while I'm flying it here. I don't have answers. But Nick and I need to go."

The man hobbled back to his spot and hunkered the best he could.

Sawyer nodded and the two set off again.

"Maybe it was some kind of madness that passed," Nick said softly. "Maybe the crazies are sane again now—"

"Shit, I hope not! If they went nuts once they could go nuts again. I'd rather find them and eliminate—"

Behind them, in the cavern they'd just left, there was screaming.

Both men turned on a dime and raced back down Broadway toward the tangle of collapsed houses they had left only moments before. Sawyer suddenly grabbed Nick and literally threw him to the floor, then flattened himself beside him. Turning wide eyes to him, Sawyer said, "I hear ... reptars."

The word stopped Nick's heart. One thought leapt into his mind. He had heard Ellie's description of the attack on Ft. Knox. Everybody had. If an entire military base with tanks and artillery couldn't stop them ... he looked at the rifle in his own hands. He and Sawyer didn't have a chance.

The shrieking suddenly stopped and in the silence Nick could hear the sound. The sucking sound and then a purr.

They peered up over the top of a neat stack of orange crates — who had brought them into the caverns and why? — in time to see Parker leap to his feet and try to run, screaming away from the creature. It scuttled after him, but not as instantaneously as the beasts could move. Sawyer had seen them, had described the rapid movements. This thing was more like ... lumbering. But it was still faster than Parker could run on his bum leg and before he'd gotten fifty yards, the reptar seized him with his claws and literally ripped him apart.

Sawyer turned to Nick, his face white, and gestured down the tunnel where they'd been going. The men backed away on their knees until they could no longer hear the sounds of the carnage, then they got to their feet and ran.

Chapter Fifty-Nine

THEY SAT IN SILENCE. Not huddled together in a group for support and comfort, though. Separate. Instinctively, giving each other whatever physical as well as emotional space they needed to process the new realities of their lives.

Star and Noah were side by side on the floor, leaning with their backs against the wall, holding hands. They were in an urgent whispered conversation with Garson, who was seated on an empty keg. He looked very old and utterly spent.

Eagle Feather was on the floor, too, sitting with his legs crossed, a thousand-yard stare on his weathered face.

Nick sat on a keg, looking at the ground between his shoes. Sawyer sat on another keg beside Ellie, who cradled Diana in her lap. The child had gone to sleep. It must be nighttime. Sawyer didn't know what time it was. What day it was. The date.

Noah had told him about Taylor and his family, and the news had knocked his legs out from under him.

He was thinking about the baseball Taylor had given to him for his thirteenth birthday. Randall Matheson had tickets to take the boys to see the Drummers play in Nashville. Several days before the game, however, he had contracted the chicken pox. It was impossible, but it happened anyway. Nobody had chicken pox anymore. The disease was on that list of diseases that had been eradicated. Somebody forgot to tell the virus that was raging around his system.

Sawyer was miserable. Chicken pox was a horrible disease even for a small child. But for a teenager it was unbelievably miserable. And he got a secondary infection around the sites of each of the nasty "pox" crusty sores and those filled with liquid like a burn. He was a miserable horror, not the best patient in the world, could remember with shame how he had yelled at his mother and little brother to leave him alone.

Their father, Randall, took Taylor to the game. But neither of them talked about it when they got home. Out of deference to the fact that he had to stay home, Sawyer supposed, they acted like it had never happened. He was almost totally recovered a week later, well enough to enjoy a birthday party and the cake and ice cream that went along with it.

Sawyer felt Ellie squeeze his hand and he looked over at her, aware for the first time that there were tears running down his cheeks.

"Taylor caught a home run ball. Roscoe Dubluski slammed it over the centerfield fence in Music City Park for a winning run in the Drummers' game with the Chicago Panthers. He was nine years old and Dad said he leapt up into the air like an outfielder and snatched it out of the hands of half a dozen men in the stands." Sawyer let out a shaky sigh, tried to get his shit together.

"He gave me the ball for my thirteenth birthday." He couldn't talk after that, and the room fell silent again.

Time passed, each lost in his own thoughts until Nick broke the silence. He directed a question to Garson, who had gone to sit by himself and was absentmindedly cleaning his glasses with the tail of his shirt. One of the lenses was missing but he didn't appear to notice.

"Do you understand any of this?" Then he tossed the question out into the room. "Does anybody?"

"Noah and I … we think the crazy people were Paco's doing," Star said. "You said you saw … a scorpion."

Nick literally shuddered at the question. "A death stalker scorpion, black … like the ones in the desert. Then I realized it was exactly like the last one I saw there … *exactly*. Missing a pincher. And I figured it wasn't real."

"Paco made you see it," Noah said. "He controlled people that way, by becoming what they were afraid of."

"We think the riot was orchestrated," Star continued.

"I'd agree with that."

"Paco was using his mind to control some of the people in the crowd. And then …" Star turned her head toward Garson as if she were looking at him, "… and then, I think Paco suffered some kind of … stroke. Brain aneurism."

"He sure as shit lost it there at the end," Nick said.

"The stroke he suffered must have completely destroyed the higher centers of his brain, his consciousness," Garson put in. "Yes, that fits. I'd come to that conclusion already. All that was left alive was the id. The primal portion, the animal in all of us. I think when his mind blew so did the minds of the people he was controlling, wiped out their consciousness, too. He died—"

"I strangled the motherfucker," Nick said.

"—but they *didn't* die. They went on living, with nothing governing their actions but primal urges."

"Gretchen," Ellie said. Just the one word.

Sawyer tried to force his mind to think, but he was getting to the end of himself. They all were.

"So there were ... a finite number of them. It wasn't something they caught or could pass on to other people."

"Oh no, it only happened to the people Paco was controlling at the time his mind blew. I don't know how many that was, but ..." He paused, and continued more slowly. "Given the presence of the reptars ... those people just attacking them mindlessly, I suspect they've all been eliminated by now. And maybe that gave other people a chance to run and find a place to hide."

"Why?" Sawyer knew his voice was strident, almost blaming, but he couldn't seem to do anything about it. "Why doesn't the limestone affect them anymore? What happened to them? What changed?"

"They unhooked from each other," Noah said, spoke aloud and unconsciously signed, too, though he was the only deaf person in the room. "From their hive mind."

"I think they figured out how by ... watching us," Garson said. "Until now, those five titans had never come in contact with humans. They watched, studied us." He took a breath. "Studied me. We, our interactions, taught them the concept of individuality. They saw that it was possible to behave as independent entities."

He drew in a shaky breath.

"Limestone drove them nuts because it caused feed-back, a closed loop with the hive minds in their heads. But if there was no hive mind in their heads ..."

"There is no feedback," Nick finished for him.

"Each of them ... Moe, Larry and Laverne ... is oper-ating now as an independent organism for the first time in their existence," Garson said. "And it's hard for them. That's what's wrong with them. Why they're behaving odd, sluggish. It must take tremendous mental effort not to hook back into their collective. Doesn't leave a lot of mind space for much else."

"But there's enough for them to function just fine as killing machines," Sawyer said.

The enormity of that sucked out of the room what little oxygen there had been.

"Eventually, they'll eliminate everybody else," Ellie said. "I've ... seen what they can do ..."

"So have I," said Sawyer and he drew her to him.

"There are ... what? Two thousand people left ... maybe twenty-five hundred," Nick said in a flat, emotionless tone. "The reptars will hunt them down and kill them all. One by one. We have no defense against them, even these slow, stupid ones. And when the fucking flood waters go down if they ever fucking do, the reptars will be waiting to hook up to the hive mind in their monster mothership so a shuttle can show up and whisk them away into the stars."

"They'll leave behind a mountain full of dead bodies," Eagle Feather said, softly, so his words wouldn't wake the sleeping child.

It was harsh and Eagle Feather wasn't a harsh man. But it was reality.

"And there's nothing we can do about it," Nick said.

The statement and the utter despair behind it hung like a black fog around them.

Then Noah spoke.

"No, not 'nothing.'" All eyes turned to him. "There's a way we could kill them, but it would be a suicide mission." He paused for a beat and shot a look at Star, who was holding his hand. She squeezed. Whatever he was about to say, the two of them had already talked it over inside their heads. "Some people would survive, though." He looked at the sleeping child. "Diana. And Ellie. Garson and Eagle Feather. And everybody else in the caverns who've managed to stay hidden from the reptars. There'd be a remnant of people not hand-picked by the Astrals to repopulate the world."

He grabbed another beat.

"But not us." He gestured at the remaining people in the room — him and Star, Nick and Sawyer. "We'd be killed."

Chapter Sixty

NOAH TURNED TO STAR.

"It was Star's idea."

She knew all eyes in the room were trained on her and she unconsciously reached down and scratched Pumpkin behind his ears. The old dog was breathing heavily, and she could hear a kind of gurgling sound in it. The others probably couldn't hear it, but she could. Anna had described for her the different heart conditions the dog might have. One of them was something like congestive heart failure. It would mean his lungs would slowly fill up with blood and … he would drown.

She had cried all night after Anna said that, with Pumpkin pulled up so tight against her she was almost choking the life out of him herself. She understood, though nobody said it to her, that back in Before, a veterinarian would have examined the dog and provided her with a variety of treatment options that could have at the very least made him more comfortable and at best might have alleviated the condition altogether. Or, it was possible a vet would have told her she needed to have the dog put to sleep.

That sounded like the most horrifying thought imaginable, though she knew dog owners for generations had faced the same awful conclusion to their relationship with their beloved companions, and somehow she'd managed to delude herself into believing Pumpkin would live forever. He'd always be there. He couldn't leave her.

She didn't want him to suffer, though! And maybe he was, now. Maybe it was agony or terror or some other thing for him to feel the pressure in his chest. But when she delved into his mind, that's not what she saw there. She saw the whole world around them in a pattern of overlaid images that were the way his sense of smell transmitted information to his brain. His sense of smell had been going for years, so the images were not nearly as crisp and clear as they once had been, and there were fewer images. Many fewer. But what she didn't get from the dog was any fear, any pain or desperation. Now, as she touched him, his whole mind filled up with her image and there was no room in it for anything else.

She had always cherished the childish delusion that the dog would live as long as she would. That she never would have to tell him goodbye.

And now, that's the way it was going to be. The two of them would die together.

"I could tell when the reptars 'unhooked,'" she said. "I could feel the hive mind, could sense the ..." She struggled for words but knew there weren't any that the people in this room could possibly comprehend. Except Noah. He understood. "It's a little like the hum of a generator, only it's not a sound. It's like a vibration, but you can't feel it with your senses. Like you strum a guitar string and you see it vibrate ... it's that kind of *thrumb* sensation."

They don't understand. They can't.

Noah was right. She took a deep breath and started over.

"Now there is no *thrumb* because there's no hive mind to make it. Just individual minds like mine and Noah's, but not hooked up to each other. I think if I tried, I could connect them to each other again, through me. Make them a hive mind, create the *thrumb*, which would cause the squawk of feedback in their heads."

"You could make them go crazy again and attack each other?"

Star hated the hope she could hear in Ellie's voice.

"Not for long. I couldn't hook them up for more than thirty seconds, say, maybe as long as a minute at a time. Even that would take ... a lot of mental effort."

"But it would be *maddening* when she did," Noah said. "Buzzing, shrieking feedback in their heads. It would be like ... Oh, I don't know, maybe like being hit with a taser. They'd want it to stop. They'd do anything to make it stop. And we can use that."

"You think we could kill them while ...?" Sawyer began.

"Oh, no, not that. They'd just be jolted, shocked is all. It wouldn't make them so vulnerable you could kill them."

"Then how could we use it?" Ellie asked.

"Do you know what 'track to source' means?" Garson asked.

It sort of explained itself, but not exactly.

"What it really relates to is irrelevant. What it means in this circumstance is that if Star connected them all through her they would be able to track to source the mind that was connecting them. They could find her. If Star did this, they could track her down, they *would* track her down to kill her."

"How does that help us?"

"Star would be bait. They'd come after her and she could lead them into a trap."

"What kind of trap?" Sawyer said.

"You're sitting on it, Dad," Noah said, "sorta."

She was, too. They all were. They were sitting on empty gunpowder kegs. In the cavern next door, the kegs were stacked up floor to ceiling — but not empty ones. Those kegs were *full of gunpowder.*

Chapter Sixty-One

"THERE'S ONLY one way to kill the reptars in this mine," Noah said. "We have to bury them. Rock is the only weapon we've got. We have to bring the roof down on their heads."

He could see the gears churning behind his father's eyes, could tell Nick was connecting the dots, too.

"How can we do that?" Ellie asked. "Can you ... set some kind of charge in the ceiling of one of the—?"

Garson held up his hand and turned to Noah. "The engineering genius here says nothing like that would work."

"The ceilings in the caverns are held up by the walls," Noah said. "To bring the roof down in one, you'd have to blow up all the walls supporting it — that would require more explosive power than we have."

"Couldn't we just blow the reptars up with the gunpowder?"

"That's a tempting option, but we don't have a detonator. All we have is raw gunpowder, not fancy explosives. Mostly, the only thing we can do with any degree of certainty is set kegs of gunpowder around something and blow it up."

"Couldn't we trap the reptars in some cavern, trick them into a dead end, maybe, and then seal the entrance?"

"They were locked inside the mine for three weeks without food or water and when I found them, they were fine and didn't even appear thirsty," Garson said. "Nobody knows what they require for survival. In some kind of insectile form like the reptars ... certain species of spiders can survive for two years without food. If we seal them in somewhere, they might dig themselves out when the water goes down. As soon as they leave that limestone behind, they will connect to the mothership and we'll have shuttles on our doorsteps."

They all talked about that as if it were a when and not an if. *When* the water goes down. They'd sold everybody on the same happily ever after. The sell had been ... if you stay in a horrible rat hole for long enough, eventually the water will recede and you can come out. Nobody's mind ever questioned that, because to do so was madness. And to consider what they might find when the water went down invited madness, too. So everybody conformed to the paradigm. Eventually, the water would recede and they could leave the caverns for a "brave new world."

"I'm sorry, I know I'm the most dense of the bunch of us, but I don't know what you're talking about," Ellie said. "We have gunpowder, but all it's good for is to blow a hole in something, or blow something up if you could set kegs all around it. What are we going to do to kill the reptars?"

"We'll collapse the mountain on top of them."

Ellie looked totally flummoxed. But Noah could tell his father was beginning to figure out what they might be talking about and Nick probably wasn't far behind him. Eagle Feather ...? He might have figured the whole thing out as soon as they started talking and just kept his mouth shut. The old Indian was good at that.

"You're talking about the mine, aren't you?" Sawyer said.

"Give the man a kewpie doll," Garson said.

Sawyer turned to Ellie to explain. "You remember years ago I explained to you about coal mines?"

"Yes, but tell me again. I died between then and now."

"Say you have a five-story building and the first floor is solid gold. How would you get that gold out? If you just started digging into the first floor, eventually the four floors on top of it would collapse and bury you. But what if you left pillars of gold, fifty feet by fifty feet every hundred feet to hold up the top four floors while you dug the gold out all around them? That's what they do in coal mines."

"And that's what the Astrals did in the limestone mine. I saw the pillars, each of them thirty feet square and spaced thirty feet apart. Those pillars are holding up the mountaintop, keeping it from collapsing into the mine."

"You know why they didn't just blow off the top of the mountain and strip mine it, don't you?" Garson's mind was always doing that, going off down rabbit trails away from the main point. "Because if they blew the sandstone cap off the mountain, there'd be no limestone waiting here when they came back next time, in a thousand or five thousand years. The top of the mountain keeps rainwater from dissolving away all the limestone beneath. Cracks in that cap allow water to drip in and form caverns, but the whole fifteen hundred feet of limestone doesn't dissolve away."

"Can we get back to the mine now?" Ellie said. Noah could tell she was beginning to catch on. "So you're saying the Astral mine isn't tunnels or caverns — it's just one big hole with columns of limestone supporting the mountain on top of it."

"The mine is roughly oval. It stretches from where I dug my way in all the way to Alabaster Hall — that's about two miles. The roof in the center of the mine is the most vulnerable. Along the edges, the cavern walls help support the roof, but in the middle, it's held up only by the pillars of limestone beneath it. Blow the posts out from under it, and the roof will collapse."

"... so you blow up the support columns ..." Sawyer said.

"... and the mountain above it will collapse into the mine," Nick finished for him.

"You don't have to blow up *all* the pillars in the center." Garson spewed out numbers off the top of his head, his calculations — twenty-one million square feet ... 133 pillars long by forty-four pillars wide and ... Then realized nobody wanted to know how to make the sausage. "We need to take out the five center pillars. A fifty-pound keg of gunpowder on all four sides of each. That's twelve-hundred fifty pounds of gunpowder with an explosive force of ... it will be enough."

"And Star can lead the reptars into the mine so they'll be there ... to be squashed?" Ellie said.

Noah watched them all thinking through the ramifications of the plan that he, Star and Garson had already gone over.

"But if you blow the top off the mountain, won't the flood waters come gushing in and flood the caverns?" Ellie asked.

"Theoretically, no," Garson said. Then he glanced at Noah and shrugged. "But reality often fails to conform to theory. We had to seal up the mine entrance the Astrals dug or the flood waters would have flowed in and filled the caverns when the flood first came. We sealed that hole by blowing up the rock around it, collapsing it in on the entrance. This would be the same thing, only on a much grander scale. We'll collapse the mountain above it into the mine, which should seal up the hole where the mine was."

"If there's even a chance the caverns won't flood, that's better odds for survival than waiting for certain death in the teeth of the reptars," Noah said.

Ellie began to circle back to the logistics of the plan.

"So Star would lead the reptars into the mine? Won't they see the kegs of gunpowder and figure out it's a trap?"

Garson shook his head. "They are too high-tech to perceive danger in something as primitive as a wooden keg."

Noah wanted to spell the whole thing out. It was what it was.

"Star and I *both* will lead the reptars into the mine. I don't have nearly the power ..." He looked at her, hoped with all his heart she knew how much he loved her.

Of course I know. Silly.

He smiled, which was inappropriate, and then he plunged ahead. "The plan is that we'd lead them into Alabaster Hall and into the mine through the entrance they created, and then get them to chase us to Noah's Hole." The opening he'd crawled into as a kid. "They won't be able to follow us out through it because they won't fit. Their only way out is the way they came in. But we won't give them time for that."

Star and Noah would play a life-and-death game of cat-and-mouse with the monsters luring them back into the mine. The monsters would follow them. They had no choice. They had to find Star to stop her from connecting their minds, driving them insane with the feedback.

He had blown right by the possibility that he and Star would not be able to stay far enough ahead of the reptars to escape once they got into the mine. It didn't need to be said.

"We'll go from here to Alabaster Hall slowly and carefully, a circuitous route, messing with the reptars' heads. Meanwhile, Dad and Nick will haul kegs of gunpowder to Noah's Hole in the back of the mine and plant the explosives around the central pillars."

The kegs weren't large — only held fifty pounds of gunpowder each — and they could be rolled on their sides.

"The rest of you" — he swept a gesture around the room — "will take Diana to the monastery. Eagle Feather will see you get there."

He paused.

"The four of us involved in the Great Boom Project — Star and I, Dad and Nick … it doesn't look good for us."

"Meaning …?" Ellie prompted, though he could tell she knew exactly what he was talking about. She just had to hear him say it.

"Meaning Star and I will be … sliding into home plate when we draw the reptars to this end of the mine."

He shot a look at Eagle Feather then. The old man's face was stoic, but he was looking at Star, understanding the import of the words.

"And Nick and I will have to stay at Noah's Hole to set off the charges once Star and Noah are out of the way." Sawyer understood.

"But you don't have a detonator, so how—?"

"Noah has done the take-apart-the-toaster thing he used to do as a kid — only with the laser sight on Sawyer's rifle," Garson said. "Pulled a bunch of the Glow Worms off the ceiling and pack them in a barrel with gunpowder. Focus the laser he has recalibrated on those Glow Worms … it might take a few seconds, but it will cause an explosion big enough to set off the other barrels."

"So you're saying——?"

"The timing of all this will be critical." Sawyer got it and had bought in. "We'll have to get the barrels out of here and——" He looked helplessly at Noah. "It's a *hike* from here to that hole."

The shortest route would be to transport the gunpowder down Kaboom to Pooh Bear, turn off on Piglet to the north end of Manitoba Lane and from there to Smiley Face. But the portion of Piglet between Pooh Bear and Smiley Face had suffered a roof fall and was almost completely blocked. Which meant they'd have to continue on Pooh Bear all the way down to the southern end of Manitoba Lane, then all the way back up it to Smiley Face. That would take way, way too long.

Noah knew his father had a map of the caverns in his head and might be the only person here who could visualize how what he was about to say would work.

"So we don't go out the front and down Kaboom. We use that little tunnel next to the Drawbridge door. It goes east *behind* Pooh Bear straight through to north Manitoba Lane. It's narrow, but wide enough to get the barrels through. It comes out maybe a hundred yards from Smiley Face and the hole."

Ellie put it together and addressed Sawyer.

"You and Nick will be outside Noah's Hole so when Star and Noah show up, you'll use the laser to set off the explosion——"

"No, not immediately," Garson answered her. "We don't want the reptars near the edge of the mine when the roof collapses. The cavern walls *might* support part of the roof there. They need to be dead center when the bomb goes off."

"How will——?"

"Star will … mess with their minds," Noah said.

Sawyer finished drawing her a picture. "When we blow those barrels, the mountain above the mine will collapse down into it, burying the reptars. We'll be in the cavern beside the mine when the roof collapses ... it'll fall on us, too."

Noah looked at Diana, the child sleeping in Ellie's lap. She would be one of the survivors who would seed the future of mankind. She was a very good place to start.

Chapter Sixty-Two

NOAH KNEW it would take the group a few minutes to digest what they'd just heard. He got that, didn't press anybody to do anything immediately — let them catch their breath. They couldn't wait long, though. Every minute those reptars were in the caverns they were hunting down people and tearing them apart — men, women, little kids. They wouldn't stop until they had wiped out every human being there.

Everybody in the group understood what their job was.

Eagle Feather would take Ellie, Diana and Garson to the monastery, Nick and his father would dig out Noah's Hole to make it big enough to roll the kegs of gunpowder into the mine, but still too small for a reptar to get free. They'd place the explosive kegs beside the center pillars while Noah and Star and Pumpkin made their way to Alabaster Hall for the two-mile race through the mine, chased by three reptars. Yes, Pumpkin. Star needed the dog to tell her where the reptars were. He could smell them and she could see those images in his head. That was their ace in the hole to stay ahead of the beasts. He knew

Star wasn't at all sure Pumpkin could do it, could run that far that fast, but at this extreme end of everything, no one had any illusions about saving those they loved. Pumpkin would not survive without Star. If she was to die, she'd take Pumpkin with her. And if the dog died in the effort, he would not have to face even a moment of life without his beloved master.

Everyone knew what they had to do, and that some of them would die in the effort.

Noah knew one thing that he kept out of his mind, though, so Star wouldn't hear it, but maybe she did anyway. He would not let the reptars get her. He would distract them, he would ... he would do *something* to ensure that Star and Pumpkin made it to Noah's Hole and out. There was no safety there, of course, but it would be a better death than being ripped apart by the teeth of the reptars.

He supposed soldiers did this kind of thing all the time, went into battle knowing they wouldn't survive. His father and Nick had been soldiers. It wasn't that Noah was afraid of dying, but the letting go. The saying goodbye. The certain knowledge that this was the *last time* ...

But before humanity's last shot at survival got under way, Noah had one final personal thing he had to do. He got up and went to where his father was seated on an empty keg, pulled another up beside it and sat down.

He knew what he had to say, just didn't know how to get there. For a very long time after Star found out about what had happened the day Noah's mother and sister had died in the fire, she had urged him to tell his father, to confess. Of course, she had said it wasn't his fault, that it had been an accident, a little boy had made a mistake. She had literally spent years trying to convince him before she finally gave up and let it lie.

There inside his head, she said nothing. Here, at the end, she wouldn't push. Either he would tell his father or he wouldn't. The decision was his.

He didn't sign it. Signing couldn't convey the impact of it, the importance. He would say it out loud. He would form the words in his mouth and say them out loud so his father could hear them. He owed him that much. And though he had fought against it since he was eight years old, Noah knew his father had a right to know.

"I have a thing to tell you that I have ... kept secret since I was eight years old."

His father's head snapped up, his eyes narrowed.

"The fire ..." And Noah discovered the words didn't want to come out of his mouth. Star gave him the strength to go on, though. He didn't have to say what fire. There was only the one fire. In all their lives, there had always been only the one fire, a blaze that had informed and defined much of his world for every day after it. "I set it. It's my fault Mom and Rosileigh are dead."

And once he started telling the story, the words came, they came fast, so fast his mouth could hardly keep up with saying them, they flowed out of him, gushed out of him, words that had been dammed up in his heart, locked away in his very soul, were set free.

He told his father about going to the garage that morning to work on the special project, the one Garson had bet him a milkshake he couldn't complete. He had to fashion an archway, three-dimensional, but supported by only a single beam rather than a configuration of beams.

"I didn't even know I was cold until I dropped a piece of balsa wood because my fingers were stiff. So I went to turn on the heater. But it wouldn't work. I tried the switch, flipped it off and on. Unplugged and replugged it. Nothing. It was dead. It was Sunday. The hardware store was closed. You couldn't get another one until Monday, which meant I couldn't complete the project on time."

Noah swallowed hard.

"And then ... I thought about the fire pit."

He could build a fire in the pit in the garage. The coals in the fire pit didn't make any smoke. That would provide enough warmth for him to work. So he had lit it, knowing it'd take half an hour or so to warm up the garage. Which would give him time to bring in the wood his mother had told him to go get.

"She had built a fire in the fireplace, the first one that winter, and there wasn't enough wood up by the house to keep it going."

So it was his job to get the wheelbarrow, take it down behind the barn to the woodpile, load it up, and then push it back across the snow-covered yard to the back porch where the woodbox sat beside the back door.

"I could ... I could hear her playing the piano upstairs, singing to Rosileigh."

Noah was crying. He didn't know when he'd started, but he couldn't stop, talked through his tears, his breathing hitching in and out, would have continued to tell the story if his breath hadn't been stolen totally away. Once he opened the floodgate, there was no power on earth strong enough to get him to stop talking until he had told the whole story.

"I could smell the smoke from the fireplace. I wasn't hurrying. In fact, I stopped and made some snowballs, to build up an arsenal — to be ready if Sam and David came over after supper."

Noah rounded the corner of the barn to start up the backyard toward the house.

"... a wind. I felt a warm wind hit my face and I could smell the smoke from the fireplace."

And then the tears stopped. The rest of the tale came out in a dead-calm voice, devoid of emotion, because all the emotion surrounding it had been stuffed so far down into his soul that even now he couldn't dig down deep enough to get it.

"The house was on fire. The fire pit in the garage. I hadn't set it far enough away from the workbench. Or something fell into it. Or ... I had caught the house on fire."

He paused to take a breath, but he still wasn't crying.

"And I could hear Mom and Rosie ... screaming."

His father gasped then, and it was the first time he had really been aware of his father's presence since he started the story. He looked, actually looked into his father's face and couldn't read the tangle of emotions there. But he could read the tears that were streaming down his father's cheeks.

At some point, his father had taken both his hands in his. Noah hadn't been aware of it when it happened, but he was aware of it now and he pulled his hands away.

"I tried to get to them. I ran across the yard and up onto the porch, but when I opened the kitchen door, there was a wall of flames."

He searched through the images for something that was not so horrible there were no words to describe it, but there was nothing. Every image was beyond description.

"Then I was on my knees. Mom and Rosie were screaming ... I couldn't stand the screaming. It went on and on and on and I put my hands over my ears so I couldn't hear them. And it was quiet, but the screaming was still out there in the world even if I couldn't hear it."

He said it then. There were no other words.

"They were burning to death."

There, he'd said it.

And the silence that filled his head then felt as dead and empty as the silence he'd heard on that day kneeling on the porch.

His father took his hand again and he tried to pull away, but his father held tight, wouldn't let go. Then he reached out and lifted Noah's chin so he was facing him.

He had earned this. What he had done had earned him the punishment of seeing his father's anger and disgust. Payback's a bitch.

"You're wrong," his father said. And for a moment Noah thought he hadn't lip-read the words correctly. "You didn't start the fire that killed your mother and sister."

Those words banged and clanged around in his head, making so much noise he couldn't have heard anything else even if he hadn't been deaf.

He shook his head. How could his father not understand what he'd said? Hadn't he been listening at all?

"No, Dad, you don't understand—"

"No, Noah, it's *you* who doesn't understand. You think you started it … and oh dear God in heaven what thinking that all your life has done to you. I'm sorry. I'm so sorry. So many things … make sense now."

What was his father talking about?

"Noah, the fire that killed your mom and sister didn't start in the garage. It started in the chimney."

Noah's whole mind went still. No other thoughts dared move inside his skull. Only those words stood hot and stinking in the spotlight of his soul.

"It was a creosote fire. I guess she built a fire in the fireplace that morning because of the snow."

A fire makes it so cozy with the snow outside.

"She must have thought just a little one … If I'd been home, I'd have cleaned out the chimney before … Creosote builds up inside chimneys and then when you light a fire the next winter, there's creosote in the chimney. It can catch on fire, start a fire inside the chimney. A creosote fire burns very hot."

He paused. Noah could see on his father's face something like his own haunted look. These were words that conjured up images that haunted his father's soul.

"The chimney fire caught the wall next to it in the upstairs bedroom on fire. The bedroom was between your mother and the stairs. She and Rosie were trapped."

Trapped and burning. The screaming. He had put his hands over his ears.

"Noah, it wasn't your fault."

He couldn't stand the sound of their dying screams. He had stopped his ears up, refused to hear. Had *decided* not to hear.

And he hadn't heard another sound since.

Noah sat stunned, couldn't move. Couldn't think. Then Nick Wilson got slowly to his feet and looked at the others, made eye contact with each one. He said only two words. "Show time."

Chapter Sixty-Three

It was up to Eagle Feather to get Ellie, Diana and Garson safely from Home Base to the monastery. For much of the route, they'd be on Broadway, the most-traveled tunnel in the cavern. But only as far as Big Toe. After that, Eagle Feather'd said he had planned a detour.

Ellie stood holding Diana's hand as Eagle Feather looked carefully up and down the caverns where Chisholm South intersected Broadway. They had seen a few people along the way, terrified people, fleeing their homes for ... for anywhere they could find where there were no reptars. So reminiscent of the first days after the white dots were spotted. People just mindlessly ran, even if they had nowhere to run *to*, they ran *from* wherever they were. Ellie was sure that people had fled to the elevators, the stairs, maybe even climbed down the chimneys to Level Two, and to Three below that.

Level Two was more serpentine than Level One, more loops and switchbacks, a maze. Level Three was more like Level One, though it was not intersected by as many other tunnels leading off from it. It was wide and winding, with fewer places to hide. Level Four and below were underwater.

Miles and miles of winding dark tunnels, with rock piles and narrow places, and holes and columns and … and … Families would be trying to hide in the nooks and crannies of those miles. From three monsters, that as far as anybody knew, didn't require food, or not much of it. Water? Nobody was sure. It was a for-sure thing, however, that the people running from the reptars would require *both* and there was nothing in all those miles of tunnels but dirt and rock. You could hide a long time in that many miles of cave. But how long without food and water? All the stores, the supplies, the water purification systems, everything that kept the people alive in the cave had been set up in the west end of Level One around the elevators and Carnegie Hall — in the Broadway, West Broadway and Corkscrew caverns.

Eagle Feather gave the all-clear and the four of them hurried across to the far side of Broadway and began making their way down it.

Ellie was surprised at how well she knew the caves, though her knowledge wasn't first hand. A long time ago, Sawyer had brought her a map of Matheson Caverns to put on her wall. Distraction. And he'd spent hours telling her about them. That's why Ellie knew exactly where they were when she pointed to a stand of rocks about thirty feet off the trail.

"It looks like those rocks go all the way to the wall," she said, "but they don't. There's an area behind them. We need to talk and that's a safe place to do it."

"Talk about what?" Eagle Feather asked.

Ellie didn't answer, just turned and took Diana to the spot behind the rocks with the others following along.

"You stay here, sweetie pie," she told the little girl.

"Keep watch." Then she led Garson and the old Indian far enough away from Diana that the child couldn't hear their conversation.

"Whatever we have to talk about, can't it wait?" Garson wanted to know, looking fearfully around in the shadows.

Eagle Feather was equally anxious. "We need to get Diana to the monastery."

"*You* need to get Diana to the monastery. I'm not going."

That was a conversation stopper.

"What are you saying?" Garson asked.

"I'm going back to Noah's Hole. To be with Sawyer."

The two men merely looked at her and she knew if they asked for an explanation, she wouldn't be able to give them one. There was no way to tack words onto what she was feeling, about the truth and certainty of what had to be. She had to be with Sawyer now. If she hadn't known the little girl would be taken care of, doted on by Eagle Feather, Garson, Anna, two dozen monks and everyone else in the caverns …

"What about Diana?" Eagle Feather asked.

"I want you to take care of her. You're the one protecting us now, not me. I'm as helpless as she is."

"What about her … future?" Garson asked.

"I had it all worked out with Anna, and then …" Her voice trailed off. "Until only a few hours ago, Diana thought her mother was moments away from death. She was expecting to hear it. She knew it was happening. And she was prepared for it."

"Why are you talking about me like I'm not here?" Diana asked, and the three of them turned to see that the child had not sat down where Ellie'd told her to wait for them and keep watch.

"This is grown-up talk. It's—"

"It's about you dying. You didn't die, though. You're fine now. So why are you talking about dying again?"

Ellie got down on one knee in front of the little girl.

"You knew I was going to die, Brother Sebastian told you about it, didn't he?"

She nodded, her eyes huge and filled with unshed tears. "And you knew that when I died, you would be taken care of. That the monks and Garson and Eagle Feather and …" She almost said Star, Noah and Sawyer, but she didn't. "You knew you would be okay when I died, didn't you?"

Again she nodded.

"And then suddenly, I didn't die. I came back, healed and well."

The smile that graced the little girl's face seemed to light up the whole cavern.

"But what if that was just for a time? What if I was given this opportunity to come back … just for a little while? Just long enough to hold you while you slept. To run my fingers through your hair one more time. To tell you I love you and to tell you goodbye. Isn't that better than the way it was before?"

"It's better if you come back and *stay* back. If you get well and stay here with me. I don't want you to go away, Mommy."

She grabbed Ellie and held on fiercely.

"I don't want to go away either. But … a lot of people have died in the world. More than your little mind can imagine. I'm just one more. And I got to come back for a time to tell you goodbye. None of those other people got to do that."

Diana pulled back out of Ellie's arms. She wasn't crying, not making the sound, but tears were streaming down her face and her breathing hitched in and out.

"Now, you're going to go. You're going to die, too, aren't you?"

Ellie thought back all those years, to the blue ball of clay in a ring box in her top drawer and how she had measured the lump in her breast against it in the early days to see if it was growing. And after she measured it, she would tell herself that the next time she did, the lump would be smaller. That the next time she checked, the lump would be gone and she would be fine. Delusion. And that kind of false hope had made the reality, when it happened, even harder to bear. She could tell Diana that she had a chance to survive — and she would have a chance, just not much of one. The cavern wall and ceiling might hold, might not collapse when the mine roof fell. It was *possible*. No, she couldn't, *wouldn't* do that to the little girl, make it harder on her than it had to be.

"Yes, darling, I'm going to die, too. I have to know that you're going to be fine without me. Can you be that brave?"

Diana barely nodded her head, and Ellie knew if she spoke she would cry.

"Give me a great big hug, the biggest hug you have. Then take Dr. Garson's hand and go."

Maybe it was the biggest hug Ellie had ever had. She sat there afterward, her arms aching to hold the little girl, to feel that hug forever. But she did have to go. She had to be with Sawyer, die by his side.

Chapter Sixty-Four

SAWYER WORKED HARDER than he'd ever worked in his life, or so it seemed, carrying one fifty-pound keg after another of gun powder out of the armory and loading it onto a cart, moving carts down the narrow, unnamed corridor between Kaboom and Manitoba Lane and down it to Smiley Face, then hauling the kegs up the hill to Noah's Hole … and then into the mine to place around the pillars.

Star was keeping tabs on the reptars, waiting for the best moment for her and Noah to set out for Alabaster Hall. She could dip into their minds individually, had not yet tried to hook the three of them to each other. One reptar was on End of the Line, west of Broadway and the elevators. One was far down Pot Belly. The third was moving down Chisholm Trail back toward Broadway. The people that the crazies or the reptars hadn't yet killed were hiding all over the caverns — in tunnels, behind rocks and outcrops, hunkered down into holes. Given how sluggish the reptars seemed to be, it appeared that it was sometimes possible to get away from them, or that's what Star was hearing through their minds. To operate as they were intended, as "killing machines," they needed to focus, no distractions. The effort to keep themselves locked down and unhooked from each other was wearing on them, taking its toll.

Eagle Feather, Ellie, Diana and Garson had set out for the monastery, which had a locked door that would survive even a reptar attack. They'd be safe there with the monks even if the Boom Project didn't work … until the food and water ran out.

Sawyer's parting with Ellie had been gut-wrenching and brief. And after he let her go. After he watched her walk away holding Diana's hand, never looking back, it didn't matter anymore to Sawyer that he was going to die. He had been prepared to lose her, as prepared as it was possible to be. For the past six months, he had been actively hoping she would die, to release her from the agony. He had accepted her death.

Then she was back. For a brief few glorious hours, Ellie was back. He got to hold her, touch her, kiss her and tell her how very much he loved her. That he had loved her for years.

"Knowing you're going to live," he'd said, so lost in the beauty of her eyes he could hardly think of what he was saying. "It's okay. You and Diana will go on, and if this is the price tag on that, I got the cash, I won't need plastic."

She had merely looked at him, had hardly said anything at all, but seemed to be gobbling him up with her eyes, imprinting his image on them to carry away with her. He had kissed her fiercely, whispered his love into her ear and she had walked away.

Now the image of her face filled his mind. When it wasn't shoved aside by Noah's staggering revelation.

Ellie had come back from the dead. Noah had

admitted he'd spent the past twelve years blaming himself for the deaths of his mother and little sister.

Sawyer had wanted to talk to his son about it, reassure him … say *something*. But there had been no time. The end would come soon. Time … for everything, had run out.

Every second's delay in executing their plan could cost another villager their life.

Sawyer's whole body was lathered with sweat. Crawling through Noah's Hole to place the charges had smeared his clothing with dirt. They had been at it for …

He looked at his wrist and saw that his watch was not there. Was it day or night? And what day? Day thirty-six, thirty-eight? Maybe later. Maybe it was still just thirty-five and he had simply elongated the time in his mind to fit the import of the events in it. It seemed like it had been years since he saw Ellie's face begin to turn pink and her blue eyes open. And it felt like it had happened two minutes ago.

"Think this will get it?" Nick asked, panting as he shoved the last keg into place.

"It'll have to. Either it'll work, or it won't."

The two men stared into each other's eyes in the yellowish lantern light, one filthier than the other, and their locked gaze said everything that needed to be said.

They had set out twenty kegs of gunpowder. The perfectly smooth stone-cut limestone didn't have so much as a crack they could wedge any kind of explosive charge into even if they'd had one. All they could do was surround each of five center pillars with four kegs of powder. Sawyer couldn't imagine the roof of the chamber could stand with that many of its support posts suddenly jerked out from under it. Of course, what Sawyer thought didn't mean jack, but the fact that Noah had given it the nod meant it was as good as humankind could do. The genius for building was certain the mountain atop the mine would collapse into it when they blew those kegs.

"That's it, then," Nick said. "Let's boogie."

Nick crawled out of Noah's Hole first. Sawyer slid out after.

Ellie was standing at the bottom of the pile of rocks.

"I heard there was a party here. That it was going to be a real blast and I wasn't about to miss it."

How … Why …?

"Don't even," she said, reading his mind like he was Noah and she was Star. "I am here. There is no way to send me away without turning me out into empty tunnels patrolled by three reptars. I can't go back now. So get over yourself. We don't have that much time, and I'm not wasting a second of it convincing you that I had come here to die with you. And you have to … let me."

EAGLE FEATHER KNEW where he was, as in on-a-map knew where he was, but he had never been in this particular cavern. It was not a visitor tunnel, no artfully placed lights behind rocks and paved walkway complete with handrails. It was narrow and rocky, and they had to climb part of the way up and over debris that had fallen down on the bottom of the cavern. It was not the scenic, tour bus route, but Eagle Feather had taken it for just that reason.

Sawyer had described it as a "back door" to the monastery. It was a narrow, winding tunnel that stretched from the back of what appeared to be a dead-end in Big Toe to the east side of Carnegie Hall, where the commercial kitchen was located. Using the back door, Eagle Feather would avoid the most popular part of Broadway, and the entrance to Alabaster Hall. This tunnel emerged not fifty yards from the metal door that protected the monastery.

The monks' compound was as secure as the locked chambers where the gunpowder was stored. It could withstand a siege. But the people inside … not so much. The water filtration system, the food supplies — survival — was stored in locked caverns along Corkscrew, the cavern that veered off Broadway at the north end of Carnegie Hall, then looped back into the south wall. Oh, the monks and the children they'd been caring for — in the nursery and at school — when the shit hit the fan would make it for a while … had better odds than any of the people hiding behind rocks in the tunnels, and right now, that was the best game in town.

It was Eagle Feather's job to protect the little girl, as it had been his job to protect Star as a child years ago. Though Diana was not the prophesied "savior" of her people as Star had been, he was no less dedicated to keeping her from harm. She might not have a "gift from the gods" to save her people, but she was the future. Her descendants would repopulate the world, and he would willingly give his life to ensure her survival.

Or to save his dear friend Garson, if it came to that. The wealth of information stored in that brilliant man's mind — a new beginning for mankind would need that.

Eagle Feather would make short work of any remaining crazies that menaced them, but he had no illusions about his chances of survival if he came upon a reptar. Even sluggish, they were still very effective killing machines. So he picked his way silently over the rocks, cautioning the little girl whose hand he never let go of to do the same. She sent rocks rattling down the hillsides, though. She was just a child. But she tried very hard to be quiet.

Suddenly, he heard movement, stopped and crouched low.

The cavern narrowed and then widened and then narrowed again, sometimes to only slightly larger than he could comfortably walk down without turning sideways. The back door offered lots of nooks and crannies back in the rocks, a place to hole up, though he had no intention of staying here.

There it was again. He shot a glance at Garson, walking behind Diana. The old man's eyes were huge. He'd heard it too.

Something was moving alright, scraping on rocks, but the caverns echoed so badly in places that it was hard to tell where the sound was coming from.

Of course, any sound when you're trying to move quietly sounds ominous. But in truth, the odds were that what he heard was some other cave dweller like himself, trying to hide from the crazies and the reptars.

There were, after all, only three reptars and miles upon miles of caverns.

He heard a clattering sound. A clacking, like … *claws* on rocks.

No, holy shit, no.

If he met a reptar in this enclosed space … He turned, making hand motions to Garson to back up, retrace his steps.

Purrrrr.

It was the sound of a big cat, a cat much larger than he had killed, a predator far more dangerous. Why would a reptar be in one of the side tunnels? Lost, maybe. Perhaps it didn't know where it was, but it would soon realize he was there with it. He had been told their sense of smell was better than a human's — not anything like a dog, but better.

He heard the sound of clacking again, much closer! Just around the corner. He mouthed to Diana and Garson, *hide.* She took off up the side of a rock pile, but in her haste sent a shower of rocks tumbling down into a crevice. So much for stealth.

Garson hurried back up the trail and wedged his body into a crack in the wall. Eagle Feather didn't think the crack was deep enough to do him any good but it was all there was.

Eagle Feather drew his knife.

Never take a knife to a gunfight.

Or a reptar fight.

One knife versus a mouth full of knife-sharp teeth. Not a chance.

He backed into an area where the cavern widened slightly. Then it was there. Not there, then there. Even sluggish, the creature moved horrifyingly fast.

Its claws clattered on the rocks, where it was climbing its way over the stones toward him, a bug with too many legs. Red eyes, monster eyes and black armor plating that would deflect any knife stroke. He did not want to die on the teeth of a reptar, but that appeared now to be a given. All he wanted was to get far enough away from it to distract it away from Diana and Garson. He took another step backward.

The reptar was the small one, probably the female, Laverne, but it was impossible to tell for sure. The titans were not gender neutral, but the reptars were.

It advanced a step, but didn't leap at him as he expected. It was closing on him stealthily, as if it were sneaking up on him — which was crazy. Reptars didn't sneak, they charged.

One of its back legs slipped on a rock and it teetered that direction. Off balance, almost toppled over. He took one more step back, had gone as far as he could before turning to run back down the narrow passageway when he heard a sound behind him.

Oh sweet Jesus, please, no. Not Diana. Why had she come out of hiding?

There was another sound behind him, an odd sound, like movement on two sides about five or six feet back.

Then he heard a low rumbling sound. A growl.

He looked then. Took his eyes off the advancing reptar and glanced to either side.

Wolves.

His breath had already been stolen by the sudden appearance of the reptar so he had no more air to gasp. But he gasped anyway. They had ... but he had *imagined* them.

Was he imagining them now?

If he was, the reptar was sharing his hallucination because its eyes darted from one to the other of them. From the corner of his eye now, Eagle Feather could see them taking their places ... surrounding their prey.

It was a pack. Five wolves. The ones he had seen but hadn't really seen ... but apparently really *had* seen when he was almost dead from blood loss the day of the flood.

That explained the track Sawyer told him he saw where the donkey had disappeared. He'd described it, the claw marks in front of the solid foot pad. It wasn't the mountain lion. They retracted their claws. It had been the wolves. They'd been poaching food and small animals the whole time the people had been in the cave. The big cat got greedy and got caught. The wolves had stayed hidden.

They'd made a den somewhere in this unused tunnel between Big Toe and Carnegie Hall. Close to their food source, but not a trail anybody ventured down. Or if they had, they hadn't lived to tell about it.

He had only a moment to think the thought, a bright comet across the expanse of his mind and then gone: if the wolves were real, then *the old Indian was real, too.*

The reptar swung its head from side to side, and Eagle Feather knew it would decimate the five wolves. They couldn't take this prey down, even the whole pack. It had armor plating their claws couldn't penetrate. Its front legs were as sharp as swords and the claws they ended in would rip the heart out of a wolf before it had a chance to blink.

Eagle Feather instinctively backed up another step. The wolves advanced a step. Now, they were closer to the reptar than he was. He could cut and run and maybe killing the wolves would distract the already unsteady reptar enough for him to make a getaway, circle around and come back for Garson and Diana. They would remain hidden until he gave them an all-clear. Eagle Feather was tensing his muscles to bolt when the reptar threw its head back and made a heinous sound. He'd never heard that reptars could make sounds, but this one could. Not a menacing sound. A sound of anguish. It shook its head violently from side to side.

Star! She had hooked the reptars into a hive mind.

The beast was already unsteady on its feet and the motion toppled it. It cried out again as it fell onto its side on the rocks.

And the wolf pack charged. They came at it from all sides, trying to bury claws into its hide and teeth into its flesh but it was like attacking an armored car. Their claws slid off, their teeth could find nothing to sink into. But the reptar wasn't fighting back. It was flailing its front legs, the clawed ones, and its back legs didn't seem to be working right at all. When it collapsed, the big wolf, the grey one, went after its eye.

Eagle Feather turned and ran back the way they'd

come, bolted around the bend in the trail as he heard the tearing and growling of the wolves at their prey.

"Diana!" he called.

"Here," a little voice called out and he saw Diana in a crack between rocks just ahead. It was a good place to hide. She was a smart little girl. It was so small only she could fit down into it, but it was deep. Nothing could have reached her when she was down in it. Garson wiggled out of his "hiding place," fortunate the reptar hadn't come along because it would have dug him out of the shallow indention where he'd sought refuge like a pecan out of its shell.

There was no more stealth, trying to move quickly and quietly. He grabbed Diana's hand and the three of them ran as fast as they could, clambering over rocks, jumping from stone to stone, terror making Garson more agile than Eagle Feather would ever have imagined.

By Eagle Feather's geography, they were now less than a quarter of a mile from the spot where they'd started, the tunnel that opened unobtrusively in the dead-end back side of Big Toe.

Suddenly, he heard a sound behind him. He shoved Diana at Garson and told him, "Run!"

Then he turned to face what was coming, what lay between them and the safety of the monastery. If he could just distract it for long enough for Garson and the little girl to sneak past it and get away …

It drew closer, the sound not quite right. Then it came into view. It was a reptar, all right, but it had been the victim of a viciousness to match its own. It was blind, both eyes chewed out by the wolves. It was bleeding from several places between the armor plates on its body, where the teeth of wolves had been able to fasten onto flesh beneath the plates and rip it out. One claw was gone. Just gone.

It came toward him, blind, weak, shambling along. Oh, if he got too close, it could still slash with sword legs, hook with its claw, chew him apart with its teeth — that now had pieces of fur and flesh dangling from them.

He stepped carefully to the side, then as quiet as a mouse, he climbed to the top of the nearest big rock. The reptar shambled by beneath the rock, unaware of his presence. Behind it was a gory trail of blood that'd been gushing from the front leg that ended in a stump.

He followed along behind the creature quietly as it staggered forward, looking for Garson and Diana. They appeared after the reptar passed where they'd been hiding. Eagle Feather put his finger to his lips, took Diana's hand and turned to resume their journey to the monastery. He'd only gone a few steps when Diana stopped and pointed back to where Garson still stood, watching the reptar shuffle slowly away toward Big Toe.

"Alien life form," Garson muttered under his breath. Then he spit in the dirt.

Chapter Sixty-Five

THEY WERE in each other's minds. Totally. Both of them. There'd been a vacant place created when Star was taken away from Noah. They'd been together on the mothership and then the shuttle separated them, deposited each of them where they'd been when they were abducted. Noah in Kentucky. Paco in California and Star in New Mexico. The vacant place had ached in her heart and mind every day as she struggled to get back to him, crossed half the country with her grandfather, fought off monstrous dope growers ... she would have crawled over broken glass ... to be with Noah, to feel his presence inside her head, and he was there with her now as the two of them ran through the tunnels with Pumpkin on their heels.

The only danger to the two of them were the crazies, if there were any of them left. No one knew how many there'd been to start with, but they had been cannon fodder for the reptars when they left Alabaster Hall, attacking the monsters with no thought for their own welfare. The reptars hadn't had to go out looking for victims, the crazies went after them with knives and tobacco sticks and their bare hands. And the reptars mowed them down.

It did give other people a head start, though, allowed them to get away at least for a little while. Now those people were cowering in homes, behind rocks, in deserted caverns, down inside crevices, anywhere they could find to escape the three monsters that would not stop until they had killed every human in the caverns.

Unless the humans killed them first.

Star had thought when she first came into the cave that she would have less trouble than most adjusting to the darkness. After all, she was blind. The reverse had been true, however. The only things Star could see were very bright lights, blobs of bright colors and patterns of light and dark. In the cave, there were only shadows. Without Pumpkin at her side, she'd have broken her neck a dozen times in the first few weeks, while she was memorizing things about the caverns others didn't even notice. What it smelled like — Carnegie Hall smelled like popcorn. Years ago, they'd sold bags of popcorn there to the tourists, but the smell should long since have dissipated. Broadway always had a breeze blowing through it though there was no reason there should be one. West Broadway, the home of the commercial washing machines and driers, always smelled like dirty clothing, and of course, South Bend, home of the sewage system that serviced the big bathrooms on both ends of the cavern, smelled like shit.

Star's dips into the reptars' minds were telling her that one of them had gotten separated from the other two. Not that they were connected in any psychic way. But the two male reptars, Moe and Larry, had stayed fairly close to Carnegie Hall. Laverne had gone off on her own, was in a small connecting tunnel. Perhaps she'd chased somebody there, got lost and couldn't find her way back. She'd come back, though. When Star turned on the Jamming Juice, they'd all come back — to shut her up.

Finally, they stumbled to a halt in the hallway outside Alabaster Hall. Star got images from Noah's mind and from Pumpkin's that made her glad she could not see.

NOAH WAS glad Star couldn't see the carnage. Dead bodies everywhere, none of them with all their limbs attached. He only allowed his gaze to flit over them, refused to register details, wouldn't let himself recognize the bodies of his aunt — Kelly Jo, Dave and Sam — just inside the entrance. It looked like someone had put two dozen people through a woodchopper and the chunks of them had flown out everywhere. He walked carefully, trying not to step on … something, but it was impossible. The blood made the floor as slick as a skating rink.

Noah, the fire that killed your mother and sister didn't start in the garage. It started in the chimney.

The words rang like gongs in his head, each one a separate, distinct vibration, all of the vibrations colliding in a single concussive force that rattled him to the core.

"It wasn't your fault," Star said in his head.

No, it wasn't. The wonder of that … He wished he'd had time to savor it — one good thing to hold onto now. That and his love for Star.

He led Star and Pumpkin around the bodies to the hole in the wall of Alabaster Hall the Astrals had melted with their mining equipment. They stopped there.

"How are you going to do it, connect them?"

"I don't know for sure. I can't explain it, but I'll be able to feel it when I go there … into their minds."

Star took a deep breath.

"No farther than I have to. It's so dark and … filthy. It's like putting your toe in sewage. You don't want to go in any deeper."

"Where are they?"

She looked blank for a moment. "The two males are nearby, in caverns with paved floors. But the female is … I don't know where she is because she doesn't know where she is. A side tunnel, rocks and dirt."

"She got lost?"

"Maybe she'll never find her way out. What I'm about to do is going to be … disorienting."

She took another deep breath, centering and calming herself.

He reached out and took her hands.

"I was so hoping we could … live in a world without monsters from the other side of the universe, that we could start over."

"Without the monsters. I wouldn't really care what was left in the world when they leave, as long as they leave. As long as they're gone."

"Diana will know a world without the monsters. She'll grow up … *free*. Are you ready?"

"No. Yes! Let's do this."

They stood like that for a time, a handful of minutes, not speaking. Just holding each other's hands, lying comfortable in each other's heads. Saying goodbye.

When he knew she was ready, Noah dropped Star's hands so she could concentrate.

STAR LET GO of Noah's hands and focused on blanking every thought and idea and image out of her brain. On being as empty as she could be. Like an empty pipe.

She reached out and immediately felt the mind of the big one, the one called Moe. The blackness and fury ... she reached out farther, found Larry. Smaller, moving.

Then she put the two of them together.

The shock felt like putting two electric cables together; she expected to see sparks flying everywhere, because there were sparks flying in their heads.

Where there had been darkness, all was bright. Too bright. The brilliance of a strobe light, but constant, not pulsing. She felt around in the bright, squinted her psychic eyes, and found Laverne. When she pulled the darkness of the third reptar into the mix, Laverne's mind ... *shattered.* It seemed almost to explode. Maybe the funneling of the two other reptars into her mind at the same time had done something catastrophic. She didn't know what, but Laverne's mind began to spark and arch, big bright lights flashed, at least that's how it looked psychically, like the joining of their minds had somehow damaged hers, continued to damage hers as long as the hook-up lasted.

The other two minds were sparking, in pain, like they were hearing the God-awful squawk of feedback, each funneling that sound back through Star to the other reptar. But enough of it hit Star, too, the sound, the concussive force of that much energy, that much ...

Star jumped back like she'd been shocked, tingling all over, feeling like her legs were too weak to hold her up. Beside her, Pumpkin was whining and Noah was saying something. But she couldn't hear him. Couldn't hear him with her ears or her mind. There was some kind of static, bright and buzzing, but gradually it calmed. The noise faded. She could hear again, both sound and thought.

"They're coming! Right now, they're headed this direction as fast as they can go. They're damaged, I think.

Particularly Laverne. But they know it's me, where I am. And they don't want another shock like that one."

Noah looked at his watch and took her hand. "Let's go!" With Pumpkin on one side and Noah on the other, she ran off into the dark Astral mine.

∼

THREE MILES OF DARKNESS … an unfathomable pit … Noah and Star and Pumpkin ran through it as fast as they could go. Noah had a lantern of sorts — just a jar filled with a strand of Glow Worms. Anything brighter would give away their position to the reptars, but the lantern gave off enough light so Noah could tell they were running straight down an aisle between pillars. On that course, they would eventually get to Noah's Hole on the far side of the mine.

Finally they had to stop, gasping for air.

"They're in the mine," Star told him inside his head. She had no air for speech even if he could have heard it. A painful stitch stabbed into his side and he couldn't imagine how hard the running was for Star, who didn't play sports, didn't run wind sprints like he and Sam and …

He let it go. Walled it off.

"The two males are … but not the third. The third isn't here."

Noah's heart leapt into his throat. It had never occurred to them that the now independent-thinking reptars might not behave predictably. It wasn't like the three could consult each other, decide on a plan of action. All three of them would be in such pain they would want nothing more than to make it stop. But what if …?

"Where is the third one?"

"She's ... she's just gone. Her mind is gone. I think she's ... dead."

Noah couldn't countenance the thought of a dead reptar. Unless she had stumbled into an abyss and fell to her death hundreds of feet below ... then something, some*body* had killed her.

~

THEY RAN ON.

Star held onto Noah psychically with the same kind of frantic desperation that she held his hand as they ran. She had to have him in her head with her, because inside her head had become an exceedingly dark place. The reptars had done a track-to-source, alright, had located her. And each of them, independently, blinked into and out of her head, tracking her. One of them was faster. It was gaining on them, but they couldn't run any faster than they already were and she had no idea where they were, how far they had to go.

It had become as dark inside her head as outside. Time didn't seem to work there. The ugliness of the reptars' minds kept blinking on in hers, psychically body slamming her, then blinking back off.

She couldn't run any farther, had run out of breath, and something was very wrong with Pumpkin.

Staggering, Star stopped and dropped to one knee.

The dog was panting, gasping for breath, and there was blood coming out his mouth and nostrils. She could see inside his mind, could see that he was trying to smell but couldn't. She could tell he was in pain.

She threw her arms around him and hugged him tight to her.

"Star, we have to—"

Then she opened up and became a conduit again, and connected the minds of the two reptars.

STAR HAD CONNECTED the two reptars again, and it looked like a Fourth of July fireworks show in her head — light and brilliance, two huge sources of power arcing off each other and the most horrible wailing *squawk*.

And then Star fell over against his leg.

Noah knelt beside her, called her name. She opened her eyes, but didn't see him, not really. But the reptars were coming! He could tell from what he could see in her mind that the big reptar was closing fast.

And he was *pissed*.

LIGHT AND DARKNESS. Blurring. It was more light than Star had ever seen. But it was light behind her eyes, not out in front of them. She was dizzy, disoriented.

Noah was carrying her.

"Noah, put me down!"

He staggered a few more feet, then stumbled, collided with Pumpkin and they all slammed into the floor of the mine.

"He's close," she wanted to tell Noah. But she couldn't.

"It's there," Noah cried, "just ahead. Another fifty or seventy-five yards. I can see the light shining through the hole. Come on."

Star lurched to her feet to run with him, but her legs would do nothing more than wobble. She staggered forward, tottering, not running. And now she could almost feel the reptar's breath on her neck.

They wouldn't make it to the hole in time.

≈

NOAH DRAGGED Star along beside him. She was stumbling and staggering, but he held her upright, mostly carrying her and ran as fast as he could. Pumpkin was … somewhere. Noah couldn't see.

He heard the clatter of claws on the stone floor behind them. He heard a purring sound, like a big cat.

He heard the reptar. Not in his head. *He heard the beast with his ears.*

The beast couldn't be more than fifty feet behind them, and the hole was probably that far in front of them.

And he *heard* the scuffling of their feet on the floor, the thunderous roar of his breathing in his ears, the whimpering sounds Star probably didn't even know she was making. The reptar was there, *right behind them.*

Noah threw Star in front of him. Literally shoved her as hard as he could. She staggered, then fell. Pumpkin appeared beside her. The hole was only ten feet away.

The reptar suddenly materialized in the glow of Noah's lantern. It was the most hideous creature Noah had ever seen, a monster born of children's nightmares. The razor-sharp teeth glistened in the faint light. The claws. He saw them as they came at him.

And then the monster fell sideways, made an awful bawling sound, like some kind of injured bull, and he knew Star had connected him to the other reptar. And he also knew she couldn't hold that connection for more than a few seconds.

Leaping forward, he grabbed her shirt and dragged her toward the hole. Heard a sucking sound behind him as he shoved her across the floor at the hole, and someone's hands reached out to grab her and drag her inside.

The reptar's purr was right behind Noah. He would feel the ripping talons any second.

"Goodbye Star," he was able to cry in his head, as he dived hopelessly for the hole.

He heard a growl then. The rumble of a big animal, an *angry* animal. It was louder than the purr of the reptar. Hands grabbed his, yanked him forward into the hole.

Pumpkin's dying yelp filled his mind. He heard it, and heard it echoed in Star's mind. And then he was out of the mine, in the cavern, panting, listening to the furious monster clawing at the rocks on the other side.

Chapter Sixty-Six

THE FIVE OF them sat in the dirt beside Noah's Hole, listening to the reptars just three feet away in the mine — they were both there now — clawing in impotent rage at the other side of the rock wall.

Star was crying, repeating softly, "Pumpkin, oh poor Pumpkin." Noah sat with his arm around her, holding her tight against him.

Nick held the switch Noah had rigged up on the recalibrated laser sight from his father's rifle.

Ellie sat calmly beside Sawyer holding his hand.

It occurred to Sawyer that there ought to be something he should say now, something somebody should say. They were all about to be crushed beneath tons of falling rocks, maybe blown apart, perhaps even drowned.

Noah was of the opinion that drowning was the least likely. Though the blast would "give the whole mountain a good shake," he thought the cave wall they were behind might hold — not likely, but anything's *possible*. And if it didn't collapse out from under the ceiling of the tunnel above and dump it on top of them, the explosion in the mine would put a cork in Noah's Hole and at the other end in Alabaster Hall, keeping the water out. Theoretically, at least.

They couldn't wait long to set off the blast. One or the other of the reptars might probe the humans' minds, figure out what was going on and try to dismantle the explosives.

Star'd said their minds would be so jumbled by the feedback that they'd be incapable of higher-order thinking for awhile after they were zapped. They'd get over it eventually, though, settle down.

Wiping the tears off her cheeks, Star straightened up out of Noah's embrace. "Now?" she asked.

"Now," Noah said.

Sawyer watched the girl focus. A pleat appeared between her eyebrows. She squeezed her eyes tight shut and held her breath. One second. Two. Three.

Then she opened her eyes and fell back against Noah, panting.

She had planted in the minds of both reptars a single image — the top of the mountain collapsing into the mine. Not the exploding kegs of gunpowder or the pillars giving way. Just the mountain collapse.

They all listened, holding their breath.

The sounds of the reptars clawing at the rock on the other side of the cavern wall instantly stopped. Then they heard the staccato clacking of too-many clawed feet running away across the mine floor. Noah looked at his watch. He had timed how long it took to run the length of the mine, would know when the reptars had made it halfway back — out into the center near the explosives.

They waited in silence.

"I love you," Sawyer said. Not to anybody in particular but to everybody in particular, to each of them individually and to all of them collectively. They had come very close to surviving the alien invasion and only a handful of people out of all humanity could say that.

"Love you, too, Dad," Noah said, and his voice was different, his speech was … Sawyer didn't know how but something was …

"I just don't want to be there when it happens," Ellie said.

"What?"

"Woody Allen. He said he didn't mind dying, he just didn't want to be there when it happened."

She smiled. The smile was the parting gift. The goodbye.

Noah looked up from his watch and nodded. Nick made eye contact with the four people who could see, one at a time, and then flipped the switch on the recalibrated laser. The world exploded into a thousand points of light around them.

Chapter Sixty-Seven

SAWYER IS RUNNING down a dark tunnel toward a light that grows brighter as he approaches it. He's carrying Ellie, limp in his arms. Heavy, not a light, emaciated skeleton, a ... *dead* weight. It's too late this time. Too late. She's dead and there's no way now to bring her back.

THE RUMBLING roar is like being inside a cement mixer, so loud and overwhelming it blots out all thought ... and that's good. Ellie doesn't want to think, doesn't want to be aware when she's crushed to death, or feel the cold water fill her lungs.

She drifts then. Nowhere. The rumble roars in her ears even after it stops. The echo of it bounces around inside her head, muffles her hearing.

But what sound would there be to hear?

Then she feels light on her face and she's glad. She had been to the very brink of death before, one or two breaths away, and she had seen the light then. It was a golden glow that grew brighter and brighter and when she held up her hand in front of it, the light cast no shadows.

She had seen it, felt its warmth, and then she had come back. She wasn't sorry. Oh, no, no, no, not sorry! The few hours of life had been a precious gift. But this time, she won't go back. This time she'll stay in the light. And that's as it should be. She hopes all the rest of dead humanity is in the light with her, can feel the warmth of it on their faces as she does now.

SAWYER LAYS Ellie's dead body gently down and kneels beside her. The light is so bright he's squinting, but that's not why tears are running down his cheeks. He's crying, not trying to hold it back. They had gotten so close. So close.

ELLIE DOESN'T WANT to open her eyes because the rosy glow through her eyelids is so very lovely. Oh, she's not afraid. She doesn't fear what she'll see when she does because she is in the light now where nothing can harm her.

She lifts her eyelids and the glare is so bright she closes them again. She caught a glimpse, though, of …

Blue and white.

She saw blue and white.

She blinks.

Blinks again and squints.

Blue sky. White clouds.

She closes her eyes, wondering, hears a muffled sound through the rumble in her ears.

Is the hereafter … heaven … whatever … *wherever* …? She never imaged it would be a—

There's the sound again.

SAWYER FREEZES AS STILL as death itself.

Did he see …? Did Ellie …?

"Ellie!" He screams the word at the top of his lungs, yells it with all the force in his soul. It comes out a strangled whisper.

Ellie blinks. Again.

"Ellie?" He speaks her name in wonder, his heart thundering so loud he wouldn't be able to hear even if his ears weren't still ringing.

ELLIE HEARS SAWYER'S VOICE, calling her name.

She opens her eyes, keeps them open this time. And breathes in a lungful of air that smells like … like the air smells after a storm.

"ELLIE, are you alright? Dammit, say something!"

"Am I … are we dead?"

She hears laughter, bubbling joyful laughter and recognizes it as Star's voice.

The world is coming into focus now. She is becoming aware of dirt all over her, in her face and her hair. She can feel grit between her teeth.

"Ellie, are you hurt?" Sawyer demands.

"How the hell would I know?"

He laughs a beautiful rumbling laugh and gathers her into his arms, holding her tight. She still doesn't know what … where …

But she's beginning to figure it out.

Wiggling out of his embrace, she struggles to sit up. She gazes around in wonder at a world lit by a bright sun. Looking into Sawyer's dirty face — with a single streak of clean down each cheek — she can't even form a question, but he answers anyway.

"Double Cellars Sinkhole. It's where Noah got out of the cavern when he was a little boy. It was blocked when the druggies set off an explosion years ago that sealed the natural entrance, and …" — he looks around — "… the shaking opened it back up again."

"You mean we … we *made* it?"

"I thought you …" He reaches out and touches her head and she winces from pain she hadn't noticed until then. She feels a trail of wet oozing over her forehead that sitting up has sent down out of her hair and when she wipes it away, she sees it's blood. "Pieces of rock fell out of the roof and you were lying so still. I panicked when I couldn't hear a heartbeat. But then, I can't hear much of anything." He pauses. "The flood's … *over*." There is a kind of awe in Sawyer's voice she had never heard in anyone's voice — ever. And would likely never hear again.

"We blew the top off the mountain." That's Noah, Noah's voice. She turns and sees him standing with his arm around Star. They're both slathered in dust. He turns to look off into the distance. "The flood waters are … gone."

"I lost track of time, stopped counting," Sawyer says.

"I didn't," Nick says, and Noah turns back around as if he heard him. Of course, he did, through Star. But it looked different, somehow, more … *natural* … in a way

Ellie can't quite fathom. Nick's standing on the other side of Ellie, equally filthy. "Did my job — fulfilled my obligations as the official Town Cryer. I get a gold star." He looked at his watch, held out his wrist toward Ellie, but didn't give her time to see anything. "Today's Day Forty-One."

There's a beat of silence as understanding soaks in.

"Forty days and forty nights," Sawyer says.

"And then it's over," Ellie whispers.

She struggles to get to her feet and Sawyer stands and extends her a hand. Being suddenly vertical makes her momentarily dizzy, but what is more dizzying is the freshness of the air. Not cave air. A breeze, a real breeze.

Green. Trees. A forest on a hillside. A silver ribbon of river in the distance. Not like it had looked before. Different.

"It's a world," Nick says, gesturing at everything and nothing.

"A world," Ellie repeats and snuggles into Sawyer's embrace. "A whole new world."

A Note from the Author

Thank you for reading *The Saved.*

If you enjoyed this book, you please consider writing a review on your favorite bookselling site so other readers might enjoy it too. Just a couple of sentences would mean a lot to me.

Thank you!

Ninie Hammon

About the Authors

Avery Blake doesn't want you to know where she lives, or what she does. She travels the world, moving from place to place quickly to ensure she can't be tracked. It's safer that way.

When she's not looking over her shoulder, you can find her in the corner of a cafe, facing the exit, typing as fast as she can.

Ninie Hammon (rhymes with shiny, not skinny) grew up in Muleshoe, Texas, got a BA in English and theatre from Texas Tech University and snagged a job as a newspaper reporter. She didn't know a thing about journalism, but her editor said if she could write he could teach her the rest of it and if she couldn't write the rest of it didn't matter. She hung in there for a 25-year career as a journalist. As soon as she figured out that making up the facts was a whole lot more fun than reporting them, she turned to fiction and never looked back.

Ninie now writes suspense--every flavor except pistachio: psychological suspense, inspirational suspense, suspense thrillers, paranormal suspense, suspense mysteries.

In every book she keeps this promise to her Loyal Reader: "I will tell you a story in a distinctive voice you'll always recognize, about people as ordinary as you are--

people who have been slammed by something they didn't sign on for, and now they must fight for their lives. Then smack in the middle of their everyday worlds, those people encounter the unexplainable--and it's always the game-changer."

Also By Avery Blake

The Invasion Series

Longshot

Invasion

Contact

Colonization

Annihilation

Judgment

Extinction

Resurrection

Save The City Series

Save The City

Save The Girl

Save The World

Stonefall Series

Alienation

Stonefall

Snowfall

Downfall

The Taken Saga

The Taken

The Changed

The Hidden

The Saved

The Next Evolution

Transition

Convergence

Evolution

Stand-Alone Novels

Analog Heart

Family Royale

Ruthless Positivity

Vicarious Joe

Also By Ninie Hammon

Cornbread Mafia

Fire In The Hole

Blown' Up A Storm

Ridin' For A Fall

So Shall The Tree Grow

Nowhere, USA

The Jabberwock

Mad Dog

Trapped

The Hanging Judge

The Witch of Gideon

Blown Away

Nowhere People

Through The Canvas Series

Black Water

Red Web

Gold Promise

Blue Tears

The Taken Saga

The Taken

The Changed

The Hidden

The Saved

The Unexplainable Collection

Five Days in May

Black Sunshine

The Based on True Stories Collection

Home Grown

Sudan

When Butterflies Cry

The Knowing Series

The Knowing

The Deceiving

The Reckoning

The Fault

Stand-alone Psychological Thrillers

The Memory Closet

The Last Safe Place